ANTONIO & ISAAC

The Annotated Account of Phillipe Wolf,

Composer & Spy

ANTONIO & ISAAC

The Annotated Account of Phillipe Wolf, Composer & Spy

a novel by Todd Shimoda

This book is a work of fiction. For clarification of how the historical characters and events are used in the story, please see the Author's Note at the end of the book.

ISBN 978-1-956358-00-1 (Hardcover)
ISBN 978-1-956358-01-8 (Paperback)
ISBN 978-1-956358-02-5 (eBook)

Library in Congress data available upon request

For more information about this novel, visit shimodaworks.com

SHIMODA

CONTENTS

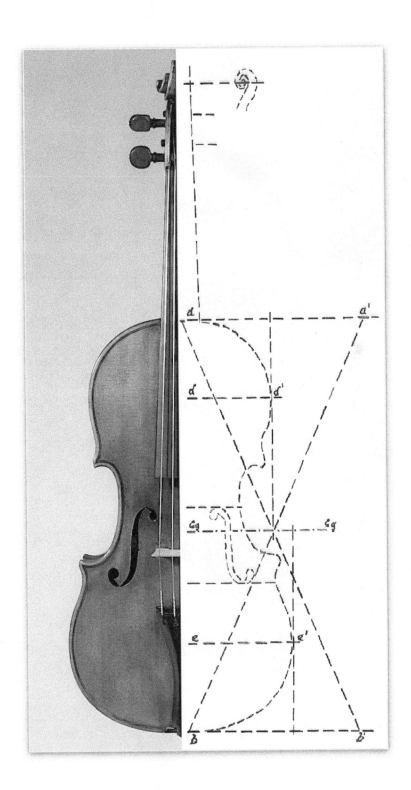

Opus 1

Counterpoint

chapter 1

Isaac Newton—eminent for his sciences, mathematics, and philosophies encompassing all higher thought, and well-established as Master of the Royal Mint, but most celebrated by me as the uncle of Catherine Barton—had kept me waiting forty-seven minutes according to an intricate clock in his parlor. Notwithstanding Miss Barton's letter of introduction, which I duly submitted to Dr. Newton[1] via his assistant at the Mint, and which effusively recommended he spare me a few minutes to discuss my matter of interest, it was well within his power to deny me an audience, even at this late moment. As the dagger-like minute hand advanced past the hour, that possibility seemed all the more likely.

I had the pleasure of meeting Miss Barton—Catherine, if I may —at the reception after the premiere of a sonata I composed. She was attending the event with a clutch of London society, including an English army captain, James Brookfield, with whom I was attached while serving as Austrian military liaison. At the reception, Captain Brookfield introduced me to one person then another; I say this casually because after I met Catherine the names of most others were promptly forgotten.

James well-nigh dragged me toward her and another woman standing at the edge of her company.

"Good evening, lovers of fine music," James said to the two. "You must meet the composer, Phillipe Wolf. Captain Wolf, may I introduce Miss Catherine Barton and Miss Rose Harrington."

---

[1] At this time, Sir Isaac Newton had yet to be knighted, hence my use of "Dr." Newton. *PW*

Straightaway, I was struck by Catherine's engaging smile which brightened the reception hall's dense atmosphere imparted by the massive wooden beams and the floor-to-ceiling tapestries covering the walls. The heavy fabrics absorbed much of the clatter and conversations, as if wads of cotton were stuffed in my ears, making the room dull and cheerless. Worse, however, a self-inflicted disappointment in my sonata clouded my mood.

The hall and my mood lightened further when Catherine said, "Captain Wolf, your thoroughly delightful composition cries out for a more evocative title than 'Sonata for Violin in E Minor.'"

"Thank you very much, Miss Barton," I replied with an appreciative bow. "I'd be sincerely grateful if you could suggest such a title."

Miss Harrington and Catherine shared a mischievous glance before Catherine said, "Rose and I invented a perfect title, but you would likely find it silly."

She turned her head away.

Was she mocking me?

"Then I'll have to pry it from you," I said. "Perhaps over a glass of sherry?"

"Captain Wolf," said Catherine, turning back toward me, her smile rising again, "you must think we lack fortitude, if you believe our secret can be pried from us with a glass of sherry."

Miss Harrington muffled a laugh with her gloved hand.

My face flushed ablaze.

Catherine rescued me, entwining her arm with mine and resting her gloved hand lightly on my forearm.

"My apologies, sir. We were only amusing ourselves at your expense. The title we invented was 'A Winter Rose Dreams of Spring.'"

"I like it very much," I said, recovering from my embarrassment. "It's in honor of your friend, Rose, I assume? Consider the name changed."

Patting my arm, Catherine said, "Captain, you're under no obligation to appease us. I'm sure your title is perfectly suited for the composition."

"It may be precise, but I agree that it lacks the feeling of your title. Although, wouldn't you say that now you're appeasing me?"

Catherine honored me with a sweet, breathy laugh. "I suppose I am. But with due seriousness, the feeling is in the work itself. Words in a title won't give it more, or less, emotion. However, wouldn't an evocative title attract more people to hear it? At least I might think that to be true."

"Undoubtedly, it would," I replied with honesty. "I'll take your suggestion to heart. Thank you."

"Excellent! We've resolved our first disagreement. And now I'll be happy to enjoy that glass of sherry."

I turned to find that James and Rose had disappeared into the crowd. After Catherine and I picked up our glasses of sherry, we shared a toast which she proposed: "To the 'Sonata for Violin in E Minor.'"

"To 'A Winter Rose Dreams of Spring,'" I said, raising my glass before sipping.

With the liquid already warming me, I asked if she was a composer, or played a musical instrument.

She answered with an amused shake of her head, "I play a little bit of clavichord and violin. However, my appreciation for music is considerable. If you don't mind, I'd like to ask how you manage to compose so well while you perform your official duties in the military?"

"No, I don't mind your question. On the contrary, I'm flattered that you enjoyed my sonata enough to ask me." Then, in *sotto voce*, I said, "There is a secret."

Catherine leaned close to me, exposing the curve of her neckline. A subtle breath of floral scent enveloped me, intimately joining us. "Yes? Do tell me."

"Except for the horror of battle, life in the military is largely one of boredom and much idle time."

A faint smile appeared as she leaned away. "As is life, taken in its breadth, I'm afraid. But is your music drawn from your experiences in war, perhaps an escape from battle, from the horror? Or is it a mere idling away the boredom?"

I could tell she had taken my response as cavalier. Rightly so, I realized with no small bloom of regret.

"The horror of battle," I began earnestly and with due repent, although what followed was not wholly in truth, "is the substance of my darkest dreams, yet it doesn't influence my music. However, your question is one I've asked myself many times, and I'm afraid I have no answer. It's simply that the music comes largely unbidden—perhaps a run of notes, or a snip of melody, perhaps with a counterpoint response."

"How fascinating! Speaking of counterpoint, and forgive me if I'm incorrect, but I noticed in the first part you played one note against another, in the second part a pair against one. In the last part you went back to note against note, as if two soldiers in battle."

"Excellently observed. Your understanding of music is greater than most others who claim to be authorities. I can't but be considerably impressed. What other insights might you have for this modest composer?"

"Captain Wolf, you have no need to be modest," she said, articulating the words as if she were perplexed. "In hearing the sonata and during the brief time we've been conversing, I believe your music comes from somewhere deep within you. Although I can't say, at least not yet, what that means in full. I hope to discover the truth."

At once, her astute perception intrigued and alarmed me. There was much to say to her, but before I could make a suitable response, another of her party joined us. She introduced me to Mr. Charles Montagu, the Baron Halifax.

Mr. Montagu was half-a-head shorter than me, his face ivory-white, the cleft of his chin deep and hidden in its shadow. Without fanfare, he launched into an apparently witty tale of folly affected by a fellow member of the House of Lords. *Apparently*, as I knew nothing of either men, nor of the folly involving an arcane political difference between Whig and Tory. Catherine, on the other hand, gave him a prompt laugh followed by her own witty comment.

Mr. Montagu laughed, roiling his jowls, and he took Catherine's arm in his. After a curt nod, he whispered this aside to me as he whisked her away: "Lovely. Perfectly lovely."

I was certain he referred to Catherine and not my sonata.

The reception dragged on slowly after that, and after I greeted all who cared to meet the composer, I endeavored to speak with Catherine again. However, Mr. Montagu was keeping her firmly within his retinue.

Away from the main crowd, I spotted James in conversation with Rose and I went over to them. Perhaps sensing what I desired, Rose said, "Let's find Catherine so she may join us."

While James and I followed her, he said, "It's your reception, Phillipe, but haven't you done as much smiling and bowing as you can stand? I believe the officers club is still open."

"Agreed. I'd like to say good night to Catherine, if possible."

Rose managed to extricate Catherine. She seemed pleased to be in my company again, judged by her smile. I apologized for interrupting her conversation with her friends. "I also must apologize for having to say 'good night' as duty is calling us back to our station."

"At this late hour?" Catherine asked.

"The vagaries of command, I'm afraid," I said.

"Yes, of course," said Mr. Montagu, who had crept behind me. "You must not cross duty, the queen of time that she is."

"Precisely correct, sir," I said. "And a perfectly lovely queen she is."

My attempt at sarcasm did not amuse him, or he chose to ignore it, as his expression went blank. Backing away, I gave Catherine a glance. She returned it before again being whisked away.

J ames and I found the officers club still open, quietly so, with only a handful of others present who paid us no serious attention. After getting our ration of spirits, we took two chairs in a nook surrounded by paintings of epic battles and valorous deeds. The pigments were yellowed with a gauze of tobacco smoke, candle soot, and the fog of tall tales.

"Congratulations," James said, raising his glass. "All was due praise for your sonata."

I joined his toast, but said, "I don't believe the sonata was all that well received, certainly not by everyone, despite the platitudes."

"If Catherine Barton said it was good then it was, for she doesn't speak idly."

With that statement I agreed, even though I only knew Catherine from the few words we managed to share. "Perhaps so. Regardless, thank you for the timely escape."

"I presume you'd like to hear more about Catherine?"

I shrugged with feigned nonchalance, but James went ahead, telling me she was twenty-two years of age, originally from East Midlands, the niece of Dr. Isaac Newton, the extraordinary genius, as I have already mentioned. Then he told me that she was in the employ of Mr. Montagu.

There I interrupted. "She's in his employ?"

"Yes. As the manager of his household in London, hired after his wife died a few years ago."

"How did that come about?" I asked, thinking aloud. Catherine didn't seem to be a household manager, although I may have lacked a good understanding of the position.

"How did his wife's death come about?" James asked.

We laughed.

He told me Mr. Montagu had been a friend of Dr. Newton for over twenty years, since Mr. Montagu's days at Cambridge.[2] When Mr. Montagu rose in political power, it was in his position as head of the Treasury that he advocated Dr. Newton for the post at the Mint. James also told me what he knew of Dr. Newton's success at the Mint, where he introduced assay standards of coinage and pursued counterfeiters. His efforts were beginning to stabilize the currency of the realm, made wobbly by war debt and the proliferation of clipped or fake coins. It was around this time that Catherine moved to London to help her unmarried uncle with his household, but eventually found employment with Mr. Montagu.

"I see," was all I could think of to say at the time.

We finished another round of spirits before retiring to our quarters. In mine, a room with only a desk, dresser, and bed, the quiet was overwhelming. I knew sleep would not come as my thoughts were overtaken with the evening's events.

Leaving the silence of my room, I walked through the grounds of the base, eventually stopping in the dark quadrangle where military parades were held. I listened for several minutes to the songs of insects pursuing solace. A symphony of natural beauty, one that I knew I couldn't replicate with my meek compositions, played on flimsy instruments. The melody was occasionally punctuated by a short silence, as if all needed a breath, or time to collect their thoughts.

Finally, when I felt sleep would come, I retreated.

After a lengthy day of unmemorable conferences with military strategists, I was working on a new composition when there was a knock on the door. I opened it to find an infantry private; his

---

2 Mr. Montagu attended Trinity College, Cambridge, from 1679-1682. Isaac Newton was a professor at the college during those years. *PW*

face so fresh and glowing, he seemed a schoolboy. He saluted me and removed a sealed envelope from his satchel. He made a great showy performance of handing it to me. I thanked him. He saluted again, turned heel, and left.

I'd been expecting the message, so he needn't have presented it as such an important missive. Earlier in the day, I sent a request to meet the Austrian consul in London, and his response informed me of the time we should meet.

As the time was set for the early evening and it was already late afternoon, I put away my work and changed into clean attire. I ate a little something and then found a carriage to take me to Mr. Lupine's residence. We always met at his residence rather than the consulate, likely because he didn't want ears on what we discussed.

He answered the door himself and ushered me into his library. It was a small but comfortable room, where barely two chairs and a table fit. A tidy fire was going in the hearth. A snifter of Austrian brandy was at the ready for me, and one for him.

"How is the English military treating you?" he asked. An old, thin scar traversed his left jawline. He'd fought in more than one duel, I heard. More than a career bureaucrat, Mr. George Lupine had also served in the military, which allowed us to converse easily.

"Well enough," I said.

"As well as the English can?"

Apparently, Mr. Lupine was not enamored with his host country.

After I gave him a brief account of the day's meetings, he said, "Nothing much of a critical nature."

"No," I agreed.

He took a drink. "I apologize for not attending your concert. And do believe my apology is sincere. I'd rather have been at the concert than at the court dinner, which was not as useful or as entertaining as I hoped."

"No apology is necessary. The concert was a small event. Although at the reception afterwards, I met Mr. Charles Montagu."

Mr. Lupine raised an eyebrow.

I told him I was introduced to Mr. Montagu without mention of Catherine. It was unnecessary, I'd decided, to bring up her name.

As if judging the potential value of Mr. Montagu's attention, Mr. Lupine thought for a few moments before saying, "What was the extent of your conversation with him?"

"Brief. Nothing of substance was said between us. I did hear him talking with others about the misfortunate of another politician, although about whom I can't say. It didn't seem pertinent. Although, admittedly, I was distracted and can't remember anything about the story."

Mr. Lupine sipped his brandy, then rubbed his scar as if trying to eradicate it. "We must be able to recall those details. Anything might be of help."

"Agreed, sir."

"Montagu's influence is weakened by his current disfavor with King William."

"Even if that's the case, he still puts forth an air of importance," I said. "He was surrounded by several others."

Including his household manager, I thought.

Mr. Lupine said, "True power lies not on the surface. Cozy with the King or not, Montagu is one of those whose say will determine involvement of the English in the war on which we are embarking.[3] Likely he's already working behind the scenes, steering the English political powers one way or the other."

"So, it would be important to know more of his stance and activities?"

"Undoubtedly," said Mr. Lupine. "Will you be able to initiate further contact with him?"

---

[3] The War of Spanish Succession, which pitted French against Austrians after the death of Spain's heirless monarch, Charles II. *PW*

This time I was the one thinking for a few moments. "Yes, sir. I believe I can find a way."

"Excellent. Keep me informed."

James surprised me with a small party at Rose's home where she lived with her cousin, Elizabeth Gammon. Her cousin's husband, Matthew Gammon, worked as the chief accountant for a large brewery, where Rose was employed as one of Mr. Gammon's office assistants. I mention this because Mr. Gammon's main task involved moving the brewery from under the cloud of an excise tax scandal—the tax in question began under Mr. Montagu's scheme to fund accumulated deficits of a nearly continuous century of war.[4]

The Gammons' house was of moderate size, the ground floor severely portioned into several rooms. In a room serving as a parlor and library, there were six of us—the Gammons, Catherine and Rose, James and me. We were enjoying ale fresh from Mr. Gammon's brewery, which he drank with a great showy smacking of his lips and tongue.

My nerves, I confess, began the evening as overly stretched catgut. But with the ale and the effortless and lively conversation, I soon settled in and spoke freely. When the war Austria was fighting against the French became a topic, I offered my opinion, "My experience fighting the French tells me the war will be protracted. It will be shortened considerably should your fine English military ally with us."

James said, "If we have the stomach for it."

---

[4] Mr. Montagu introduced the concept of National Debt to cover the rising costs of the Nine Years War and future wars. Newly imposed taxes on ale and spirits would be used to pay off the debt. Along with beverage taxes inevitably came tax scofflaws, putting breweries under the purview of tax collectors. *PW*

Catherine said, "Indeed. So soon after the last war our appetite for conflict has greatly diminished."

We laughed at Catherine's furtherance of James' metaphor.

"But on the other hand," Catherine continued, "if France is allowed to spread its influence, there might be a larger conflict in years to come."

Mr. Gammon said, "Which would likely further increase the tax on certain beverages." He raised his glass heartily, causing ale to slosh over the lip.

Rose said, "And higher taxes mean our customers would be forced to drink less ale. But enough talk of war and taxes. Catherine, Elizabeth, and I have a little surprise."

They walked over to a harpsichord in the corner of the room, and on top of nearby table were a violin and a viola. Rose sat down at the harpsichord, while Catherine picked up the violin and Mrs. Gammon picked up the viola.

Catherine announced, "In honor of Captain Wolf, we shall endeavor to play his composition titled 'Sonata for Violin in E Minor,' which we renamed 'A Winter Rose Dreams of Spring.'"

She gifted me one of her sly smiles before adding, "Please accept in advance our apology for the poor musicianship to which you will be subjected."

But their rendition was anything but poor. They, the self-professed unskilled novices, played the sonata with more true feeling than the musicians who would claim to be the best in London. Not only due to their precise skill with the instruments, but because the composition changed in their hands into one with more range of emotions I had hoped to evoke, from the depth of despair, to a warmth that might rescue a lost soul.

We had more lively conversation afterwards. When I was able to speak with Catherine alone, I thanked her for the performance.

Catherine said, "It was my pleasure to be able to play it. I hope we were able to capture a bit of the meaning imparted by your score, especially the complexities of the counterpoint. I sense there's a theme of much greater purpose than a simple melodic exercise. Can you tell me more, please? That is, if I'm not imposing on your secrets as a composer. I've never been able to speak with a composer about his work. The process is fascinating to me."

I wish I could say I impressed her with my exposition on the magic of composing, but I struggled to find the words. What I wanted to say is that first comes the ecstasy of inspiration, of an infinite potential of ideas. Then, after the inspiring and energetic start, the real work begins and the composer slogs away to the end, when the composition is deemed finished. The regret and disappointment begin soon after with the realization that the final work doesn't match the initial, seemingly brilliant idea. Between those times, there's some point when the composition begins to change, and something else entirely, something indefinable, of unknown origins, begins to emerge. I remember vaguely trying to explain this, and found myself repeating what I already said, as if I didn't know what I was talking about in the first place, or more likely, that I was trying to convince myself of my veracity.

As if hearing my thoughts, she said, "I understand it's difficult to discuss the thoughts which often come from a mysterious place, perhaps in the night when we are deeply asleep, or during the day when involved in some other task."

This time I was the one who smiled and nodded, encouraging her to continue, but she needed no such license. "As we practiced your composition, each of us had her favorite part, as well as her interpretation of what certain passages might mean, or of the feeling intended. Mine is the passage near the end of the first part with its great pause. The silence creates such a strong impression, a deep ravine of emotion, bringing it forth as much as any musical note could. I believe this feeling, coming from the depth of the silence, is the crucial meaning of the score. Please tell me I'm correct?"

Silence was my answer as I considered all she said and tried to think of an articulate answer.

"You don't wish to speak of it?" Catherine asked, an edge of impatience to her voice. Then, in a softened tone, she said, "You don't have to tell me. It's that I find your ability to capture feeling in music so intriguing."

"I wish that I could be so forthcoming," I responded quickly, nearly stepping on her words. "Yes, you're correct. The pause, the full note of silence, carries a great weight in the composition. Should I say that it's the essence of the piece? Yes, I might just be able to say that. I'm thrilled that you can see it, that you feel it. As for what it means, it's something I carry deep inside me, hence my silence when you asked the question. Not that I wish to maintain a great secret, certainly not from you. No, there's a great deal of my own inadequacy when I try to speak of it. Perhaps that's why I try to say it through music."

Catherine considered the words tumbling out of my mouth. In our wordless quiet, there came a rill of laughter from the others. We glanced at them and then smiled.

She said, "Whatever you carry in your heart is yours until you desire to share it. But maybe there's a way to bring it to light?"

"And how would that be accomplished?"

"Through your music, as you said, of course."

Her "of course" again made me question myself. I'd only considered music as balm, a muffling of pain. Or an expression of it.

"I don't know if I'm capable," I said quietly, thoughtfully.

She scolded me, "Forget your timidities. Now, what would it take to expose the darkness, for lack of a better description, you hold onto with such strength?"

I admit I didn't immediately know how to answer her question. But then I was struck with a sudden vision, at the time seemingly out of the blue, but I believe it was not. Instead, it is most certainly the sum of all Catherine said to me, about silence, about voice, and about desire. So much she said impacted me in the depths of my mind, even during the short time I'd known her.

"I can only think that a perfect composition played on a perfect musical instrument would be successful in that regard."

Now Catherine was thoughtfully quiet, as if replicating the silence in my composition, before saying, "Then that's what you must do."

After the party, the rest of which I barely remember as my thoughts were overtaken with our conversation, I returned to my quarters and set to composing a new concerto for the violin. But the attempt was not successful, not at all, as if I started swimming to the New World—I could see in my mind what it would be like to be there, but I knew I had no chance of making it.

T he following morning, I realized I hadn't learned much of anything about Mr. Montagu during the conversation at the Gammons' house. I'd have to make up for the failure, perhaps during a conversation with Catherine. As I desired to speak with her anyway, I sent her a letter, asking if we could meet at her earliest convenience to speak about music and instruments, especially about violins.

For a handful of days I didn't hear from her. I was in despair, near to giving up when I received her post.

We arranged to meet in a district where several purveyors of musical instruments were located. The district was called the Minories, and was near the looming Tower of London which housed the Royal Mint. As we walked, Catherine apologized for not responding sooner. Her life as house manager for Mr. Montagu had become very occupied.

I politely refused her apology and taking her opening to my advantage I said, "You must be constantly busy with Mr. Montagu's obligations."

"Obligations," she repeated and then was silent, for what reason I couldn't guess.

I added, "I understand he has much to do with the politics of the country."

"Ah, those obligations. Yes, I suppose he does have many. He also has many social functions. He participates in several literary circles, especially. Although his political obligations and his social events often go hand in glove."

"Undoubtedly so. What about music circles?" I asked. "You and he attended my concert."

"He goes to a concert on occasion, though not nearly as often as he attends literary functions."

Not wanting to push my mission further, I again told her that her apology was not necessary because I should have no expectation at all that she would be available to help me, nor that she needed to express any interest in my musical quest.

With her straightforward way of telling me I had erred in my judgment in refusing her apology, she told me I had a duty to accept it. I did so immediately, which made her laugh. With all of that settled, she asked me, "Do you have a particular instrument in mind?"

"I must admit I've barely made a start on the composition, so I can't say for certain. However, I believe it should be a violin. No other instrument has the depth of feeling that can be coaxed from it."

She announced her agreement with a single word—"Good"—and we began our quest. The shops were small and crammed with instruments from brass to strings to percussion. Catherine and I tested a few violins, but with only a few notes we could tell these were not superb instruments. Nearly giving up, we came to a small shop wedged between two larger buildings. The sign above the door read simply "Penbook" and there was only a single violin bow displayed in the window box. It rested on the burgundy felt which covered the bow's case.

Catherine said, "Penbook seems to care about quality more than quantity."

"Very promising," I said, and we entered the shop.

The tinkling of a well-tuned bell announced our presence. Inside, the shop was narrow but long. Along one side, the violins, violas, and violoncellos[5] were displayed elegantly—the violins and violas on the wall, and the violoncellos in cases set on the floor. Along the other side were a settee and chairs.

"Welcome," said a voice seemingly from out of nowhere. "I'm Penbook."

I found the source of the voice—a shortish man nearly hidden by a winged chair.

"Hello," we said in return.

"How may I be of service?"

Catherine and I stepped forward while he remained at the chair, as if needing it for support. We stopped before we got too close, possibly frightening him to death.

"We're interested in a violin, Mr. Penbook," I said.

"I have a few, to be so bold as to state the obvious," Mr. Penbook said, gazing around the shop.

I said, "Then to get straight to the point, our interest is in not just any violin."

"That depends on what you mean," said the proprietor, "But I dare say I have a few 'not just any' violins."

Without even a trace of the exasperation I was feeling, Catherine said, "We'd be pleased if we could try your best."

"First," said Mr. Penbook, clearly annoyed by the sharp tone to his voice, "I must ask whom I'm going to be pleasing?"

I introduced both of us without embellishment, as I believed he would not appreciate the full story of how we came to be in his shop.

---

[5] Now known more commonly as the cello. *TS*

Besides, his blank countenance after I announced our names meant they bore no meaning for him.

"Your descriptive word 'best,'" said Mr. Penbook, moving slightly away from his chair, "depends on the context in which the violin will be played. Is it for the beginning player or the top violinist in the royal court orchestra? Will it be played in the salon of a house or the largest concert halls of Europe? Is the music to be played subtle in tone or in full measure? Those are but a few of my questions."

Catherine summoned a smile from somewhere and said, "We're interested in a violin a top musician would be happy playing in the best concert halls in Europe. And the compositions would be of equal rank."

"Who would be the composer?" asked Mr. Penbook.

Catherine placed her hand on my shoulder. "Why, here he is. Captain Wolf."

Mr. Penbook took a long look at me. "Forgive me. I lack knowledge of you or your compositions. But never mind, allow me to show you the finest violins in London."

His initial reticence overcome, he demonstrated three violins for us, playing a few bars of a concerto that extended across octaves. Each violin bore remarkably different sounds, one sweet and light, one opposite of that with deep, broad, and almost guttural tones, and one that was smooth, across low and high tones, but without much excitement.

"Those are excellent violins, if different in tone and power," I said. "The first one ... where is it from?"

"The workshop of Amati, an Italian luthier. The second is from a French luthier, and the third from Jacob Stainer, one of your Austrian countrymen."

I'd heard Stainer's violins being played; they were powerful, but the Amati impressed me more. "Might I have Miss Barton play the Amati?" I asked him.

He made a great show of his hesitancy, no doubt intending to build up the value of the instrument. Finally, he handed the violin and bow to Catherine.

"Remarkably light and balanced," she said and then played a few notes from my Sonata for Violin in E Minor. "Well lively. Is it what you are looking for Captain Wolf?"

This time I hesitated. "Close, perhaps. I find it difficult to say exactly what it is we want to hear."

Mr. Penbook clucked and took back the violin. "You'll simply find no better violin in London. When you have better in mind what you need and have tried all the other instruments, you'll return here."

He replaced the violin in its case and retreated to his place next to the chair.

Dismissed from his presence, we walked out of the shop. Catherine said, "I'd love to share a pot of good coffee, if you can. I have a little time before I must return to the house."

"I do have time as well," I said.

She took me to an establishment where women were welcomed—in most London coffeehouses they were not. This one also catered to writers and artists and musicians, according to Catherine. Most were blurry eyed as with lack of sleep, and yet speaking loudly and on top of one another. Matching the atmosphere, the coffee was also lively.

"Mr. Penbook was rather haughty," Catherine said, "but he raises a good point. If we could describe exactly what we wanted in a violin, then we'd have a better chance of finding it."

"Agreed," I said, enjoying her use of *we*. "I'll think more about the music."

"That would be a good path. But I also think it would be good to understand more about the actual construction of a superior violin. Do you know much of the materials and craftsmanship involved?"

"Very little, I'm afraid."

Catherine let a moment of silence slip into the conversation before she said, "I have a thought, perhaps a strange sounding one. I suggest you speak with my uncle, Isaac Newton. He's not a musician, nor have I heard him express interest in music, but he's a man of the highest intelligence. He loves a puzzle that captivates him so much he must solve it, even before eating or sleeping."

I jumped at the idea, not only that he might help me, but also that I would be more encompassed in Catherine's life. Whether it would result in good or bad consequences, I failed to consider at the time.

chapter 2

My reminiscing ended when Dr. Newton wandered into the parlor as if unaware he entertained a visitor, or as if deep in thought on another matter. Perhaps both were the case. He wasn't tall but his straight posture and fine physical condition made him appear taller and much younger than his fifty-some years. When he became aware of my presence, the gaze he turned on me was as focused as Catherine's had been when we first met, although nothing so pleasant.

He must have seen me staring at the clock because without words of greeting he said, "Huygens created a splendid timepiece despite his mistaken ideas of many natural phenomena. Given the course of events, it appears that fabricating the mechanisms of a clock distracted him while calculating the mathematics of pendulum motion or from arriving at accurate philosophies of the natural world, particularly the fundamental nature of light. Yes, yes, I understand a precise and dependable clock is valuable, but I would have told him to leave the practicalities to others.[1] I'm sure you would agree, wouldn't you, Captain Wolf?"

As I didn't understand with what I was agreeing, I didn't know how to answer, at least not in any sense of a clever response. Trying something, I blurted, "I agree we need to be of a focused mind to perform our best."

---

[1] Ironically, as I later learned, Dr. Newton ground and polished glass for the lenses of his telescopes and created other physical measuring instruments as he required. *PW*

Contrary to Newton's criticism, Christiaan Huygens hired a clockmaker to construct his clocks. *TS*

Dr. Newton's large eyes pinched nearly closed above his long, pointed nose, making him appear as if he were inhaling something malodorous. Moments went by, doubling my worry.

Finally, he spoke. "You're arguing a generality when I asked your thoughts on a specific case."

"I see … well then, regarding Mr. Huygens, I can't say I would agree or disagree since I've never met the man, nor have I read any of his ideas."

Dr. Newton appeared to soften. In pity? Abruptly changing the course of the conversation, he asked, "If I were to ask you the speed at which sound travels, what would be your answer? I ask this because music is the result of sound. Thus, you should know at least this much about the basic phenomenon of your interest."

My viscera twisted into knots. I hadn't anticipated an intense interrogation upon the first moments of meeting.

"I can't tell you for certain, not precisely, at what speed sound would trace. I can say it moves quickly."

"Quickly?" said Dr. Newton, the word spoken in distain.

"Very quickly?" I said while thinking of an example. "If I stand on the stage of a large concert hall and play a note on an instrument, there is a tiny lapse in time when the note, the sound, strikes the back wall and returns to my ears. But, as the sound travels fast, it isn't enough to make a difference since it's instantaneously registered by the audience."

Now Dr. Newton's expression turned sour. Clearly my stumbling answer distressed him. "I'm afraid your answer doesn't rise to an acceptable level for your quest. Thus, my next question is this—how shall I help if you care nothing for the very basic phenomenon of your subject?"

Standing in his parlor, with all social proprieties disregarded, knowing not what Catherine told her uncle about me and my endeavor, while being accused of lacking any fundamental knowledge of sound and thus music, I felt as if I were facing a firing squad. I endeavored to rise above the occasion of my imminent death.

I took a deep breath and let it out as I answered his protestation. "You're correct, sir. If I'm to have you assist me in this matter I must go back to the fundamental aspects of sound. I sincerely apologize. I shall take leave, no longer waste your time."

I waited to be dismissed without a further word. But, he was to not let me off the hook so easily.

"If you don't know the speed of sound, other than it being 'quick,' and even if you don't understand the limitations regarding the lack of certain knowledge, surely you must know how one might endeavor to measure the speed of sound?"

Thinking of a logical and reasoned answer, my desperate gaze reverted toward Huygens' clock. Time, or rather measuring time, should be part of the answer, because I knew that speed is related to time. In battle we can estimate the distance of artillery ordinance by the delay between muzzle flash and hearing the explosion.

Confident of my logic, I gave my answer, "In battle, it's important to know the distance of the enemy's cannon fire. We have a rough idea of this from the delay between flash, which is observed instantly and the sound of the powder exploding, which comes at a slower pace. Using this idea, but in reverse, if we know the distance to the observed cannon, and we measure the time delay with a device, such as Mr. Huygens' clock, we can determine the speed of sound."

At first, Dr. Newton again appeared to be in great distress; however, his expression softened almost immediately. "Your method is crude, and it wouldn't rise to a level nearing rigor, but you're on the right course. You've made many assumptions, the sum of which would compound into grievous errors. One assumption is that you're seeing the muzzle flash instantaneously. Not only is there nothing instantaneous about it, indeed, light, which you are really seeing, has a speed itself. Light is made of corpuscles which move through the air, or transparent material, and vary depending on the corpuscle's characteristics. Although, your clockmaker Mr. Huygens would dispute this."[2]

"Hmm, I see," I mumbled when he paused and glared toward the clock. I didn't understand his description or explanation of the nature of light, but neither did I want to interrupt him for clarification.

"In addition," he continued, saving me from further indictment, "your argument includes your *perception* of the flash, which passes through your eyes and into your brain, before impinging on your awareness of the light. This process takes a measurable amount of time. Furthermore, your assumption that a clock such as the one sitting here is precise enough to measure your delay is also not correct. You would need one far more precise. Perhaps, were he alive, you could enlist Huygens to develop such mechanical precision; although, I believe he would fail at the task. Furthermore, how do you start and stop the clock, or whatever time measuring device you use?"

I wanted to shake my head and admit I was lost, but instead I looked thoughtful and eventually said, "With a mechanism to control the clock, or by noting the time when the flash is seen and the explosion is heard?"

Dr. Newton jumped on my answer as if he had anticipated it. "Sight and sound, and the reaction to those perceptions, are inherently imprecise, no matter how well trained you think you might be. Regardless, your measurements would not be reliable. And another

---

2 Christiaan Huygens, 1629-1695, believed light travels in waves, like ripples in a pond, as opposed to Dr. Newton's corpuscular theory. *PW*

"Corpuscular" refers to "particles;" so according to Newton, light consists of tiny particles traveling through air or other medium. Newton also knew something of the anatomy of the eye, having performed an experiment on himself—insetting a small dowel behind an eyeball and stimulating the optic nerve. *TS*

factor, which is really discussing many things at once, is that you've neglected confounding variables."

He stared at me for an uncomfortable moment before asking, "Do you know what that indicates?"

Again, I did not know entirely what he was asking, and my recollection of his exact words may not be correct. However, I was relieved he was continuing to ask me questions instead of completely shutting me out.

I mustered a veneer of bravado and said, "I assume by 'confounding' you mean things that would interfere with the experiment. I know I'm speaking too generally in contrary to your desire for specifics."

My mind frantically searched for something specific. "I suppose that one could be the size of the powder charge."

Unfortunately, I again received his distressed expression. He said, "Why would this be a confounding variable?"

My throat grew dry and constricted. "I believe that the sound from a larger charge would travel faster."

He appeared to be slightly surprised at my answer. "And why would you *believe* that?"

"Because louder sounds travel faster?" I said, realizing at once that it was a feeble response.

"But why, sir, *why*? What's your hypothesis?"

My what? Although I had a feeling of an answer, I had no immediate response that would not likely dig my grave deeper. My silence was met with his. Worse than the dead quiet, except the delicate whirring of Huygens' clock, Dr. Newton's mind seemed to have slipped into another world. I searched his countenance for a clue as to his mood. Was he about to explode into anger? Or in a paroxysm of laughter?

Instead, his lips made a slight quivering movement before he turned and left me alone.

Not knowing if I'd been summarily dismissed, or if I should wait for his return, I remained frozen to the spot, wondering why my response would elicit such a reaction. If I'd said something utterly wrong, I thought he would have pointed out my error without hesitation.

On the other hand, I might have made a valid assumption, one that told him I didn't need his assistance. Surely that couldn't be the case. I tried coming up with other confounding factors that might affect my hypothetical experiment; however, my mind was so frantically engaged with coming up with reasons why Dr. Newton abandoned me that I failed to come up with a single one.

Seeking to calm my mind, I turned to music, running through the preliminary bars of my composition. I had at last begun the work, relying on the inspiration of my afternoon out with Catherine. I settled on C major as the key and its outright expression of joy. Now, I added a plodding, heavy few bars to reflect the mood of my solitary existence in Dr. Newton's parlor.

"Excuse me, sir," the housekeeper said as she entered the room. "Master Newton is detained. I beg your patience and wish to offer you tea or coffee[3] while you wait until he's ready to rejoin you."

"Thank you kindly. I need nothing. Do you know how long Dr. Newton will be unavailable?"

"If I knew that I would be the wisest woman in the world." She gave me a nod of sympathy and turned to leave. Then she stopped and said with a sly smile, "Instead of tea or coffee, perhaps an ale?"

I smiled. "I would covet an ale, if you would be so kind."

"A wise choice, Captain. Our ale is brewed by the master himself."

She returned quickly with the refreshment. While I sipped Dr. Newton's excellent ale, well balanced with sweet and bitter, I tried to

---

[3] Newton enjoyed coffee although not likely as much as Voltaire who reportedly consumed as many as fifty cups a day. *TS*

think of some other confounding variables, that is, other than my attempt with the powder charge, which drove Dr. Newton away. Perhaps the weather? Could the temperature, the air's heat or cold, change the speed of sound? Maybe the time of day ... that is, could the amount of sunlight affect the speed of light? Or the terrain over which the sound travels?

However, I thought, Dr. Newton's exit may not have been because of my inability to come up with valid variables, but rather that he was distressed with my general lack of precision or lack of care in how I approached him with my request. Clearly, I realized without a doubt, I didn't have, even minutely, his intellect and reasoning skills. But in my defense, I wasn't given a chance to explain my quest.

I finished my ale and was near ready to give up when Dr. Newton burst back into the room. Without explaining his absence, he launched into an excited dissertation. It was as if he'd never left.

"The speed of sound is one-thousand, eighty-eight feet per second in air.[4] Of course, the medium in which it flows affects the exactness of the calculation. Think about two different types of sounds. I'm sure you have a tuning pitch pipe, which produces a singular, signature note. This isn't the same with your cannon shot, the sound of which consists of notes produced by the vibrations of strings or reeds, or of an inestimable orchestra, each member playing random notes on their instrument as loudly as possible at the same time."

He paused. I nodded, not in complete understanding, but enough that I was encouraged to urge him to continue. That seemed to please him.

---

[4] Newton's calculations based on pressure waves were correct but failed to take in to account a fluctuation in temperature, as pointed out later by the French scholar Pierre-Simon, Marquis de Laplace. The speed of sound is 1,126 feet/sec (343.2 meters per second) in dry air at 68 °F (20 °C). *TS*

"It's the frequency of the sound wave, the essence of musical notes!" he exclaimed. Then he went over to a desk where he found a piece of paper and a quill pen. He dipped the point in a jar of ink.

As he moved the pen over the paper, he said, "The detonation of a powder charge causes an explosion of all frequencies. Of course, waves travel at the same speed, otherwise your large concert hall would change the timing of low notes versus high notes, making the music sound oddly disconcerting. The pitch produces a concise pattern which travels in its signature wave form, and thus we can precisely calculate the differences through whichever medium it flows."

He showed me his sketch—partly musical notes on a scale, which I understood, and partly a series of undulating lines, which I did not. Clearly, he expected the drawing to help.

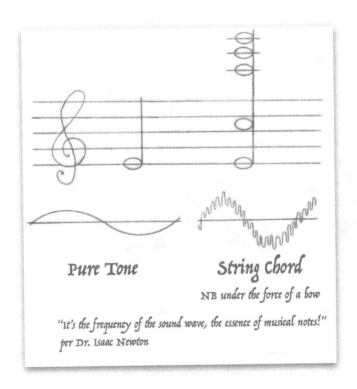

Pure Tone

String chord

NB under the force of a bow

"It's the frequency of the sound wave, the essence of musical notes!" per Dr. Isaac Newton

"Now what can you say about your experiment with the cannon shot?"

He was again putting me to the test. I responded with my first thought, "The speed of sound would depend on the weather?"

Dr. Newton's eyes flicked back and forth before his gaze rested on me for longer than the briefest moment it had been before that evening. Whether I saw fire or ice in that gaze, I cannot rightly say now. All I felt was a dread that I'd been exposed to be in heart and mind a weak man, one of little consequence and, worse, that I was incapable of rising above my lowly station. What Dr. Newton spoke next, though, was nothing short of an unholy evisceration.

"Make no egregious error concerning my intentions. I know why you're here, Captain Wolf. I know the exact details of your quest. I know more than you know, likely more than you'll ever know. I'm in a position to assist, but you do not, apparently, have the raw intellect to handle, to comprehend, even the most basic of my requests, or my simplest queries. Nor do you have the patience to perform the least amount of thinking that my questions require of you. But, after all of that, I must admit, incredulously, I'm intrigued by your quest, by your obsession. Hence, despite my better judgment, I cannot turn you away.

"The creation of a violin for your musical composition, an instrument sufficient to reach the notes and the volume of sound that Catherine has described to me, requires a rigorous process and as much deep thought and rational experimentation as the creation of any scientific instrument, or in the understanding of a natural phenomenon. Guiding any and all these numerous decisions and implementations are at once the elemental and profound discrete facts upon which all must rest. Take a single factor or variable, the thickness of the varnish applied to a violin, for one example. How do you decide on the thickness of one layer without understanding the myriad of effects one layer makes on another?"

After I'd gathered my wits from my dressing down, I said, "I do understand that there are many elements a master luthier must consider. Then he must be able to execute them in a more than workmanlike manner. My hope is that you'll be able to help me sort out all the elements, to determine the ones of most value and their impact."

Dr. Newton surely thought me an ill-mannered child when he peered at me with disdain. "Sir, you're making this extremely difficult not only on me, but on yourself." And with that said, he again walked out of the room.

But what had I said? I rather thought I spoke in agreement with him, and in the manner that would make him amenable to help with my task.

After another twenty minutes passed on Mr. Huygens' clock, I knew Dr. Newton had abandoned me.

chapter 3

My first encounter with Dr. Newton, as disheartening and unpleasant as it was, instilled in me a curious vitality. All things shone brighter. Smells were sharper, sounds clearer. I experienced a surge of musical passion, composing pages of score at one go.

On the other side of that coin, though, I'd let down Catherine after she introduced me to her uncle. I started a letter of apology to her several times, but always failed to find the right tone. *My dear Catherine, I am truly distraught* ... distraught? So weak! *My Dear Miss Barton, I first must thank you for introducing me to your uncle, Dr. Newton* ... argh, she knows her uncle's name.

My disappointment also weighed on the heavy side as I was unable to induce Dr. Newton to speak one word regarding Mr. Montagu. Of course, I simply had no chance of inserting the question of political power and influence into the conversation as I struggled with the speed of sound, confounding variables, and apparently my general lack of knowledge of everything else in the world.

A morning after a restless night, I met with James and several other English officers, including the high-ranking general—the Earl of Marlborough.[1] We gathered in the chambers called the Royal Battle Room. With its towering ceiling, grand paintings of past generals ever more valiant than those in the officers club paintings, the room gave our assembly a vigorous mood of heroic urgency.

Although I wondered if the room was named for royals in battle, or royals battling each other.

---

[1] Born John Churchill, he survived a charge of high treason only eight years prior. The Earl of Marlborough would soon become Duke of Marlborough and command the English army. *PW*

The Earl spoke at length, as generals are wont to do. The gist of his speech questioned the inevitability of the English joining the Austrians and our allies in fighting the French. As much as he despised the French, he made a point of raising the question more than once: Was it England's responsibility to support the Hapsburgs over the House of Bourbon?[2] As much as he would love to give the French a good fight, he saber-rattled, the English had other conflicts to deal with, as well as recovering from the war ended not too many years ago.

The hesitancy not only stemmed from the military, he continued. Those in the highest reaches of power were averse to another war. But if drawn into the conflict, he said with voice raised, then the English shall be in it to prevail as quickly as possible. Therefore, he pronounced, he was making plans with all due secrecy to determine the most strategic and effective use of the forces under his command.

At last, after the drawn-out speeches, I was subjected to an interrogation aimed at finding out what I knew of the current state of the Austrian campaign against the French. I was forthcoming of our progress, which had been advancing slowly but steadily into captured territories. Of course, I advocated for the assistance of the English military—the "finest in the world," I declared to the obvious pleasure of those in attendance.

The council meeting ended when the general's stomach began rumbling like distant cannon fire. James and I were able to escape from the general's party to enjoy ale and pie at an out-of-the-way tavern by ourselves.

"How do you think it went?" I asked James after we slugged down a half a mug of ale.

"Well enough. You were very artful in your answers."

---

[2] The power struggle between the Austrian Hapsburgs and the Holy Roman Empire, and the House of Bourbon in France, was at the heart of the War of Spanish Succession. *PW*

"I hope it was enough to persuade the Earl to push the war effort here."

"As much as the general wishes to believe his power can reach that far, it's fortunate that he has little say on whether we go to war or not."

"I assume it's your royal monarch who has the ultimate say?"

"Perhaps, but the real power, or rather the conflicted nature of power, lies within the Whigs and Tories. They battle behind the curtain to decide the course of action. The winner will have the greatest advantage over the course of the nation, which is to mean an advantage for their personal power as well."

After I let the weight of James' point sink in, I asked, "Would Mr. Montagu be one of those embroiled in the conflict?"

James nodded. "At the heart of it."

"And his stance?" I asked, hoping I wasn't too direct.

James seemed unperturbed by the question, answering forthwith, "I can't say I know, or if he knows it himself, at this early stage."

That was important to hear, I thought, but didn't press this line of inquiry further. We enjoyed the food and more ale. The sustenance relaxed me, and I found myself relating to James my encounter with Dr. Newton. In our state of near inebriation, the tale became more comedic farce than tragedy.

"What has Catherine said about your encounter?"

My hesitation answered his query.

"Phillipe, by now she will have heard from him. You have to tell her your side of the misery circus. I'd recommend she drink sherry while listening, then perhaps you can turn it to your advantage. Otherwise ..."

"Otherwise?"

"Otherwise, she'll believe you no end a coward, or at least a man who has not only wasted her time, but also wasted the most precious time of her uncle."

I was already aware of that, but to hear it from James made it seem more severe and of greater consequence. "Though what should I say to her?" I implored. "Especially after this long delay?"

"You simply need to apologize profusely and speak with her in all honesty. Catherine can tell if you aren't speaking the truth."

That wasn't something I hadn't already surmised on my own.

Mr. Penbook rose from his chair when I entered his shop. Inside, the warmth of the air had a gentle moistness to it, like a southern sea. The flicker of recognition he gave me didn't betray if he was elated to see me or not, but he said without a trace of disdain, "Welcome back to Penbook's. Have you decided on an instrument, sir? Or should I say, Captain? I believe you were leaning toward the Italian Amati."

"I'm still leaning that direction."

"An excellent direction to lean."

"However," I continued in an earnest tone, "I'd appreciate understanding more about the violin and what makes it better than others." I thought of Dr. Newton's exhortation to think of the creation of a violin in terms of variables. But I didn't want to go into that painful memory with Mr. Penbook.

He was unperturbed by my request. "Of course. But first things first, shall we agree on a price?"

"That will be satisfactory," I said, anxious to hear if his price was within reach of my funds. "What would be your price?"

"This fine violin, exported from Italy, is worth considerably more than forty pounds sterling. But I'll sell it for that amount."

A rich sum. My funds could cover it but would leave me with only a few pence. Our negotiation went on for an aggravatingly long time, until we finally agreed to thirty-two pounds. He tried to make me feel I got the better of him, but I was sure the reverse were true.

As promised, he gave me his opinion of why the violin was superior, pointing out the beauty of the wood and clarity of the varnish, the care taken with the joinery, and, in general, the excellent craftsmanship. He then played a few bars before extolling the golden, rounded notes as if describing a sensuous lover.

When he finished, I thanked him and asked him to tell me more about the region in Italy where the violin was made.

"In the city of Cremona, there are several luthiers. By the way, a superior violinist, named D'Amico, lives in Cremona. I imagine he would know all the luthiers there and the quality of their instruments."

I hadn't heard of the violinist, but I'd heard of Cremona. Unfortunately, the city was currently occupied by French military forces.

With the Amati violin in my possession, I managed to compose a few more lines of my concerto. The Amati was indeed a superior violin, discernibly so even in my inexpert hands. However, I felt it lacking in the middle range, the higher register needed more brightness for my purposes. I didn't know how a luthier would change the construction of a violin to accommodate those proposed improvements. But as I composed, I developed an idea of what to do with the instrument, that is, more than inspiring the composition.

Before implementing my plan, I met James and Mr. Lupine at separate times. In a room at the end of a back hallway in the military headquarters, where James and I were assured of a private conversation, I hatched a strategy for action instead of more sitting in endless meetings.

"How is your French?" I asked him.

"My French?" he said with doubtful consideration. "I suppose it's passable. I studied it for a few years and was an interrogator of French prisoners of war. Why?"

"If you're willing and believe that action and good information is critical to an early end to the war, any war, then I propose we travel to Italy, to a city named Cremona, where the French have a stronghold. There we can infiltrate the city posing as French bureaucrats."

James sat up in his chair where he was slumping. "Intriguing. But what kind of bureaucrats would go to an occupied city during a war?"

I told him about the Italian Amati and Mr. Penbook's advice of finding a luthier worthy of creating a superior violin. "We could pose as purchasers of musical instruments for the court musicians."

"Killing two birds with one stone," he said with a smile. "It's a good idea, I believe, but why would you want me along?"

"If it were only me, then would my reports upon returning be considered unbiased?"

James made fists then unclenched them, as if preparing for a fistfight. "Not likely, no. Then I should practice my French."

"I'd be of help with your practice," I said. "My mother is French and that's what she spoke to me as a child."

"Interesting. But you were born in Austria?"

"Yes. My mother was exiled there before I was born. It's a long story."

"I should like to hear it sometime. For now, we should discuss your plan in more detail. I'll need to have my part in it approved."

We spent a good part of the day with maps, writing down strategies, and even getting in some practice with French. James' fluency was indeed passable, although his accent needed the most work. With a few more sessions, it might be more than passable.

Mr. Lupine was also amenable to the plan, when I met with him later that evening. "It's not without risk," he said.

I agreed. "No, it's not. The rewards would be great."

He nodded once. "And what of Montagu? Have you been able to find out anything of his stance?"

"I've yet to hear anything definitive, either from his own lips or the words of others. I've been establishing solid contact with Dr. Newton and Catherine Barton, as well as with Captain Brookfield. The proposed plan to infiltrate Cremona, if successful, would further solidify those relationships."

As he did when thinking, Mr. Lupine absentmindedly stroked his scar, and sipped his brandy. "I'll submit your plan for approval."

N ot long after the plan was approved by the English command, and while we waited for approval from the Austrian military, I received a post from Catherine, asking to meet me at the coffee-house where we had been before. When I arrived, the proprietress whisked me into one of the private rooms in the back. Catherine was already there and we greeted each other warmly.

"This is for you," I said after we settled at our table.

Gazing at the case I placed in front of her, she said, "The Italian violin from Mr. Penbook's store?"

"The very one."

"Excellent. But why do you present it to me?"

"I believe it's the best violin in London at this time. I want you to play it whenever you wish, but hopefully while playing my concerto. If I ever complete it. But I also would like you to lend it to Dr. Newton, so that he might hear what a superior, if not perfect, violin might sound like."

Catherine opened the case. "It's more beautiful than I remember. I shall look forward to playing it, and to practicing your concerto."

Our coffee service arrived. We enjoyed some of the strong and enlivening drink. Placing her cup on the saucer, Catherine said, "Speaking of my uncle, he asked after you."

"I doubt in good reference."

"Contrarily, he said nothing of negative consequence. Although, my uncle being himself, he also said nothing of great encouragement. Still, that he said anything at all is in your favor."

"What did he say exactly, if I may ask?"

"To be truthful, not very much, as he merely asked if you were still pursuing your stringed instrument experiment—as he called it. I know my uncle's feelings more than most, although even that's not very much. But I can assure you that when my uncle's curiosity is piqued by something, he won't let it go."

"That's good to hear," I said. "But I failed to purport myself well in our first meeting. I have thought about it very much—thinking about what I might have done better. Should I have been more prepared? Or should I have been more explicit in what I'm trying to do?"

Catherine shook her head a little while smiling. "I'm afraid you're wasting your thoughts. You could spend a decade preparing and not cover all matters he might bring up or, might I say, torture you with. But in the end, you mustn't be afraid of him."

"He can perceive fear like a wild dog?"

She laughed. "I don't know what he can sense of another person, or if he can at all. If he can, he would likely not care one way or another. His mind is keen, but more than that, he's many steps ahead of your thoughts. That's what makes any preparation difficult, if not impossible."

That she told me this did give me a measure of comfort. Whether that was her objective or not didn't matter, for I appreciated her words. "Thank you," I said. "I'll pursue my dream with your uncle."

"I believe he would be disappointed if you gave up and never spoke with him again. I wish I could tell you more how to approach him, but I doubt I would be able to provide clear and complete guidance. That said, I do suggest that perhaps you read some of his works. I have read much of it. I confess it's difficult reading. Some of it I understand better than others. Indeed, his ideas of motion have a counterintuitive sense to them."

"That's good advice. I shall do exactly that. Do you have other suggestions?"

She thought for a few moments. "Beyond his oft-impenetrable intellect, his early life was one of turmoil, and I sincerely believe this contributed to making him a … complex man. His father died before he could know him. His mother left him with his grandmother when he was three years old, and she sought another life with my grandfather, whom my uncle despised.[3] That makes him my half-uncle, to be precise. He has buried this abandonment deeply and won't discuss it at all. But I know it still affects him."

That could explain his abrupt behavior. "Thank you for telling me this. It's very insightful and will be helpful to me. Has he discussed his childhood with you?"

"No, not at all. I believe that he wouldn't want to. When I mention anything from that time, he quickly moves the conversation away to other topics."

Even knowing him only through my one encounter, I believed it was completely in character for him to do so. He certainly had with me. "I should avoid that conversation then."

Catherine thought for a moment while sipping coffee. "If anything, Uncle Isaac is unpredictable, even as he focuses on explaining nature with unchanging predictions. I can't advise you there. But you're an intelligent man. You'll be able to measure the worth of discussing any topic."

I thanked her, even as I doubted it fully true. I said, "I understand from James that your uncle and your employer met at Trinity College."

---

[3] Apparently, Dr. Newton despised his stepfather enough to once threaten to burn his house down over him and Newton's mother. *PW*

"Yes, true. Uncle Isaac was, officially still is, a professor. Charles Montagu, Baron Halifax, was a student."

"What did Mr. Montagu study?" I ventured to ask.

"Philosophy and letters? I believe so. He focused on poetry, and that's how he first became known, before progressing into the realm of politics."

"An interesting path," I said lightly, not wishing to tread too firmly.

"And not always a smooth path. The winds of power change directions at a whim."

"But he's catching the wind now?"

Catherine looked away, perhaps wondering what to say in response. "Perhaps there's a light breeze blowing in his direction," she finally said.

Not wanting to press further, I ended my questions about Mr. Montagu. We enjoyed our coffee. Catherine played the violin in our private room. I wished the afternoon to never end.

While James and I planned our expedition to Italy and I waited for an invitation from Dr. Newton, I valiantly read his tome, *Philosophiae Naturalis Principia Mathematica*. The ideas were complex and the writing in Latin,[4] both which slowed my comprehension. His mathematics were most foreign to me, but I believed I understood his drawings, perhaps because of my training in military maps and sketched plans. Beyond these general topics, what I gleaned most of all was how deep a thinker he had become, and not only in understanding the motion of worldly objects and heavenly bodies, but in the ability to see what is not immediately obvious to those of us with lesser powers of observation. His reasoning and in-

---

[4] Originally published in 1687, the *Mathematical Principles of Natural Philosophy* was not translated and published in English until 1728. *TS*

tellect far exceeded mine, so much so I would never reach his level even if I studied his expositions for a hundred years.

His brilliance forced upon me a realization that compared to Dr. Newton's grand explanations of the natural world, my objective of a grand composition played on a superior instrument lacked substance. I needed to add depth to the meaning of what I was trying to accomplish. What that might be, I had no idea at the time, but knew that finding out was important.

I also realized that Catherine did not merely suggest I read her uncle's work for my education, but that there was something within it I needed to grasp, or to discover, which would help me in dealing with him. This came to mind while I was reading the volume in my room at the officer's quarters at the military barracks, struggling to keep my eyes open, wishing I could be with Catherine. I perked up when I read in his first book, Section 8, Proposition 48—rules that determine the speed of waves in fluids. In air, the speed depends on the density of the air and amount of water vapor. He estimated that the speed of sound is one-thousand eighty-eight feet per second, just as he told me in our first meeting. If, using my rudimentary mathematics, a cannon blast happened a mile away, the "boom" takes a little under five counted seconds to reach my ears.

Applying this to music, the sound from a violin takes a minuscule portion of a second to reach the ears of someone sitting in the middle of a large hall. And the same sound deflecting off the back wall returning to the ears of the same listener would be about twice as long. But this secondary sound would not be as loud for a person sitting in the back of the hall, yet longer for a person sitting in the front. I have experienced this phenomenon, although the effect depends on the shape of the hall, the materials covering the walls, the number of people in the audience, and probably many other factors.

At least I felt that, if only for a few moments, I was using my reasoning to an advantage, which might be approved by Dr. Newton.

chapter 4

The housekeeper greeted me with a bemused smile, likely astonished I was back for more of Dr. Newton's torture. I followed her through the house, passing the library with crimson painted bookcases, skirting the dining room with crimson wall fabric, and then walking up a staircase festooned with crimson balusters. At the top of the stairs, we went down a corridor and entered a large room where Dr. Newton was standing bent over a long table. Around the room on other tables were mechanical devices, glass lenses and prisms, balls and blocks of various materials, stacks of papers, and mysterious tools.

On the table were three violins. One had been sawn apart, as if drawn-and-quartered in an execution.

My throat caught my heart as it leapt. Had he disemboweled the Italian violin I had given to Catherine?

The housekeeper announced me. Dr. Newton waved me in with a quick flip of his hand, then gestured for me to come over to him. When I neared, I saw that he was writing notes on a drawing. While he wrote, I managed to get a better look at the violins and released the lungfuls of breath I'd been holding—one of the wholly intact instruments was the recognizable Italian Amati.

"Thank you for seeing me again, Dr. Newton," I said. "I trust all is well with you?"

His hot gaze was a saber ready to cut. "Captain Wolf, I've granted you this visit, and we have much ground to cover in a short time."

So much for pleasantries. I vowed to never again presume they were necessary.

When I was close to him, he turned the drawing and pushed it toward me. "What do you make of this?"

I murmured when I saw he had drawn a set of lines, arcs, and circles, and had written tiny script at various places on the paper. My murmur was one of shock at the details, at the complexities it proposed, not to mention the amount of work he had expended on the drawing. Then I noticed a date and time written in a corner—the date was the current day, the time only two hours earlier. He created the intricate document quickly. But I needed to say something of substance besides praising his quick hand, and so I inspected his work more closely.

The diagram was roughly divided into thirds. The top third was a line that repeatedly sloped up then down, crossing a line labeled as "time." The middle third consisted of a view of a section of the top of a violin, with the *f*-shaped sound holes drawn and lines connecting them, and with a circle drawn between them, connected by dashed lines. The bottom third showed a cross-section of the violin, drawn at the bridge, showing the bass bar, the bridge, and the sound post.

I recognized that the drawing portrayed the main functional sections and parts of a violin. His notes broke down the complexities into smaller complexities, each, no doubt, with further intricacies not yet explored. As if a military map could be taken down to the individual level of officer, sergeant, and infantryman.

But what was he expecting me to say about the work? I thought back to Catherine's suggestions, about keeping her uncle's attention. In one sense, I did have something to say: that I'd examined his drawing, noted its features, and had drawn some conclusions from it. Likewise, I must not be too concerned with trying to know what Dr. Newton would want me to say. I had to stand as I would in the face of the enemy—prepared and with a plan, but willing to change course if needed.

I said, "What do I make of your drawing … well, it shows the important pieces of a violin. There's a string, which generates sound when under the bow. Then we see the front where the bridge is placed, and where the bass bar and sound post are placed underneath the top, in relation to the sound holes. Lastly, we see how those pieces are seen from a side view of the instrument. The size and relationship of the pieces are also described with notations and measurements."

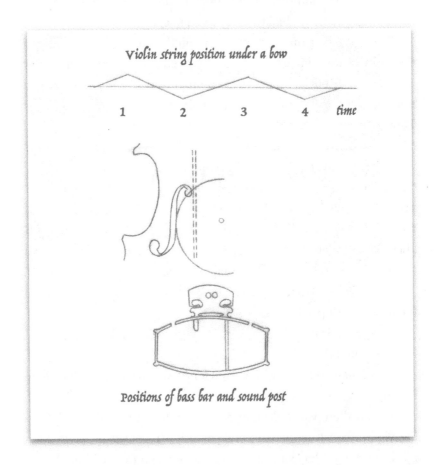

Violin string position under a bow

1   2   3   4   *time*

Positions of bass bar and sound post

I paused for a moment, then said with as much confidence as I could muster, "Taken as a whole, it's a functional drawing showing the essential elements of a violin. Much as in your *Principia*, where you show the relational aspects of the Sun and Planets to Earth."

Dr. Newton tilted his head and made a sound that must have been a laugh; although it might have been a cough of disgust.

"Captain, you've been reading since our last meeting. Then you should have no need of my assistance with a mere violin if you understand the motion of heavenly bodies and the nature of force and motion. You have all the knowledge you need."

Not expecting that response, my mind went dead until I sensed the satirical tone in his comment. "My knowledge of such matters has increased, but it's minuscule compared to yours. I merely mention the fact that I appreciate the details of your drawing as much as I appreciate—"

"As much as you appreciate my efforts to explain the natural world in a way never before accomplished," he finished for me. "That fact should not be necessary to mention. But I do in turn appreciate you taking the effort to learn those derived explanations of natural phenomena. If you absorbed those explanations, you must be able to use something from your readings to understand the mechanics of a violin, some knowledge that will help you with your quest."

"Yes, Dr. Newton, so much so. For two things, I learned about the nature and speed of sound."

"And what is that?"

I repeated the number I had memorized.

"Commendable," said Dr. Newton. "And what does that figure tell you?"

I knew there was a deep and complex fundamental principle for the violin's construction, the craftsmanship involved in its creation, but I did not yet have a clear and concise response for him. Desperate to say something, I could only mutter one word that bore a relation to sound: "Pressure."

Dr. Newton had been adding something to the drawing while I was thinking. After my clipped answer, he stopped writing. "Pressure? What about pressure? Would it be the essence of sound? How do we quantify pressure?"

His questions were rapid-fire, slings of arrows shot at me.

Thinking quickly, I said, "Pressure is related to force."

Again, Dr. Newton seemed to be attentive to my answer, maybe, I wondered, even a little impressed? I had, after all, absorbed something from reading his work.

He said, "Force? You are saying force is somehow related to pressure, which in turn is related to sound? Can you explain further?"

Believing I was on the right track, I said, "A force creates a change in the object or entity in question, and the change is manifested as a pressure, which moves the air enough for our ears to detect it as sound."

Dr. Newton laughed loudly, startling me.

"More than a little crude," he said, crossing his arms and looking amused. "Your thesis is redundant and tautological, not well-formed, but on the whole, much closer than I would have predicted you would be. You have the correct order of the three factors and their causative features. Granting you that much, I believe we can proceed with our further examination of the violin and how to create one that you require in your quest. We shall discuss that later.

"First, what do see that is different between the violins we have on display here? Other than the fact that one has been taken apart. To be clear, I mean *see* not *hear* a difference. The latter will be addressed after we determine the visual."

I moved toward the violins, and again felt a warmth of familiarity as I gazed on the Italian Amati on which I spent a good sum.

"I see two violins, other than the one you have taken apart," I said. "One of superior craftsmanship. The varnish has a richer color and depth. The purfling[1] is much more skillfully executed. The *f*-holes sharper and cleaner, and more similar between left and right.

---

[1] Purfling is the thin, inlaid strip of wood laid just inside the perimeter of the body of a violin. The relative beauty of the purfling is a true measure of craftsmanship. It is also functional, as it helps prevent cracking along the edges of the body. *PW*

There is a better balance, more symmetry between the sides in general. On whole, the Italian is the better violin, at least from a visual inspection."

Gaining confidence, I asked Dr. Newton if I could pick them up.

"Of course," he said.

I picked up the non-Italian violin first, balanced it in the air, then held it in the playing position. Next, I did the same with the Italian. "This one also has a superior feel to it, a better balance and weight."

Dr. Newton then asked, "Do you believe these differences correlate to sound quality? Is beauty to the eye equivalent to beauty to the ear? Or do we even know if we can judge beauty correctly?"

So much was involved in answering any of those questions. I didn't know where to begin my thoughts, let alone begin to answer his latest barrage of questions.

Perhaps sparing me, Dr. Newton went on, "If you know the answers, the truths, then you are the wisest man ever lived. The correct answer is that you don't know. That is what brings us here. If we knew the answers, we would not need to examine the differences, come up with hypotheses, and test them."

After his lecture, I had nothing to say, although I assumed he desired no response.

Indeed, after a moment he continued, "Here's an easy question. Is the same type of wood used on the front and back of these violins?"

I didn't immediately know the answer to his easy question. But I assumed he wouldn't have asked the question if the wood were the same. "I don't know definitely, but I presume not."

"Why would you presume not?" asked Dr. Newton, in a surprisingly calm voice.

I was about to answer, but I thought for a moment too long.

"Examine the violin in cross-section," he hinted. "That might help."

Doing that gave me time to think of a response as well. "They must be from different wood. The front and back are performing dissimilar actions when the violin is being played."

"Which are?"

I knew he was going to ask me that. "The bridge is on the front of the violin. And the strings are supported by the bridge." Obviously, I thought.

He let me pass on that weak answer. "What kind of wood is used for the front, and what kind for the back?"

Not knowing for sure, I said, "I've always heard maple is used."

"For the front or back?"

I frowned and picked up the Amati. The back was of two pieces, the distinctive markings radiating away from each other. "This back is maple," I said confidently.

Dr. Newton didn't confirm my answer, so I assumed it was correct. Instead, he walked to the end of the table, where he stopped and glared at me. "Captain, come along over here."

I followed him to another table where a string had been stretched between two dowels fixed into the table. "The distinctive sound of a violin is the result of interactions between its many parts. The first part is the strings."

He plucked the string and it made a single distinct sound that resonated weakly. "As you said, the plucked string creates a pressure difference that radiates through the air. But what about a bowed string? Please … the bow."

I reached over to the other table and picked it up.

He said, "Use it to play a note. You're much more experienced than I am."

Without protesting that I was not even a mediocre violin player, I drew the bow across the E string. I stopped when Dr. Newton waved his hand. "Now, how does the bowed string create the note you played?"

"It causes it to move," I replied, knowing my answer would be unsatisfactory.

"But how does it move?"

"The bow drags across the string, making it move rapidly?" I answered in a weakly questioning tone.

With a sigh, he said, "Yes, a string moving rapidly means it's vibrating. But how does the bow make it move rapidly? If you would look closely and observe, and slow down the motion in your mind, you would see that the bow pulls the string forward for a minute distance before the string moves back. And what causes this to happen? That is, why does it happen rather than the bow simply gliding across the string?"

I leaned closer so I could get a favorable position to see the string as I drew the bow across it. I squinted, and tilted my head left and right, but I couldn't see the motion he described.

When I straightened up, he said, "It's difficult to see such a phenomenon without proper training. And, of course, what I mean by *see* does not mean to literally see. You might, for example, be able to feel the phenomenon rather than hear it."

Again, drawing the bow across the string, I tried to feel for the skipping motion. Again, without success.

"Or if that fails," he said, with unusual patience, "what you must do is create a similar situation but with more observable tools."

He held up his right index finger. "Place your finger lightly on the tabletop at an angle of forty-five degrees."

I followed his instructions.

"Now push your finger forward."

It slid across the table smoothly.

"Now return it to the starting position and push down slightly harder while moving your finger forward."

I did so with largely the same results, except I could feel the pressure more strongly. There was a rubbing sound as my finger moved across the table.

"This time, press much harder."

Pushing hard enough, my finger didn't move for a moment then it jerked forward to a stop, then jerked forward, then stopped. I continued to push my finger jerking across the table until I could reach no further.

I smiled and said excitedly, "I understand now. The bow acts like my finger bearing down on the table. Skipping across the strings."

"And what is the phenomenon that makes such a skipping motion?"

I tried to recall anything from *Principia*. I did manage to dredge up one of his laws, the one about about motion.

"Objects at rest tend to stay at rest, objects in motion tend to stay in motion?" I hoped my understanding and translation from Latin was adequate.

After a long moment of dead silence, he erupted in laughter again, more loudly than I had heard anyone, who wasn't inebriated, laugh before. "Good Lord! Inertia? How incredible that would arrive into your mind. Inertia! Heavens yes, in a way, I suppose it is partially due to inertia. But before you next decide to propose another law that for every action there is an equal and opposite reaction[2]—which one could argue is also part of the phenomenon—let me tell you that the phenomenon I refer to is called *friction*."

He went on to explain about the forces of a surface interacting while sliding against another.[3]

---

2 Newton's Third Law of force and motion. *TS*

3 From Latin word *frictionem* (nominative *frictio*) roughly translated as "rubbing with force." *PW*

Not widely used until about 1720 in the scientific sense, friction, or the static frictional force of an object starting to slide on a surface, is proportional to the normal force (the weight of the object) through a constant. When the object starts to slide, kinetic friction takes over, which generates heat. *TS*

Perhaps emboldened by his reaction, my mind was suddenly focused. I risked mentioning another of his laws relating force, mass, and acceleration.[4] "Would not the fact that it's related to the amount of force needed to overcome friction and also how much air is moved?"

Rather than laughing this time he appeared serious and dropped into what mental plane I could not imagine. Taking up his pen, he dashed notes on the drawing. Upside down, I couldn't make out what they said. But I felt a momentary rush of satisfaction knowing I said something to pique his mind. My hopes were that it was in a good sense.

After a few minutes, he raised his pen. I waited for him to briefly explain his sudden thought, but instead he gave me a lecture. "The transmission of energy from the strings, vibrating at varying wave forms, is through the bridge and sound post to the body of the violin, specifically to the top and back. The tension and type of strings, placement and tension of the sound post, quality of the bow, and the construction of the body, all contribute to the loudness and tonal quality of the sound. But we must further explicate those dimensions on the mechanistic generation of sound to understand which is critical and at what varying degrees."

Dr. Newton then fell into his silence. But he didn't leave the room and continued with his writing well into the night while I watched.

---

[4] These are the fundamental concepts in Newton's Laws of Motion. *PW*

chapter 5

When I left Dr. Newton's house, my mind was a jumble of thoughts that nearly laid me out as much as any fight in a battle. I believe I'd made inroads with Dr. Newton and with my quest, although it came at the expense of my own lucidity. Worse, I had little faith I would be able to sort out all I learned, all that Dr. Newton had given me to comprehend, before I left for Italy.

Fortunately, I had the drawings and notes he gave me after that long evening.

When I reached my room, I found a note attached to the door. James needed to meet with me and could be found in the officers club until it closed. I hurried over and when I arrived, James was ensconced in a circle of officers, all floppy with drink. After I was served my drink, I joined them, or rather attempted to join them, as they paid me little mind. Three or four stories were being told at once. How they got into that entanglement, I don't know. But they were too far gone into their narratives for me to enter the conversation.

James finally freed himself from the group and escorted me to the side of the club. We found a table and sat there.

"How was your meeting with Dr. Newton?" he asked straightaway.

"In most ways better than my previous meeting. He most certainly has taken my request seriously, as he endeavors to explain his discoveries or theories and ask me questions. But he expects me to understand before the breath of his explanation or question is gone from his mouth. Even as I think of an answer, he's already another two or three, or maybe a hundred, questions ahead of me."

James shook his head in sympathy.

"But he did give me some drawings with mathematical formulas and notes, so that I might be able to show them to a luthier when we arrive in Cremona."

"That's what I want to talk with you about," he said glancing over to the group. "Finish your drink."

I did so and as we walked through the grounds of the compound he told me this: "To get to the point, I've been warned away from going to Italy with you."

His coldly direct statement was a kick to my gut. I managed to say, "I must ask who warned you, and what reason was given?"

"It was through a chain of command, but I can't say who initiated the claim. The reason, to put it bluntly, is that you unnecessarily cost men's lives in battle. That's why you were taken off the battlefield and assigned to be posted with us."

The silence that pervaded the short distance between us became a gulf.

James said, "There's always death in battle. Perhaps all of it unnecessary, or all of it necessary. But no one should be assigned that blame."

I let out a long breath of air. "If I told you there was some truth in the matter, although it's not as simple a matter as you heard, would you not go with me on the mission to Italy?"

James, without hesitation, said, "From what I know of you, from what I have seen since you have been in London, no, it would not matter."

"Thank you," I said, hoping to leave it at that. Fortunately, he didn't want to continue with the topic.

Shortly after that revelation, the expedition to Italy was fully approved. Of course, I wanted to see Catherine before leaving. Luckily, Mr. Montagu was away at his country estate, and Catherine and I could meet in the music room of his home. There, I showed her what I had finished of the concerto. She said not a word as she reviewed the score, then immediately began playing.

Upon finishing, she praised it. That was good to hear, but then she offered her suggestions for improvement.

For one: "I think these notes, here, lack a certain brightness in comparison with the previous bars without a transition. It's almost as if you were suddenly overtaken with melancholy while enjoying a walk in the park with your lover."

The fog I had been in trying to compose the work lifted a little. "Perhaps that's exactly how I was feeling at the time."

"My dear Captain. I don't mean to intrude on your work, or tread on your composing style. I think you might need to ignore my comments, especially since this is a very personal work."

"No, no. I didn't mean that. I take all your advice to heart. Don't refrain from making comments when you desire. I value your opinion above all."

Without a word, she played a few notes. When she lowered her bow, she said, "That's what I mean. I'm certain, you can hear the abrupt change. If there was a transition, even a short one, the ear might not be so offended. Perhaps like this."

She started back several bars, played up to the offending abrupt transition but instead of my notes, she played her own, a delightful run that extended the theme of the previous bars without making it repetitive or trite, while building up to the more profound section. It was as if a sun-filled afternoon sky had changed with a few wispy clouds that gathered and became darker, gathering into a storm.

As I hastily jotted notes, I said, "Magnificent. It both extends the previous mood of joy while deepening the profundity that follows. Thank you."

"You're most welcome."

We worked for a few more minutes, not always as successfully as the first moment of collaboration, but we were able to work together with little effort. This was a pleasant revelation for me, one that I hoped to enjoy in the future.

Then, she spoke at length about something so deep and nearly unfathomable to me that I can only recapitulate in my own words, which barely capture her complex and astounding thoughts, both light and dark at the same time, which blended into a powerful attack on my sensibilities.

"There's a certain way of living that requires an amount of effort which most do not aspire to attain nor ever will because they do not have the courage nor the resilience to overcome the obstacles. In essence, this way of living is one of patient perseverance in the light of seeing what's most important. On one side of the matter, there's the most singular existence of *being*, encapsulated in the essence of life, *a* life, one unique and never repeated. And yet there's the other side, where one life really means nothing, at least next to nothing, considering the sheer number of unique individuals who have existed and will exist. How do we reconcile these two extreme concepts? Can we? Or do we have to find our own unique way of existing?

"We only have but a brief time to make sense of our existence, whatever we believe is its true essence. There can be no predetermined course nor result from our inquiry because in the course of the process there's a continual change of position, a constant renewal or abandonment of beliefs. There can even be a wholehearted change of mind, often sudden and dramatic, usually unexpected. Perhaps it's like the cycle of life—the newborn's universe is entirely self-contained, pure sensation with no meaning other than when desire is fulfilled. And then, seemingly ahead to the end in an instant, when we are about to die in our old age, we know that despite our best efforts, we are being subsumed into the vast ocean of the world and heavens with as much nothingness as we began."

Opus 2

Secrets Cast Upon Secrets

chapter 6

The guard at the Po River gate leading into Cremona bestowed upon us a most severe gaze of suspicion after we handed him our documents. My papers introduced me as Phillipe Rémon, principal financier with the Royal Musicians Office. James had become Jacques Marchand, also in the employ of the office as my assistant, which the guard should have no trouble interpreting as meaning my bodyguard and protector of the funds we carried to make our purchases.

I hoped the guard's severity was because we were buying stringed instruments in an occupied city in the middle of a war, rather than that he suspected our documents were forged. Unfortunately, my concern grew when the guard summoned his superior officer from the dark recesses of the gatehouse.

"Good evening, gentlemen. I'm Lieutenant Laurent," said the officer.

I said, "Good evening, Lieutenant."

James turned sideways and coughed, feigning a traveler's illness to muffle any residual English accent when he mumbled, "Good evening, sir."

The guard handed the officer our papers, mine first. The officer quickly leafed through them. He looked at me and said, "Mr. Phillipe Rémon?

"Yes, sir," I answered in a civilian's tone of respect.

"The Royal Musicians Office? I'm not acquainted with this division of our bureaucracy."

While casually shrugging, I said, "Apparently, the treasurers can't trust musicians to purchase their own instruments. We heard of the great stringed instruments coming from this region of Italy, and since it's under control of our military, I felt compelled to make a trip here to see, or rather, hear for myself."

My little speech came out well, I felt. I'd practiced it enough.

Lt. Laurent snorted with the jaded agreement of one who had dealt with too much bureaucracy—military, royal, or otherwise.

Then he glanced at James' papers before asking him, "And you are Jacques Marchand, the assistant to Mr. Rémon?"

James sniffled and said, "Yes, sir."

I quickly added, "He's humbly in service to me and shall perform all duties as required. Even with his illness he'll dance on command."

The officer laughed. "Our humble assistants run the world, eh, Mr. Rémon?"

"Indeed, sir, indeed," I answered. "I wouldn't have made it here, nor would I be able to complete my tasks and return safely without Mr. Marchand."

There was a slight drop of the corners of the officer's mouth, a brief clouding of his gaze. Something was off. Perhaps I was too effusive with my agreement, or my phrasing a bit awkward.

But the lieutenant gave the guard a crisp order, "Do not delay these gentlemen any further."

With our freshly stamped papers, James and I secured a carriage and driver. Glad to be off horseback, we rode through the city that seemed strangely quiet. Cremona certainly bore well its immediate charm with cobbled streets, hidden alleyways, shop fronts and taverns and inns that seemed to emerge from solid walls. The townspeople peeked in and out of pigeonholes as we passed, their expressions drawn in tightly, as if not wanting to give away their feelings. The few we passed on the street—men and women carrying wares and foods in baskets and sacks—kept their heads down or turned to the side as they hurried to their destinations.

James tapped my arm and pointed ahead.

A French platoon marched toward us. Our coachman tugged on the reins and the horses moved the carriage to the side to let the soldiers pass. Their steps were sharp and lively, eyes bright in the dying light of the day. Their uniforms were clean, well-tailored. Most of the soldiers were smiling, some murmuring to their compatriot on the left or right. Knowing soldiers as well as I did—French or Austrian or otherwise—this platoon was not on its way to its post, but marching away from it, toward their barracks where the soldiers would soon be free for the evening.

I could feel James' gaze on me. I'd grown tense, leaning forward as if to bolt from the carriage. Without returning his gaze, I relaxed, sat back and observed the details of the platoon. When they passed, we resumed our journey.

James whispered to me, "Sixteen soldiers, two officers."

I nodded. "Each supplied with a musket, pistol, and dagger. Their post must have ended shortly before sunset."

The locals who had disappeared when the platoon approached, returned to finish their errands. We clipped along for a few moments until we came to small open courtyard where some of the men of Cremona were gathered in small knots. They were close enough that I could see their looks of suspicion fall upon us.

As we rounded a corner, another platoon came toward our carriage. This time the driver didn't have time to edge to the side of the road, but as the platoon reached us, they split and marched around the carriage. They weren't wearing the same uniforms as the soldiers in the French platoon, nor carrying the same weaponry. Most had only a musket.

When the last soldier was out of hearing range, I asked James, "Irish mercenaries?"

"Yes. Heading to their night posts I would guess."

Without further encounters, we came to our lodging in a pensione. Employing the help of an Austrian sympathizer, we had been able to secure the room before entering the city. The unremarkable building, made from weathered stone and bleached, pock-marked wood, was tucked back in a corner in an alleyway so narrow that our driver had to stop and let us walk the rest of the way. James and I marched in single file, lugging our bags which banged against the walls of the buildings.

At last we entered the pensione. Seated behind a small table reading a book was an elderly gentleman with skin as wrinkled as the bark of a gnarled oak. Before greeting us, he pulled open the curtain behind him enough to peer around it and call out something I didn't understand. Then he stood and gave us a little bow of his head. "Welcome," he said in Italian.

"Thank you," we answered in Italian. We'd learned as much as we could before leaving London, along with our practice of French.

A man older than the proprietor emerged from behind the curtain and began to hoist our bags. When we protested, he grumbled at us as if we were mischievous children.

The proprietor said, "It's his job, has been for fifty years. If he stops working, he will die. So he believes."

We let the older man lug our bags while the proprietor led us into a back room of the surprisingly long building. Our room was meager, but most importantly, it had a door that opened to a private court-yard—a second egress if needed. The proprietor showed us how to open a gate that led into another of the city's narrow streets, before leaving us alone.

James dropped onto one of the beds and sighed in relief. I col-lapsed onto the other bed.

Our journey had been long, not so much dangerous as tedious— a creaking merchant ship to the Lowlands, then a long horse ride through the German states, Saxony, and Bohemia, until we reached Austria and Vienna. Immediately after arriving, stinking of horse and dust, we were escorted to our briefing with the military intelligence forces.

After only two days in the capital, we began traversing through the lands of neutral Venice, before entering the French-contested states of Lombardy and Milan. Fortunately, our forces had some success pushing the French further south. However, we were soon in occupied territory, and our senses perked up when we encountered military patrols. We skirted around them, although the strategy extended our journey.

James was particularly quiet during the travels, perhaps concerned by the warning against me, despite his declaration that it was not the case. Perhaps he was merely bored by the tedium of travel.

Whatever the reason, the long periods of silence gave me time to contemplate my composition, as well as try to understand the writings and drawings given to me by Dr. Newton before I left London. However, despite the time available to me, I hadn't managed to add much to the composition—a few bars of new score and some changes to the existing, in which I endeavored to match Catherine's description of the arc of life and her awareness of it. For instance, the opening chords bridged into a run of notes capturing the initial naïve awareness of existence, the nothingness of our thoughts as infants, when all is perception and no conscious rationality. Sadly, being away from Catherine dampened my ability to create, and my mood grew darker the farther from London we traveled.

In the past, a dark mood could help me compose. The strong emotions reached deep into the place where music was conceived. But not this time. Catherine must have built a new place in my head, or heart, and being away from her had closed the door to that place.

If I'd made any progress at all in my quest, it would have been grasping the intricacies of one of Dr. Newton's drawings. My path to understanding, which was born out of the maddening and failed attempt to understand all his designs at once, was to find a single thing to completely understand. Once the single thing was demonstrably secure in my mind, only then would I move on. The strategy proved successful, not in making much headway, but at least I had one piece of the great puzzle.

The first of his drawings that I grasped was the single note versus the chord produced by a violin. Of course that would be obvious since I'm a composer and used to seeing notes on a score. The sketch, however, pointed out the complex nature of sound and violin, reminding me that I had much to learn.

The other drawing I understood, if I could explain it as well as I thought I understood it, was the friction created by the bow on the strings. After all, that's where the sound begins. I supposed this bit of understanding came from the finger pushing demonstration Dr. Newton had me perform. Then if true, I could increase my understanding of his science and mathematics with other physical demonstrations.

After trying to contrive another demonstration, unsuccessfully, I rolled over to ask James, or rather Jacques, if we should forage for dinner. But he was dead asleep.

chapter 7

Our first morning in Cremona began early. After James left to reconnoiter the city's defenses, I began my duties as Chief Financier to the Royal Musician's Office. My first step was to find Mr. Penbook's recommended violinist, Mr. D'Amico.

On the streets, I blended into the morning's coming-and-goings of the residents—stocking their markets, opening stores, stopping in the churches. Several French patrols marched to their posts; most of the soldiers moved listlessly, some yawning, all likely suffering from a late evening out.

Mr. Penbook had no idea where I should begin looking for the violinist; however, his description of the musician's physical description was vivid. He was tall as me, with a full head of black unruly hair matched by the fullness and wildness of his beard. His fingers were preternaturally long, which allowed him immense range on the neck of a violin.

Congruent with his appearance, according to Mr. Penbook, Mr. D'Amico's playing could be wild, untamed. I hadn't heard of him myself, and I'd missed him in London by more than two years before I arrived.

"He can wreak havoc with any *forte allegro* run, and yet can also draw out the subtle quiet of any *pianissimo*," said Mr. Penbook. He shook his head at this and whispered the violinist's stage name, "Il Diavolo," the meaning of which needed no translation.

The owner of the pensione didn't know where the violinist lived, but believed his home was near the Duomo, which happened to be across from a street lined with workshops owned by makers of stringed instruments. It would be logical, I thought, that a violinist would live near luthiers.

The Duomo—the Cathedral of San Domenico—and surrounding piazza was easy enough to find. The only people in the piazza were a trio of elderly men standing near a fountain, which had a trickle of water flowing out of the mouth of a worn stone carving of a fish. In my weak and odd Italian, learned mainly from Italian opera, I asked if they knew where the violinist D'Amico might reside.

They stared blankly at me, then blankly at each other before rapidly speaking at the same time, the words interspersed with guttural pops of percussive sounds.

"Il Diavolo?" I tried.

That brought their out-of-tune libretto to an end. One of them, the younger of the three, waved me over. When I neared, he spat to the side, then pointed over my left shoulder.

I turned and looked at a large but otherwise unremarkable building.

"He lives there?" I asked.

The man gestured again, grunting something I didn't understand. I followed the line that his steady finger pointed out. It seemed to be the upper floor of the building. I pointed to that floor, at the middle window.

"There?"

"Yes, yes, yes," he said in exasperation.

I thanked him. In response, he nodded several times and waved his hands about like a conductor, urging me to go.

I went into the building and climbed the stairs. The odor was dank and musty, as if the building had been shut after a flood years ago. At the top of the stairs, there was a landing and a hallway of several doors. It wasn't clear which would be the middle window from the outside, but then I heard a violin being played behind one of the doors. The music—a difficult, furious piece—went on for several moments while I listened in awe.

Abruptly the music stopped. I knocked on the door. There was the fall of footsteps. Then the door flew open.

If I hadn't been prepared by Mr. Penbook, I might have turned heel and run. The violinist's hair and beard were like the manes of wild animals, still quivering from his walk to the door. His eyes fiercely gazing at me made him seem as charmingly wicked as the Devil.

"Yes?" he said, in a voice that was deeply hoarse as if he'd been talking all day.

"I'm sorry to disturb you," I said in Italian, at least that's what I intended to say. "I'm here on the advice of a violin seller, who said you might be able to help me locate the best luthier in Cremona."

My request seemed to not surprise him, so I began my practiced speech about the Royal Musicians Office before he interrupted me.

"I understood what you said. It's an odd request, one I have never heard before," he said in passable French.

"I see," I said, relieved we found a language in which we could communicate, although not sure why my request was odd.

After a pause, waiting to be invited in for further discussions, or for an answer to my question, I asked, "I sincerely apologize for coming unannounced. But if you have a little time, could you assist me with my search?"

He stepped back while opening the door completely, then bowed from the waist, as if at the end of a performance. He stood up, and his hair flopped over his face, completely obscuring it except for the tip of his nose.

I followed him into the parlor, its ceiling high, as high as two floors in the homes I have known. Chairs were placed about haphazardly, each covered with a slip of differently patterned fabric. In the center of the parlor was a music stand and a small table on which sat a violin and bow.

With a quick flourish, he picked up the violin and bow. Without another word, without an introduction or explanation, his hair still covering much of his face, he began to play. I didn't immediately recognize the music; it was beautiful yet raw as if still being composed. It was perfectly suited for the violin, which I began to think was his reason for the impromptu performance.

As suddenly as he began, he stopped. He must have known my thoughts, saying, "The music works with my violin perfectly. Or does my violin fit the music?"

I believed his question to be rhetorical, so I didn't answer.

"This violin is an Amati, precisely a Nicolò Amati,[1] whose work-shop is across the piazza." He pointed with the tip of his bow toward the window. "It has boundless voice while maintaining tone, wouldn't you agree?"

To demonstrate, he again put bow to strings.

When he stopped, the notes echoed from the ceiling, perhaps beyond. I readily agreed.

Holding the violin out to me, I took it gently. As with the violin I received from Mr. Penbrook, its perfect balance, weight, and obvious quality of materials and craftsmanship were obvious even to my lim-ited knowledge of how to judge the quality of violins.

"Specifically, it's a Grand Amati, larger than Nicolò's classic smaller pattern. Unfortunately, the Amati family has fallen into dis-repute since Nicolò died. The generation at the workshop is headed by Nicolò's son, Girolamo, who has this much craftsmanship as his father."

The violinist held up a hand with only a little finger extended. As fitting with Mr. Penbook's description, his little finger was unnaturally long. But his point on the lack of talent of the younger Amati was understood, even if exaggerated.

Walking with a long, slow gait to the window overlooking the pi-azza, he opened the drapery. I didn't know whether to follow him,

---

[1] Nicolò Amati, 1596-1684, was a grandson of Andrea Amati (~1505 - ~1578) who is credited with creating the first violin as an evolved de-parture from the lute. *PW*

and if so, whether to continue holding the violin or set it back on the table.

"Girolamo Amati's workshop," he said, "is on the corner. Over there."

I decided to carefully place the violin on the table and join him. We were now looking across the piazza, our line of sight angling to the left.

"Then there is Vincenzo Rugeri's workshop, Francesco's son. As with Nicolò Amati, Francesco[2] did not pass along all his talent to his three sons, although Vincenzo has the most potential."

He paused and looked at me as if to make certain I was following. I nodded several times to assure him I was paying attention.

"Next is Andrea Guarneri's place. A decent if not superior maker of violins, a former apprentice of Nicolò Amati. Sadly, Andrea died not very long ago. His sons have taken over, but unlike Amati and Rugeri, they seem to be in the same league as their father, especially the younger, Giuseppe.[3]

"Now we come to the one who is overtaking them all. Antonio Stradivari."

He pointed to the building on the corner, sitting at the head of the row of workshops.

"His work is impeccable," he said. "More importantly, his sales will soon be that of the others put together. He works with his two sons, and others in his family help run the workshop. Stradivari is always tinkering with his designs, a trait I find attractive, although the results are not always in the right direction for my tastes. He certainly has driven the other luthiers mad because of his success."

---

[2] Francesco Rugeri, or Ruggeri, ~1628 – 1698, had three sons: Giovanni Battista, Giacinto, and Vincenzo. Indeed, Vincenzo had taken over the Rugeri workshop. *PW*

[3] Later famously known as Giuseppe Guarneri del Gesù. *TS*

I said, "I'm sorry not to have heard of him. Has he been working for a short time?"

The violinist shook his head. "To the contrary. He's been working for more than thirty years. But he didn't come from a family of instrument makers, although I heard he worked for a while as an unlicensed apprentice of Amati.[4] That's likely, as his first violins were of the Amati form, until he began creating his own patterns. Perhaps more telling is a truth that Stradivari worked for a carpenter and so gained experience with wood and tools."

Here, the violinist paused. I couldn't tell if he was finished or thinking of something more to say. I was taken with his description of Antonio Stradivari's "tinkering," which sounded like "experimenting." Dr. Newton would surely approve.

I jumped in with a question, "With all that said, you must be directing me to see Antonio Stradivari's workshop?"

Mr. D'Amico closed the drapery and went back to the table where his violin rested. Picking it up and the bow, he ended our conversation with, "As I stated, what you require depends on your needs. But yes, Stradivari is where you should start."

After thanking him profusely, which he seemed to take as applause as he made another bow, one grandly overdone and yet not ironic, I went back outside to the piazza. Standing in front of the row of homes and workshops of three-floors each, narrow, crammed together, I had a sudden wish that Catherine were with me. I would feel much more confident with her ear to listen to the violins, as well

---

[4] One of Stradivari's first violins bearing his label (year 1666, at age about 32) declares him "*alumnus Nicolaii Amati*," although there is no record of him as an apprentice at the Amati workshop. However, it is unlikely that he could have learned the basics without apprenticing. He might have apprenticed with Francesco Rugeri, who also may have been an Amati apprentice. An instrument labeled with Amati's name, rather than Rugeri's, would have been worth more at sale. *TS*

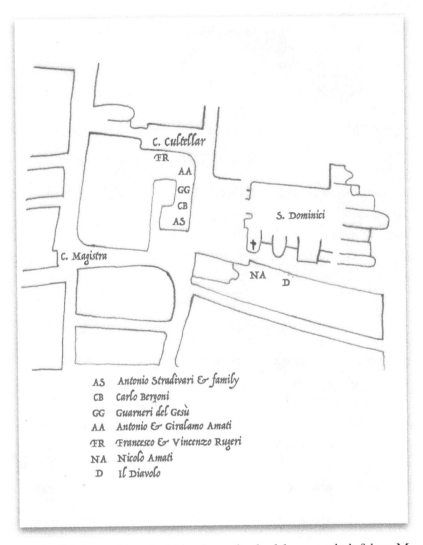

AS   Antonio Stradivari & family
CB   Carlo Bergoni
GG   Guarneri del Gesù
AA   Antonio & Giralamo Amati
FR   Francesco & Vincenzo Rugeri
NA   Nicolo Amati
D   Il Diavolo

as to dialogue with a luthier, since she had been so helpful at Mr. Penbook's shop.

Of course, she wasn't with me when I stepped over to the Stradivari workshop. Without a formal letter of introduction, I didn't know if I could simply walk in. When I was about to reach the door, a pair of men exited hurriedly, almost as if being pushed. Each lugged slabs of wood under their arms. A young man appeared at the door, chattering away, still making a point about the quality of the wood the men were trying to sell, at least from what I could comprehend.

When the two woodsmen were past me, valiantly making their case to the younger man even while in retreat, I raised my head expectantly. The younger man turned his gaze toward me and exclaimed in Italian phrases of which I couldn't catch the meaning. Repeating his words, his voice became staccato and impatient. I assumed he was one of the sons Mr. D'Amico mentioned.

In my operatic Italian, I tried to make it known that I wished to discuss the purchase of a violin and perhaps other instruments. The man's brow smoothed, and his frown changed to a broad smile. "Are you French?" he asked as he ushered me into the house. "I speak a little French."

I wondered if my Italian had a French accent, or if he assumed anyone not speaking fluent Italian would be French. "I apologize for my poor Italian."

"No matter!" he said and clapped me on the back. "We speak the language of music here."

"Excellent," I said. "It's a universal language."

He nodded, shrugged, and shook his head in a confusing sequence. "I'm Omobono Stradivari. Youngest but most important son of Antonio Stradivari." He grinned, I assumed at his description of his standing with his father. "How shall I introduce you to my father?"

"I'm Phillipe Rémon. Oldest and most important son of Louis Rémon. Also, principal financier of the Royal Musicians Office."

"The latter is music to my ears. Which instruments are you here to purchase?"

"Let's say I am interested in discussing all instruments, but particularly a violin."

"Yes, let's say that."

Omobono held out his arm to guide me into the ground floor workshop, where inside were violins, violas, violoncellos, and other instruments hanging from hooks and twine along the upper reaches of the wall. Amid piles of wood pieces in various stages of shaping, the racks of tools and templates, and benches and tables, were two men. One, older looking than Omobono, was bent over a piece of wood inspecting it with a focused gaze.

The oldest in the workshop, wearing a knitted cap and white apron, whom I assumed was Antonio Stradivari, was working on an f sound hole on the belly of an unfinished violin.

"One moment, wait here," Omobono whispered while patting the air in front of me.

I stayed in place while he went over to the older man. Omobono leaned next to him and spoke quietly in his ear.

The older man jumped up as spryly as a man much younger. He approached me as if greeting a long lost friend.

"Sir! Welcome to the workshop of the Stradivari family. I'm Antonio Stradivari. You've met my son Omobono. And this is my son Francesco." The older son stood and bowed formally, awkwardly, then returned to his immediate task.

After I introduced myself, Mr. Stradivari said, "Please follow me into our parlor. It's more comfortable."

"Thank you," I said, "except I would like a tour of your workshop before I leave your home. I'm fascinated by the craft of creating such beautiful musical instruments."

"Yes, of course. We shall do that," he said, as he removed his cap and apron. "For now, come with me. My wife, Antonia, will be happy to serve us refreshments. Omobono, let her know."

The youngest son sighed and went off with shoulders slumped. He must have thought he would be participating in our forthcoming negotiations rather than conveying messages to his mother.

Mr. Stradivari led me into a room across a narrow corridor. The walls were covered with framed letters, sketches of musical instru-

84

ments, and portraits of musicians. When we were seated, Mr. Stradivari clapped his hands together. "This is indeed an honor, sir. We have never been graced with the presence of a representative of the Royal Musician's Office. Tell me more about it and why you've come all the way to Cremona."

It was no surprise that I was the first from the office. "In short," I said, "I'm entrusted to bring home the finest instruments, those with a superior sound complimenting our new compositions and performance halls. At least one such instrument will be a violin of the highest quality."

As I spoke, he studied me intently. When I stopped, he said, "It's a pleasure to welcome you to Cremona, where the best stringed instruments in the world are crafted. Of which, Stradivarius instruments are the best of the best, I can say with utmost confidence."

I should admit I'm roughly translating our conversation, which was a mix of Italian, French, and a smattering of Latin.[5] There were stops and starts, rephrasing, along with nods and shakes of the head, and much talking with hands. But after a short while, our impromptu language moved toward a fabric of comprehension.

"Thank you," I said. "It's a pleasure to be here. The reputation of your instruments is far and wide."

A broad smile expanded his face. "Thank you most kindly. Please tell me more of your mission, particularly about these new compositions and performance halls you mentioned. Are you in need of a full set of concert instruments? We also make lutes, guitars, harps. Even mandolins."

I told him we were more interested in standard concert instruments, and then I mentioned names of composers I knew and de-

_____

[5] Something like, "É un grande piacere ... un grand plaisir ... dare il benvenuto a Cremona, i migliori strumenti a corda ... instruments à cordes ... nel mondo vengono prodotti qui, Stradivarius sono i migliori di quelli, naturalmente ... dico deprecabor." *PW*

scribed some of the performance halls I had been in, including those famous in France into which I'd never set foot.

"I can assure you that my instruments will fit those needs superbly," said Mr. Stradivari. "Ah, here are Antonia and my daughter Caterina."

The two women emerged from the back of the house. They smiled genuinely while apologizing, unnecessarily, for taking so long. Mrs. Stradivari looked to be much younger than her husband and not much older than Caterina. So I assumed that Antonia Stradivari was his second, or later, wife.[6] If she was, she was a second wife who was with child.

Mr. Stradivari introduced me. Mrs. Stradivari smiled brightly, made a proper French court curtsey, and said, "What a great honor to meet you, sir. Our home is full of joy at your arrival."

Her effusive greeting did warm my heart. So far, the Stradivari household was a great difference from my experience at Dr. Newton's home. Mrs. Stradivari and Caterina treated me to wine and bread, meats and cheeses, and dried fruit. Of course, I realized they were foreseeing a large order from me, and I didn't dissuade them from that impression.

I said, "Thank you for your wonderful reception. I'm the one who's honored that you welcome me into your home."

"You're always welcome here," said Mrs. Stradivari. "Caterina and I will leave you to your discussions. If you need anything, please tell my husband to fetch me."

"I'm very grateful. Thank you."

---

6 Antonia Zembelli was Antonio's second wife, whom he married in 1699 after his first wife, Francesca, died in 1698. Antonio Stradivari was 55 and Antonia was 35 when they were married. Caterina was the daughter of Antonio and Francesca and was ten years younger than Antonia. Antonio Stradivari, who lived to be 93, fathered eleven children, six of whom outlived him. *TS*

As I enjoyed the refreshments, more a meal, Mr. Stradivari spoke of several instruments he crafted for this prince, or that king, or for a renowned musician. He imparted a string of details needed to satisfy their requirements—the thickness of the belly, the overall length, the placement of the sound holes, the varnish, but most importantly, the wood. More precisely, the different types of wood he used and their ages, origins, and other points which he ran though like a priest in a hurry to name those who died during a week at the height of the Plague.

As Mr. Stradivari spoke, I wish I'd been able to write it all down, instead I focused on coaxing the offered details into my memory. I wanted to be able to report them to Dr. Newton … should I be allowed a return visit to his home. Unfortunately, I had to give up as there were simply too many.

"But in the end," Mr. Stradivari said, "I make my instruments perfectly, no matter what the circumstances."

"I haven't a doubt they are superior, Master Stradivari. Perhaps you should show me a few instruments that you would have for purchase? I'd also be very pleased to see your workshop now."

Mr. Stradivari looked disappointed. I must have sounded too impatient. But then he stood and said, "I'm afraid I currently have no instruments for sale. I do have a few older instruments, but I only use them for comparison these days. Frankly, sir, all we have time for are requests. But allow me to show you the instruments we are finishing for others."

We climbed three flights of stairs to a rooftop terrace. There, instruments were secured to wooden racks. "This is the *secadùur*, what we call the drying loft in Cremonese dialect."

He directed me to a rack along one wall. "Here we have a violin and a viola for a Venetian musician. And over there, a full set for a quartet in Spain."

"Even in times of war, music goes on," I said.

"Thank the Lord," Mr. Stradivari said.

I inspected the instruments closely. The workmanship, the attention to detail was superior to any instrument I'd ever seen. The purfling was masterful, incredible, as if placed by a supernatural hand.

Before leaving the terrace, I paused to look out over the city. "A beautiful sight," I said, while noting its excellent strategic view.

"Also the best place for the breeze to help cure the instruments. Come, let me show you around the workshop."

Down in the workshop, Mr. Stradivari's two sons were hunched over parts of instruments, while a young boy swept the stone floor. Mr. Stradivari showed me a block of maple and its grain, demonstrating with his hand the angle at which it would be cut. Then he showed me a few of the templates of varying sizes which he personally developed. Next in our tour were the ribs—thin strips of wood bent around the template frame. He described how he heated the wood with hot metal to make the wood flexible, but without scorching it, or "killing it," he said in loud voice toward his sons.

They ignored him.

Next, he briefly described the main steps involved in creating the back and the belly, especially pointing out the thickness and points along the cross sections from up and down the spine. When I asked him for the specific widths he frowned and didn't answer me directly, except to say that it depended on the wood and the type of instrument.

He presented a few of his bridges, little works of art, then pointed out the inlaid purfling using poplar, so superbly done as I'd noticed in the drying instruments. The sturdy necks with the scrolls at the head were beautiful. I wondered if the carving enhanced their functional purpose. When I asked, he said that nothing was done by way of mere beauty, except when that was the purpose.

I was left to puzzle that on my own, as we rapidly moved on.

In a separate room for varnishing, pots and pans, glass containers and baskets, brushes and cloths covered every flat surface. The smells were effervescent and sharp, a sorcerer's cauldron. Mr. Stradivari seemed particularly enthusiastic about the varnishes, and I recalled Dr. Newton stating that he believed it to be one of the important variables in the construction of a violin. Or should I say, he *hypothesized* it to be important. But Mr. Stradivari was most secretive about this aspect of his craft, for when I asked him about the specific ingredients and number of layers, he answered, "There are many ingredients, each with a determined purpose, used in layers which are correct for the instrument, especially the individual portions of wood from which it was created."[7]

From there, we returned to the sitting room. Mrs. Stradivari and Caterina had refreshed our drinks. Caterina gave me a glance out of the corners of her eyes while filling my glass. I thanked her and she smiled warmly in return.

While I enjoyed the wine, Mr. Stradivari said, "Thank you for your attention to my humble workshop. You noticed my two sons working on the instruments, but I must tell you they are only allowed to work on areas on which they have years of training. Of all the critical areas I alone craft those."

He paused here, I assumed to make sure I understood his last point. I nodded that I heard and he went on: "I believe you would now desire to hear some of our instruments. The tone, the dynamic range, the power, the sweetness, of course, are most important, most significant, in any instrument. I assume you can play?"

"I play very little, embarrassingly so. But I can try, I know enough of the needs of the players to detect what's acceptable."

Mr. Stradivari grimaced at my comment. "I can assure you none of my instruments would ever be described as 'acceptable.' That wouldn't be adequate for me. I would rather destroy an instrument than have it judged 'acceptable.'"

---

[7] Here I paraphrase somewhat as he spoke in hushed tones, and in stops and starts, as if deciding what to tell me, or just as likely what not to divulge. *PW*

He paused here, but before I could give him an apology, he stood and turned to walk out of the room.

I thought I'd lost the luthier, as I had lost Dr. Newton many times, but then he began to call out, "Omobono, bring the MB violin and a bow."

MB? When he turned back toward me, I asked him what the designation stood for. He waved his hand, as if batting away the question. "I cannot answer completely, or I would give away too much, but it's based on this template." He found and unfolded a template drawn on a piece of paper.[8]

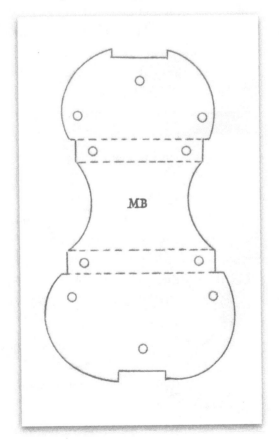

_____

[8] MB likely meant *modello buono*, or "good model." *PW*

I could only glance at it before he refolded it. As with the layers of varnish, I wondered how I would be able to obtain the perfect violin for my composition if all the ... *variables* ... were to be secrets. I decided I was pushing him too far, too fast.

Omobono trudged into the sitting room with a violin and a bow. He handed the violin to his father, who plucked the strings and adjusted the tuning. Mr. Stradivari rested the violin under his neck and took the bow from his son. He played a few simple notes, and satisfied with the tuning, gave me the violin and bow.

The feel of the violin, the way it rested in my hands, gave me an unqualified thrill. It was light and livelier than other violins I'd held. Of course, I couldn't play well, but I could draw the bow across the strings enough to hear the violin come to life and bring forth a voice of clarity and brightness. And with surprising power.

I examined the instrument, looking for clues for its superior sound. It did appear to have finer, more precise craftsmanship than I had ever before seen in a violin. Perhaps that also had something to do with its superior sound, but I doubted that was all there was to the story.

"A brilliant sound, isn't it?" Mr. Stradivari asked.

"I won't dispute that, sir," I said. "Indeed, without a doubt it's exquisite."

Mr. Stradivari had a blank expression for a moment, then smiled, but appeared less than satisfied with my response. He said, "Of course, this room isn't the best for hearing our instruments."

"And I'm not a violin player," I added.

"Then we should set up a small concert for you in a hall with good sound."

"That would be wonderful, if it can be set up soon. I don't have too much time here in Cremona."

"We can arrange it for the day after tomorrow. You'll still be here then?"

"Yes. I would appreciate very much the opportunity to hear your instruments." Thinking of my encounter with Il Diavolo, I said, "I forgot to mention that I'm here due to advice from the violinist, Mr. D'Amico. Would he be able to play the violin?"

Mr. Stradivari was clearly surprised. "Il Diavolo? He plays an Andrea Amati. I would never have thought he would have a word, good or bad, to say about my violins. But since you advocate for him, and he for me, I shall see if he's free to play. I hope he doesn't request an exorbitant fee."

"If he requests any fee, I'll pay it," I said. "I also have a further request, if you would be so kind to indulge me."

From my bag, I took out the copy of my unfinished composition. "Would it be possible to have him play some of this score?"

Mr. Stradivari studied the sheets. "I'm no musician, but I can see it's an interesting piece. Is this a commissioned composition for your royal musicians?"

I hesitated, then said, "Something more personal, shall we say?"

He nodded and didn't press me. "I shall ask him."

With that, we'd agreed on the next steps. Mr. Stradivari gathered all in the house to send me off with a familial farewell. Mrs. Stradivari and Caterina presented me a wrapped package of food. Omobono offered to show me the sights of Cremona that evening. I thought that a guide through Cremona would be helpful in James' and my reconnoitering the city. I accepted his offer, subject to James' approval.

Beaming with pleasure, Omobono said he'd wait for us to call on him at the Stradivari home.

chapter 8

At the pensione, James was more cheerful than I had seen him since our trip began. Before I could ask why, he asked me, "Was your day successful?"

Since leaving the Stradivari home, I'd been asking myself that very question. The luthier was unrestrained in telling me about his craft but at the same time secretive concerning the details of his processes, materials, and ingredients. I was apprehensive in ever getting direct answers, but I did feel hopeful that Mr. Stradivari would be able to craft a superior violin for the composition ... if I could afford it and the other instruments with the limited funds given to me by the Austrian military treasurer.

I told James about the maniacal violinist, Il Diavolo, then recounted my reception at the Stradivari home. "Mr. Stradivari and his family were most welcoming. He showed me his workshop, and listened to my requirements. Most excitingly though, he's organizing a concert so we can hear the quality of his instruments."

"Excellent," James said. "That will be a good support for our cover story."

"Our masquerade will be fully in place," I said in agreement. Then I asked him, "Did you gather much intelligence today?"

"A fair amount. There's considerable activity throughout the city. But I felt as if eyes were watching me most of the day."

"Did you see anyone following you?"

"Not directly so much as that. It was only a feeling."

"I trust your feelings. We should take care."

James nodded. "I'm more afraid I won't be able to remember all that I saw—the number of platoons and their positions, weaponry, timing of movements, locations of arsenals, and so on."

"That's much to remember. But we can't simply make a record of our observations, can we?"

"No, that would mean sure death if we're caught with that information in our possession."

"Tell me what you remember," I suggested. "The two of us will reinforce each other's memory."

He did that, but my ability to keep track of such volume of well-observed information was also stretched to the limit. I repeated what he told me, hoping that the repetition would ingrain it in my mind.

As the evening set upon us, and I could handle the mental exercise no more, I mentioned that Omobono offered to show us around the city.

James said, "That's a good plan. He will have access to places we might not be able to enter."

"We should do it then."

When we arrived at the Stradivari home, they were still working. I introduced James, Jacques, to all. Omobono was happy we accepted his offer. Or, likely, he was glad to get out of the house and avoid the last hours of work.

He took us to a taverna, where the customers were only local residents of Cremona. It reminded me of an English tavern only more raucous. In a corner of the establishment, we were served wine and plates of food we shared between the three of us. Omobono had a great appetite for the food, but more for the wine.

At one point, James asked him, "What do you and the others from Cremona think of the French military?"

After a good swallow of wine, Omobono said, "We love them. We hate them. Please, take no offense to you and our countrymen. The French army is good for the economy. They have good appetites for our food and wine and pay well. But that often leaves us begging for our own food and wine, or paying a high price. In this place, for instance, the prices used to be half what they are now. Even then I don't know what the owner has to do to secure his supplies."

I asked, "What's the morale of the French soldiers? I suppose they don't appreciate your culture, being the provincialists we are."

Omobono shrugged. "Maybe not, but the soldiers seem to like our women." He found his statement full of humor.

We laughed along with him.

James said, "I have to agree, the women are lovely."

Omobono laughed again. "I suppose you'd like me to introduce you to a few lovely women?"

James raised his eyebrows and looked at me. "I suppose we would not be opposed to that at all, would we, Phillipe?"

"Of course not, Jacques."

Soon after, we were ensconced in another taverna crowded with local men and women, and also many French soldiers. The patrons mingled closely together, and were vociferous in conversation and much laughter.

I sipped from my glass of grappa, which our host insisted we try. My tongue and throat burned with each sip. While Omobono tried to find women willing to spend the evening with us, James and I listened for any conversation of us and our mission. I heard little of interest, mostly complaints about boredom and being posted far away from home.

When the crowd pushed close to us, threatening to consume us, and before we became too intoxicated, we apologized to Omobono and took our leave. He didn't seem disappointed, as he was in lively dialogue with a young woman. I wouldn't doubt he'd already forgotten all about us by the time we set foot outside the taverna.

James and I strolled in the fog, trying to lift the fog imparted by the grappa. Perhaps James' fear of being watched was contagious, as I felt the presence of at least two behind us, matching our pace. Speaking in French and in low tones, I said, "I can't see the nose on my face in this fog, let alone the noses of those behind us."

"Nor can I," James said. "But perhaps that's because of all the drink. That grappa is wicked."

"Let's hurry home then. But I need to relieve myself. You go ahead."

He hesitated, then understanding my plan said, "Yes, I shall go ahead."

At the next corner, I slid into the narrow alleyway and ducked into a doorway. Holding my breath, I waited for interminable moments as the fog rolled across me like a living animal, or the ghosts of an army slaughtered long ago who hadn't forgotten one moment of agony, one drop of blood, one last gasp of life.

Two shadowy figures drifted through the night and stopped in the frame of the buildings. I slid deeper into the doorway.

At last they spoke, mumbling something I couldn't hear, before they traipsed together following behind James. When a few moments passed, I stole along the wall until I came to the road. The two figures were swallowed by the fog. I started to follow them as they followed James, far enough behind so it would be a simple matter to disappear if they suddenly turned toward me.

James led them on a rambling jaunt, until they stopped and began to grumble to themselves. I moved into a niche between two buildings. The two turned back and, still talking, walked past me. I followed them for a few minutes, until they entered a building with two soldiers posted out front. A French flag was hanging over the door. The building was the headquarters of the occupation forces.

Without further encounters, I made it home to our residence, where in our room James was on his bed leaning against the wall. He gave me a smile of relief. He nodded with no surprise when I told him where our two friends had ended their evening stroll.

"Maybe they weren't following us at all," he said.

"That could be," I said, but thinking they must have been on our tails.

"You seem shaken."

"Shaken? No, merely tired," I said as I stretched and yawned like a cat. "It's been a long day."

"Not another grappa?"

"You have some?"

"I found a bottle in a cupboard at the front of the pensione." We set upon it, downing another portion or two, before passing out.

I woke in the middle of the night with a fierce pounding in my head, tempestuous ocean waves crashing against my skull, but also titillated with an idea.

A wake well before James, I foraged a pot of coffee, day-old bread, and thick slices of hard cheese. Spread out on the small table of our room were pages of musical score, writing utensils, and a partial map of the city sketched from memory. I created a few trials of my idea before I was satisfied with it.

With a groan behind me, James announced he was still living.

After I shared some of the breakfast with him, I showed him a page of music score.

He gave it a quick glance. "More of your concerto, Phillipe? You know I can't read music."

I sat back with my arms crossed. "You'll have to learn to read this music."

He rubbed his temples. "What?"

"It isn't music. Well, it is in a sense. There are a series of notes, although if played, they wouldn't sound very good."

James grimaced, then sipped coffee. "Enough," he said. "Tell me what you're getting at."

On the map, I traced a portion of the defensive wall from the outlook in the northeast section of the city. "This section of fortified wall is represented by the first line in the score."

I paused to see if James understood. He looked perplexed, or maybe the grappa still clouded his reason. I tried another portion of the wall. "From this road to the next, the length of wall is the second line of the score."

James brightened. "What? Are you creating a musical map?"

"You might describe it as such."

He pointed to the first bar of the first line. "I presume these notes represent something other than notes?"

"Correct. A whole note is equivalent to a platoon, for example. Another line represents time of day. I'm still coming up with the coding symbols."

"Very inventive. All right, I'll learn your musical notations. We can go out later to add to your composition, and avoid being followed again. We must be more careful."

"Especially more careful about drinking too much grappa."

"Especially in tavernas frequented by French soldiers." James again rubbed his temples.

"You should eat, drink more coffee," I said. "When you're ready, we can start on our composition."

James pretended to play a violin.

W hen we finished setting up our musical codes, we went out to reconnoiter. It seemed to me on first impressions that the military forces had increased in numbers, although there was no increase in quickness in the step of the soldiers, who strolled more than marched to their destinations. Their attention seemed to be far away, as if I could have gone up to them and shouted, and they would not have paid me any attention.

James and I ended up strolling along the periphery of the main fortified wall where the guards were more alert. When we strayed too close, they glared at us. We feigned to be involved in important business as we moved away.

We walked in and out of the narrow streets and alleys. I knew that we were being followed again. James knew it as well. We slowed, whispering in French about mundane topics. We counted steps to measure distances from gates to barracks, from barracks to officer quarters. I tried to think like Dr. Newton might, in a modest way, converting distances to time—how long would it take a platoon to respond to an assault of a gate.

When we were about to turn back toward our lodgings, we came upon a small church along the southern wall. Carved in the cornerstone was "Parrocchia di Santa Maria Nuova."[1] With a quick tilt of my head, I motioned for James to follow me inside the sanctuary. A few candles were lit, casting dim orange-yellow light. We sat in a pew at the back and bowed our heads.

In a few moments, the door opened. I held my breath. There were no footfalls of someone entering the church. After another few moments, the door closed.

We waited a good while, not praying, although perhaps we should have been, before we left.

---

[1] The New Parish of Santa Maria. *PW*

chapter 9

The next morning the fog had lightened but the remaining wisps chilled me to the bone as I took my turn to walk through the city watching and counting the movements of the forces. When I returned, I added the coded numbers to the score.

In the early afternoon, James and I set out for the concert hall that Mr. Stradivari had arranged for us. Inside, he greeted us with his enthusiastic nature before showing us to our seats strategically in the middle of the hall. On the stage, Omobono and Caterina were helping the musicians, including Mr. D'Amico, set up their stands and music. Il Diavolo gave us a showy flourish of a greeting. Caterina acknowledged us with a bow of her head. I gave them a nod of appreciation.

Mr. Stradivari said to me, "I presented Mr. D'Amico and the musicians your score, so they've had some time to practice it with their own instruments. However, this will be the first time they've played the score with our instruments." He leaned into me and said with quiet confidence, "I'm sure the musicians and the instruments will be excellent. But you be the judge."

"I'm excited to hear the composition played on your instruments," I said, adding, "and I'm grateful that you've been able to arrange the concert in such short time."

"I'm the one who is grateful that you've come all this way to consider our instruments. It does say that we're producing the finest in the world. Consider the violin you'll hear tonight for instance. The wood for the belly came from a singular, hand-picked spruce tree.

"The viola you'll hear is a departure from the typical viola, which is usually a proportionally-shaped larger violin. Instead, my design has dimensions which are relatively narrower and longer. Only slightly, yet enough to create a sound that's superior and more complementary to that of the violin. Creating this viola was difficult, as the grain of the spruce was more uneven than I prefer. But the wood had an undeniable spirit I sought to preserve."

Barely pausing to catch his breath, he went on, "Now the violoncello—ah, such a story of perseverance. If indeed there's any instrument that shouldn't have been completed, it's this one. Twice it had to be taken apart to refine its thicknesses because the sound was not perfect. Indeed, in the end, you would be surprised to find that if you precisely measured how thin the wood becomes."

As he told us the story of the four instruments, I listened carefully, absorbing the specifics of design and craftsmanship. But his speech was more of a story than a technical discourse; the instruments were his children and he lovingly related their upbringing.

On the stage, Omobono cleared his throat. "We're ready. Shall we begin?"

Mr. Stradivari asked James and me, "Did you have other questions?"

I answered for both of us. "We're ready to hear the music."

"Excellent," said Omobono. "Our estimable musicians will first play excerpts from a concertina in A major, composed to allow each instrument to be emphasized at places in the score. However, the violin, with its sweet yet powerful tone, shall take over the hall in this concert."

Omobono was clearly striving to be the merchant of the Stradivari family.

When Mr. Stradivari, Omobono, and Caterina were seated behind us, the music began. After only a few bars, I was transfixed by the sweet power of the instruments, especially the violin wielded by Il Diavolo. If anything could be said in opposition, there was perhaps too much sweetness and not enough power.

Of course, it might have been the musicians and not the instruments. Il Diavolo was living up to his name, and the others had to match his style.

They played two other pieces—a sonata and concerto. Both were equally good at showing off the range of the Stradivari instruments. Next, they played my composition, the unfinished Violin Concerto in C Major. They certainly played it well enough, but as Mr. Stradivari noted, they had little time to practice it, and in a few spots, it was a little off from what I'd written, or at least how I imagined it would sound. That said, Stradivari's instruments did add much to the composition.

Nearing the end of the composition, a dull ache overcame me, sinking me into the seat. I was wishing that Catherine were in the hall with me.

When they finished, our small audience applauded only to be interrupted by Mr. D'Amico, who waved the Stradivari violin in the air. I was afraid he was about to fling it into the hall.

"Please, please, allow me a moment," he said in a booming voice as if the hall were full and he had to yell to be heard above the din. "We haven't done justice to test this violin. I must play a piece I've written." He began without further explanation.

The piece started quietly, slowly, as if a child's plaintive plea. The violin came alive, more so than in the previous compositions—especially mine, I admitted to myself. The music volume and the speed built quickly. Notes piled upon notes, and not even I as a composer could untangle them. Il Diavolo became as animated as the music, his hair wild in the fury. Then strands from the bow began to fray and fly about, matching the hair on his head.

I glanced back at Stradivari, expecting him to be horrified at the torture punishing his violin, but no, he appeared rather amused at the sight.

After many bars of playing with demonic energy, the music slowed gradually, until it again became the plaintive plea. The last note, a bright B sharp, lasted long, as if the last breath of air from the child. We applauded loudly. Il Diavolo gave us one of his theatrical bows while holding the violin in the air.

Mr. Stradivari thanked the musicians, and he invited us all to his home and workshop for a reception. "Omobono and I will meet you there after we take care of the instruments and close up the hall."

Turning to leave, I noticed a French officer exiting the hall. As we made our way up the aisle, I asked James if he saw the officer.

"I saw a figure leaving just now but couldn't say if it was an officer or not."

We hurried out of the hall, but there was no one outside the doors. Then James elbowed me and whispered, "Over there."

The officer from the guardhouse, Lt. Laurent, was standing across the street. He tipped his cap and strolled off.

A t the Stradivari home, when our wine glasses had been refilled more than once, Mr. D'Amico, James, and I were in the courtyard. Il Diavolo said to me, "Your composition is very unusual. It doesn't fit in with other standard music styles. Not concertos, nor sonatas, certainly not symphonies. I say that with all measured admiration for I'm not one to be subsumed by what music society views as acceptable."

I thanked him. "It's a personal piece of music."

"If you mean that it comes from deep within you, drawing from what has meaning, then all good music is personal. All good playing should also be personal."

"I agree," I said.

"Now that we've agreed to that, I must say your composition is too ... restrained. Maybe too precise. I apologize, I'm not coming up with the correct description. Can you grasp what I'm saying?"

"Not entirely," I said with a strain of defense in my voice. "But I shall consider your evaluation."

Il Diavolo shook his head several times. "I hope this didn't offend you. Please take or leave whatever I say."

"No, it didn't offend me. Upon due consideration, I'll undoubtedly further discover that you're correct."

The violinist graciously allowed me the last word in the matter.

Not long after that, I happened to find myself alone with Caterina. Or perhaps it didn't merely happen. I don't remember. Whatever the reason we found ourselves alone, I was pleased we did. She asked me if I enjoyed the concert.

"I did very much. The musicians were marvelous, and of course your father's instruments were superior."

She nodded in appreciation of my compliment. "Mr. D'Amico's performance matched his stage name of Il Diavolo. I was worried for the violin, yet it survived. Even more, it seemed to take the diabolical playing as if it were enjoying the onslaught of notes."

"I confess, a few times I held my breath at Il Diavolo's attack."

"But he could also play peacefully and joyfully, especially during your composition, in which I found great pleasure."

I thanked her profusely.

"What's your inspiration, if I may be so bold to ask?"

A good answer did not come immediately to mind, and my tongue being tied was obvious, as Caterina politely said, "No need to answer, sir. It must be difficult to put into words. I'm sure composers, any artists, prefer their works to stand on their own, with no further explanation."

"No, it's not that," I said. "The inspiration is deeply buried."

Caterina accepted my declaration, even as I sensed she wanted to dig for it.

Our conversation ended when Mr. Stradivari came into the courtyard. He asked if I enjoyed the food and drink. I had, very much so, I answered. He said I should have more, while apologizing at the same time for the poor quality, blaming the French again for taking the best provisions. I answered it was all delicious, and that I had plenty of both. Regardless, he told Caterina to refill my wine glass.

"I would be pleased to," she said and left with my glass.

Mr. Stradivari then said to me, "Your composition is wonderful."

"Thank you. It's still very much in progress. Your instruments make it sound better than I imagined it could."

He looked pleased.

I said, "To get straight to the point, I'm authorized to purchase a full set of instruments for the Royal Musicians Office. In particular, a superior violin as I mentioned. However, all instruments shall have specific requirements."

Mr. Stradivari said, "All musicians have specific requirements. Of course, you can tell me their desires, which will help guide me. But none of them know how to create a more perfect instrument."

I didn't know what to say to that. Trying to appease the luthier, I said, "I believe that you are the best craftsman of violins in Italy, if not anywhere in Europe, but I might surprise you with some specific ideas of how to create a more perfect instrument, at least for my ... our needs. I have drawings and measurements that I'll offer for your consideration."

"Sir," Mr. Stradivari said after a pause, "I doubt I need any further direction. However, I sense your urgency and your genuine desire to attain perfection. So, I'll indeed allow you to submit to me whatever requirements and suggestions you have."

"I'll also be open and willing to accept your keen judgment."

With a broad smile, he said, "To show you my sincerity, I'll let you borrow the MB violin to demonstrate the superiority of the Stradivarius back in France to your discerning musicians."

"How generous! I accept your offer."

"Excellent. I'll examine your drawings more closely. Let's go into the workshop."

In the workshop, we sat at a worktable that Mr. Stradivari had cleared. Caterina found us and placed a glass of wine near me. She also carried another glass, which she offered to her father.

"No, thank you," he said. I had not seen him drink much wine, nor eat more than a few small bites of food. He seemed to be in his own world of thought. Much like Dr. Newton.

"I didn't think so," Caterina said. She took a sip from the second glass of wine. "What are you two discussing?"

"Mr. Rémon was about to tell me how he came to have these drawings. Please, tell me, us, your story," said Mr. Stradivari.

I didn't know how to begin my story. I could have told him that even as a child, I found an escape from sadness and tragedy through music, which continued through school and into the military academy where my mother sent me after the death of my father. I could have said I taught myself how to compose by listening to musicians and writing down notes. Of course, I skipped over meeting Catherine who knew my compositions grew from the tragedies of battle, and I didn't say that I was holding onto a dream of being with her.

Instead, I valiantly went through Dr. Newton's drawings and his sciences and mathematics, without giving away his name and nationality, which would have raised questions. As best I could, I summed up his calculations of pressure and the speed of sound, and even showed them his fingertip demonstration of friction.

Mr. Stradivari listened with patience, despite the restlessness I could feel was rising in him. When I paused, Caterina jumped in. "How wonderfully interesting," she said.

"I've never seen anything like this," said Mr. Stradivari. "I don't know what to make of it. I can grasp some of it, the rest will take me some time to study. Although, I feel that even if I do fully understand, I doubt that I'll change the way I go about my work. After all, a violin is not a building, or a bridge, or a boat, where precision matters most of all, and each detail can be chosen in advance."

After a pause, he further added, "A violin is an embodied voice, captured from the gathered materials and given new life by the maker."

With that he stood up and said he must get back to work. Caterina and I left him alone.

chapter 10

While waiting for an agreement from Mr. Stradivari on purchasing a set of instruments, James and I continued our other mission. One evening, we visited a taverna recommended by our host at the pensione. We were warned French officers would be there. Their presence was perfect for our mission, but also undoubtedly risky.

We secured a table in a quiet, dark corner, and ordered a meal and grappa. The fiery liquid was growing on me. We drank for a while, trying to hear anything from the officers in the restaurant. We picked up bits and pieces of good information: complaints about lack of fresh troops, low morale of troops, which officers were in line for promotions, or demotions. Other than that, there was talk of family in France, trading information about female companionship, and a debate on the superiority of French or Italian wines.

When the level of conversation dimmed, and the restaurant grew less crowded, James and I finished our meal. Outside, we walked the other direction we had the previous evening. The air was warmer, drier, keeping the fog from appearing.

We found ourselves alone and began to speak softly in English. James said, "It looks like the forces here are becoming complacent, feeling no pressure from the war. They don't have that look of battle-readiness."

I agreed with him. "But they have the city well-fortified. Any invading force would have a difficult time penetrating the fortifications without many casualties. We need a way of taking advantage of the complacency we've seen."

This time, James agreed with me.

We were making our way back to our pensione when we heard the clunk of a boot heel on the cobblestones behind us. We glanced at each other, realizing we might have made a mistake in discussing our mission. We hurried ahead silently until we were nearing the parish church.

Before we reached it, James ducked into a narrow alleyway. I slowed and continued toward the church, then stopped before I entered the door. Behind me I heard a grunt that died into a muffled moan. When I turned, James and our shadow were grappling like Greek wrestlers. I ran back to them. The shadow had the upper hand by the time I neared them. The man held James by the throat and in his hand, raising higher, was a dagger. I managed to grab his arm, just before the blade plunged down. But then he lashed out at me with his other hand.

James, gasping for air, tried to tackle him, but the agile man twisted to the side and regained his balance. Now he faced off in front of the two of us. James and I moved to the sides of him, opposite one another.

Like a mad dog, the man lunged at me, mouth agape. I stepped back out of the way of the knife. James charged, tried to grab his hand, but missed. The man snarled, kicked James out of the way. Before he could move toward me, I was on him.

I had both hands grasping his wrist in the hand that held the dagger. James punched him in the stomach and a *whoof* of air discharged from his lungs. While he was momentarily weakened, I pulled down on his wrist, turning the dagger towards him. He resisted with a groan. I fought not only him but struggled against my revulsion at the violence until without recourse I plunged the dagger into the man's chest.

He quivered, shuddered, then after a horrible spasm, as if he were bursting out of his skin, went limp. James and I held him from falling. There was much blood, its sharp metallic smell in my nose, mingling with the earthy odor of other fluids.

I recall, clearly, Catherine's words on the arc of life haunting me. But I didn't have long to consider this—we heard approaching footfalls and then voices.

"The church," I whispered.

With the dying man between us, James and I dragged him as soldiers would carry one of their own who had passed out from too much drink. I started singing a French drinking song, my voice lurching, as were my steps.

We reached the church as the soldiers passed by. One of them shouted, "Praying won't help the drunken bastard!" His compatriots laughed.

We dragged the corpse inside, laying him on a back pew in the nave of the church. In the candlelight, I recognized the soldier. I looked at James, he back at me, after recognizing the soldier from the Po River gate who stamped our papers.

We moved away, both of us trying to catch our breath.

Whispering, as if the dead might overhear us, James said, "Do we just leave him here?"

"I don't know. We can't carry him out the front door. The French will be looking for him soon."

"Where else could we take him without being caught?"

"Wait here," I said. "I'll see if there's another way out."

I ran through the nave, my footfalls echoing off the stone walls. Along the right side in one of the vestibules, I found a door behind a curtain. I opened the door, revealing a dark, narrow stairway. I took one of the candles from the sanctuary and started down the stairway. At the end of the stairs, in the dusty depths, I came to another door. I opened it and found a long corridor lined with smaller rooms—storerooms, workrooms. I walked down the corridor and at the end found a wine cellar.

"May I be of service, sir?"

I gulped and turned to see a priest. He was neither short nor tall, neither thin nor portly. His request was not threatening; instead he seemed to be genuinely asking if I needed help.

He added, "Inspecting the church's wine?"

"No, not that," I said in French-laced Italian. "I apologize for intruding."

"But you aren't French, are you? Or should I say, you and your companion in the church aren't French? I overhead you speaking in English."

My mind spun into a dizzy torrent of options. But before I could decide what to do, the priest said, "If you aren't inspecting the wine cellar, then perhaps you're looking for something else?"

"Something else ... yes."

The priest waited for a moment, then introduced himself as Giovanni Cozzoli, rector of the parish.

"A pleasure to meet you, Father Cozzoli," I said as calmly as I could. "Officially, I'm Phillipe Rémon, here in Cremona as the financier of the Royal Musicians Office."

"And unofficially?"

"Perhaps that's better not said."

"Perhaps not," he said. "But I should say I'm no friend of our French occupiers, if that's helpful."

I believed him without deliberation. "Then, yes, you might be of service. We had a run-in with a French soldier who would have exposed us. I'm afraid he has expired."

"I see. God rest his soul. Let me attend to him."

We walked down the corridor to the stairs. His pace was deliberate, reverent, and I matched it, even as I wished for him to hurry.

Up in the church, James gave me a worried look. I gave him a reassuring nod toward the priest and introduced him. "This is Father Cozzoli."

James edged away from the dead soldier hidden in the dark pews.

"He knows," I said.

"He knows," James repeated but with a tone of worry.

The priest walked between us to the resting place of the soldier. He bent down and began intoning his rites.

James and I backed further away to leave them alone. I whispered, "He heard us speaking in English, but he claims not to support the French."

"Is he telling the truth?"

"I'm fairly certain. He's a priest, after all."

James looked over to him. "You have more faith than I do."

"At this point we have to trust him."

James sighed, then agreed. "What did you tell him?"

"Nearly nothing. Only that the soldier was going to expose us and we dispatched him."

"I suppose he will have many more questions," James said.

The priest finished and approached us. "I assume you were looking for another egress from the church," he said.

"We can't leave him, his corpse, here. Is there such a way out? Preferably not into the street."

"You were close to one," he said. "Through the wine cellar. I'll show you."

We lugged the soldier's corpse down the stairs and into the wine cellar. We came to a well-disguised door, which the priest unlocked and opened. On the other side was a dry moat. Beyond the embankment were the dark woods and fields surrounding the city. We hurried outside and made our way as fast as we could across the moat into the woods. When we couldn't move another step, we lowered the body to the ground and searched for a suitable place for his burial.

Finding such a place, we rolled the remains of the poor soldier into a gully. Without ceremony, we covered him with dirt and stones and, finally, a thick layer of dead, thorny brush.

Opus 3

Action, Reaction

chapter 11

"Why can't you tell us what you've been doing while you were away for so long?" pled Catherine.

James and I glanced at each other before I answered, "Please accept our apologies. We're obliged not to say."

In a mocking tone, Catherine said, "Shall we resort to prying it from you with a glass of sherry?"

I laughed. I hadn't heard laughter coming from me in a long time.

James and I had been away more than three months, including travels to and from Cremona, and with an extended stop at the military headquarters in Vienna to report our findings. The weeks seemed to span more than a year, the return trip especially long. Instead of James being the quiet traveler, this time it was me.

Killing the soldier affected me more than I could have imagined, even as I knew it was necessary. Our confidence sank in moving freely about Cremona—it was likely only a short while before his corpse was discovered. We desired no further contact with Lt. Laurent, who without doubt harbored suspicions of us, especially after the disappearance of the soldier.

Staying out of sight limited my ability to see Mr. Stradivari, so he and I concluded our business more quickly than I desired. In the end, we settled on a price for the instruments, other than for the principal violin which we agreed to further discuss on my return to Cremona, when that would be, I couldn't have known at the time. I found myself saddened to be leaving so soon, as I enjoyed being with the Stradivari family, especially watching the master luthier at work.

"Even with a glass of sherry," I said to Catherine with a bow of my head. We were in a reception hall at the military headquarters, hence our reluctance to speak too loosely. "I really can't say precisely what occurred, but I can say that as part of our travels, we were loaned a violin from the master Italian luthier, Antonio Stradivari."

I escorted her and Rose over to a table at the side of the hall. On the table was a violin case. I opened it and presented the Stradivarius MB violin to Catherine.

She gasped. "It's incredibly beautiful, Captain Wolf. I've never seen such exquisite craftsmanship. The precise lines, its balance and weight, and the varnish is like a deep well, swallowing me up."

"Catherine!" said Rose. "Such poetic praise."

"Feel for yourself," said Catherine, offering the violin to her friend.

Rose accepted it, cradling the violin as if it were an infant. "Yes, it's incredible. I see what you mean about swallowing you up. Please, play something," she said as she carefully returned it to Catherine.

Catherine asked me, "Shall I play some of your composition, Captain Wolf?"

"Perhaps something else. I haven't had much time to work on it."

She gave me a look of some disappointment, then played a simple melody. The first notes were so sweet, she seemed taken aback, and skipped a note or two. We in her audience were amazed—all our ears tuned to the music as if it were the only sound in the world.

Catherine did not stop there—she moved into a powerful run of notes, testing the violin. And yet, I felt, she was barely pushing the instrument. I shivered in the excitement, even more strongly than when I first heard the violin in Cremona.

When she finished, we applauded. Catherine waved away our praise. "Such a marvelous sound."

James and Rose left to walk in the garden surrounding the hall. Catherine and I sat in silence for a few moments while she admired the Stradivarius before restoring the violin to its case.

"Captain Wolf," she said, matter-of-factly, "during your absence Uncle Isaac asked me where you were. I told him you were off on a mission. He had nothing more to say, but the fact that he spoke your name means he still has your request in mind."

"You believe he won't mind if I ask him to continue our conversation?"

"I cannot presume to answer for him, but I'll be happy to convey your desire. I assume you want him to inspect the violin from Cremona?"

"Very much so," I said. "I also have much to tell him about what I learned. And, I want to tell you."

"I want to hear it all. At least all you can tell me. I often wondered what you were doing, how you were feeling, what you were seeing. I'm envious of your travels, I admit."

"I can tell you that our mission went well. Purchasing instruments from Mr. Stradivari of Cremona was our raison d'être into Italy."

"But it's occupied by the French. So you must have had to pretend to be Italian to gain entry?"

"We posed as French bureaucrats from the Royal Musicians Office," I said after a pause. I was already trusting her with more information than I should have.

"Incredible! Although, infiltrating enemy lines would make you a spy, enjoined with all the risks associated with such adventure. Then I'm fortunate to see you again. I fear the conflict will worsen, dragging us into an interminable war. If only King Charles had an heir; it all might have been avoided. At least that would have lent time before a war, perhaps allowing for a bloodless resolution."[1]

"A perfect outcome that would be, although given the divisions and powers involved, they would have been drawn into war even with a passive alternative."

"I do see that likely as well. So, Captain, why are you now telling me of your involvement?"

---

[1] Other political forces would make a bloodless resolution unlikely. *PW*

"To be forthcoming, I feel it important to have you in my confidence. I do know that we have only the briefest of acquaintances, but I feel I can confide in you. You would offer sincere counsel when needed and without judgment."

"I'll do my best," she said. "But I can't promise I'll always be so open, nor will I always be present when needed."

"I didn't mean to imply that you must be always at my beck," I replied in haste.

She looked away, briefly, as if something caught her attention, before turning back to me. "Since you're now forthcoming, as you say, please tell me more of Mr. Stradivari."

In the moments of hesitation before replying, I realized something was occupying Catherine's thoughts. I didn't ask what that might be, understanding that it was not something I was yet entitled to know. Or ever to know.

"Mr. Penbook was correct," I started, not knowing where else to begin. "There are several outstanding instrument makers in Cremona. The violinist Mr. D'Amico, known as Il Diavolo, was helpful in pointing me to the Stradivari workshop."

I told her of the impromptu concert he performed for me in his room.

She sat on the edge of the sofa, enraptured by my story of his ferocious playing. I stretched my recounting of the encounter to include details that I didn't need to embellish.

"Heavens," she said, when I paused to take a long breath. "If only I could have experienced such a spectacle."

"He performed at an informal concert later, playing our unfinished concerto, and other pieces."

I dove into a lengthy account of the time between the first meeting with the violinist and the concert, recounting my discussions with Mr. Stradivari, describing his workshop, and especially his secretive nature. Even then, I only pressed upon her the brief summary of what transpired.

"I thought of you," I told her. "I thought of you while all of it was happening, and really there's so much more."

"I desire to hear it all, perhaps best at another time. I can't stay too much longer. My duties call."

"I understand," I said, believing I'd overstepped the boundaries of our relationship. "I'll eagerly anticipate another time."

Catherine gave me a tilt of her head. "I as well. I'll deliver the Stradivarius to my uncle as soon as I can."

"Thank you. If he will allow me an audience, I'll try not to provoke his anger."

She laughed. "As I've said, it's impossible to anticipate what he will say. Besides, you're doing well enough to be invited to return. Now promise me you'll tell me the rest of your story in Italy."

"I promise. As soon as you can meet with me."

"Agreed. And may I ask a favor of you? When you see my uncle, will you please ask him about trouble at the Mint? I've heard grumblings but know nothing of the cause, and Uncle Isaac claims there is nothing to worry about. He might be more forthcoming with you."

"Of course," I answered quickly. "I won't leave his presence until I have the full story."

"Then I wish you good luck. As you well know my uncle can be impetuous."

"Why, no, I've never seen that side of him."

We were still chuckling as her and Rose's carriage arrived and they departed.

Over the next few days, James and I found ourselves involved in lengthy strategy assemblies with military officers. Most of the discussion was dull and unimportant, and I often found my mind drifting to my conversation with Catherine and anticipating my next meeting with Dr. Newton. However, at one of the assemblies, James and I briefed a visiting general from the Austrian military, who was attending at the personal request of the commander of the Austrian military, Prince Eugene of Savoy.[2]

The general—Viscount Pichler, whose voice reminded me of a guard dog's growl—demanded much from us: "How do we know your observations remain valid? I believe they would have changed considerably in the last month since the prince has been advancing on Lombardy.[3] The French are moving forces up from Cremona to Chiari."

"It's true, of course," I answered with due patience, "our records are only valid for the time we were there."

The general rolled his eyes at his commanders seated around him, then barked, "I am aware of that, gentlemen. But what about other equally important states and strategies of the enemy? What's the morale of their troops? What are the plans for defense of the city? Where would reinforcements come from? Where's the weakest point in the defenses? Which gate will they defend the most? And, most disturbingly, buying fiddles is your cover story?"

James jumped in before I could retort. "Yes, sir, we understand. We do have answers for most of your questions, and admittedly, some which we do not. I request time to consult my colleague, Captain

---

[2] Prince Eugene's fame as a military strategist and commander was already well-established, due to a victory in a battle during the Ottoman Wars. Ironically, he grew up around the court of Louis XIV until his mother, Olympia Mancini Savoy was exiled from France after being associated with the L'affaire des Poisons.

The Poison Affair led to the execution of three dozen for murder and witchcraft, and many others were incarcerated or expelled from France, including some in the inner circle of the court such as Prince Eugene's mother. The prince was rejected for service in the French Army and after his mother's banishment he joined the Austrian military. PW

[3] The region in northern Italy that includes Cremona, also called Po after the river. PW

Wolf. We shall prepare a more thorough report addressing your concerns."

"Time?" sputtered the general. "I wish I had time to see my children, to enjoy a good meal and bottle of wine, to lay with my wife. If you wait for enough time, it's too late. One simple answer can change the entire focus of the battle. Let us say that the French are in Milan, but their position is weak. Perhaps the troops' morale is poor, and desertion is high. Louis will send reinforcements, believing the Emperor would not be able to make a comparable increase in the Austrian's forces, but he cannot make those reinforcements available until the spring. So the French generals move their forces into Cremona for preparation of a push. We need to know when they ..."

I must confess that as the general lectured us a wonderful run of notes came to mind, perhaps as a balm to the general's growling, or that his speaking of aspects and scenarios reminded me of Dr. Newton, which in turn reminded me of Catherine. The run of notes embraced that emotion of being at a distance, yet that can be felt, still, as I understand Dr. Newton's concept of gravity, the force that can apply itself over a great distance, with seemingly no intervening substance needed.

"Captain Wolf would agree, I'm sure. Captain?" James had been saying something I missed in my composer's reverie.

"Yes, correct, sir," I said, knowing whatever James had said, I would have answered in agreement.

W here was your mind?" James asked me when we escaped to The Hare and Tortoise. "Or do you need to answer that question?"

I shook my head, as I guzzled a long draught of ale.

"'No' is correct," James said. "I know when you're composing—your head sways in time to whatever piece of music is in your head."

"The general noticed it as well?"

"I doubt that. He was emptying the drivel from his own head. We didn't accomplish a thing of value in Cremona, according to his speech."

"That's why I stopped listening," I said.

"I thought he would have been appreciative of our efforts to infiltrate into the heart of the enemy's fortified city with our brilliant ruse. And yet it was not a ruse, at least not fully so. That's what makes it so brilliant. Still, you must pay attention when a general has the floor."

He was right. "My apologies. But it's a good thing we left so many unanswered questions, at least according to the general. It's clear we need to go back."

James said, "I hope not too soon."

Again, I agreed with him. "Whenever it is, I hope the soldier we killed has been forgotten. Or if he hasn't been found, he's been labeled a deserter."

"Either way," James said, "I believe our friend, Laurent, will be watching us closely."

"True," I said. "If they've found the corpse, we'll be suspected of the assassination. If so, the lieutenant will arrest us, and torture us as long as possible before executing us."

"Pleasant thoughts," said James.

I changed the subject. "Catherine told me she has heard of a matter at the Royal Mint that is troubling her uncle. I agreed to ask him about it. You haven't heard of anything, have you?"

James gave this some thought. "The only such trouble I can think of is the hunt for counterfeiters, the coiners as they're often called. There's controversy, I hear, of a particular criminal who has flaunted his invincibility for years, and has something of a popular image with many of the city's criminals. If the Mint deputies catch him, and if convicted, the punishment would be execution. He will be hanged, drawn, and quartered.[4] So the stakes are high."

I said, "I can't see Dr. Newton, despite his severe and righteous assertiveness, allowing such a horrific execution."

"He has no choice in the matter. In his position he must gather evidence, present it to the court, which will undoubtedly agree with the evidence, and sentence the convicted coiner to the fit punishment."

After a gulp of ale, I moved the conversation back to the matter at hand. "I believe the general was never going to laud us with praise for our efforts."

"Never," James agreed. "He was acting as required for his rank, which does not include praise, certainly not enough so that we might upstage him."

"So, during our next trip to Cremona, we must do more to impress him."

James raised his glass and we toasted. "We will, my friend. I've been thinking that the gates could be easy prey—there are only so many ways to protect them. How they plan to repel a prolonged siege is more difficult, as we would need to discover those plans."

I added, "It also requires more details of the reinforcing armies that could come to their aid."

"Surely that would not be our responsibility? We can only provide so many of the pieces of their plans. And what of our cover story? Will we keep using the 'fiddles' as purpose?" James grinned at the reference.

"We have to use the same cover story. In that regard, I hope to meet Dr. Newton soon and learn more about the sciences and mathematics to bring to Mr. Stradivari."

––––––––––

4 The Treason Act of 1695 required more due process than previously, including a counsel for the accused and more than one witness. *PW*

"I wish you well. You haven't had the most enjoyable of times with Dr. Newton."

Summoned to the Austrian consul's home, I was personally greeted by Mr. Lupine and ushered into his library. As during my last visit, there was a fire in the hearth despite the warm evening. Two snifters of brandy were already poured and inviting, sitting on the table between the two chairs in front of the fire.

"Welcome back to London," he said. "I hear your mission went well. Is that a true and accurate assessment?"

"Well enough," I answered.

After we sipped some of the brandy, Mr. Lupine sat on the edge of his seat, obviously wanting to get straight to the heart of the matter.

I'd come to realize there was a great undercurrent of shifting allegiances, power struggles, and disingenuous loyalties, enough so that I had best keep anything that would potentially harm Catherine and her uncle, or Mr. Stradivari and his family, to myself. In other words, I wasn't sure how much I wanted to divulge to the consul.

"Anything spoken here is in confidence," he said, sensing my hesitation.

"That goes without saying," I answered his proviso. "It's rather a matter of deciding where to start. In the broadest of terms, I suppose, it can be considered a limited success. Captain Brookfield and I were able to enter the Italian town of Cremona. Our ruse of buying stringed instruments worked well and we were able to sustain it while discovering as much about the French positions within the city."

Mr. Lupine nodded. "And what is your general assessment? Is the city pregnable?"

"Not without further awareness of their defenses, reinforcements, supplies, and other details."

The consul dreamily stroked his scar, maybe wishing to hear details of a more violent nature. "Is this what you told the military leaders?"

"For the most part. We presented our observations as accurately as we could."

"I'd be interested in hearing this directly from you."

After considering how best to answer this, I reviewed for him our observations—the numbers, strategic placements, weaponry, and troop morale. While I spoke, Mr. Lupine listened intently, likely imagining my report and translating it from numbers and impressions into a visual montage, as the military officer would be preparing for a battle.

"Excellent," he said.

We sipped brandy.

"Now," said Mr. Lupine, "on the matter we discussed before you left."

"Concerning the English supporting us in the war?"

"Yes, in particular Mr. Montagu being an important person in that effort. While you were away, the debate over the English position has grown contentious. Are you able to find out more of Montagu's influence?"

I didn't know if I would ever be in Mr. Montagu's presence again, but I answered, "Yes, I believe so."

"Very good. Then do all you can to keep your ear to the inner debate and inform me of the arguments."

"I will."

"But be careful."

There was no reason, at the time, for me to believe I had anything to be careful about. But I assured him I would.

chapter 12

Dr. Newton kept me waiting only thirty-three minutes, as precisely measured by Mr. Huygens' clock. My standing with the great genius was improving. When I arrived earlier, the housekeeper greeted me with friendly airs and settled me into the reception room. She returned shortly with an ale, as if anticipating the wait I was to endure. Again, I was pleased with the fine balance of Dr. Newton's brew.

When informing me of her uncle's acceptance of our meeting and delivery of the Stradivarius violin to him, Catherine warned he was more distracted than usual. I accepted her warning and thanked her profusely for arranging a meeting. She said there was no need for thanking her, rather it was she who was appreciative that I was capturing her uncle's attention, as difficult as that could be at times. I responded that I would approach him about the troubles he was having at the Mint. Again, she expressed her appreciation, which I took to mean she was genuinely concerned about her uncle.

I recalled this exchange not for any surprising revelations (which it did not have), nor for the height of passion it reached (which it did not), nor for the promise of something more or better for us (which it utterly did not). No, because in a way, it was one of the last innocent moments we shared.

Just as I finished my ale, Dr. Newton appeared, this time looking straight at me as he entered the room. Not only straight at me, but his gaze bore through me as if I were one of his experiments. I didn't know which was worse, my presence barely acknowledged or tortuously in his aim.

"Captain Wolf. My niece told me to welcome you back from your journeys."

"Thank you. And please, give your niece my thanks."

"I assume you'll be able to do that yourself," he said impatiently. "I've been examining the violin Catherine said you were able to secure as a loan from an Italian luthier."

"Antonio Stradivari."

"It's a superior instrument," he continued without pause, as if the name of the maker were inconsequential. "I shall tell you the results of my preliminary analyses, but first I must inquire about the principles the luthier imparted to you."

My thoughts immediately became a jumble. Mr. Stradivari's principles ... I didn't recall that I learned anything that would be classified as a *principle*. I learned many things, to the point I realized there were many more I would need to learn to approach understanding all the intricate skills, knowledge, and experience which Mr. Stradivari invested in his craft.

My mind conjured up his workshop, the varnishing room, the secadùur. I recalled the countless details Mr. Stradivari told me or that I observed. But to call any of them, or all of them, principles, that I couldn't say. But I couldn't remain silent either.

Selecting what I thought to be the most important things I learned, I said, "Mr. Stradivari did explain to me that knowing the wood and how it should be shaped is vital. He mentioned symmetry, so I assume that to be most critical. He also explained that crafting each piece involved an important skill, as an example, not scorching the wood when heating it so it could be bent. And the varnish involved many ingredients, each with a specific purpose, although he hesitated, no, refused to tell me anything in depth—"

Dr. Newton had raised his hand. I stopped talking not without some relief. "Captain," Dr. Newton said, "Those aren't principles, those are recipes. We aren't preparing dinner, are we?"

I decided not to reply with the obvious answer and further antagonize him. But if not the details I learned, then what did he want to hear? It was then I recalled Dr. Newton's three laws of motion—

those laws have the scope of principles, do they not?[1] But if I were to make a wrong assumption? My exasperation grew, even as I was drawn into Dr. Newton's way of thinking and discussing all these things. I wanted to steer him into a more pragmatic line of discourse. So to make some progress, I hoped. And I realized I needed to have a concrete understanding of Dr. Newton's violin design principles to give to Mr. Stradivari when I returned.

"I understand the need for precision in my descriptions," I said to end the silence. "I shall endeavor to be more precise. I recall now what Mr. Stradivari said about the construction of one of his instruments, 'The viola was difficult as the grain of the spruce was uneven but it had an undeniable spirit.' He sought to preserve it."

Dr. Newton folded his arms across his chest, appeared to be about to say something, then abruptly left the room. My failure to extend our conversation more than a few minutes crushed me. But before completely disappearing from my view, he stopped and turned. He gazed at me curiously, as if I were a dog not following his master. Taking that as my command, I followed him.

We ended our little march in his work room, where he went over to an array of tools. After selecting a wood saw, he walked back to the table on which were the violins—the Stradivarius had now joined the Amati violin I'd purchased from Mr. Penbook. Dr. Newton picked up the front of the violin he'd previously sawn in half. With surprisingly deft skill, he used the saw to dissect a sliver of wood from the violin. He handed it to me and said, "Tell me, Captain, do you see the spirit, the soul, of this sliver of wood?"

---

[1] While it is not exactly clear what Wolf heard or understood in this discussion with Newton, there are both large and subtle differences between scientific principles, laws, facts, theories, and other classifications. Newton was likely referring to general, underlying beliefs based on experience that guided Stradivari in his craft, and likely not scientific laws explaining natural phenomena. TS

I knew the question was one of Dr. Newton's traps, but I bravely answered anyway, "I don't know what a soul is, to be frank. Thus, sir, I wouldn't know where to look."

"Then why would you report to me that your Cremonese luthier was seeking to preserve the soul of a piece of wood?"

"I believe he said 'spirit,' but I can't be precise as I'm translating into English. However, he could have been speaking in metaphor."

I thought I made a good point. Unfortunately, Dr. Newton grimaced.

"A metaphor? You mean soul, or spirit, or whatever word he actually spoke, encompasses the physical nature of the wood he uses? His 'soul' accounts for all the variables he desires in the wood?"

Dr. Newton lifted the drawn-and-quartered violin. After inspecting it, he said, "I can think of twenty such variables in a cursory glance—density, moisture, grain direction, grain size, thickness, to mention a few."

He pointed to the sliver I was still holding and said, "Perhaps you should take this section of wood to the luthier and have him point out the soul."

Turning the sliver in my hand, I tried to imagine how Mr. Stradivari would answer, if he weren't insulted into silence.

Dr. Newton continued his lecture, "Theologically, there is no mention of a soul to be found in trees.[2] Thus, his reference is nonsense. The real question should be what is the essence of wood that creates sound which we perceive as musical notes? But before you answer, please bear in mind that I am requesting a generally available or applicable foundation of knowledge, in other words, one that might apply to all such cases."

Here, I became completely befuddled, disappointingly so since I thought I had begun to make headway in my discussions with him.

---

[2] Dr. Newton would not have said this lightly as he was also a theological scholar. *PW*

What did he mean? Was this at all related to his previous mention of principles? Was he still wanting me to divulge Mr. Stradivari's principles?

I'm sure I spent too much time thinking about a response, time during which the learned man was already a half dozen ideas or further questions ahead of me. I needed a new strategy in dealing with him. In battle, if a tactic is failing move to another.[3]

The strategy I came up with was to not answer his direct question, instead, I would change to a new but still related topic. I tried this, which came to mind without much forethought, "Might not the wood itself carry the notes of a scale—one section of the wood carries the E string, one section the A string, one the D, one the G.[4] Furthermore," I went on without pause, trying to keep Dr. Newton from coming up with his counterargument, "might not notes depend on how the wood is selected and carved? And if that's the case, then might there be notes, or the chords of notes, in other substances as well? Or, extending this idea, are there musical notes in all substances?"

I thought my points and questions wholly blather, so I was thoroughly surprised when Dr. Newton blinked and, ever-so-slightly, smiled.

He bounded away from the work bench, heading toward the door. This time I didn't wait to be summoned; I followed him directly. We hurried as if time were of the essence. Through the house, toward the back, we entered a room that contained many strange contraptions and a vast library. In fact, the room might have been a library at one time, but now the books overflowed from the shelves,

---

[3] Or as a commanding general once advised me, "If your strategy stinks of offal, let it go, don't wallow in it." *PW*

[4] More precisely, the violin strings are tuned to a perfect fifth from each other: G3, D4, A4, and E5. *PW*

piling up on the floor, leaning against the walls, sliding under furniture, making it more a poorly maintained warehouse than a library.

Dr. Newton set about making space and moving one of the contraptions near a window. This contraption was a substantial prism of glass mounted on a metal stand. Taking the better part of ten minutes, Dr. Newton fiddled with it, twisting the frame and adjusting its distance from the window. He finally exclaimed and pointed to the wall behind us.

A patch of the wall covering had been removed, leaving a blank white square. On the square was a rainbow of colors created by sunlight of the day streaming through the prism. Dr. Newton picked up an ink well and quill pen from a desk and moved to the wall, where I joined him.

With the expertise of a draftsman, he drew eight horizontal lines which were separated equally from the violet on top of the colored bands to the red band on the bottom. On the left side of the bottom line, he drew a circle.

He pointed the quill point at the circle and said, "If I were to tell you that was the note D, corresponding to the color red, what could you tell me about the rest of the notes traversing the colors?"

His request, what he might be looking for in an answer, was not immediately clear. Once again, he had me stumped but this time, being a question in music, I felt I had a chance to come up with a sufficient answer. Clearly, I thought with sudden confidence, Dr. Newton was hinting at a run of notes.

"It's a scale," I said with confidence.

"Which scale?" Dr. Newton asked.

"A scale starting with D ... the Dorian minor scale. That is, the C major scale but starting on the second note."

Dr. Newton nodded as I spoke, while filling in the notes on his makeshift sheet music. "E, F, G, A, B, C, then back to D. Yes, the Dorian scale, each note corresponding to a color that makes up white light. Red, orange, yellow, green, blue, indigo, violet. An octave of notes, an octave of color."[5]

With that quick explanation, Dr. Newton's light shone directly into a dark corner of my ignorance. A rush of the pulsating excitement loosened my tongue. "As I spoke earlier, the wood itself must be imbued with musical notes. Extending this idea into a principle, and as revealed by your light prism demonstration, music can be found in other substances, some as non-material as light. In order to extract the music, there must be a ... a manipulation of the substance, crafting a violin in the case of wood, moving light through a prism in the case of the color spectrum."

---

[5] The analogy is more like a major sixth than an octave, since orange and indigo are technically half steps. Also, Newton wrongly believed violet to be a continuance of red in the spectrum similarly as notes recur in octaves.

It's also controversial that Newton could see indigo in the spectrum, also called Newton's Indigo Paradox by novelist Eric Paul Shaffer. *TS*

Satisfied with my reasoning I stopped there. But it was also because worry nagged the back of my mind—was I crawling to the edge of a cliff?

Dr. Newton's head swayed slightly as if listening to music, or weighing the logic of my statements, in turn valid then not. I was about to employ my new strategy, leapfrogging to a new topic, when he said, "Not nearly as incorrect as you have been thus far. You made a strong move toward a more universal principle, although you ignored, or forgot, the fundamental nature of sound. Or you do not understand the fundamental nature of light. Perhaps both of those cases are true."

I rubbed my forehead to assuage the pain of thinking. I took a deep breath and released it. "I understand," I said, though certainly not fully. "If I were to grasp the fundamental nature of sound and light, would this help me, and Mr. Stradivari, create the perfect violin?"

"It would," he said, rushed with frustration. "That logical process begins the inquiry from the top. We can also start from the bottom. How would you think we shall do that?"[6]

I resisted the urge to rub my forehead again while he drummed his fingers on the wall near his musical scale. The spectrum of light suddenly disappeared, as if magically induced by his percussion. But then I realized the sunlight had moved to an angle where the prism no longer captured it.

What did we have before there was the spectrum? We only had the violins in his workshop. Without further thought, I said, "The violins? The differences among the violins?"

Dr. Newton shook his head, but then he smiled.

---

6 Newton is playing a philosophical game here, which could be called "guided emergence vs. reductionism." In other words, can we determine the origin of a phenomenon by reducing it to its elements, or does it emerge holistically through complex interactions? Is it something greater than the sum of its parts? *TS*

Back in his workshop, we spent the evening and well into the night making a list of the differences.[7] As scribe, I struggled to keep up with Dr. Newton; indeed, he gained vitality as the hours passed. The list grew and shrank, items changed as quickly as they were proposed.[8] It was near midnight when the housekeeper interrupted us, asking if we needed anything before she retired for the night. If it were Dr. Newton alone, I was certain he would have waved her away. Instead he repeated her request to me, but I replied that I needed nothing. I must have looked tired because he then told her we were finishing for the night. As exhausted and hungry as I was, I remembered to bring up the subject of the counterfeiting as requested by Catherine. He appeared surprised but asked me to make an appointment with him at the Royal Mint.

---

[7] The list remained with Dr. Newton. Later, I re-created it as well as I could; my list can be found with my other records. *PW*

[8] Newton is playing another philosophical game with Wolf—list making, also called a structural elements game by Allan Collins. *TS*

chapter 13

Soon after my meeting with her uncle, I was able to join Catherine at Mr. Montagu's home while he was away at his country estate. When she and I settled in the parlor, she asked me about my latest visit with her uncle.

"As usual, I'm afraid I failed to meet his standards," I replied. I related our severe disagreement over Mr. Stradivari's claim of finding the spirit, or soul, in the wood of the viola. She gasped in disfavor when I told her about the sliver of wood Dr. Newton carved from the violin and demanded I show him its soul.

However, she was very favorably interested in her uncle's demonstration with his prism, especially his comparison of the spectrum of colors to a musical scale. In fact she had me tell the experience more than once, each in more fine-grained detail than the previous. With greater appreciation than I'd ever felt before, she applauded my insightful reply to Dr. Newton concerning musical notes existing in the wood, as colors exist in light.

"So perhaps I made a little, well, a tiny bit of headway. And one or two of my comments seemed to have amused him."

"Is that true? I can't say I've ever seen him amused. He might occasionally find something ironic, something contrary to his strict sense of logic."

I tried to explain how I fumbled through his questions and how I tried to relate them to his laws of motion. "Then I tried once too often, stretching my analogy too far. He laughed."

Catherine's eyes grew in amazement. "He laughed? Out loud?"

"Vociferously."

Now Catherine laughed. "My dear Captain Wolf! What I would have given to hear that. I have never even heard him more than give a quick, quiet little chuckle. Anyone who can amuse my uncle is already in the top tier of those my uncle has interacted with in his life. Now, he won't hold back when he takes pen to paper if he feels aggrieved in some way, no matter how slight. I've had a chance to read some of these missives to those on his wrong side. Mr. Flamsteed[1] for one. Mr. Leibniz[2] for another."

"I didn't feel so fortunate when he was laughing," I admitted. "In fact, I felt the fool."

Catherine smiled sympathetically. "I'm very sorry. I'm certain you didn't feel fortunate. It must have been horrifying and embarrassing."

"It was. Although unlike our first two meetings, our last encounter didn't end suddenly when I said something which angered him."

"Excellent."

"I managed to remember to offer my help concerning his duties at the Mint."

"Also excellent. That's music to my ears."

"Speaking of music," I said, removing the sheets of music from my satchel, "here are the latest sections of our concerto."

She accepted the score and perused it. "If you keep adding to it, you'll have a symphony before long. I do see much improvement. I'm excited to hear what you've accomplished. Allow me the honor of playing it."

"The honor would be mine."

---

1 John Flamsteed, English astronomer and one-time friend of Newton, tightly held onto his moon transit records that Newton desired. He and Newton once fought, physically, over the observatory instruments Flamsteed controlled. *PW*

2 Gottfried Leibniz, German mathematician and philosopher, and Newton engaged in a decades long dispute over who first developed the mathematics of calculus, as we now call it. All evidence points toward an independent arrival at the concepts. *TS*

While she played the score, I was moved back in time to my room, when in the dead of night, when the officer's quarters were quiet, I would light a single candle, placing it far enough away so I could make out the notes I put down, but not close enough to wash away the moody darkness. In this way I could focus, purge the day's mundanity of political and war strategy. But more importantly, it kept me afloat in the deep pool of pain into which I'd plunged. The water was black, the depths unreachable, no island of sanctuary to save me.

The notes were my breaths, at the tempo of heartbeats, floating in bubbles of raw emotion, chasing away thoughts. The music ran deeply, as I sank further into the pool. But I began to hear, viscerally so. More than melody, more than counterpoint, the raw feelings became a language. A language only understood by me, a language that could only be spoken by the most perfect of violins.

Then I was taken back to the last conversation Catherine and I had before I left for Italy, recalling her eloquent description of the arc of life, of the beauty, the joy of it as well as the sadness. The new parts I'd written most surely captured the melancholy which came from my long absence.

Catherine replayed the new sections, drawing out the intended enormity from the music, matching the light and the dark aspects she had portrayed with her words. I knew how difficult it would be to fully capture her thoughts and emotions behind the words. I had so much further to go. But also, I realized how great would be the finished work if it only captured a portion of her understanding of life.

But more than that, I realized, I was trying to capture the entirety of her being.

"Here," Catherine said, pulling me back into the present. "I think if we changed these few bars, like this," and she hummed a few notes.

"No," she said, "more like this." She hummed it again, adding more emphasis on the new notes. Then she played it on the violin. She looked at me when she finished.

She was right. I nodded with great enthusiasm,

"From what I've heard so far," she said, "it's incredible, so much more than I could have imagined. I've been trying to decide which composer it reminds me of, or which other compositions, but I can't come up with one. There is some of Mascitti's lyricism, Pepusch's melodic genius, and Purcell's soaring expressiveness, but there is nothing exactly like it.[3] Certainly nothing from those composers approach your sheer ambition."

I will remember those words forever. "If only my execution can match my ambition," I said quietly, to myself more than to her.

We worked on the composition without break for two hours when James and Rose arrived. While we settled in for a light meal, Rose asked how we were doing with our composing. Catherine spoke first, "Very well, I think. But I can't speak for Phillipe."

"Thanks to Catherine," I said, "it's much stronger than I could have imagined. We made great progress, and I'm considerably inspired to continue."

"That's good, perhaps you can now focus on your other duties," James said. "You should have seen him in the meeting we were having with a general. I'm endeavoring to get across our successes in Italy, thwarting the general from having us demoted, and what is my friend here doing?"

---

[3] All Baroque composers: Michele Miscitti, Johann Pepusch, and Henry Purcell. I would later cross paths with Pepusch. German-born, he lived the latter fifty years of his life in England. *PW*

Catherine said, "Was he writing down musical notes instead of military notes?"

"Almost as bad," James said. "His head was swaying in time to some inner music, his hand twitching as if the baton were in his hand. I was afraid he was going to start humming a melody."

"An exaggeration," I said, "but not entirely untrue. I was controlling my real thoughts on the general's misguided criticism."

James said, "I warned our Austrian friend here to be careful, or we might get booted out of the military for musical insubordination."

"Frightful," said Catherine with a grin. "But then you might be able to focus on something more creative with your lives."

"That would be perfect," I said. "A poor but honest artist."

Rose said, "Rich at heart and mind. And you, James?"

"I'm afraid I haven't a creative bone in my body. I'm destined to die a soldier."

"We hope a very old soldier," Catherine said. "I'm worried we are getting dragged into this succession conflict. Yet, it seems inevitable. When the king of France cocks his head and makes his pronouncement, we English must cock our heads the other way."

Rose said, "Yes, peace and music instead of war."

"Would that be the case," James said, apparently eager to change the topic. "I think we should finish our meal so we can hear Catherine and Rose play."

After dinner and the petite concert, James and Rose drifted into the garden to continue their own conversation. Catherine and I were in two chairs seated across from each other at a slight angle that drew us together intimately. We were quiet until Catherine said, "Maybe it's naïve to believe such a radical change would ever be possible."

"As a man who has been in battle, I would say that such a change would be most welcome to most of those in the military."

"For you?"

The cloud, the life-taking darkness, came over me, choking out any words.

Catherine must have sensed my discomfort. She reached out and placed her hand on mine which rested on the arm of the chair.

"Thank you," I managed to say. "I've really enjoyed our time together tonight. I'm hoping that we can do it again soon."

She smiled. "I too have enjoyed it. It's so difficult for me to get away. My life is rather consumed with my employment. But I'll try. I was thinking earlier, perhaps it would be a good idea to have a small party at Mr. Montagu's home. We could play some of your composition. And of course, we would use the violin from Italy. I'll invite my uncle so he can hear the joyfulness it can bring. If, of course, you believe this would be a good idea."

"Yes! Thank you for offering."

"Wonderful. I shall begin planning it right away."

In appreciation, she leaned forward, granting me the privilege to kiss her.

And so, I did.

Not many days after, I received a note from the Royal Mint saying the Master requested my presence. I arrived at the appointed hour at the Tower of London, and was escorted through shadowy corridors, past guards at every corner.

In a large suite, Dr. Newton was seated at his desk and speaking with two men, one who looked like a clerk and the other an officer in uniform. The three glanced over when I entered, Dr. Newton giving me a quick nod. While it wasn't an effusive greeting, it was more enthusiastic than his previous ones. I nodded back more than once, as I found myself pleased to see him in a different setting.

The three concluded the business quickly and they left me alone with Dr. Newton. He stood up and started in right away, "I understand from my niece that you have certain skills in the area of subterfuge."

The statement had the tone of his rhetorical questions, so I didn't feel it necessary to confirm that Catherine was correct.

Indeed, he continued without a response, "I've done this myself when I was Warden of the Mint, wearing a disguise to gather knowledge of a coiner. You may have heard of the case of the criminal William Chaloner,[4] the most egregious and despicable of the counterfeiters who delighted in fraud and fun[5] against the Mint. I'm sure you can ask anyone for more concerning the events that transpired. But now that I'm the Master and have become more well-known, I should need some help with another particularly stubborn opponent who has not seen the evil and risk of his criminal ways."

He paused. I wasn't sure if I were to give my consent without further information or ask him for that first. Again, he continued without a word from me.

"I assume you'll agree to help with this matter. Of course, it must be strictly in confidence. I won't speak of it outside of these walls and only to my most trusted assistants here. You must do the same."

Again, a pause. This time I jumped in. "Good sir, I would be happy to help you. But I can only agree to certain things, especially as I am in your country as a guest of the military. I can't do anything which might jeopardize that relationship."

Dr. Newton looked annoyed at my response. "I wouldn't want you to do anything to endanger your position, but if anything should happen in that regard, I'll defend you in whatever manner necessary.

---

[4] I had not, but later discovered the details of his case. Chaloner was a successful counterfeiter and was equally successful at evading the law and avoiding convictions. Dr. Newton eventually provided damning evidence and Chaloner was hanged, despite personal appeals to Dr. Newton. *PW*

[5] "Fun" refers to deceptive, non-violent criminal activities intended to enrich the criminal and disrupt institutions. *TS*

What I propose should be relatively simple and safe. It's a matter of not having the person here I can trust, nor one with the right temperament and reasoning. And I certainly can no longer go out as anyone but who I am. Not after the Chaloner case."

I realized this concern is why Catherine asked me to find out what was happening. "I shall assist you in whatever way I can."

"Then please, have a seat."

We sat in chairs in the corner of his suite, which was filled with weight scales and other instruments of precision, metal samples, charts and maps, and sheaves of paper with all manner of writings and formulas and tables of numbers.

Dr. Newton began without further ceremony, "A metals merchant, Robert Percy, is suspected of counterfeiting coins with an alloy of inexpensive metals. 'Suspected' being the official designation but I'm certain of his guilt in this matter."

He pushed a coin across to me that appeared as if conjured. I examined it and was surprised it wasn't genuine.

"A sophisticated facsimile, very troubling so," said Dr. Newton. "While we've traced some of the activity through the materials that point to the man, we need to have a witness actually see him with possession of the coins and willfully distributing them."

"Do you have an idea of how best to accomplish this?"

"Nothing so much as certain yet," he answered. "He remains very much in the shadows, unlike the boastful Chaloner. However, upon careful examination of patterns of where the coins appear, there does seem to be a connection to the metals industry. Criminals, like all humans, establish patterns."

Applying my military experience, I said, "It's only when we are in the unusual situation that we must break the pattern."

That stopped him in thought, for a reason I didn't know.

"But," I quickly added, "those patterns provide us a way of attack."

"Yes, yes, yes," he said in a quick staccato. "Plan strategies, evaluate weaknesses, marshal resources."

Adding military strategist to Dr. Newton's list of accomplishments, I said, "I assume that my friend Captain James Brookfield can work with me, especially since he knows the city better than I do."

Dr. Newton agreed to that and supplied me with the knowledge he could impart, including the charts and maps illustrating the patterns he mentioned. He asked me if I could commit the information to memory. "I cannot have any of this fall into the wrong hands, nor seen by the wrong eyes."

"I understand," I said, and set about to commit it to memory.

But there was much to learn, times, locations, people. I asked for a blank sheet of paper and a pen. Dr. Newton gave me a questioning look. I said, "Please bear with me."

He obliged my request and watched over my shoulder as I created the lines of a musical score and began writing down musical notes. After less than a minute, he made a slight chuckling sound and said, "A very clever musical cypher, Captain."

He pointed out a note and said, "This note corresponds to the number five, correct?"

"Yes," I answered, surprised he untangled the puzzle so quickly. I hoped it was because he was brilliant, and not because my cypher was so easily broken.

chapter 14

Before James and I could begin our subterfuge pursuing counter-feiters for Dr. Newton, we received an invitation to attend a meeting of the Kit-Cat Club. Surprisingly, the invitation came through Mr. Montagu's office. James claimed no part in securing the invitation, so I assumed it was through the efforts of Catherine, as I couldn't imagine Mr. Montagu being so generous on his own ac-count. Whatever the reason, I was certain that Mr. Lupine would be happy to hear of the invitation.

James had previously attended one of the club's meetings, and he was able to relate the club's history. Briefly, it began as a literary event held in a bakery that served pies, or "cats." Over the years, the club's purpose moved toward supporting the Whig party's schemes.[1]

We arrived at the Cat and Fiddle shop near The Fountain tavern on Strand. Still early in the evening, the meeting room was already lively with conversation, and filled with the warm and inviting smells of freshly baked pies and other savories. Everyone had a drink of something—wine, ale, cider, or stronger spirits.

Mr. Montagu personally greeted us. "I'm pleased that you can grace our modest club with your presence."

His sincerity was tinged with a bite of sarcasm.

"We very much appreciate your far too generous invitation," I said with a bite of my own.

---

[1] "Kit" originated from the given name of a pastry maker, Christopher Cat, whose surname also means "pies" in English vernacular. A friend of Mr. Cat and one of the club's founders—a bookseller named Jacob Tonson—served Kit's pies—hence Kit's cats—likely to entice others to come to meetings in early days of the club. The group quickly rose in political influence from its beginnings as a group of poets and pie-eaters. *PW*

He introduced us to some of the club members, announcing their professions as well, a collection of barristers, writers, business owners, artists. Then James and I were seated at the end of a long table—the opposite end where Mr. Montagu and the other apparently important members held court.

The pies were delicious.

There seemed to be an unannounced ending to the informalities and eating, and a round of discussion topics began. The discussion, however, was more about who could shout the loudest, or make the wittiest comment, rather than offer the most intelligent point. And yet, there was some rationality in the chaos, at least I began to see a pattern. One of the members announced a question, who was then roundly denounced for bringing up such a trivial matter. Another member would restate the question, twisting it around until it seemed to make no sense, except through some alternative logic. Then another member tried their hand at the question, while the jeering and shouting grew louder, especially as the morphing became more and more irrational. Finally, with the question now unrecognizable, the person to whom the question was originally addressed began his answer. But the answer, or response, seemed to find its way from the illogical to the logical. Only to be denounced by the din and insults from the others.[2]

When it came to the question of the war, one of the refined gentlemen shouted, "And now we are being dragged into another war against France, and allied with whom? Weak-sister Austria? Can we possibly be ready for another bloodbath? What is this madness?"

Jeering erupted.

---

[2] I discovered this verbal jousting was the Whigs' backhanded swipe at the perceived lack of logical and sensible reasoning of the ruling Tory party members and the King. *PW*

Another shouted, "What of the Treaty of London? Has not this matter already been settled?"[3]

The jeering escalated, with hissing thrown in.

"The Treaty of London?" spoke another. "Wouldn't the paper it was written on be of greater value wrapped around one of Kit's cats?"

Laughter roiled through the room.

Another club member shouted, "Madness is only in the mind, yet blood doth boil unseen deep in flesh, so why are we to go to war with our weak sister?"

Clearly this volley was meant for me. I was about to answer when James touched my arm. He whispered for me to wait for the game to be played out.

Shouts and boos and guffaws, and other nonsense was thrown about until Mr. Montagu raised his hand. "Now, gentleman ... and others ... we shall have to ask one of our guests to resolve this question. We have here, whom some of you've met, a military officer from the weak sis—er, Austria. Or *is* he an officer? Might he be just a music man? Or maybe he's neither and is imposter all around? Shall we ask this *captain* to answer for himself?"

After the sarcastic applause died, I said, "If the world fought with music, with a conductor's batons and musical instruments, Austria would rule every sovereign nation. And we would have all of your wives and sisters."

---

[3] Officially, the Second Partition Treaty, or in full—*The treaty betwixt the Most Christian King (ie France), the King of Great Britain, and the States General of the United Provinces for settling the succession of the crown of Spain and the dominions thereunto belonging in case his Catholick Majesty (Charles II of Spain) die without issue.*

At the time England and Scotland were separate countries; however, the formal agreement signed by William III (also William of Orange) was as King of Great Britain. The United Provinces were the Dutch Republic. *PW*

Loud laughter and howls followed.

Clapping his hand on my shoulder, James announced, "This man saved my life. I haven't one moment of hesitation to enter war with the Austrians by our side."

Mr. Montagu said, "Thank you, Captain Brookfield, for pleading the other captain's case. Forgive me, but you make him sound as if he's a one-man army."

Hoots and whistles erupted.

James raised his voice. "An army without Captain Wolf makes that army look small."

I further rebutted, "My friend, Captain Brookfield, is the brave one, to risk his life to make any potential war, any future battle, go as strongly in our favor as anyone can expect."

Mr. Montagu shouted above the din, "And what does this exactly mean? What's going on that we should know about? Perhaps we should bring in some of the soldiers under his command."

James said, "Let's move beyond the personal. What do we have to gain or lose if France controls the Spanish Kingdom?"

There were shouted answers to that question, all denouncing France. This went on for several moments, until a senior member raised his hand and started another question. I was relieved to be off the stage. Glancing at Mr. Montagu, I found him staring at me, as if contemplating a fox that he was about to shoot at the end of a hunt.

Later, on our way out of the club, we passed a shelf with a row of toasting mugs, each inscribed with verse. I found this one at the end of the row:

To Mrs. Barton,

Beauty and wit strove, each in vain,
To vanish Bacchus and his train;
But Barton, with successful charms,
From both their quivers drew her arms,

The roving god his sway resigns,
And awfully submits his vines.[4]

Beneath the verse was signed the name of the authoring poet: "Ch. Montagu."

The next evening, James and I were at Kilwraith Tavern, a pub located on a rancid street near the central docks, squeezed between vegetable markets and fish mongers. We fit right in, as if born on the street, with our disguises of unshaven faces, tussled-with hair, and workaday clothes. The place was crowded and rowdy, as much as the Kit-Cat Club had been, although with a rougher clientele. We kept our heads down and drank steadily so that we didn't make too much of an impression, at least not enough to rouse suspicion. Although I don't think we had too much to worry about, as it was well into the evening and the locals well into their drink.

As we glanced around, I spotted the two men who were described to me by Dr. Newton. They were not as scruffy as most of the other patrons and seemed to be wary and engaged in a serious discussion at the same time. One had red hair, the other black. I told James where they were. He gave them his gaze, then nodded at me.

We finished our drinks. I went over to them while James hung back near the door to the tavern. In case they declined my forthcoming offer, James could follow them, perhaps to the leader of their counterfeiting ring.

The men stared at me when I neared their table. They looked at each other, giving the other a shake of his head and a shrug.

"Sorry to bother you gentlemen, but I have a proposition you might be interested in."

---

[4] See *Barn Elms and the Kit Cat Club* for other verses. *TS*

"We take no *propositions*," said the man with red hair. "Anyway, who are you on God's earth?"

"At this point it doesn't matter. I'll tell you in good time, Mr. Ague."

His eyes squinted at me. "How do you know my name?"

"You and Mr. Button come highly recommended."

The other said, "Who would say that?"

"Again, at this point it doesn't matter."

Mr. Button laughed and spat on the floor.

I said, "I assure you I'm serious. I can say that what I have to offer would double your usual take."

Mr. Ague said, "How do you know what we take? How do you even know what we do?"

I started to answer, but Mr. Button said, "Let me guess, it doesn't matter at this point."

I nodded.

Mr. Button said to his colleague, "I suppose it wouldn't hurt to hear."

"Excellent," I said, "my partner and I can answer all your questions."

I gestured toward the door. James gave them a subtle nod. "Can you join us at another establishment not too far from here where we won't be disturbed by so many others?"

The two men quickly drained their mugs.

We went to another pub not far away, where James and I had secured a private room. We got a round of drinks and told them of our plan to use their help to pass off counterfeit coins. I showed them a roll of freshly minted coins given to me by Dr. Newton.

Both men inhaled sharply. "These are counterfeit?" asked Mr. Button.

James and I nodded.

"Incredible," said Mr. Ague, turning one of them in the light. "I can't tell them from the real thing. Except for the fact they look too perfect, as if right out of the press. They would stand out too much."

"Exactly," James said. "We need some roughers and conduits to pass them off without creating suspicion back to us."

"By roughers, you mean ...?" said Mr. Ague.

"Exactly what it sounds like. Rough them up to take the shine off."

"How's that done?" he asked.

"Carefully," I said. "Too much and the counterfeit metals are exposed. We can show you how."

"And what are these ... conduits you mention?" asked Mr. Button.

James said, "We have a network of establishments which can be used to take the coins without question. But as with the roughing, setting up the network has to be done in a very careful manner so as not to arouse suspicion nor to create any linkage back to us."

Mr. Ague asked, "Which establishments might these be?"

I said, "We must remain discrete in this matter at this point."

Mr. Ague said, "But we—"

Mr. Button gave his partner an elbow. "But we must also be discrete. You propose to double our current take?"

James and I nodded.

Mr. Ague glanced between the two of us, then said, "When do you propose this venture to begin?"

"As soon as we agree," I said, "The men we wanted to work with lacked intelligence and reliability. So, we had to look elsewhere. We need to start now to keep promises to our connections."

"Immediately," James gave them the concise answer.

"But we have current commitments," said Mr. Button.

"Yes, we do," confirmed the other man.

"Understandable," I said, "We're prepared to give you a down payment now to begin with us immediately, but also to take care of your current commitments."

"But how will you do that?" asked Mr. Button.

I raised my finger and wagged it.

Both men laughed. Mr. Button said, "As long as this down payment isn't some of your dodgy coin."

We assured them it would not be dodgy coin.

Catherine and I were able to get away together one afternoon. We brought the MB Stradivarius, which she fetched from her uncle, to Mr. Penbook's store. The elegant shop owner was not seated in his winged chair but cleaning his wares and shelves with the fluffiest feather duster I'd ever seen.

"Captain Wolf and Miss Barton. Welcome back," he said as he deposited the duster behind his chair.

"Thank you," we said.

"And what have we here?" he asked, gesturing with an upraised hand at the violin case.

"A violin from Cremona," I said, "on loan from its maker, Antonio Stradivari."

Catherine added, "A most superior instrument."

"Let's have a look then. Over here, please." He brought us over to a table polished to a gleam.

I set the case on the table and opened it.

Mr. Penbook murmured in appreciation. He reached for it, then paused. "May I?"

"Of course," I said.

Mr. Penbook slide his hands under the violin, one under the back and one under the neck. "Ahh," he again murmured. "Such fine balance." He turned the violin at all angles, examining it with a close eye then a far eye.

I said, "Your suggestion to contact the violinist Mr. D'Amico proved most expeditious in pointing me to the Stradivari workshop."

Mr. Penbook gave me a curt nod but said nothing while he continued his inspection.

Catherine said, "The Stradivarius violin can sing every emotion from ponderous tragedy to delicate tendrils of love. It can be colossal in tone or a sweet whisper."

Mr. Penbook gazed up to Catherine. "Then I would be remiss not to hear for myself. Would you please be so kind to play?"

"I would be so pleased," she said and took the violin from him, even as he seemed to be reluctant to let it go.

We left Mr. Penbook's with his assurance the Stradivarius was indeed a most excellent violin. His short list of attributes included the tone at all ranges, the superior craftsmanship, and an undeniable yet undefinable presence. He also made me promise if I was to return to Cremona that I would act as purchaser of a set of instruments for him. I didn't make that promise but told him I would do my best considering the situation in Cremona was complicated by the hostilities. His expression sagged in disappointment, and so I lightened his mood with reassurances that I would meet with him before I returned to Italy.

In the carriage leaving the shop, I told Catherine her playing was superb.

"Thank you," she said. "I enjoyed playing the violin very much. I hope you don't have to return it too soon." She was quiet for a moment then said, "Mr. Montagu told me of your heroism in Cremona."

"James exaggerated during his speech at the Kit-Cat Club. He saved my life as much as I did his. We were being followed in a dark street. We discovered the soldier following us. James was attacked and engaged him. I managed to help James escape."

"Heavens," Catherine said. "Do be careful when you return."

We rode in silence for a while longer before she said, "Tell me the truth, Captain Wolf. Did you kill this man you were fighting?"

I let out a long breath. "Yes, unfortunately I had to or we would have been discovered." I paused before adding, "I have to tell you that at that moment I recalled your powerful words about the arc of life, about when we return to nothingness …"

I could say no more as her lips covered my mouth and she arched her body toward mine.

chapter 15

Our subterfuge for Dr. Newton resumed on a cloudy, windy afternoon with the occasional spit of rain. A few days earlier, James and I delivered a sample of counterfeit coins to Misters Ague and Button for them to rough before circulation. After another day, we retrieved the coins and were now ready to report our judgement on their success. It would not be good news for them.

We met in the back of the tavern, in a yard house of crates and barrels waiting to be repaired. James and I arrived several minutes late as we made sure it was just the two of them before entering.

Sitting on barrels, swinging their legs impatiently, the two men glared at us. If they were dogs, they would have bared their fangs and growled.

James said, "Gentlemen, be calm. Our apologies for being tardy."

I said, "To come straight to the crux, the coins you roughed are not up to our producer's standards."

Mr. Button, the dispassionate one, remained aloof while Mr. Ague squinted in confusion and sputtered, "Standards? What are these lies? They were the same as—"

The other shushed him as if he were a talkative schoolboy. He asked us, "Exactly how, sirs, are they not good to his eye?"

I took a small sack from my pocket and opened it, holding it out in front of me. James dipped his hand in and took out one of the poorly-made counterfeit coins Dr. Newton had forged.

James handed it to Mr. Button. "We couldn't flog this to a beggar."

The man took it and inspected it. He handed it to his colleague.

"But this isn't one of the coins we roughed for you," said Mr. Button.

I said, "Perhaps it doesn't look like what you give us, but this is what it looks like when we got it. Something happened to it. Corrosion perhaps, or reaction with another metal. That's what our producer said."

Mr. Ague shook his head. "This can't be ..."

James said, "Don't doubt my colleague here. He doesn't like to be doubted. Regardless, we can't use them. Whatever you did to them is not satisfactory. We need to see your governor to settle the matter."

Mr. Ague started to say something but the other jumped in first, "That won't be possible."

James took another coin out of the bag and tossed it to Mr. Button. "This one is just as bad. We won't be able to accept your refusal."

"Is that a threat?" asked Mr. Ague.

James laughed. "Now, isn't that a question!"

Mr. Ague took an ill-advised step toward us.

Mr. Button, who was still inspecting the coin, reached out and held back his accomplice. "Gentlemen, I'm sure there's a logical explanation for this. Let's not resort to unseemliness. Let us take your sample of coins to show our governor and we can find the meat of the matter."

I said, "You mean for us to go with you."

Mr. Button said, "Now that, I'm afraid to say, would be impossible. Our man doesn't receive strangers."

"We can't trust you to carry our message," I said. "He will receive us or I'm afraid his empire will come crashing down on his head."

"As will your world," James added, pointing to the two men.

Mr. Button gave this some thought while Mr. Ague could only look perplexed. Finally, the former said, "I suppose we have no choice but to let him decide what to do."

I said, "Precisely. But first, you should decide if you want your man to find out about the problem with the coins from us or from you."

They looked at each other. Mr. Button said, "We'll inform you when he decides what to do."

"Make it soon," I said. "Or we'll move on."

As one would expect, the alley behind the Lion brewery stunk of spillage, even after the full rain that finally broke from the clouds. The spillage mixing with the runoff comprised of bobbled ale, scattered sweet malted grains, petals of bitter hops, fermenting yeast blooms.

Workers wearing stained aprons milled in and out of the great sliding doors of the brewery, or were clumped in small packs, grunting their conversations, smoking tobacco, or fisting rolls of pink ham into their maws.

James hadn't been pleased we convinced Rose to tell us how best to gain entry to the brewery, even if it was a rival of her cousin's and not likely that our subterfuge would be traced back to her. I agreed we should not put her in danger in any way, nor cause trouble for her cousin. Rose claimed she was happy to help us, although only if we remained out of trouble ourselves.

We promised.

Entering through the back alley allowed us to get far into the brewery without being challenged. We surveyed the operations as we walked through the grain boxes, hop baskets, and rows of vats, the air thick with fermenting grain mash, the cloying sweetness sticking in the back of my throat. There were cleaners and haulers and stirrers reporting to the brew master who was dressed in fine clothes, as if a gentleman on a stroll, except for his long white apron and the instruments and writing tools in the pocket on the left side. We nodded as we walked past him. He gave us a long look, then another, but didn't challenge us. He went back to signing papers and giving orders.

At the end of the rows we turned sharply and walked toward a corridor. These were the offices, according to the interior plan Rose had sketched for us. At the first office door, James stopped while I walked ahead. I reached the door, pausing to take a breath and let it out before opening it and going inside.

The room smelled smartly of tobacco, tea, and ink. Two men were seated at desks, and both continued writing for a moment before looking up. One said, "Yes?" with impatience. When he didn't recognize me, he glanced at his partner, who shrugged.

The second man put his pen down and folded his hands in front of him. "And, so?" he said.

I closed the door behind me. "Titus George," I announced my pseudonym, and that was all I said.

Again, the second man, clearly the one in charge, said, "And, so?"

I frowned and shook my head as if in disgust. "Titus George," I said more emphatically. "Didn't you hear?"

This set the first man off and he stood up from his desk. "Hold your tongue, or I'll cut it out."

The second man waved a hand at him. "Mr. George, I apologize if I am to know who you are or your purpose. Perhaps if you could give me a clue to engage my apparently feeble memory."

"You're Mr. Ravenscroft," I said. "Chief Accountant for Lion Brewery."

With a suspicious glare, he said, "Correct. And this is Mr. Killsworth, head brew master."

I fished a coin out from my pocket and held it out at arm's length. "Well then, Mr. Ravenscroft and Mr. Killsworth, what do you think of this?"

The accountant squinted at the coin, gave me a puzzled look, and said, "A coin of the realm? I should be so impressed with a guinea?"

I stepped forward and placed the coin on the desk in front of him. He picked it up and inspected it. "And, so, Mr. George?"

I asked him if he thought it genuine.

He flipped it front to back, then weighed it in his palm. He handed it to the brew master who performed the same inspection. He nodded.

"It would seem so," said Mr. Ravenscroft.

"What if I were to tell you it was not?"

The man considered that statement. "You can't be saying it's counterfeit? A fake? I can't believe it."

"Believe it, or don't believe it. I can take my offer elsewhere."

The accountant stroked his chin. "What offer are you talking about? I heard no offer, only a likely bogus claim. And who are you anyway?"

"You haven't heard an offer yet, that's true. As for me, I represent whom I can only call our producer. The offer comes from him through me. It concerns such coin and the ale taxes you might, or might not, be paying. Are you now willing to hear the offer?"

The accountant crossed his arms. He smiled then told his colleague to fetch two men named Harley and Gerald. The man strode past me. I assume Harley and Gerald would throw me out on my ear.

He managed only a few steps before he was shoved back into the room. James came into the room and closed the door.

I said to the two surprised, now angry, men, "Now I won't be asking. You'll have to hear my offer."

The accountant said, "One shout from me, and you'll both be dead."

James said, "But not before you've expired."

I let James' threat sink in before I said, "Excellent. It's simple, really. I know that you require some assistance in paying your ale tax, and we want to pass the kind of coin I just showed you. In other words, if you help us, we'll help you. I'm sure you can see how easily that works."

The chief accountant for Lion Brewery, Mr. Ravenscroft, sighed then nodded dully.

T he note of only a few words from Catherine asked me to meet her at the coffeehouse at a given time on a given day. There was no choice offered in the matter, and I assumed the window of time she specified was narrow and set in stone. Of course, I arrived at the coffeehouse at the precise time. I would have been there even if I was supposed to instead meet with the Holy Emperor.[1]

I didn't see Catherine among the patrons when I arrived, but a young woman working in the establishment noticed me. She came over and said, "Captain Wolf, I would venture?"

I thought she was going to tell me that Catherine could not keep our appointment. Instead, she asked me to follow her toward the back of the coffee house. She pulled back a heavy curtain revealing a private alcove. Catherine was there, I was relieved to see, standing near the narrow window.

She smiled and waved me over to the table with two chairs. We sat down. She said, "Our coffee service shall be here in a moment. Are you well?"

"I'm well," I said in response. "And you?"

"Also well. Thank you for meeting me," she said.

"I need no gratitude as the pleasure is mine."

---

[1] Referring to Leopold I, Holy Roman Emperor, who sought to impose the Spanish crown inheritance to his younger son, in defiance of King of France Louis XIV, during the War of Spanish Succession. Leopold and Louis were first cousins. Leopold was a patron of music, as well as a composer. *PW*

I recount these few words of greeting for the formality, the uneasiness of their tone. It was not how I expected our meeting to begin, given the intimacy we shared during our previous encounter.

"I hear from Rose that you and Captain Brookfield are well into the counterfeit coiner's world. Thank you again for helping my uncle. You must accept my gratitude this time."

"Yes, accepted. We are indeed well into that world. Shall I tell you how far we have progressed?"

"If you wish," she said. "But I have no desire to interfere or otherwise judge your progress. Nor should I give you any bad luck in telling me."

"I'm sure you could bring no bad luck on any person," I said.

She smiled wryly, as if hearing a poor attempt at humor. "You don't know me well enough then."

"I shall endeavor to learn more," I said, although my response sounded odd to me even as I spoke it.

The matron of the house returned with our coffee and set up our service in quick order. When she left and as we drank from our mugs, I told Catherine the primary elements of the subterfuge James and I had put into play, so far successfully, at least I believed so. We'd set up a presence in the world where we should soon begin to see the counterfeiters in action. I ended my brief story saying, "Rose has been most helpful."

Catherine considered this for a moment. "Excellent. But I do wish to say again, please be careful."

With that caring declaration, I felt some warmth in the room. I promised her I would be careful.

"Good. Now I wish to say that I've begun preparations for the concert at my employer's home. It will be in three weeks' time, if that's satisfactory."

"Wonderful," I said.

"Your composition will be the highlight of the evening." Catherine paused before saying, "How is it progressing?"

"It's coming along," I said, without telling her that I hadn't had much time to work on the score.

"I'll be pleased to see it. I should need to practice it soon, along with other performers as well, who are much more skilled than I. When will we be able to have the score?"

"Soon, I hope."

"Can you put a day on it? So, I can arrange a practice session."

I found myself loath to do so, not having any confidence in when I would be able to finish the concerto. In fact, I felt as if I were undergoing one of Dr. Newton's friction experiments.

"I would have to put some thought to it," I said.

"I understand," she said.

The chill returned, which I disliked very much. "Shall we say … a week from today?"

Catherine brightened. "That will be wonderful. I'm sorry if I put you in a vise. The thing is, I must entreat my employer to allow the event in the first place, and the second place, it must rise to a certain standard, high enough to attract the right audience for my employer, and in third, it must be successful."

That was putting me tightly in a vise.

Catherine must have sensed my feelings. "I don't wish to increase my debt to you, nor be a further burden."

"No, neither will ever be the case. It's I who must not be the burden."

Catherine considered this, her expression one of sadness, I believed. But it was fleeting, as she reached behind her chair and produced a violin case—it was the MB Stradivarius. She asked me, "Did you bring your music?"

I removed the score from the satchel. "As much as I have finished."

She turned through the pages, stopped at one, then opened the violin case. She studied the page for a few moments, then began playing.

The part she had chosen portrayed a deep welling of fear, a darkness that exuded from a place I never thought of, not intentionally. The unknown hollowing out of my soul, I might have said, if I could have thought of it at the time.

In this intimate room, lit only with a candle, the part was made even more opaque yet touching in a way I never imagined it could be. Catherine's playing of it brought out a layer of feeling I hadn't considered.

Was it also the Stradivarius?

Yes, I believed so. Catherine's playing of the instrument was so constrained, as if building the tension of the music from within the violin, from the very wood that Mr. Stradivari carved and shaped and varnished. As if the music had been encased for the hundred years the tree had grown. The depth of sadness was coming out after being locked in the fibers.

"What were you thinking when you composed this portion?" Catherine asked.

I realized she had stopped playing moments earlier. "Thinking?" I repeated.

"Or feeling?"

I recalled what she said to me before I left for Italy. "More feeling than thinking," I said. "I believe it might have been inspired by your words before I left for Italy. Your treatise on the arc of life. How when we look back on life it feels as if there was nothing and everything at once."

Catherine considered this, but before saying anything to my response, she played the section again. It changed, subtly at first. Quieter, I realized, then her playing grew in voice, compounding the darkness, the fear, the sadness, then sinking to an inescapable depth.

chapter 16

My afternoon with Catherine ended shortly after she had played the new sections of the concerto and proclaimed them "wonderful," although I couldn't help but feel it was encouragement for me to get on with composing. She announced, again formally, that she had to leave. We kissed, not lingering, and with her finger placed on my lips, I was instructed to stay alone in the coffeehouse for a few moments. After doing so, I walked out, looking around but didn't see her or anyone I recognized.

It was clear there was a change in our heretofore rich, yet innocent,[1] relationship.

I thought about asking Dr. Newton if he knew anything about this change—I was again waiting for him, while drinking an ale in his parlor. The thought of asking such a personal question made me sputter a laugh decorated with bubbles of the ale. I couldn't imagine him speaking of intimate matters.[2] But I could be wrong about that, probably was wrong, I decided. Of course, I didn't want Catherine to hear that I was discussing her with her uncle.

Instead, after only nine minutes of waiting,[3] I was shown into Dr. Newton's workshop where he immediately launched into a protracted dissertation on his list of the differences between the Stradivarius and

---

[1] Again, I used the word "innocent" ... but in what form? I asked myself this question many times, and could not come up with a clearer description, nor think of a better word. *PW*

[2] In defense of Newton's humanity, he sent Catherine this note when she was ill with smallpox and recovering in the country: "Pray let me know by your next how your face is and if your fevour be going. Perhaps warm milk from ye Cow may help to abate it. I am Your loving Unkle, Is. Newton." *TS*

[3] ! *PW*

the "poorer" violins. He'd even named them: Poor A and Poor B. The latter was the one he had sawn in half, or drawn-and-quartered as I had come to think of it.

I wrote down as much as I could, which was not much, as he spoke rapidly. Only when he stopped to ask me if I was following did he pause. I would nod, and he would go on.

As much as I could understand, the most important and fully described points dealt with the thicknesses of the back and belly. Dr. Newton demonstrated the tool he created to measure thickness. It was made with thin, connected lengths of metal, one end bent so that it could be inserted into the violin through an f sound hole. Along one of the lengths of metal, precise markings had been etched. When the ends of the two lengths were drawn together, the edge of the connecting cylinder would fall somewhere along the gauge. The location of the reading and the distance were recorded.

"Here's a cross-section of one of the violins," Dr. Newton said as he presented a drawing. "What can you deduce from it?"

Immediately, I knew the question was broad and full of traps, as my experience with Dr. Newton's questions taught me. I studied the drawing. There were two lines one on top of the other. The bottom line was horizontally flat, the top curved. The curve was complex, like an archer's bow. At regular intervals, short, vertical lines joined the two longer lines. At the bottom of the intersections, numbers had been written: 4,5 3,3 6,4 and so forth.

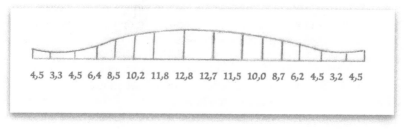

4,5 3,3 4,5 6,4 8,5 10,2 11,8 12,8 12,7 11,5 10,0 8,7 6,2 4,5 3,2 4,5

The numbers on the drawing reminded me of my musical code to track the French forces and the coiner transactions. On Dr. Newton's drawing, the curved line was the path along the surface of the violin, the line on the bottom, a baseline, the vertical numbers corresponding to distance and thickness—the arching, as I recalled Mr. Stradivari called it. But what did Dr. Newton want me to *deduce* from it?

If I told him what I believed the lines and numbers to be, he would likely respond, "But that's not what I asked."

I focused on the numbers, finding they ran toward the greater and lesser without precise consistency. So maybe they weren't the measurements I first believed. Whatever I was going to answer, I needed to do it soon. I could feel Dr. Newton's anxiety building, like the heat of a barrel blast.

"There lacks a consistency in the measurements," I said, regretting it immediately, even though I had at least said something.

"That's an observation not a deduction," he said.

I should have known he was going to say that. He remained silent, almost patiently. Giving me a second chance? If so, I was grateful. I focused on what it meant to deduce, which I assumed was making a conclusion given a fact or some facts.[4]

I came up with this, "Because there is no clear pattern to the numbers, I would say that this drawing is of Poor A."

Dr. Newton did not immediately berate my response. Instead, he asked a further question, "When you say 'because there is no pattern to the numbers,' and then leap to your proclamation that it is Poor A, you forgot to include the most important part of the deduction."

I caught on. "Because no pattern exists, there was less care taken in crafting the violin." Then I quickly added, "And taking less care creates a poorer violin." Confident I had satisfied the conditions for Dr. Newton's deduction, I stopped there.

Dr. Newton drew up his face into his look of disgust. He rubbed his forehead, the first time I had seen him with that much consterna-

---

[4] Close. *TS*

tion. "So many assumptions ..." he said to himself more than me, I believed, from his low tone, nearly a mutter.

"You made so many assumptions," he repeated aloud.

Disappointment again clouded my optimism. "I apologize," I said, not knowing what else to say.

"An apology is not what is needed or required. What do you believe I meant by assumptions?"

This time I was the one who rubbed my forehead. My brow wrinkled in response.

Dr. Newton did not wait for me to make a list. "The most egregious is that you jumped from one conclusion, which might or might not be true, to another. Then you came up with reasons to justify your great leaps."

I was frustrated, feeling helpless. "What should I have done instead?" I pled like a whipped schoolboy.

"Quite simply to begin with, you should have asked for more information. I didn't preclude you from requesting that, did I?"

"I suppose you did not. I assumed—I believed you were wanting me to decide which violin the drawing referred to."

"That would be true," he said. "But the selection is the least interesting part of the deduction."

"I see." After a pause to think, or decide whether to run from the house, I said, "Then am I able to ask the meaning of the numbers written on your drawing?"

Dr. Newton gave me a wry smile. "That question is, of course, entirely allowed."

He explained the numbering system, which turned out to be straightforward, once he had explained it. Rather than direct measurements, the numbers represented a deviation from a normal number. The numbers showed where symmetry did, or did not, occur.

The normal number was also important as it differed between the violins.[5] My understanding of it allowed me to ask another question.

"Might I also see the other drawing and be given the two normal numbers?"

Dr. Newton laughed. I would have to remember to tell Catherine her uncle found amusement again.

Without admonition, he let me see the other cross-section drawing, which also had a curved bow-like line on the top and a straight line on the bottom. He pointed to a number I hadn't noticed at the edge of the drawing, then pointed to the same place on the first drawing.

The number on the first drawing was smaller than the one on the second. Also, the numbers along the bottom line showed more symmetry on the second. I now had more information to make my deduction. But that also left me befuddled. If I couldn't decide which set of drawings and numbers allowed for a superior violin, then they didn't do me any good, at least not on their own.

"There's clearly a difference," I said, pointing out what I had noticed. "I must next decide which set of measurements corresponds to which violin."

Dr. Newton's expression soured, again, so I thought quickly about something else to say. But I was too late.

"Frustration is my least favorite sentiment," he said. "It ties up my guts like putrid meat."

I must admit, I nearly laughed at his description. But I didn't want to pile anger on top of his least favorite sentiment. "No," I said. "*Deciding* is not the correct action. I must *deduce* what the differences mean."

---

[5] I'm likely not accurately describing Dr. Newton's system. *PW*

The analytic method sounds close to a statistical analysis, perhaps a type of regression, where the error from a predictive model determines the significance. *TS*

The answer must also have something to do with a concept, or principle, or law, that Dr. Newton had already told me about. But which would make the most sense in this case? Friction? Forces?

Pressure!

Words fairly tumbled from my mouth. "It's about pressure. The bowing creates forces on the bridge, which in turn puts the air in the violin under pressure."

Dr. Newton showed me a drawing while he spoke this question, "And how do the forces create the pressures?"

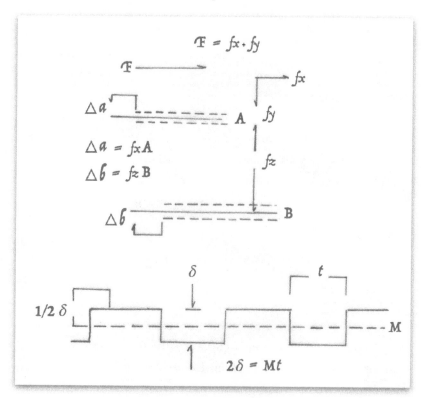

I didn't know what to say; I believed I had completed the chain of events. Looking at the drawing didn't help.

"The feet of the bridge press against which part of the violin?" Dr. Newton prompted.

The top, of course. I didn't think it was necessary to add that, but I answered with a question, "Are you referring to the top plate of the violin?"

"I can't follow your deduction if you don't give me the full chain of your reasoning."

Another wave of defeat engulfed me.

"All right," I managed to speak. "The player puts bow to the strings, which through friction makes the strings resonate. The bridge is moved by the resonation, down to the feet of the bridge, which moves the top plate of the violin, causing the air inside to be under pressure, which moves the bottom plate, the back of the violin. The air moving through the *f* holes creates the sound we hear."

I took a deep breath. My little speech was likely the longest I'd given in his presence.

Dr. Newton tapped a finger against his head. "Was that so difficult?"

Exceedingly so, I thought, as I breathed in relief.

He went on without waiting for my answer, "Of course, that leaves us with many questions. For one, what are the values we must specify to make use of this particular mechanism to perform at its optimum?"

He paused and looked at me.

"A fair question," I said.

He smiled wryly. "Tell me, now that you are an expert in deduction, where does this reasoning power come from?"

That threw me over a barrel. Where does what come from?

"Our minds?" I offered tentatively.

"Does it?" he said sharply. "Descartes might say so.[6] Yes, we use our minds, but from where does a thought originate?"

_____

[6] René Descartes, 1596 – 1650, French philosopher, mathematician, and scientist. Newton is referring to Cartesian, or mind-body, dualism. The mind is immaterial and the body material, although they do interact, as in "I think, therefore I am." *TS*

I was sorely perplexed by this line of questioning.

"If examined closely," he went on, "would we find our minds and bodies to be separate? Or are they inextricably intwined? Maybe minds are mere expressions of our souls, as your luthier might say. If so, does all rational thinking come from somewhere outside of our souls? Furthermore, does this mean there are no mechanisms in the natural world? Is everything merely a consequence of thought?"

With that final question, he wandered off, disappearing from the room. His questions must have intrigued him mightily. Or he was certain I would be unable to answer them.

chapter 17

Mr. Lupine habitually traced his scar while he went on at length. The gist of his exposition, spoken in his diplomatic monotone, was that the war, the War of Spanish Succession as he pronounced nobly, had reached a stalemate. The Austrian forces in Italy bogged down into unproductive skirmishes, the Low Lands campaign had yet to begin in earnest.

"We need the English to get involved soon," he said, ending his speech.

"I understand the urgency," I said. "What are we doing to encourage them?"

"We have been making our case at high levels, but there's a strong move away from involvement."

"Mr. Montagu can still be persuaded, can't he?" This is what I believed after the Kit-Cat Club meeting James and I attended. He hadn't made a definitive pronouncement either way.

"Even if so, the Honorable Member of Parliament[1] seems to be losing his power."

"It didn't seem that way," I said. "His full force and power were on display at the meeting of the Kit-Kat Club."

Mr. Lupine considered this. "I believe there would be no diminishment of his belief that he has power, even if it becomes true."

I could not disagree with him about that.

---

[1] Correctly, he was Baron Halifax and *The Right Honourable* Charles Montagu MP FRS at this time, but in a few years would be known as The Lord Halifax in a bid to survive impeachment from the House of Commons. He eventually became the 1st Earl of Halifax. *PW*

"MP" is Member of Parliament, "FRS" Fellow of the Royal Society. *TS*

He continued, "But beyond the Kit-Cat Club, I hear rumors of an even stronger shadow government that needs to be turned in our favor. Unfortunately, I don't know the particulars, but I believe Montagu is at the heart of it."

After long moments of silence, I said, "I see."

"I believe you're in a better place to find out more," he said after his own lengthy pause.

"I'll do what I can."

"Good. It will have to be soon, as I also have approval for you to return to Cremona to pursue further intelligence of the French forces there."

I was surprised. "I assume Captain Brookfield would be going with me again? When are we expected to be in Italy?"

"I haven't received the details, but I believed it would need to be before the end of summer."

There was much to do before then.

J ames and I were alone in the officers club one early afternoon, sipping light drinks. I said, "Something intriguing seems to be afoot."

"There usually is," James replied. "What do you know?"

"I heard Mr. Montagu is gathering power behind the scenes."

James tilted his head in a questioning gesture. "Are you referring to his role in the Whig Junto?"

"Tell me more."

James gathered his thoughts with a long drink from his glass. "Do you think, do you believe, there's an invisible undercurrent of power, one that keeps flowing no matter what happens in the world?"

"I can't say for certain," I said, after considering his question. "There's the inevitable march of time, which defeats all. If you speak of the power perpetuated by men or women, there also seems to be an inevitability of action."

And reaction, I almost said. Dr. Newton was permanently in my head.

"I believe," I continued, "power that's visible is easier to attack, easier to destroy. Power that hides in the shadows is more likely to survive. But even that doesn't mean it will always be there, existing through eternity, an unending, continuous flow from the same source."

"No, maybe not," James said. "There may be ebbs and flows, sometimes the power may be diverted, but in the end, it can't be completely stopped."

"What of Mr. Montagu and the Whig Junto?" I asked. "Is that the invisible power you refer to?"

"It's a group of influential Whigs, the perpetual undercurrent of which I spoke. Yes, Montagu's visible influence is weak, which is likely what you heard. But within the junto, it's as strong as ever."

James paused and looked straight into my eyes. "Don't underestimate him."

Hearing his warning, I nodded.

Misters Button and Ague arrived at the barrel yard house well after James and I had already found the place empty of workers. Without any pleasantries, Mr. Button said, "We will take you to see our governor, but we must make sure you are without weapons."

James and I raised our arms as they did their business and judged us weaponless.

We rode in a carriage through the streets paralleling the docks before turning onto a side street. There we stopped at a block of buildings with an internal courtyard. We got out of the carriage and were escorted into one of the buildings. There was a strange hushed quiet throughout, as if all shoes were covered in felt and voices in whisper. We entered a room where a dozen or so men were hunched over metals in raw and finished form, with scales and glass beakers at their sides, and bound ledgers open.

We walked past them and through another door. This room was expansive, with floor-to-ceiling bookshelves as if we were part of a university library. Standing behind a wide desk was a beefy man, who could have been Mr. Ague's older brother, by the translucent paleness of skin. Three other men were standing in front of a set of papers spread out tidily. They turned around when we entered, and their quiet conversation died.

With a questioning look, the pale man appeared greatly annoyed with our presence. "What is it?"

Mr. Button said, "I'm sorry to bother you, Mr. Percy, but these are the men I spoke to you about earlier."

He shook his head and sighed, then waved the three seated men out of the room. When they were gone, he sat down but did not gesture for us to take the seats at the table.

"All right," he said impatiently. "Go on."

Mr. Ague said, "These two men presented themselves and lodged a complaint about our recent roughing job."

James produced the coin he had taken from the bag.

Mr. Percy turned a shade of flaming pink. "You brought this into my presence? You know that's utterly unacceptable."

Mr. Button took over the conversation. "Sir, please, take a look."

James placed the coin on the table.

Mr. Percy glanced at it, then picked it up and inspected the back and front, and then the sides. "What is your game? This isn't one of … this isn't something I've ever seen before. It certainly isn't like the coins we roughed for you."

Mr. Button said, "These men claim the coins quickly decayed into this condition."

Mr. Percy again gave the coin his eye. "Impossible," he muttered.

He got up and went over to the bookcase. Sliding a book over, he opened a hidden panel, fiddled with a lock I couldn't see, then took out a wooden box. He brought it over to us and took out a handful of coins. Counterfeit I assumed.

He pushed one next to the coin he got from us. "They should look like these. I hardly think any natural process could have caused such a difference."

James and I stepped closer and feigned great purpose in making our inspection of the two coins. After a due amount of time, I turned to James and said, "I see his point."

"I do as well," James said.

Mr. Percy clucked. "It's Ague and Button who have apparently funned you. As you can see, I'm a man of a reputation who would not resort to such foolishness."

As I gave him a slight bow, I said, "I beg your pardon, sir. I see it's Misters Button and Ague who have given us cause for ire. We shall no longer work with them."

Mr. Percy said, "I won't blame you for that." He turned to Mr. Ague and Mr. Button, "Perhaps we should have these two gentlemen take over from you?"

The two looked none too pleased about that suggestion.

I ignored their displeasure. "I have another proposition, assuming your suggestion was not entirely in jest."

"It was not. What's your proposition?"

"We have another brewery in line for passing some of our coin."

Mr. Percy studied me. "Which brewery is that?"

"Of course, I can't tell you without some assurance we can work together."

Without much further thought, he said that he would consider our proposition.

J ames and I walked into the Lion brewery, armed with sheaves of taxation records, barrel counts, purchase and sales records, among anything we were able to secure through Dr. Newton's connections at the Mint. Rose had also graciously reviewed the materials and explained the details to us. We had prepared as well as we could.

We presented ourselves to Mr. Ravenscroft, who was by himself this time. He quickly shuffled through the papers. While he did that, I said, "As you can see, we have a full accounting of your records. It points to the fact that you could use an increase in your profits to compensate for the increase in taxes."

"We can all use an increase in profits," he said. "But that doesn't mean it's a good thing to pass counterfeit coins. I prefer my neck without a noose around it."

"Understandable. We shall make our joint venture without risk to your neck, or any other bodily parts."

A wry smile arose on Mr. Ravenscroft's thin lips. "And how is that possible?"

James and I looked at each other and laughed.

"What's the humor?" said the accountant, his smile disappeared.

"Our apologies," James said, then he turned to me. "Tell him how we have eliminated the risk."

I spoke at length about the *metallurgy* and *weights* and *corrosion* and on and on about the science of why our coins were undetectable. Dr. Newton might have been pleased at the precision of my vocabulary, or maybe not, but it was certainly enough to convince the accountant.

"I see you have a good handle on the manufacture of your product. But it's still counterfeit. It only takes one slip up to trace it back to our accounts."

I nodded. "Duly so, that's the truth. The venture would not be without even a minuscule risk. But not only do we have the product, we also have a well-honed system to allow the flow of coins to be untraceable to your accounts."

This time it was James' turn to explain. "Without giving too much away, and the less you know, as they say, the better, we have a loyal and dedicated assistant who handles the flow of the coin on both ends of the transactions. That way, it will be in the shadows, even to you. Also, the flow will be without a traceable pattern. Such patterns allow the Mint to catch the less sophisticated coiners. You will notice the variance in profits, always trending upwards but again, not in a detectable manner."

Mr. Ravenscroft turned his back to us, gazed out a window for a while. He then said while still not facing us, "I see how the brewery could profit, and with little risk if your coin and strategy are good. But then how might I be able to be compensated for my personal risk?"

James and I had already planned for this need. I replied, "It goes without saying that you'll be justly rewarded. We typically offer a percentage of the profit we acquire, payable in legitimate funds, or in other tangible assets, however you would like them. And we would do this in the most discrete way."

Mr. Ravenscroft turned around, his thin-lipped smile firmly in place, as if he'd swallowed a whole sweet plum.

The matron of the coffeehouse escorted me back to the private room. I'd been good to my word, working hard on the concerto, especially now that our subterfuge was firmly in play.

Catherine was already there with a pot of coffee and mugs. The latest version of my, our, composition was open. On a side table, the Stradivari violin rested, waiting to be played, anxiously so, I felt as I sat near it.

"I was just about to play some of the new score," Catherine said. "But let's have coffee first."

We did just that, and she again thanked me for helping her uncle. I confided some of the scheme to her and cautioned that it was not by any means completed, or successful, yet.

"As long as Uncle Isaac is not in any further danger, it's been thus far successful."

"I believe I can say that's true. At least I can say that he's not in more danger due to the counterfeiters. But, if I might be privileged to ask, would he be in any political danger?"

Catherine took a long sip of coffee. I sensed I'd tread onto the wrong path.

Quietly, as if someone had an ear to the door, she asked, "Why? Have you heard something?"

"Nothing substantial," I said, trying to lighten my query. "Something about your employer's power is lessening. And if that were to be the case, then might your uncle's position be in danger, as well?"

"If you're referring to Mr. Montagu's group," she said after thinking for a moment, "then yes, perhaps it would be a true statement that his power is lessening, because the power of his collective itself is lessening. Although, I wouldn't assume that Mr. Montagu's personal influence is in the same situation. Nor would I assume that my uncle is in danger, no matter Mr. Montagu's status."

"I'm relieved to hear both," I said. "I appreciate you being forthcoming. I know so little of the ruling structures in your country."

"It's a complex, limited monarchy,[2] which does suit our current temperament. But it does allow an ebb and flow of those who might want to … shall we say, guide the course of events. And often it's like a ship in a storm, creaking from side to side."

"Thank you for the enlightening image."

"You shall see more of it at the concert, as many of them will be attending."

"I shall be on the lookout, and perhaps I will learn more."

---

[2] A constitutional monarchy, as well. *TS*

"If they aren't being too guarded. But we should really begin to practice. I have some suggestions, minor ones, in a few spots."

We played through the spots, the mood lightening as we did. Her suggestions were excellent, and they inspired me to make other changes that I noted on the score.

Catherine said, "I sense some change in the mood of the piece. A bit of a sadness creeping into the underlying tone."

I hadn't realized it. "Coming up with this version of the score, even though it was nearly finished, has been a struggle," I said.

"Are other things occupying your thoughts?"

"Likely so," I said.

"Tell me."

"The most pressing thing is that I must go back to Italy, within this month. Not long after the concert."

She frowned and let out a long breath. "I'll be sad when you are gone. And worried."

"I'll also be sad, as I was the last time. But I'll dutifully complete my task, with care to not give you any reason to be concerned."

"I'm happy to hear those words. I'll hold you to them. Do you have much to prepare before leaving?"

"A considerable amount. Not only for the mission, but also to continue the work I'm doing for your uncle. I must also have his details for the violin that Mr. Stradivari will craft for us. Regarding that, I do worry about taking up his time, especially with my way of aggravating him."

"That is much to do before you leave. As for my uncle, I would recommend you find common ground, which I've discovered to be a way to soften his critical nature. Perhaps that will help you find a way into his inner thoughts."

"Thank you," I said. "Is there a particular inner thought that I might find this common ground?"

She thought for a moment. "Something of everyday life that triggers the deepest connections between the world and the individual."

Then through a broad smile she said, "Ask him about the falling apple."[3]

---

[3] The story associated with Isaac Newton that the world is most familiar with, more than the facts of how he developed his theory of gravity, or any of his other contributions. However, Newton was known to tell the apple story. The story, myth, exaggeration, of Newton's *eureka!* moment is a noteworthy epistemic game. *TS*

chapter 18

T he next time James and I were being escorted into Mr. Percy's office, I noticed on his bookshelves a familiar volume that I hadn't seen during our previous visit—Isaac Newton's *Philosophiæ Naturalis Principia Mathematica.* I wanted with utmost desire to ask why a counterfeiter would have Dr. Newton's most difficult publication. Perhaps Mr. Percy and I might even have a discussion of force-and-motion laws, or how the planets revolve around the sun. I certainly didn't remember a connection to counterfeiting in the three volumes, not that I'd scrutinized every single line.

"Gentlemen," Mr. Percy greeted us. "Please tell me my faith in you hasn't been misplaced."

James said, "It hasn't. We've determined a method to rough the coins that won't ruin their otherwise perfection as counterfeits. Also, we established a working relationship with a brewery to handle a share of the coin."

Mr. Percy studied our faces as if judging our veracity. "Very enterprising. This brewery ... which one is it?"

James and I gave him our own pause before I answered him. "If we tell you, I assume that means you are in our fold completely. We would then like to assist you in managing your other connections."

"I believe we can agree to a beneficial relationship. However, I'd like to proceed with caution."

"As would we," James interrupted. "But we can't be strung along, either."

Mr. Percy's cheeks went a light shade of red. "I can assure you, when I take on a partner in full, it must be without concern on either side."

"We understand that, most certainly," I said. "However, we must be able to make a full go of this, or we will have to take on other opportunities."

Mr. Percy tapped his finger once, twice, thrice on the table. "I hesitate not because I lack confidence or trust, but that I've built a sound endeavor and have no wish to see it jeopardized."

"Certainly," I said. "That's why we want to be a partner in that very structure. We have no desires other than that."

That seemed to be what he wanted to hear.

"All right. Let's get down to business."

Having secured the details of our preliminary arrangement, James and I headed out to a late-evening drink at a pub through the warren of alleys that led away from Mr. Percy's place. In a block of deserted storage yards, a group of men, four or five, I couldn't tell, appeared from the shadows and without a word set upon us with fists and clubs.

Fending off their blows as best I could, James and I managed to disable two or three of them. With that, we were able to break away and outrun them.

When we were safe, breathing heavily and wiping away blood, James asked the question I also had on my mind, "Who was that mob?"

"I don't know. I couldn't see their faces to tell if we were previously acquainted."

"Then what did they want?"

"I don't know. They didn't seem to want money. They would have threatened us first for it."

James grimaced as he rubbed a hand across his ribs. "If they wanted to kill us, they would have been swift with lethal force or weapons. They wanted to inflict pain."

"And pain it is."

The bruises were fading to green when I was able to visit with Dr. Newton. It was an evening meeting in his home, and again I was having an ale while watching Huygens' clock. James and I had not found out who was in the gang, or who set them on us, if that were the case. If the mugging was planned, that raised the question of how they knew when and where to attack us. Whatever the reason, we were more cautious, as they did not finish their job, and perhaps were planning more.

Dr. Newton came into the room before I had finished my ale. He carried a book with him, his right index finger stuck in the pages about halfway into it.

"Yes?" he asked me.

I was perplexed, wondering if he were surprised to see me standing before him with an ale. I had, of course, arranged the meeting with the full listing of topics to be discussed. Dr. Newton spoke before I could loosen my tongue.

"Which is it to be?"

I was again confused, before I realized he wanted me to start. "The counterfeit case should be first."

"One moment then," he said then walked out of the room while opening the book to its marked place.

I hoped he wasn't going to finish the book before he got back with me.

The housekeeper came in after only a few minutes passed on the clock. She escorted me into the dining room where two plates had been set, one on each end of the table. There was also another full mug of ale near the plate where I was seated. She took my satchel containing the documents I'd prepared and set it on the hutch.

"The master will be in shortly," she said positively, but also with a shrug. "Please start your meal before it turns cold."

I was glad I did as I had nearly finished it before Dr. Newton re-appeared. He might well have finished the book. He sat down at his end of the table. "Tell me of your progress," he said, without a word about why he was detained.

"I prepared a report for you," I said and got up to fetch my documents from the satchel.

As I walked to the hutch, Dr. Newton said, "I hear from my niece Mr. Montagu will be hosting a concert, and it will include your music. I'd be curious if you have a pattern that you seek to achieve?"

"A pattern? As in how the work progresses, or if the work reaches the objective of what I first envisioned?" I picked up my satchel and brought it over to the table.

"Both," he said while gazing at the satchel for a moment, then toward the windows. "In my own work, my mind can be a horrible, untamed creature, twisting to attack anything that might be close."

His statement, spoken in a flat, unfamiliar tone, struck me more strongly than anything he had said before, and he had spoken many profundities. I found myself stuck in time, my own mind swirling and confused, as if Dr. Newton had removed a mask.

Finally, I managed a banal observation. "But your mind, as witnessed through what you say to me, is the opposite of that. Entirely rational and reasoned."

"Perhaps what comes out of my mouth, or what I put down on paper. I'm speaking of the internal storm of thoughts. I'm asking if you have some of the same when composing? Are you trying to make something significant out of the chaos?"

"I suppose I am," I said slowly, as I thought of a decent, and truthful, response. Perhaps this was our common ground. "There's much more going on than mere melody, or rhythm, or harmony. There's a swirling of emotion, an underlying swell of unknown power that seeks to control the work."

Dr. Newton's brow furrowed, raising doubt that I had furthered his thoughts on this matter. Indeed, he tapped a finger on the satchel.

"Your report?"

"Yes," I said as I took it out. "We've had continued success infiltrating the ring, gaining the confidence of Mr. Percy. He didn't give us the complete accounting of his counterfeiting trade, but enough for us to begin."

"Good," he said.

High praise, I thought.

With boosted conviction, I pointed out the code on the musical score. "As we agreed, the documents are in code, which already deduced the underlying method."

He studied the musical notes, telling me what he could decode, and what he couldn't. The former was much more than the latter.

"Yes," he said after we worked through it all. "You're correct, this is an excellent start. A good basis for the evidence we would need for prosecution."

"Thank you, sir. The only problem right now is that I must leave London for Italy, likely for several weeks. I've covered my absence with Mr. Percy, telling him we will be building up our reserves of coin, solidifying our confidences."

Without responding, Dr. Newton studied the report. I tried to anticipate what he would find to criticize.

Instead, he said, "Since you'll be traveling to Italy, then we need to arrive at the full list of parameters needed for your superior violin. Do we not?"

"Yes, if you have time."

He gathered up my report, got up from the table, and walked toward the door. I followed without hesitating, knowing well enough we would be going to his work room. Indeed, we ended there. He placed the report on a stack of papers on a desk. Then waved me over to the table where the two violins rested.

"What insights have you had since our last meeting?" he asked.

For this question, or one like it, I had prepared at least a modest thought or two. "It's really about moving air with precision, isn't it?

The force that the violin belly and back exert on the air to create the pressure waves. It must be critical that these two pieces of wood be formed correctly, that is, the best mix of strength and flexibility."

I paused there, wanting to hear one word of encouragement.

"But what of the asymmetry we discovered last time we met?" he asked.

At least there was no word of discouragement concerning my statements. In fact, he was giving me a clue about what to say. A worm of inadequacy burrowed into my mind. I looked at the violins on the table, hoping for a spark of inspiration. They appeared to be the same from side-to-side ... except for the strings, the lower G3 to the highest E5. There was the corresponding bass bar glued to the belly underneath the bass string, while the sound post was placed closer to the treble string.

"The range of strings, each tuned to a perfect fifth from the strings next to it, create differing notes, different sound pressures, I suppose, which create the combined tones of the musical sounds we hear."

Admittedly, I was rambling.

Dr. Newton picked up the cross-sectioned violin, then stared into the cavity for a moment. "You are proposing a determined reason for the asymmetry? It isn't just the imperfections of the craftsman?"

I had to choose an answer, and said, "Yes. It must be."

"And if so?"

And if so ... yes, what indeed if so.

Dr. Newton must have reached the limit of his patience, for he pounced on his own question. "If so, then the most superior crafts-man knows this is the case and can precisely calculate, *calculate*, with precision the exact asymmetrical parameters required."

After replacing the violin on the table, he stretched out a large piece of paper. With a pen, he quickly traced the outline of the intact violin body. Placing the violin to the side, he drew other lines offset by regular intervals from the traced line. The finished sketch reminded me of ripples of a stone thrown in the middle of a pond.

He repeated the process with two other outlines, each time the lines skewed more to one side of the outline. "What are the differences in the drawings?"

It was an easy question to answer, too easy on the surface of it. I said, "The interior lines have been shifted to the right."

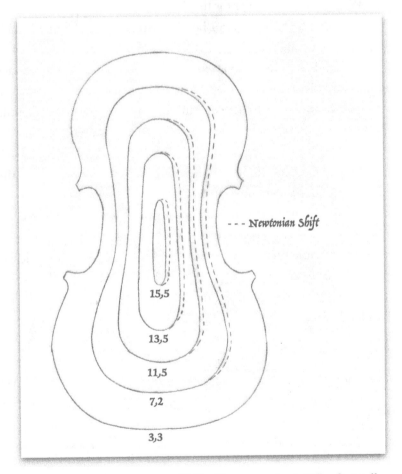

"What does that represent?" Dr. Newton asked. "No, first tell me what the interior lines represent."

"Predicated on what you showed me last time, they are lines of equal thickness. The shift then represents varying degrees in the shift of symmetry."

My description seemed right and logical to me.

"Which one would produce the superior sound?"

It was a much more difficult question to answer. "I suppose that the middle one would be."

"What's your reasoning for that?"

"It seems the others would be too extreme, one too much shift, the other not enough."

"A prejudice toward the average."[1] He sighed, then said, "That's not the way the universe works. There will always be an explanation, one that's beautiful and satisfying. In this case, we can determine the effects of the shift through the proper calculations or set of calculations."[2]

On a fresh sheet of paper, he began to sketch more lines, write down calculations, sometimes furiously.

I knew that my time with him was up, as he already dismissed me from his mind, if not his home. I was about to leave when I remembered what Catherine has advised me. "Excuse me, sir, before I leave, I wish to ask you about the story of the falling apple."

He raised his pen immediately and squinted at me. "Dear Lord. This has nothing to do with gravity."

James, Rose, and I were among the first few to arrive at Mr. Montagu's home bedecked all aglitter for the concert. Catherine greeted us with great effusiveness and introduced us to the few who were already there, except for the master of the house.

---

[1] Also known as bias toward the mean. *TS*

[2] Newton did believe the universe to be orderly, mechanistic. *TS*

"Mr. Montagu is with a few close friends in his private drawing room," she told us, a lilt of impatience in her voice. "I suspect he's warming them to the occasion with a glass of his best whisky."

I could have used a glass of whisky to ease my nerves. As if she knew my thoughts, she waved over one of the servants. "Please let him know what you would like to drink. I must attend to the other guests."

"I'll help you," Rose said and left with Catherine.

As James and I waited for our refreshments, I asked, "Who are the close friends being entertained by our host?"

"I couldn't say, but one would assume his close friends from the Kit-Cat Club among others of his inner circle."

In my head, Mr. Lupine's voice exhorted me to hide behind the curtains and hear what was being discussed. Too late to hide, but maybe not too late to put an ear to the door.

"Excuse me for a moment," I said to James.

"Need to compose yourself?" he said.

We laughed and I left him to his own amusement.

Wandering the house in search of the men, I heard voices coming from the library. I didn't need to put my ear to the door as it was open and the men were fairly bellowing, often several at once. Trying to discern the nature of their vigorous discussion, more of an argument, was a trial. When I could make out some of the words, there were names and events I was unfamiliar with, and perhaps, they were speaking within their own secret terminology or pseudonyms for the persons referenced.

I listened only for a few moments before leaving and rejoining James. He and I drank until the group of men filtered into the parlor. It was then that Catherine found us and steered James and me toward Mr. Montagu.

"Captains, welcome to my home," Mr. Montagu said when he observed our presence. His eyelids drooped enough for us to know he had shared more than a warm-up dram of whisky.

Catherine said, "We're very excited to hear Captain Wolf's composition."

"Yes, very excited," said Mr. Montagu, his tone dry and sarcastic. "Perhaps later you can finally tell me how a military officer has time to compose music. For now, I should greet the other guests."

He gave me a formal nod, which I returned. Over his shoulder, Catherine gave me a "forgive him" smile.

James and I continued to wander around the room, which had livened up now with the addition of members of the Kit-Cat Club, who loudly held court in niches of the room. In the near center of the parlor, there was a cluster of animated men and women. When we got close, we could see a man who was the center of attention. His head was large, full of cheek and jowls, and a neck that quivered as he spoke with enthusiasm.

James said, "It's Jonathan Swift. Famous for his barbed poetry and essays."

When we were close enough, I could hear Mr. Swift denouncing a government official: "His decrees and laws and regulations carry the weight of goose down, all stuffed into a pillow that is so light it can float away to the moons of Mars.[3] One never has to take them seriously, for he'll make a contradictory rule the next day. Before the first mug of ale."

We'd listened for a while, when I noticed Dr. Newton arrived and was speaking with his niece and Mr. Montagu. They appeared to be discussing something in seriousness. A few moments later, Mr. Montagu moved away, leaving the two alone. I tapped James on the arm and said, "I'm going to join Catherine and her uncle."

James nodded. "Please do."

---

[3] Jonathan Swift, imaginatively or presciently, correctly predicted Mars would have moons. Swift also later expressed some distain for his host's political and intellectual accomplishments, saying that Montagu provided only "good words and good dinners." *TS*

As I neared them, I tried to catch Catherine's eye. Dr. Newton had his arms crossed; his gaze averted as Catherine spoke in rapid but hushed tones. When she noticed me, she spoke even more rapidly as she reached out toward my arm. When I was close, she held my forearm and pulled me closer.

Dr. Newton finally looked up and gave me a nod. "Ah, Captain Wolf. We were just talking about you. I have something you might be interested in."

Catherine said, "Yes, uncle, you do, but I would like you to remember this is a social event, as well as a musical one, so we wouldn't want to take Phillipe, Captain Wolf, away from that."

"Don't worry, dear niece. I won't ruin your party."

"You know that's not what I mean, Uncle Isaac."

He said, "Equally, you know that's not what I meant."

She gave me a look of exasperation and with James at her side left us alone.

Dr. Newton unfolded a piece of paper. There was one of his drawings, clearly something to do with the violin design as I could make out the outline. We went over to a table, on which he spread out the paper. He began to explain the many lines, some straight, some curved. I admit I had trouble keeping up with his rapid words and flourishes, but the gist of the matter was that he discovered several recurring patterns he believed would be required in a superior violin.

He spoke so quickly and with my attention distracted to the coming concert, I was unable to take in much of what he said.

Then we were interrupted by Catherine who directed us toward the dining hall. Dr. Newton continued lecturing me as we walked and until we were ushered to our seats. But I couldn't believe my good fortune when I was seated next to Catherine. The dinner went well, with discussions ranging from the War of Spanish Succession, to Mr. Montagu's recounting his instituting the concept of a national debt covered by ale and spirit taxation. James and I gave each other a glance, both of us wondering if Mr. Montagu was aware of the sub-terfuge we were executing for Dr. Newton.

Later, I caught Mr. Swift's diatribe against women in the arts—they were too dainty was his claim in essence. Catherine gently chid-ed him with the story of Aphra Behn[4] who was not only a poet, playwright, and fiction writer, but was also a spy for the court. She was considered an equal by many poets, writers, and other libertines of the era.

Mr. Swift gave Catherine a bow and proclaimed he was shown to be wrong … "in this instance."

I did my best to participate, especially in the discussion of the war. At one point in this discussion, Mr. Montagu turned my way as he spoke on his lack of trust in the abilities of Leopold's military. I avoided his gaze, pretending I didn't hear his directed slight.

After the lengthy dinner, we gathered back in the parlor where our concert had been set up. I was sitting off to the side and had a view of both the musicians, led by Catherine and Rose, and the au-dience. My excitement built through the introductory pieces selected by Catherine and Rose. My heart was pounding as Catherine ex-changed a violin for the Stradivarius, then began to play the Concer-to in C Major. She was playing beautifully, when I looked out of the corner of my eye toward the audience to see their reaction. Cather-ine noticed and gave me a quick smile, but I could see a few of the guests' heads lolling to the side, heavy with slumber.

Mr. Montagu and Mr. Swift were in conversation, the topic most likely not about the music. Near them, clearly oblivious to the con-cert, Dr. Newton was scribbling on a sheet of paper.

---

[4] Aphra Behn, 1649-1689, was an author and playwright, and indeed, served as a spy in Antwerp for the English king, Charles II. *PW*

*L*ater, when most of the guests had left, I lingered to say my thanks to Catherine. I searched for her, hoping I would be able to say a proper goodnight, perhaps with a stolen kiss. In the shadows of a corridor, I finally found her. But she was already kissing someone.

Mr. Charles Montagu.

Opus 4

L'Anima

chapter 19

Before James and I left London for Italy, Dr. Newton had delivered to me a bound sheaf of papers. The informal book provided a well-organized accounting of his investigation into the MB Stradivarius but also in the broad sense of instrument design derived from his experiments and knowledge of forces and other natural phenomena. I pored over the document, at first only understanding a few of the details even though we had discussed much of it.

However, the more I studied it, the more Dr. Newton's propositions became clear, although this was largely because of the diagrams. The mathematical equations sent my head spinning, and I only grasped the most basic of those. Most difficult was his description and explication of the asymmetrical pressures inside the body of the violin—his "shift," which he showed me in his workroom. I was encouraged that my efforts in regard to the composition and violin design were not in vain, at least I hoped Dr. Newton's continued interest was evidence pointing that way. Yet I was concerned how well I would be able explain Dr. Newton's work to Mr. Stradivari.

James and I stopped again in Austria, where we attended many strategy sessions with military leaders. Most sessions involved listening to the field commanders argue for their preferred strategy or against a rival's strategy. Our final meeting was with the general Viscount Pichler who remained skeptical of our spying mission, particularly of our cover story of buying instruments in Cremona. We repeated the story of our previous success in Cremona, although again we did not bring up killing the soldier.

In the end, as there was no other viable opposition our mission was approved.

Investigation of the "MB" Stradivarius Violin

From the Physicks of Stringed Instruments AND the Nature of Sound

ISAAC NEWTON

1. Fundamental description of sound
2. Physical elements of the violin in question
3. Forces in effect during playing with a bow
4. Variations of dimensions and other measurements
5. Materials and construction differences
6. List of confounding variables and other extraneous factors

After the final and lengthy session, I invited James to a concert. He tried to beg off, but I convinced him it would be excellent and the event was in the exquisite Hoff.[1]

"Consider this," I said nonchalantly, "there will be many of the most attractive music lovers in attendance."

So we went.

---

[1] *Newe Saal oder Danz Plaz zu Hoff* is the full name of the venue. *PW*

The first composition was a lively Corelli,[2] a violin sonata, made more dynamic by the sound in the large Hoff. I estimated the reverberation of a quick sixteenth note, upon which I recalled my first meeting with Dr. Newton and my poor response to his question about the speed of sound.

Also coming to mind during the concert, unfortunately, was the disaster that was my own concert at Mr. Montagu's home. The misery of watching the audience, nearly all of them, not paying the least attention, was still raw. I resolved, though, to complete my concerto, played with a perfect violin, and make even the most uninterested Londoner sit up and listen.

Suddenly, viscerally, I wanted to know what Catherine was doing at that moment, perhaps enjoying a concert with Rose. Or hosting a dinner party, later to be thanked for her successful event with a kiss from her employer. I forced that scene from mind.

After the concert, James and I went for dinner at a nearby café where many of the attractive music lovers also enjoyed a post-concert meal. As we ate, James said, "You seemed to be tense during the concert. Was there something displeasing about the music?"

I took a drink of the wine, put my glass on the table, and crossed my arms.

Before I could think of what to say, James spoke up, "Truly, you've been tense, no, miserable, since that damn dinner at Montagu's. And I'm sure it was due to the poor manners of all during the concert. But it was a dinner party, where the food was plentiful and the spirits more so. That's why the guests were there. That, and to be seen at the socially-important event. They weren't there for the music. If some were sleeping, if some were gossiping, well, they wouldn't know good music from bad. You should rid yourself of your morose persona before it affects our mission."

---

2 Arcangelo Corelli, 1653-1713, was an Italian composer, known for developing the sonata and concerto. *PW*

"I apologize," I said, knowing he was right. But I hadn't been able to tell him about the knife to my heart I witnessed in the shadowy corridor. "I'll be done with it now."

James relaxed into his chair and gazed around the café. "Let's introduce ourselves to some of your Austrian music lovers."

The guardhouse at the Po River gate was crowded with several soldiers. One of them studied our papers and entry permits from our previous visit.

"I assume that's a violin," he said, pointing to the case I held.

I opened the case to reveal the MB Stradivarius. He appeared to be about to let us in without a question, when he took a second look at the entry permits, then summoned the officer-in-charge.

Most fortunately for me and James—Jacques, I should say—this officer-in-charge wasn't Lt. Laurent.

The officer appeared unimpressed by our presence, asking us no questions, barely glancing at us. He took our papers, however, and went back to his desk. I could just see him as he searched through a large ledger. I looked away when he glanced up at us.

The officer came back and handed our papers to the guard with a grunt. The guard stamped our papers, wrote the date underneath the stamp, and handed our papers back to us. He gestured with his head for us to pass. Not a kindly reception, but I was pleased to get through the gate, even as I wondered what was in the ledger.

Riding through the streets of Cremona, we immediately observed more troops on the streets from our previous visits. More patrols marching, more off-duty soldiers gathered in the squares or loitering on the streets. They paid us no mind.

We arrived at our pensione, the innkeeper acknowledging our arrival without much more than a nod of recognition and expectation. The older man was still working, and again insisted on dragging our bags to our room.

As we had arrived in the early afternoon this trip, James and I ventured out. We stayed away from the outposts at the city gates, observing them from a distance as best we could. We kept a good pace so to not be seen with suspicion.

When we were famished, we stopped at one the taverns that we remembered was good. It wasn't busy so we got a table in a quiet corner, where we could talk in a whisper when not being served. James mentioned the increase in troops in the city.

"I'd expected some more, but not this many," I said. "They must be reinforcing Cremona as a defensive position."

"Or massing for an offensive push?" James said.

I agreed that was a good possibility. "We'll have to find out their mission."

After our meal, we went to the parish of Father Cozzoli. Inside a few parishioners were in the pews, quietly praying. We sat in the last row. In a few minutes, the rector entered the sanctuary and gave a short sermon in Latin, after which he led us in a prayer and a hymn.

James and I lingered while the others filed out of the church. When all were gone, we got up and walked to the priest who was still in supplication. He ended his silent prayer.

"You've returned," he said.

I said, "We wanted to thank you again for helping us."

The priest gave us a subtle nod to the side door. "Let's move where we can speak more freely."

We followed him into the back of the church, into the priest's office where he hung up his robe. There was a small table and chairs, and a short case of books. When we were seated around the table, he said, "Have you returned to accomplish more of your mission, whatever that may be?"

James looked at me. I said, "We should say little."

The priest thought for a moment, then he coughed. "Excuse me, I'm not well. You must have come back to our church for a reason, other than unnecessarily thanking me."

"Father Cozzoli, if you are so inclined," I said, "you might tell us if any events of interest have transpired since our last visit."

"I'm so inclined. The French have moved in more troops, putting a strain on the city and its inhabitants. There are more restrictions on movement, fewer materials and food to go around. They initiated a curfew for all inhabitants of Cremona unless given special permission to be out."

I asked him if our misadventure caused any problems for him.

"Not for me, no," he said. "But I'm not usually out late at night."

His news and humor were a relief from my worries.

James and I thanked him, then took our leave.

I awoke early. While I took my breakfast in the pensione, I reviewed the documents from Dr. Newton. There was so much to understand that I felt I was slipping under water, grasping at one principle or equation only to have my understanding float away. In the end, I decided to pare it down into three main points that I would be able to discuss coherently with Mr. Stradivari.

The first was the ultimate source of sound being the changes in air pressure inside the violin body. The exact physical properties, that is, the mathematical description of the changes in pressure, provided by Dr. Newton would have to remain a technicality I could learn later. I hoped Mr. Stradivari would understand it from his point of view as a luthier. All other aspects of the violin construction arise from the pressure of air. At least that's how I understood the application of forces via Dr. Newton.

The second main point was that the vibration of the strings, caused by the bow being drawn across the strings, generates the energy transferred through the bridge onto the belly of the violin. In turn, the changes, whether sustained or short, bass or tenor, depended on how those vibrations were critically transmitted through the bridge.

The third point was a set of questions arising from the first two points. How much does the quality of the wood effect the sound quality? How critical is the shape of the violin? What effect does the varnish have on the wood? And what characteristics did it impose on the wood, especially in relation to pressure and resonance?

Satisfied, at least in my mind, that I would have a somewhat intelligent conversation with Mr. Stradivari, I finished the meal and gathered my notes, my composition, and the MB Stradivarius from our room. I told James, who was just waking, I would be back later in the day but to not wait for me. He waved me away without a word.

I hurried through Cremona, only glancing at the soldiers or locals I encountered. When I came to the plaza fronting the homes of the violin makers, I slowed and took a few deep breaths. Dampening my rising enthusiasm so I would seem calm, I knocked on the door to the Stradivari home and workshop.

Caterina opened the door. She smiled greatly and exclaimed, "Ah! It's Mr. Rémon!"

"Caterina," I said. "A pleasure to see you again."

"Come in," she said, then guided me into the sitting room. "I trust you have been well. I'll let my father and mother know you are here."

I barely had time to start arranging my papers when Mr. Stradivari came into the room, Omobono following closely behind.

"Welcome back, Mr. Rémon!" said Mr. Stradivari. "We have been talking about you just recently, wondering how you were getting along with your musicians and your composition in particular."

"I apologize for being so long in returning."

Mr. Stradivari shook his head. "I'm sure it's difficult to get so many musicians to agree on anything. And with the war making things difficult especially securing funds and traveling with all the restrictions."

"That's all very true. Still, I'd hoped to be back sooner, since I have been in possession of your fine violin for so many months. As you can see, I have returned it exactly as you lent it to me."

I removed the violin from its case and made a formal transfer. Mr. Stradivari accepted his violin but did not inspect it. He gave it to Omobono, who did examine it. Satisfied, Omobono placed the violin in the case, closed it, and whisked it away.

Mr. Stradivari gestured toward two chairs in the corner of the room. "Please, let's talk for a while. I'm very interested to hear about you and your travels. I get out of my workshop so little, it's good for me to hear something of the world."

I wondered what I could say without giving away my identity. "In the world of music we hope to be uninvolved in the daily despair of the world, in the conflicts and the politics, if I might say that in confidence."

"I believe the same. I only want to create the most beautiful instruments. Something that can help transport us into another realm of existence, one pure and untouched by the tragedy of human power struggles, the selfish desires of the basest who would sow pain and suffering for their own benefit."

"You sound much as one of my, our, most generous patrons," I said, thinking of Catherine. "You're right to be focused that way. If only all others would feel the same."

Mrs. Stradivari came into the room, enthusiastically greeting me as well. She was no longer with child, so I congratulated them on the birth.

"Thank you. So kind of you," said Mrs. Stradivari. "A girl, Francesca Marie."

"Wonderful," I said.

"We'll be right back with some refreshments," said Mrs. Stradivari. "Now don't let my husband talk your ear off. He can be very long-winded."

"Antonia! Mr. Rémon and I are having a very productive conversation."

Mrs. Stradivari smiled affectionately, as if placating an elderly uncle.

When she had disappeared back into the house, I said to Mr. Stradivari, "Your wife and children bring light into a room."

"Usually," he said, laughing. "They can be very demanding. But yes, they do provide a light in my life, as does music universally, as we were discussing. How about your family, sir?"

"I'm fairly alone in the world," I said, not wanting to complicate my deception. "My career has taken me away from a stable life. But I do have a wonderful person in my life."

"Good. That's important. Freeing in so many ways. It's the same for me. Having a family with many children and a life with many responsibilities, provides a satisfying sense of purpose as much as it carries weight. Plus, it's good that they can help with the business. At least those who are interested."

"I'm pleased for you," I said. "Your satisfactory family life can only lead you to continued and further success."

Mrs. Stradivari and Caterina returned with refreshments. Mr. Stradivari said, "It also helps to have food and drink. Although, it's been more difficult to get them, not to mention supplies for our business."

His statement reinforced what the priest told me. With some guilt, I took a sip of wine before I said, "Worse than our previous visit?"

"As of late it's been stifling. So many soldiers and checkpoints and bureaucratic obstacles." He glanced at me and added, "But I stay away from the military as much as possible."

"That's well considered," I said. "Should we forget the occupation for now and discuss musical instruments?"

"Yes, of course. We're still working on the set you ordered. I admit, our progress has been slower than usual due to the occupation, but we are taking extra care for you."

"That's good, yes, thank you."

"And the violin, the special one, for your composition? Have you finished it?"

I gestured to my stack of papers in which was a copy of the latest but still unfinished composition. "No, not completed in full, but coming to the end," I said, despite my lack of confidence.

"I enjoyed what I did hear of the composition. I'd like to see your progress."

"Thank you," I said. I found the score and handed it to him.

After only a few moments, he said, "Even with my limited ability to read music, I would say you've made many changes. I can see where the music moves from a slow and peaceful section to this dramatic and lively section. I'll enjoy hearing this on a Stradivarius."

Pleased, I said, "I would as well. Besides my composition, I have some documents on the specific qualities of the violin. They're similar to those I showed you before, prepared by my learned friend. I was able to meet with him a few times to discuss the matter of the violin. While he does not have experience in the creation of a violin, he has one of the most superior minds in the known world. He knows of the movements of planets, forces—"

"As much as our countryman Galileo?"

I'd heard of the Italian astronomer. "That I can't say. But I'm sure my friend owes Galileo an intellectual debt."[3]

"Much as I owe the luthiers who came before me," Mr. Stradivari said.

---

[3] Newton did famously say that he was able to accomplish what he did by "standing on the shoulders of giants." What he meant, however, has been debated. *TS*

I found this an interesting statement. "Who are those makers who provided you with their knowledge?"

"The Amati and Ruggeri families were generous with their time. I'd worked with wood before, but not in instruments."

"Your family was not instrument makers?"

"No, my father and his father were engaged in senatorial pursuits.[4] It was Nicolò Amati who helped me understand the subtle points of craftsmanship."[5]

"As my friend has been so kind helping me understand what makes a truly great violin—"

Mr. Stradivari interrupted me again. "With respect to your friend, I can't understand how anyone who doesn't craft violins nor apparently have background in music would be able to provide you with help in creating a superior violin."

I took due note of Mr. Stradivari's rising annoyance, but I pressed ahead. "I realize that it does sound rather pretentious, but I know of no other man capable of such knowledge, other than yourself. Please, let me show you some of the essential characteristics he has produced for me."

I spread out the drawings before him.

"Here's one." I selected the one with the bridge on the top of the violin showing the sound post and bass bar and noting the resulting changes in tone with changes in position. The figure culminated with a mathematical notation.

Mr. Stradivari studied the drawing and notes for a long time, turning them this way and that. "Your colleague has shown how varying the placement of the sound post varies the tone of the in-

---

4 Perhaps referring to the legal profession or political appointments. *PW*

5 It's not clear what he means by this statement about Amati. As previously noted, there's no documented evidence, such as a census record, that he was an apprentice in the Amati workshop. *TS*

strument, if I understand what he's doing here." He looked up at me. "This is well known to any luthier."

"Yes, of course," I said. "I believe he's creating a formula which predicts placement of the post to create a certain tone. That's what his mathematics does so precisely." I pointed to the equations.

Mr. Stradivari glanced at them before shaking his head. "But I don't understand his mathematics. Nor do I understand the need for them. However, I'll listen, so, please explain them to me."

"I wish I could fully explain, but my powers of understanding are not developed sufficiently. I do have other similar drawings and formulas to offer."

I showed him the others—the string vibrations, the pressure waves inside the cavity, positioning of the f sound holes, and a table of dimensions that Dr. Newton created from meticulous measurements.

Mr. Stradivari began shaking his head as he jumped to his feet to get into a better position to point to the drawing of the pressure waves in the body of the violin. "This one I particularly don't understand, here, these lines showing … pressure? This idea doesn't seem important to the creation of a good violin, since they should be the same for every violin. It's more important how the air moves in an individual violin. Come, let me show you. Bring your papers with you."

In the workshop, Omobono and Francesco were at their work benches. Mr. Stradivari asked Omobono to bring a violin hanging from a rack, then we went to a worktable, where there were two violins, completed except for the bridge and varnish. Mr. Stradivari took the finished violin from Omobono and placed it next to them.

He asked me for the drawing of the pressures inside the violin. When I had placed it on the table, he pointed out Dr. Newton's comparison of dimensions of the two ordinary violins compared to the MB Stradivarius.

"I agree with the differences noted. But you should know that the dimensions are not set by one luthier or another, especially not a body sending out edicts as those from the Church. These dimensions vary considerably according to the needs of the musician, or the music currently in fashion. Each maker also has certain prejudices toward one shape or another. Any statement as to superiority is not valid."

Feeling he was about to divulge something of his craft he held close to his heart, I said nothing, hoping my silence would urge him to continue.

He did. "I have been humbly making violins and other instruments for forty years,[6] and I have never made the same instrument twice."

He then started a long discourse into the minute differences between the violins, for instance, Violin #1 was one-sixteenth of an *oncia*[7] greater in length than Violin #2, twice that of Violin #3. The extra length added a tiny amount of power in the lower notes, or vice versa, the shortened length added a ray of brightness. There were several such minute differentiations, I committed them to memory as accurately as I could considering he never paused, as if one thought led to another, and then the next.

He left me dizzy, as much as Dr. Newton would leave me after one of our sessions.

---

[6] Forty years would put his age of beginning to work in the craft at sixteen, likely then an apprentice. As previously noted, his earliest known label claiming a completed violin was in 1666, at age 22. *PW*

[7] Oncia is the Italian pre-metric system "inch," equivalent to about 43 millimeters, or about 1 and 2/3 inches. One-sixteenth oncia is about 2.7 millimeters, or about the thickness of a US nickel coin. NB: there are other interpretations of this measurement system. *TS*

chapter 20

L ater that evening, James and I went to a taverna recommended by our host at the pensione. There would be French officers there, he warned. While risky for us, their presence would be perfect for our mission.

We secured a table in a quiet dark corner, where we enjoyed a local stew of beans and vegetables in a rich sauce, and freshly baked bread. The inns serving French officers were getting good supplies of food.

"You had a successful day with the violin maker?" James asked quietly.

"Not as well as I'd hoped. He didn't receive my explanation of Dr. Newton's design principles with great regard. I wouldn't say he took it as an insult to his craftsmanship, but he wasn't swayed by my first attempt. I fear I presented Dr. Newton's work to him too soon and with too much vigor."

I told James about our extended discussion about the sound post.

"He has his own genius," James said. "As with Dr. Newton, he seems to enjoy the challenge of your quest. What's the next step?"

"We'll continue to discuss the details of the special violin to match my composition. I'll also see how the set of the other instruments is progressing."

James nodded. "I hope it goes well ... and quickly. We never know how much time we have here."

We ate for a while in silence, picking up bits and piece of conversations from the officers, mainly complaints about slow delivery of supplies, unreasonable changes in training schedules. Other than that, there was talk of family and lovers at home in France, successes and failures in finding female companionship in Cremona, and their poor diet, despite the delicious food in the taverna.

Nothing of great strategic importance.

When the level of conversation dimmed and the inn grew less crowded, James and I finished our meal and left. We walked the other direction we had the previous evening. The weather was warm and the fog from our previous visit had not returned. There were many soldiers out in the city.

We rounded a corner and ahead, in a narrow alleyway, several of them spilled outside of a rowdy drinking house, milling around, some talking, some nodding or shaking their heads, some barely standing in their inebriation.

It was a simple task to blend in with the soldiers—we could carry ourselves as soldiers who were off-duty. The conversations were varied but the most vociferous men were arguing, from what I could gather, about a trio of soldiers who deserted but had been captured in the first village from Cremona where they stopped. They ate and drank then fell asleep. A patrol looking for deserters stopped at the same café. The patrol soldiers ate their meal before waking up the deserters with pitchers of cold water. They dragged them behind their horses to the prison.

"Imbeciles," was the general assessment.

I asked the soldiers what happened to the deserters. One told me, "Stripped of rank, sentenced to fifteen days bread and water, then to three months of cleaning up after the officers' horses."

"Severe punishment," I said. "It sounds like a sentence Lieutenant Laurent would hand down."

None responded at first. Perhaps they didn't know him. Then one said quietly, "If Lieutenant Laurent had been involved, they wouldn't have gotten off so lightly."

Emboldened, I said, "I seem to recall one of his men deserted. There was a crackdown, wasn't there?"

The soldier who spoke up said, "And some heads were cracked. Luckily for that deserter, he escaped. Never seen again."

Another soldier said, "Probably in some godforsaken village with a wife and a child on the way."

I said, "And now wishing he had stayed in service."

That brought out laughter.

James and I moved on before any suspicions arose about us.

We wandered without a plan, until we noticed two officers finishing buttoning up their uniforms as they hurriedly crossed our path. We followed them, realizing when two officers were in haste, something important was happening.

As we followed, keeping a safe distance, a sense of dread began to fester, first in my chest, then in my gut. Whether it was the way the officers hurried, or if there was a realization that James and I were headed into danger, I didn't know. Maybe it was none of that, maybe it was a premonition that our mission wasn't going to end well.

We followed them and eventually we came to the municipal building—the Hotel de Ville—where the two officers, joined by others coming from all directions, ran up the stairs. The entrance was guarded by two soldiers, so we stopped in the darkness between two buildings. The upper façade of the building was lined with stone statues, as if also in guard.

"We need to go inside, don't we?" James said after staring at the building for a few moments.

"We should try. There must be a back door, maybe one into a storeroom, or workers' entrance."

"Yes, there must be," James said.

With another twinge of dark rot inside me, we edged along the alleyway. We saw no one else coming toward the municipal building, so we slithered along the edge of the piazza, then around to the back of the building.

Straightaway, we found a door, but it was bolted shut. James pushed on the door just above the handle. The latch inside rattled a little, enough for James to shrug and put shoulder to door. It rattled louder. We both put shoulders to the door, but it did not give. We looked at each other, shrugged, and tried again. Another two times and the latch gave and the door flew open. We fell into a dank passageway.

After we closed the door and reset the latch as well as we could, we hurried into the darkness toward a dim light at the end of the corridor, passing storerooms and other nooks filled with supplies. At the end, we paused at the entrance to a large hall. We listened to the voices and footsteps coming from the room in the building. The loudest commotion was coming from our right. Looking that way, we didn't see anyone, so we bounded down the hallway. Coming to a staircase, we slid underneath it.

The voices were coming from upstairs. As we were about to start up, two arriving officers headed toward us. We ducked back under the staircase. Huffing deeply, the officers must have been running for a long distance. Between breaths, they complained about the lateness of the meeting.

When they were at the top of the stairs, we hurried behind them before some other late arrivers came in. We bounded up the stairs and got to the top in time to see the two officers turn into a room near the end of another hallway.

We ran after them. When we reached the room, we stopped, and I peered around the doorway. There was a general din coming from inside, but I couldn't see in far enough.

Then we heard steps coming toward us. As we hurried back in the direction we started from, I heard the door to the room being closed. We stopped in the shadows of a stairway.

"Now what?" James said.

"Wait here."

I moved back to the door, listened at it, but couldn't make out any of the words being spoken. I looked up and down the hallway. Motioning to James to follow me, I walked to the room just past the meeting room, and, taking a chance, went inside.

Luckily, there was no one to challenge us.

James closed the door behind us. Three desks were against one wall. On the opposite side, three framed paintings were hung. This wall was adjacent to the meeting room. James and I each put an ear to the wall. The voices were still muffled.

I jostled one of the paintings—it was loosely hung. I took it off the wall and set it aside. With my dagger, I began to dig into the plaster. James followed suit. After only a few minutes, I'd bored far enough to create a pinhole through to the other side. I put my ear to the hole on our side of the wall. The voices were as clear as if we were in the room.

It took a few moments to grasp the gist of the discourse, which was that there was going to be an offense thrust in the north of Italy. A portion of the troops in Cremona—roughly a third, I believe was the proportion I heard—would join the forces in the north. The remaining troops would be split, half to be ready as reinforcements and the other half to stay and maintain the defenses in Cremona.

The officers disagreed with the ratio, and argued about which divisions would be going to the frontlines and which would be staying. But the conflict was short-lived as a superior officer announced his decision on the ratios and divisions.

The rest of the meeting was spent assigning the logistical tasks to officers. I did hear one familiar name—Lt. Laurent. He would be planning the requisitioning of additional supplies for the troops leaving and assuring adequate supplies en route.

The meeting started to break up with an explosion of voices and movements of the officers. James and I rehung the art and kicked the plaster dust around the floor to hide it. When we heard doors open down the corridor, we ran to the back of the room and tried to hide behind columns.

But they would not be enough to keep us from being seen.

I pushed open the window behind us. James and crawled out onto a ledge. There was enough room for us to shuffle over to the row of statues that adorned the façade. We tried to make acquaintance with our new friends, but they remained silent.

Whe waited until well into the night before we safely escaped the ledge, crept through the municipal hall, and retreated out the back door to return to the pensione. I couldn't sleep and got out of bed when dawn was giving way to the sunrise. It was too early to visit Mr. Stradivari, so I walked around the periphery of the city in the fog that had returned. Tired soldiers were marching to their early posts.

By mid-morning, the sun had burned away the fog. I arrived at the piazza fronting the row of luthier workshops and the home of Il Diavolo. I took a chance that he would be in, and I walked up the stairs in the building that was still dank and musty. At his door, I stopped and listened.

The music I heard muffled through the door—a furiously paced violin solo—sounded rough to me, demonic, but not with the expected skill of Il Diavolo. I waited until there was a pause before I knocked on the door.

The muted strains of a violin began again. I was about to knock again, but the door opened. Il Diavolo, squinted at me. His hair was wilder than I last saw him. I wondered if he was indeed a devil, through sorcery commanding a violin to play by itself.

In a flash of recognition, he called out, "Rémon!"

He clapped me on the shoulder and drew me into his room where a young man, no doubt a student, was awkwardly but enthusiastically playing a violin. Il Diavolo glanced at me and shrugged, then waved at him. The student stopped and gave his teacher a questioning expression, likely waiting to know what he did wrong now.

"That's enough for now," said Il Diavolo. "Yes, please, enough."

The student's shoulders drooped. He gathered up his sheet music and trudged to the other side of the room where he put away his violin. Before leaving, he bowed deeply and mumbled his appreciation.

After the door closed, my host said, "Welcome back to Cremona. Have you returned in search of the perfect violin?"

"If that's how you know my quest, then yes."

"I'm sure Stradivari will be pleased to see you again, or have you already seen the master?"

"We have met once and have conversed about the violin. I confess, it didn't go as well as I hoped." I briefly explained the documents I brought from Dr. Newton.

"Even without seeing the documents," he said, "I can guess Stradivari's poor reaction to the arguments, no matter how logically they were derived. I don't know him well, and have spoken only a few words to him, but I don't see him as a man deeply interested in natural philosophy or mathematics, at least not in regard to crafting an instrument."

"But, sir, that doesn't mean the scientist's thoughts should be ignored." There was desperation in my voice.

"Maybe so, maybe not, but if he told me how to play the violin based on his experiments and rationality, would I change the way I play?"

"I suppose not. But even if the points were valid?"

"My questions would be then, will your learned man's methods create a violin the same as one of Stradivari's? Or would Stradivari's methods, his way of crafting, arrive at the perfect violin before the learned man?"

His questions were an insight that gave me pause. "Interesting questions. I don't know, of course. What do you believe?"

He shrugged. "The questions weren't posed because I have an answer. Far from it, I haven't an inkling. I can vouch that he never merely makes copies of his violins, nor fully copies any other luthier's instruments."

"What drives his changes?" I asked. "He must have an intentional plan. He must not be satisfied with his work, at least to some degree?"

Il Diavolo gave this a moment of thought. "Perhaps that's right. More likely he's reached a level of confidence in his work, allowing him to expand his abilities and try subtle variations based on specific needs of a musician, or to see what change in tone, in power, can be achieved."

His words struck me as true.

At this point, I didn't know what else to ask the violinist about Stradivari's methods. I knew I must ask the luthier himself. I also had a sudden insight into what Dr. Newton had been telling me, indirectly so, about his way of coming to the truth, that is, the perfect violin, through quantifying all variables, reasoning about them, and developing mathematical formulas. Mr. Stradivari's approach was the antithesis of Dr. Newton's. The luthier created instruments, whole cloth, discerned their properties, found what he liked or didn't like, and changed the next violin to eliminate the less favorable qualities or enhanced the ones he did favor.

Interrupting my thoughts, Il Diavolo asked, "How are you progressing on your composition?"

I wished I had a better report for him. "I was making good progress, finishing enough to have it played at an informal concert. Unfortunately, it must have been premature, for it wasn't enthusiastically received."

Although, I thought but didn't say aloud, it hadn't been received at all, for no one had been listening.

"Rémon, it's a mistake to play a work to an audience before it's ready. If I could see your progress, I might be able to understand what happened at the concert."

I removed the most recent score from my bag. "I've added revisions to it," I said.

The violinist quickly looked through it. "I see what you are trying to do with the piece."

He picked up his violin and played a few bars in the middle of the piece.

"I like that," he said. "It has a certain ... relentless quality to it."

He played another section. "This, however, is lacking in fierce emotion, as if you're ... sighing. Now, there may be the right time for a sigh, a plaintive moan, but this isn't it."

I wasn't completely understanding the comment, but to have any critical ear and voice offer an opinion, did raise my spirits.

"One other immediate suggestion—you should change the viola part for another violin. It would be more in keeping with the thematic tone."

"I'm not seeing your point," I said.

"Then may I keep the score and change it to demonstrate my opinion?"

"I would be very pleased if you would."

He nodded, and became absorbed in the music. I left him with my concerto, curious what he would do with it.

A t the Stradivari home, Omobono greeted me effusively. I believe he considered me his customer since first bringing me into their home. As he escorted me toward the workshop, he asked how my stay was going.

"Very well," I answered with my own effusiveness. "It's marvelous to be back in Cremona."

The luthier's son beamed. "Excellent. Ah, here comes my father."

"Mr. Remón, Welcome back!" said Mr. Stradivari as he shooed away his son. "Excellent timing. Please, follow me."

We headed toward the workshop, but instead of going in, we went into a smaller room off to the side. In the room was a long table, on which he had spread out Dr. Newton's documents. On the table, there were also a violin, paper templates, and metal instruments, likely used to take measurements as they resembled Dr. Newton's device.

We sat side-by-side.

"Mr. Rémon, I have to say I find your friend's work and technical descriptions very intriguing. Likewise, I have to say I still don't understand much of it, but that which I do, I have general disagreement. Indeed, if he were in the room, I would have a long discourse to set him straight. Since he isn't, I'll have to present my side of the matter to you. Is that acceptable?"

"Without a doubt. Let me say that I have absolute faith in both you and in my friend."

Believing I was not sounding like a mere financier, I added, "My only role here is to facilitate the creation of a superb violin, as well as other instruments for the royal musicians."

"Let me say again, I always strive to create the most perfect violin. I don't need anyone to facilitate or provide me with drawings and mathematics of any kind. But I'm interested in what your friend has spent time thinking about." He waved a hand over the work spread out on the table.

"Yes, I do understand. I'll let you speak, as I'm interested in what you find intriguing."

That seemed to calm him. He said, "Good. First, as I pointed out yesterday, I certainly know about the sound post's position[1] and effect on the tone."

He showed me the drawing Dr. Newton had prepared and then a similar drawing of his own. There were slight differences, mainly in

---

[1] As Dr. Newton demonstrated, the position of the small dowel makes a great difference in tone. To be precise, if it is slightly toward the outside of the violin, the tone is brighter; toward the inside, the lower notes are enhanced. *PW*

the notations used by Mr. Stradivari. "Do you know what we call the sound post? In Italian, it's *l'anima*. In French, *âme*."

The soul, I thought, in English. There was that word again. I asked Mr. Stradivari, "You've mentioned the spirit before when talking about wood. Is the sound post's 'soul' the same as the 'spirit' of the wood?"

Rather than answering, Mr. Stradivari peered inside the violin through an *f* sound hole with the help of candlelight. "Look."

I squinted through the sound hole until I could see the post. "Yes, I see it."

He tapped along the front piece until there was a solid sound directly above the sound post. With a piece of soft graphite, he made a tiny dot on the face where the sound was solid. He placed the violin body on a tripod stand that was padded with strips of felt. Using a small felt-wrapped wood dowel, he tapped the face along the midline.

Mr. Stradivari looked up at me. "Listen carefully," he said and repeated the tapping.

I wasn't sure what I was supposed to hear, but the tone was somewhat muffled. The note seemed to be close to a B, slightly flat,[2] when the tap was at the center of the face.

Then he picked up a long thin pair of tweezers that was bent at the handle. He inserted it into the violin, probed the cavity, then twisted the tweezers for a moment. He peered inside again, before repeating the procedure.

Apparently satisfied, he tapped around the previous mark until the sound was solid. He made another mark with the graphite. Then he again tapped the felt-covered dowel along the centerline of the violin face.

"There," he said with finality.

---

[2] Without the sound post, the body of Stradivari's violins typically resonate around the note B. *TS*

I listened carefully. The tone had changed very slightly, perhaps now an E sharp.

"You see," Mr. Stradivari said. He showed me the minute differences in the graphite marks. "All you need to do is listen to it, how it cries or sings in joy. That's l'anima, the 'soul' of the sound post. And the spirit in the wood of the violin married together."

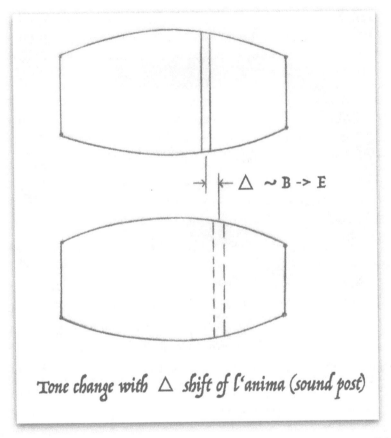

Tone change with △ shift of l'anima (sound post)

At this point, I tried to think of what Dr. Newton would say. My assumption was that he would say something to directly challenge the craftsman, such as, without a prefacing apology, "But if you know the mathematics and physical reasoning behind the phenomena you'll be able to design and predict any of the interactions between the sound post and the violin body."

Of course, I didn't say that. Instead, I said, "Yes, I can see how you would be able to produce the correct tone with your experience and craftsmanship. My friend would point out the mathematics and science behind the differences."

Mr. Stradivari pondered my statement for a moment. Long enough for me to worry that I'd offended him.

Then he broke into broad grin. "Of course, he would. And I'd respond with the voice of l'anima. Just as I showed you now."

With that response, Mr. Stradivari seemed confused by what I said. However, before I could clarify, he asked me, "What makes something alive, like a tree? Even an object, such as a violin, has a spirit that when played comes alive. It's not something that can be reduced to mechanics and mathematics as your friend proposes."

Again, I was certain Dr. Newton would disagree.

Mr. Stradivari continued, "For instance, regardless as much as he wants to create precise mathematics, the best position for the sound post can only be determined with the ear. Granted, there are some general considerations."

He showed me his drawing and pointed out how moving the post toward the f sound hole brightened the sound for the treble strings, and in the opposite direction, the tone becomes more somber, favoring the bass strings. Moving the post forward or backward, affects volume and richness. "But in all cases, it's only a critical and trained ear that matters."

"I'm sure he would agree with that," I said, although, I could only think he would point out ways to measure these variations more precisely.

"More than just position," Mr. Stradivari went on, "the crafting of the sound post is critical to its effectiveness. It has to fit precisely, matching the inside of the belly and the inside of the back."

He stared at me. "Do you see what I am saying? There are so many things involved."

I nodded. "I do understand." So many variables.

"And here," Mr. Stradivari said while pulling another of Dr. Newton's diagrams toward us. "Here we have, what I believe we have, is the action of the sound post on the inside of the belly and its effect on the sides. He calls this movement the result of pressure waves?"

"Yes," I said. "That's what I understand. He has developed some equations related to the force which creates the wave. The force is a result of the mass of air and its acceleration. This, according to my friend, is how sound travels, and what makes it travel at a given speed."

Mr. Stradivari thought for several moments. "In a broad way of thinking, I can see how this would explain certain fundamental principles, but I don't see how this could help one create a superior violin. Your friend is simplifying the whole instrument into two planks of wood with some squiggly waves supposedly doing all the work."

Mr. Stradivari found a piece of paper and a stick of charcoal, and placed them on the table.

"Here, look at this," he said with no small amount of impatience while he made a quick sketch. "It's true as your friend says, the back and the belly are carefully crafted arcs of differences in thickness, making them more like bows, each with a precise spring. The thinner the wood, the more spring. But," he paused to give me a glare to make sure I was paying attention, "there's a limit on how thin it can be since the wood needs sufficient strength to keep it from cracking under the strings as they are tightened and played, as well as changes of moisture in the air."

I nodded that I was understanding, enough so that I could ask him a question. "Then how do you determine that point of perfect thickness, or rather the thinness?"

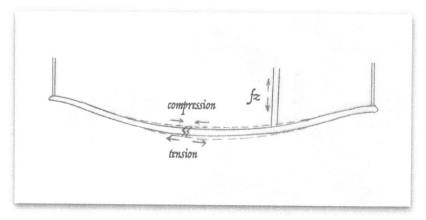

He grinned. "Yes! How do you? And not only must it be thin, but it must be thinner in places and thicker in other places. More than that, these differences must be the right places."

"Yes, I can see that. How do you determine the differences?"

Mr. Stradivari brightened from the frown he was beginning to wear. "If I knew how to define that in words, I'd tell you. But I can't. Again, it depends on what the wood tells me. And as you know, wood cannot speak in words. There's a feeling. Can you understand? It's the same with people, is it not? Do we not know a person from the words they say?"

"No, well, not entirely," I said, perhaps too emphatically.

He ignored my response. "Me, for instance. What am I to you besides an old maker of violins and other instruments? What do you think?"

"I know you're very serious about your craft. You don't waste your skill and talent, not for one moment."

He waved away my comment. "You can gather that from my words though, can't you? What about my inner, inexpressible desires? My failures as a man?"

I really didn't know what he wanted me to say. I took a shot in the dark. "I sense, if that's the right word, that you do not know how you create such wonderful musical instruments. I think you mention spirit because that's what you put into your craft. I sense that if you try to put it into words, you'll lose that ability. You will lose your soul."

It's the same way with my composing, as I recalled when I tried to explain it to Catherine.

Mr. Stradivari blinked once, then twice, while staring at me. Then he laughed from deep within his body. "Sir! You're no doubt correct. And how can you tell that about me without my words?"

Again, I spoke without much thought. "It's the way you hold a violin. The way you touch a piece of wood. The way you get excited when showing me your workshop. I suppose there are many things that I don't know. But what about me, what can you discern about me?"

Mr. Stradivari grew thoughtful. "I sense, if that's the right word as you say, that you have an altogether more serious reason for being here in my workshop buying instruments for musicians. Something is directing you."

I was immediately struck by his response. Was I giving away our undercover mission?

"This composition of yours, for instance," Mr. Stradivari continued. "It's a work of passion, isn't it?"

Relieved, I smiled slyly. "You're right about that. I'm writing it for a special and deeply personal reason."

He nodded. "I'll leave it as your secret then."

"All right, yes. And what about your secrets? Will you divulge more to me?"

"My secrets? I have no secrets."

"I believe you do. Starting with the wood you use."

Mr. Stradivari stroked his chin. "I do have my forest," he said quietly. "Although, it's been difficult to get there recently, with the war."

"Where's the forest?" I asked. "Without giving away your secret."

He waved in a vague direction. "To the north, to the mountains there."

In that general direction, he would have to go through both French and Austrian patrols. "Perhaps I could help you travel to your forest."

"How could you do that?"

I smiled. "Another of my secrets."

He laughed. "Then perhaps I'll plan a trip there."

After a dinner with the Stradivari family, Mr. Stradivari and Francesco returned to the workshop and Mrs. Stradivari began to clean up, leaving James and me to be entertained by Omobono and Caterina. Omobono was restless, bounding out of his chair and pacing around the room to emphasize points in the conversation. When he made one particularly enthusiastic leap, Caterina glanced at me, rolled her eyes, and smiled.

"We should go out, gentlemen," Omobono said, bouncing up again and looking out the window. "We'll be able to find a good time somewhere in this provincial city. Now if we were in Naples ..."

Ever chivalrous, I said, "We shouldn't go out unless Caterina comes with us."

She laughed and said, "No, please. I should help Mother."

"Then, I'll stay and help too," I said.

Omobono said to James, "I see your colleague is intent on avoiding the evening with us. Shall we go without him?"

James gave me a quick glance, to which I gave a little nod. "I think we should," he replied to Omobono.

"Good. Then let's go before the evening's over."

When they had departed, Caterina left me briefly, returning to say her mother didn't need any help. "Sorry to make you stay," she said. "But as long as you have, I would like to show you the city at night from a special viewpoint."

I was intrigued, of course, and readily agreed. I followed her up the stairs to secadùur. She closed the door behind us and took my hand. We went to the open window.

The city was dark except for a few torches, and it was quiet except for a few residents walking through the streets. The steeple of the church rose into the darkness and disappeared.

"It's beautiful," I said.

"But not as beautiful as Paris, is it?"

I hadn't been to Paris since I was a young boy, the last time my mother was able to visit the city before it became too dangerous for her, due to her association with critics of the French royalty.

"Paris has its beautiful spots," I said dreamily, as if reminiscing aloud. I told her about the monuments built to glorify the Sun King,[3] the cathedrals, the wide boulevards lined with shops.

My voice trailed off. While I was speaking, Caterina closed the distance between us, until our sides were just touching.

"Please, tell me more," she said.

I felt badly, not because of our intimate contact, but because I was unable to tell her the truth about me. I did say, "Paris is not all glitter and grand buildings and fancy dress. There are sections in the town, some areas as large as the whole of Cremona, where human misery abounds. People live on crumbs of bread, scraps of vegetables."

Rather than pulling away after the depressing turn in the conversation, she turned toward me. "It's very sad that people live that way. We have poverty here, as anywhere in the world, I'm sure, but not as horrible as that."

---

[3] Louis XIV disliked Paris, as he had been evicted twice in his youth. He created his palace in Versailles, although he continued to build monuments in Paris. *PW*

"It's very sad." I recalled Catherine's thoughts on the arc of life. "It does seem a waste of lives, that one person can live in luxury and another in poverty."

"It does, doesn't it? Why is one's lot in life a matter of birth? Why should we be stuck in that life? What should we do with the life we have?"

Those questions echoed Catherine's thoughts as well. "I don't know the answers," I said.

She turned away from me. "They are unanswerable."

We watched the night for a while, the torches extinguishing, all sounds dying away.

"You were born into a good family," I said.

Caterina laughed. "I don't know if that's true. But my father does very well in providing for us. We want for little."

Before I tell her how much I admired her father, she touched my arm and pointed down to the street. "This is what I really wanted you to see."

I looked in the direction she was pointing but didn't see anything. I softened my focus and slowly a movement appeared in my line of vision. It was a slow roiling, a churning of an ethereal substance.

It was fog, but it seemed more living creature, an ephemeral dragon, creeping through the night. It obscured the buildings, dimmed any light. When it reached the piazza it spread rapidly, as if freed from chains. The edge collided with the Stradivari home and workshop and crawled up the wall. Cold tendrils spilled into the loft and engulfed us.

When the loft was full of the chilly fog, Caterina again took my hand and led me down into her tiny room under the attic eaves. We quickly undressed, crawled under the blankets, and warmed each other.

The next morning, James and I woke up late. His evening with Omobono lasted as long as mine with Caterina. I'd left in the middle of the night, creeping through the Stradivari house like a pilferer.

James and I went out for a meal and a walk along the city's perimeter to monitor changes to the defenses. At one point, James said, "It took you a long time to help Caterina and Mrs. Stradivari clean up after dinner."

"We did have much to clean," I said.

"I didn't realize we'd made such a mess." James started to say something else, but he let it go.

Unfortunately, when we returned to the pensione, Lt. Laurent was waiting for us.

"Lieutenant! It's good to see you again," I said, trying to sound enthused.

"Enjoying the incredible wonders of Cremona, gentlemen?" he asked.

We both nodded. I said. "What did we do to deserve the pleasure of your company?"

"I just want to let you know I'm aware that you're in Cremona. How are you coming along with the luthier and your musical instruments?"

"Well enough," I answered. "We're moving toward an agreement to purchase several."

"Excellent," said the officer, although I wasn't sure if he was being sarcastic. "I hope for your continued success."

"Thank you," I said.

"How much longer do you think you'll stay?"

I looked at James and we gave each other a shrug. I answered for us. "We have no definite date of departure. The instruments all have very specific requirements."

Lt. Laurent made another little snorting sound. "They get more attention than my soldiers."

I said, "I don't know if that's the case. I'm sure all the soldiers are a priority."

"Unfortunately, no," he said. "Some even go missing. Vanish without a trace."

He looked from me to James. We remained silent. Without saying another word, he turned precisely and left us.

chapter 21

In the dark of night, obscured by fog, always the infernal fog, Mr. Stradivari and I hurried to the Parish of Santa Maria Nuova. There, we walked through the church, leaving donation coins for Father Cozzoli who kept the doors unlocked for us. To avoid any questioning of our destination as it would take us through disputed territory, we decided to sneak out of Cremona rather than go through a gate.

We descended to the wine cellar. Mr. Stradivari paused in the cellar, perusing the bottles with a lighted candle. "I had no idea the parish held such riches," he said. "But the Church does look out for itself first."[1]

I was tempted to take a bottle or two for our trip but decided we shouldn't without asking the priest—his continued cooperation was vital to our mission.

Once we were out of the wine cellar, the night grew suddenly colder, the fog congealing around us. I followed Mr. Stradivari as he strode down into the dry moat, up the other side and then along a narrow cart path that I never could have found on my own. According to Mr. Stradivari, our travel was going to take two long days to get to the forest, if we were fortunate enough in our travels to avoid patrols, foul weather, highwaymen, feeble horses, and bad food.

---

[1] Stradivari was arguably entitled to criticize the Church as he was an elder of the Parish of San Domenico. *PW*

Although, the church where he was entombed was sold in 1868 and during the demolition, Stradivari's bones were tossed who-knows-where. Except for his skull, which was retrieved by an unknown man before it was lost. Before leaving with it, he held the skull aloft and exclaimed, "Ah, Stradivari!" *TS*

As the sun began to rise, we reached a livery stable where we hired two fit horses. I was surprised to find Mr. Stradivari was a fair horseman, as he kept up the pace. It felt good to be traveling again.

We didn't stop until we reached about one third of the way on the trade route between Cremona and Brescia. Resting with our horses next to a stream, we ate bread and cheese we brought with us. An occasional farmer's cart or supply wagon traversed the road, but thus far there were no French patrols.

"How often do you visit the forest?" I asked Mr. Stradivari.

"It used to be once or twice a year but now it's difficult to find the time because of the number of orders we have for instruments, and with the occupation. I've gone all the way to Venice to select pieces of maple from the Balkans. But mostly, I simply dislike being away from the workshop. However, this step in the creation of an instrument is too important to abandon or leave to others who don't fully grasp its importance."

I wondered if he meant his sons, and I wanted to ask him how much of the craftsmanship he left to his sons and other apprentices. "Your knowledge of the trees is important as you say, but it seems to me that all the steps, all the materials, are equally important. Like one bruise on an apple, one poor piece of wood, or a poor execution, especially due to the work of others, would spoil the remainder."

Mr. Stradivari didn't respond. I wondered if I had said something insulting. Or maybe said what was too obvious. I felt as if I were again in Dr. Newton's inquisitor's chair, waiting for the condemnation of my spoken thoughts.

"What you say is true," he finally replied. "However, some of the craft can be taught more easily than others. Some steps are more important than others. Apprentices have levels of skill in one way but not another. Some may do well at preparing the blocks, or mixing varnish, or carving a scroll. Some may be only good at sweeping up sawdust. Rarely will any excel at more than two or three skills."

"As it is with your sons?" I asked.

He didn't speak for a long moment. I assumed my question lacked propriety.

"My sons ..." he began then stopped. Instead of answering, he asked me, "Do you have children?"

"I haven't been fortunate enough to have children. Perhaps I should say, I haven't been fortunate to find a woman who wants to join me in that pursuit."

Mr. Stradivari let out a warm laugh. "Not to laugh at your situation, but indeed, that's important."

"You have been very fortunate in that regard, sir. Mrs. Stradivari is wonderful."

"Ah, Antonia. I must agree with you. As for my children, namely those who help me directly, Omobono and Francesco, I can only be grateful they can do as much as they do. But I cannot, as much as I've tried, mold them, craft them, into superior luthiers. Perhaps I gave up too early, perhaps I was reluctant to fully invest enough time in them. The fault may be mine, perhaps an inability to express what I'm doing and to teach it.

"Each child is born with their own abilities. In the end, no matter what you desire to do, it's a matter of knowing by observing, listening, feeling. Or more a matter of caring to observe, listen, feel."

"And your daughters?" I asked with some trepidation.

"Gulia is well-married,[2] and Caterina is most generously helpful, not only with the household but with our business as well."

Did he give me a sly glance at the mention of Caterina? I thought so, but it might have been only my imagination.

We rode persistently until the sun was directly overhead. Our horses were often in near full stride, as if bent on completing our journey to the forest in one go. During this period of rhythmic gait, I

---

[2] Born 1668, Gulia Stradivari married into a well-to-do aristocratic family in Cremona. The connection might have worked in Antonio Stradivari's favor in developing clients for his instruments. *PW*

was contemplating Mr. Stradivari's hierarchy of skills involved in creating his superior instruments, when, as we rounded the tight curve around a knobby hill covered in scraggly trees and rocks and brush, I heard several horses just ahead.

Too late to avoid the coming party, which I presumed to be a French patrol, I gave Mr. Stradivari a nod of reassurance. He gave me no sign that he understood what I meant by my gesture, but neither did he betray any panic. We didn't break stride and as we rounded the curve, we rode headlong into the patrol.

They were indeed French, and they were startled by our sudden presence. I reined my horse to the side of the road to let them pass. I slowed my horse and gave them a polite nod in deference.

I thought we had gotten away without being stopped, but then in a change of mind, or realization that it should be duty first instead of reaching their destination, the officer leading the patrol pulled hard on the reins of his horse. He shouted for the soldiers at the rear to delay us. He turned his horse and came back to where we were being held.

"Where are you going in such a hurry, gentlemen?" asked the officer. His craggy face, like chipped limestone, twitched with irritation.

I answered him in French. "Good morning, sir. We're going to the Fiemme Valley, hunting trees."

He gave me a perplexed look. "Hunting what?"

One of the soldiers boxing us in, answered for me, "Trees, sergeant. He said 'trees.'"

The officer said, "I asked him."

"Trees," I said, in the politest tone I could muster.

The officer now appeared ready to draw his sword. "I'm not in the mood for riddles."

"I apologize if my response seemed so. But really, we will be hunting trees. My colleague," I nodded toward Mr. Stradivari, "is the most celebrated luthier in Italy. He's making a set of stringed instruments for our royal musicians for which he needs the best wood."

The officer gritted his teeth as if chewing on stringy meat. "Where are you coming from?"

"Cremona," I answered for us.

"Cremona? A long way for you to go for a piece of wood. And who are you?"

I explained my role with the Royal Musician's Office.

The officer shook his head and sighed in exasperation. "In the middle of a war we need Italian violins. What in God's name is wrong with French instruments?"

I gave him a vigorous nod. "Indeed, an excellent question, sir. If the musicians wanted mere instruments, then I wouldn't have to look far from home. But they are demanding the highest quality violins and other instruments."

The officer pondered that and, apparently finding logic in it, asked Mr. Stradivari, "And what makes yours better than ours?"

Oh no, I thought. How long would we be here while he answered that question? I gave him a good glance, but he was already replying to the question.

"Sir, I wouldn't be so presumptuous to make any such claim. Perhaps suffice to say I have provided instruments for other royal musicians including those in the court of King James."[3]

The officer frowned, then growled, "Don't expect protection from us when you run into the Austrians." He ordered his second-in-command to search our bags before he turned his horse and rode on.

---

[3] Stradivari was commissioned to prepare an entire set of instruments for the English King James. The records of this commission and delivery, however, have not been found. *TS*

We reached Brescia and stabled our horses just as the sun was setting. I was tired and sore from the long ride, while Mr. Stradivari seemed to be ready to go another cross-country trek. We hired a carriage to the home of a musician and client of Mr. Stradivari. The violinist, Mr. Moretti, welcomed us into the narrow, crumbling building that was surprisingly warm and comforting inside, full of light from a plethora of candles. The tension in my body and the thoughts in my head running amuck quickly dissolved and quieted in the home.

After we cleaned ourselves of dust, he served us a meal, during which our host and Mr. Stradivari discussed the health of Mr. Moretti's violin. There was considerable back-and-forth on many aspects, but in the main, the instrument was performing well. However, about one point of concern, the violinist insisted there was a flaw. To demonstrate, he got up from the table and played a few notes.

"There, you heard it, didn't you? A small, but noticeable wavering, a tremolo, when I move off the E string."

Mr. Stradivari's expression was one of skepticism. "Play it again, more slowly and softly."

After complying, Mr. Stradivari looked to me. "Did you hear an offending vibrato?"

I asked the violinist to play the notes again. I supposed I did catch a slight tremolo, although it could be just the way he was playing the notes and not the instrument. I admitted I did hear something that time.

Mr. Stradivari nodded. "You have a good ear. I heard it as well." To Mr. Moretti, he said, "May I see the violin?"

He was handed the instrument, and began an elaborate examination, holding it near a candle while squinting all along the joints, then tapping on its belly and across the back. He adjusted the tuning knobs while plucking the strings and repeated the examination.

Finally, he announced, "The bass bar should be adjusted. Shall I bring the violin back with me to make this alteration? We can retrieve the instrument on our return to Cremona."

Mr. Moretti enthusiastically agreed with the luthier's recommendation. As if to celebrate, he entertained us with a few selections of his repertoire while we finished our meal and a bottle of wine. After, we conversed about music and instruments, musicians and luthiers, food and wine. The two men avoided talking about the war, no doubt because of my apparent French roots.

One curious bit of the conversation did stick with me in a vague, dreamlike way. Admittedly, my mind was wandering, sleepily, when I caught this from Mr. Moretti, "I don't know how to explain … I must crawl into the music, become absorbed by it."

Mr. Stradivari said, "I don't know what you mean. I would have believed the opposite; that you would have to absorb the music."

"I see …" said Mr. Moretti. "I regurgitate the composition to feed it to the audience. Like a mother bird!"

I laughed. Mr. Stradivari did as well, before he said, quietly, thoughtfully, "Maybe I crawl into my instruments, into the wood, like a woodworm, to find its true spirit."

For some reason, Mr. Moretti thought that to be too hilarious to remain in his chair. He got up and danced a jig while laughing and playing his violin like a traveling fiddler.

We left the violinist's home early to retrieve our horses and resume our journey. The sun had been up only a little while when we reached Lago di Garda. In a glen by the lake, we stopped for a rest. Mr. Stradivari seemed more tired and subdued this morning. I said, "Mr. Moretti was an excellent host."

Mr. Stradivari made a little nod of agreement. "He's very particular about his violin. He watched over every step of its creation. I nearly had to ask him to leave the workshop, but Omobono was able to keep him away much of the time. As you saw, Moretti likes his wine."

"Do you really believe his bass bar needs adjusting?" I asked the luthier. "I wasn't entirely convinced that the tremolo wasn't his playing, rather than the instrument."

Mr. Stradivari said, "I'm not convinced the bass bar is the problem. But I'll take it back with us all the same. I can have another violinist play it. But even if it is Moretti's playing, I should be able to make an adjustment that counters his wobble."

By crawling into the bass bar like a woodworm? was my irreverent thought.

When we were rested and ready to go, I heard something strike a stone, making it skitter. I froze and listened, then heard the whispery breath of a horse not too far away. I gave Mr. Stradivari a glance and a reassuring nod then calmly stood and walked toward my horse. Mr. Stradivari did the same. We readied to mount and ride. Before we could, an Austrian mounted cavalry soldier appeared at the edge of the trees.

"Good morning, gentlemen," he said in Italian, nasally with his Bavarian accent. The soldier asked us our destination.

"Good morning," Mr. Stradivari said.

I merely nodded my greeting, letting my companion speak for us.

"We are journeying from Cremona to the Fiemme Valle in the Alps. I'm Antonio Stradivari, a humble luthier in search for a good tree or two for my instruments. I call the place *Il Bosco Che Suona*."

I translated, "The Musical Woods."

The soldier wasn't impressed. "And who are you?"

"I'm assisting Mr. Stradivari," I said simply.

He kept his gaze on me longer than I thought necessary. "You'll have to turn around. This route is restricted."

Mr. Stradivari spoke up, insistently, "But we must go now. It's a critical time for certain trees which may need to be harvested."

The soldier was still not impressed. "It's not possible. You must turn around."

I was reluctant to play my card now, but I felt I must avoid wasting this trip. In our mother tongue, I said to the soldier, "Sir, I must talk with you in private. It's a matter of utmost importance."

That startled the soldier, who blinked in confusion. After a moment of consideration, he turned his horse. "This way."

We rode to the other side of the glen.

"Thank you for letting me explain the situation," I said. "I'm Captain Phillipe Wolf, here in Italy secreting myself in Cremona and the immediate area."

I briefly told him my cover story purchasing instruments.

The soldier's confusion did not go away. I gave him a rundown of the chain of command in the Austrian headquarters.

"You must tell this to my commander," he said. "He's just up the road. Head that way. Both of you."

I returned to Mr. Stradivari and we rode in the direction ordered with the soldier behind us. We soon came to a small patrol of Austrians. The soldier rode ahead. He spoke to the officer, while he looked us up and down. After several exchanges, during which the officer appeared more confused than satisfied, he motioned me over.

"I'm Lieutenant Klein. My man just told me a strange story I find difficult to believe. Perhaps if I heard it from the source. He tells me you are from the Austrian military, yet you're traveling with an Italian violin maker?"

"For the most part, that's correct. Mr. Stradivari is a luthier. As for me, I'm Captain Phillipe Wolf of the Third Regiment, posted to London as military liaison. I'm in Cremona, working undercover as a French bureaucrat."

"And why are you here in this part of Italy?"

"My cover involves purchasing musical instruments from my traveling companion." I explained Mr. Stradivari's need to visit the forest.

"Third Regiment, you say? Where were you posted in the winter of 1696?"

I responded without hesitation. "The Netherlands. Rijswijk. To help pressure the French into signing the peace treaty."[4]

The lieutenant seemed satisfied. "Peace doesn't last so long, does it?"

"Unfortunately, no."

Before being released, I told Lt. Klein about what James and I overhead in the headquarters. The officer was very interested and asked me to repeat exactly what we heard. I also told him about the French patrol we ran into south between Cremona and Brescia. He said, "They were likely a scouting patrol from Soncino. We were looking for them."

"They seemed to be on the run."

"You did well to escape them."

"Thank you."

The lieutenant thought for a moment and apparently had nothing else to add. "Good luck with your mission, Captain."

"And you, yours, Lieutenant," I replied.

Mr. Stradivari and I soon left the main road near the lake and began to climb a steeper path. We didn't encounter another patrol. He hadn't yet questioned me about our encounter with the Austrian patrol.

We dismounted to ease the burden on our laboring horses. Mr. Stradivari led us deeper into the forest, where the air quickly became crisp and cool. The forest grew thick with tall spruce trees. Mr. Stradivari looked around the forest as we walked, his gaze alighting on trees, one at a time as if they were old friends.

We went deeper into the forest and just before dark, we came upon a camp—wispy smoke rising from a fire, three huts surrounding

---

[4] The Treaty of Ryswick (Rijswijk) ended the Nine Years' Year, also known as the War of the Grand Alliance. *PW*

the campfire. Behind the huts, under a wooden lean-to, cut trunks of the exact same dimensions had been precisely stacked.

A woodsman, sawdust sprinkled in his hair, came out of one of the huts and greeted Mr. Stradivari with great enthusiasm, exclaiming how long it had been since he'd seen him. Mr. Stradivari returned the greeting before introducing me. The woodsman smelled of astringent pine sap and smoke.

We took care of our horses while the woodsman prepared us a rustic meal, to which we added the last of our bread, cheese, and dried fruit. While we ate and drank—all tasted of heaven after our long day—Mr. Stradivari was caught up on the state of the forest, particularly several trees by name, for instance, Fork, Hip, Lonesome.[5]

According to the woodsman, all the named trees were doing well but it was up to Mr. Stradivari to be the final judge. They also discussed the forest in general, and the weather, particularly the rain amounts and snowfalls in the recent seasons. Thinking of a question Dr. Newton might pose, I asked Mr. Stradivari how the rain and snow affected the trees for use in his instruments.

Instead of answering directly, he walked over to the woodpile, perused the stacks, then motioned me over. When I was standing next to him, he pointed to the cross section of one of the pieces of wood. I bent down and looked at it.

"These circular marks … here," he said. "Can you see the differences in their separation?"[6]

---

[5] Later, I came to learn the name origins: Fork – a tree near the fork of two small streams. Hip – one at the bottom of the valley's eastern flank. Lonesome – one standing by itself in a meadow. *PW*

[6] Growth rings were known from ancient Grecian times. Using the patterns for dating became a science—dendrochronology—from the latter part of the nineteenth century. *TS*

Even in the dim light I could see that some were more spaced than others. "Yes."

"The wider the separation, the better the growing conditions."

That made sense, of course, as I'd noticed tree rings before. "Is it better for use in instruments for the separations to be wide or narrow?"

"Which do you believe to be the case?"

I couldn't come up with an answer, although I was thinking—hypothesizing as Dr. Newton would say—that the wider separations meant a healthier tree, and thus, better wood. I offered that to him.

He smiled and shrugged. "Perhaps that's true. Perhaps not. I haven't found there to be a difference, but there are many reasons we could consider. In the end, I find a musically superior piece of wood to sound better than another piece."

With a rap of his knuckle on the wood, then another, he demonstrated the differences in sounds. I confess, I didn't hear much difference, not enough to make a judgment. I asked him to repeat his knuckle-rapping. This time I distinguished one piece had a slightly duller tone than the other.

"Is that the difference?" I asked him.

"There's a lower tone in one, although it could be a difference between the two in size, or in how they cured, or in their sap, or when they were harvested. Not to mention, it might be due to how much they want to be an instrument."

I nearly laughed at his last statement, but wasn't certain he'd spoken in jest.

Other thoughts about his observations that Dr. Newton would propose came to mind—*variables* for one—although the last reason Mr. Stradivari gave me was difficult to perceive to be a true characteristic of a tree.

My goal suddenly seemed all the more distant.

In the morning, I arose to find the woodsman and Mr. Stradivari looking over the wood pile. They'd taken out three of the pieces and were discussing another one. I only caught the end of the discussion—they decided to leave the piece in the lean-to and continue to cure.

The three of us set out toward the forest. Mr. Stradivari and the woodsman identified a few trees they felt were good candidates. I tried to keep track of their discussion as much as I could, but they spoke in their own dialect. I gathered that good trees were a certain diameter, and of an observable symmetry from one side to the next. They tapped the trees with a metal rod at a prescribed height. But in the end, there was a certain feeling which went unvoiced that they used to reach their decision.

They focused on more than a dozen trees, agreeing when they might be ready for harvest, and the best time to harvest them. A winter's full moon deemed to be the best for most of the trees, although they did not explain further. They discussed where to cut it, how much time the cuttings would need to cure, among other decisions.

Then we came to the open meadow where the tree named Lonesome grew. A straight tree, though scrawny compared to many of the other trees. Its limbs were sparse, its bark rough.

"A pure and moral tree," Mr. Stradivari said. "A tree that has struggled to survive where others have failed."

There were a few straggly saplings in the meadow, some withered and near death.

The woodsman said, "The soil is not conducive to the growing of spruce."

Mr. Stradivari agreed. "And yet Lonesome is making a life here. I believe this tree will make a most superior violin."

I experienced a wave of enthusiasm, perhaps even excitement, emanating from the luthier. I pursued my curiosity by asking, "Because it's growing where no other trees can? Or because of its moral fiber as you alluded to?"

We walked closer to the tree. Mr. Stradivari put his hands on the trunk. "It sings to me."

I listened but didn't hear it sing. I put my hands on the tree. The bark, rough and prickly, felt like the bark from any spruce.

Mr. Stradivari said something that I would never forget.

"Perhaps we should make your violin from Lonesome."[7]

During our return to Cremona, packing a few blocks of cured spruce with us, I thought of Catherine, wishing that she had been there to see the tree in the meadow, to hear and feel Mr. Stradivari's emotional response to it, and to hear his pronouncement about creating the violin for our concerto. I also believed she would have had many more questions for the luthier than I did. Questions that might press Mr. Stradivari further to divulge his secrets, to burn off the fog through which he spoke. She would have gotten to the heart of the matter concerning how the trees grow (or sleep!), how he hears them sing, what it sounds like, why the phase of the moon is important to harvesting them, and other points of his secret knowledge I hadn't thought about.

Along the way, we were again detained by an Austrian patrol, fortunately led by the same lieutenant. He asked if we'd encountered any French patrols. I told him we hadn't. The officer told us there were changes in movements, and that we might encounter French patrols south of Brescia. After I thanked him for telling us that, the officer released us without another word.

We stopped in Brescia. It was after dinner at the home of the violinist, Mr. Moretti, when Mr. Stradivari and I were alone that he spoke quietly, "Mr. Rémon, I must ask you something that I've been

---

[7] An interesting parallel story: a violin sound post was made from the Miracle Tree in Japan, which survived the Fukushima tsunami of 2011. *TS*

thinking about. The way you have dealt with the military patrols, both Austrian and French, but especially the Austrian patrol, is perplexing. Are you someone other than who you say you are?"

If I said I was surprised by his question, I would have been deceiving myself. But I didn't know what to say in response. To deny it would have been insulting to him, to give full disclosure might risk our mission.

"Not fully, I admit. I have a dual purpose for being in Cremona. I can't say exactly what that is, but I assure you, I am sincere in purchasing the instruments, and resolutely determined to have you create the perfect violin for the concerto I am composing."

Now I was the one being secretive.

Mr. Stradivari was quiet for several moments. "I thank you for that piece of the mystery. As for your other life, I cannot let that put me, my business, nor especially my family in jeopardy."

A statement of strong validity. "No, I never would," I said as sincerely and honestly as I could make my voice sound.

After another moment of silence, he said, "Good."

But he did not appear to be fully convinced.

chapter 22

J ames was lying awake on his bed in our room when I returned
to the pensione. His hands were locked together behind his
head as if he were daydreaming.

"Welcome back," he said.

"It's good to be back."

He got up and poured me a grappa.

"Thanks," I said and took a long sip.

"How was your adventure?" James asked as I emptied my travel
bag.

How was it? I'd asked myself that question. Exhilarating and in-
formative, and then depressing and troubling in the end with Mr.
Stradivari's disenchantment.

"I believe it was successful," I said, "in that we brought back
slabs of spruce Mr. Stradivari deemed satisfactory for creating his
instruments. He showed me the tree he felt would make a superior
violin, perhaps for mine. Although, that's now in question."

James sipped from his glass. "Something happened?"

"We ran into patrols, both French and Austrian. I dealt with
them, but in doing so I aroused Mr. Stradivari's suspicions that I'm
not the Principal Financier for the Royal Musicians Office."

James frowned, turning the glass in his hands. "Were you able to
dissuade him of his suspicions?"

"Unfortunately, not likely. I assured him there was no danger to
him and his family, but it didn't seem to do much good. I didn't think
I could lie to him. I'm sure he would know if I were."

James downed the rest of his grappa and put the glass on the
table. "Is our real mission in jeopardy?"

"I don't think that."

"It will be if Stradivari informs on us."

Obviously so. "I don't believe he'll go that far," I said.

"But you can't say for certain, either, can you? After all, how well do you know him?"

"Granted, I don't know him well. He does remain secretive in many things. But I also convinced him that the other reason for our being in Cremona, the purchase of instruments, especially the violin, is genuine."

James inhaled a deep breath. "But without assurances to that effect? It might be more beneficial to him to inform the French command. They might grant him special privileges."

James made a strong argument, but I couldn't see Mr. Stradivari doing that.

"I think not. He's never expressed any word of sympathy for the French occupiers."

"He was enthusiastic to work with us when we portrayed ourselves as French."

"I'm certain he would have expressed the same enthusiasm regardless of our origins."

James didn't disagree, but I didn't know if he was convinced either. But then I wasn't sure of the entirety of Mr. Stradivari's motivations either. I needed to approach Mr. Stradivari soon to make certain I was still in good stead with him. Perhaps I could enlist the help of Caterina. I told James I would smooth things over with Mr. Stradivari.

"And how about you?" I asked, changing the subject. "What has happened while I was away?"

James rubbed his forehead. "The curfew and travel restrictions grew worse. It's more difficult to gather our information. But I've seen the signs that the French are changing their patterns to match what we overheard."

"Did you encounter our friend, Lieutenant Laurent?"

"Luckily, no. I imagine he's occupied with the plans."

He went on to tell me about the increased presence of guards at the gates, the constant training of both defensive and offensive tactics, and a reduction of soldiers out carousing at night. He ended with, "There's an edge to the troops and the citizens."

And that puts us on edge too, I thought, but did not need to say aloud. We worked late adding our observations to the coded musical score.

With deep lines etched in his forehead, smudge pots under his eyes, and his hair and beard more unkempt than I imagined was possible, Il Diavolo did not look like he'd reduced his carousing. He pushed strands of hair way from his eyes.

"Rémon!" He clapped me on the shoulder and ushered me into his room. We took our chairs in his sitting room. "I wanted to talk with you about your composition. But you were nowhere to be found. Then I hear you've been gallivanting around Italy with Stradivari. How was the forest?"

I briefly told him about my trip, saving my request for his advice. I was intrigued with his declaration about wanting to discuss my composition. "I'm interested in your thoughts on my score."

"Ah, yes, well," he said, almost as if he had forgotten he'd mentioned it. He bounced up and searched through his stack of compositions piled on a desk. "Here, yes, here," he stuttered.

He put the score on his music stand and took out his violin. He tuned it for a few moments, muttering that he needed the instrument looked at by the Amati workshop.

"Although," he said, "maybe I should get Stradivari to give it a good going-over."

For some reason, he laughed loudly. Maybe it was the thought of Stradivari working on an Amati. Were they rivals? Or was it that Mr. Stradivari might have been an Amati apprentice?

Finished laughing and tuning his violin, he played the first few bars.

"This is a good start, although it would be stronger if it were *un po allegro.*[1]"

He demonstrated it at a faster tempo, then even faster.

It was better, although I believed he would have liked anything faster.

"But more than that, the second part is completely wrong."

As he turned to that part in the score, I tried to anticipate why he would find it objectionable. I really hadn't thought much about the composition lately, as I needed a rest from it, but I thought he would say it was too pastoral, without an edge. Or maybe it was just too slow.

Again, he played a few bars before he stopped abruptly. He asked, "Do you hear it?"

I didn't know what I was supposed to have heard, other than it was the viola part, not the violin. When I didn't answer, he played a page more, then went back and played the violin part.

I stated the facts: "You're playing the viola part, and then the violin part."

"Well, yes, of course," he said with no small note of exasperation. "That was the point. Doesn't the viola part sound more alive, more passionate, when played with a violin?"

Of course, it was brighter, I knew that. So, was that it?

Then I understood—the two parts were meant to be equals, not one in subordination to the other. There should be independence of feeling, if not fierce conflict.

"Oh! I see," was all I could say. With that understanding, we went to work on some specifics of the new direction of the concerto.

When we had done as much as we could without some more creative effort on my part, I told him I'd fallen out with Mr. Stradivari.

---

[1] "A little fast." *PW*

Not divulging the reason, at least not the complete truth, I asked for his help in restoring my relationship with the luthier.

"I'll try, but the man is stubborn. How would you propose I go about it?" he asked.

I'd thought of a plan. Before I spoke of it, I went over to the window and gazed down to the Stradivari workshop. I couldn't see inside but was sure they were hard at work as usual.

I turned back to the violinist and said, "I've become close to Caterina Stradivari."

Il Diavolo raised his devilish eyebrows.

"Perhaps if I could talk to her," I said, "I could persuade her to smooth things over with her father."

"You want me to set up a meeting with Caterina for you?"

I nodded. "If possible."

He grinned. "I'm sure I can succeed in that mission."

James and I spent much of the next two days collecting troop movements, at least as much as we could while limiting our own movements. When we weren't making short, surreptitious reconnaissance outings, I worked on the composition. Surprisingly, given the good amount of time I had to compose, I was unable to concentrate.

I missed Catherine greatly, even as the pain of seeing her kissing Mr. Montagu had not subsided. I wanted to believe there was nothing to it beyond a flirtatious fondle by an employer who had too much to drink. She could hardly have pushed him away. But neither did she seem to be repulsed.

Thinking back on it, I realized that I'd gone looking for Catherine as the gathering was ending, perhaps expecting to find out what happens in the Montagu home. I certainly couldn't have thought Catherine was waiting for me to be the one to kiss her. So was I suspicious she might be with Mr. Montagu? Likely so. As with other times of distress, our emotions cloud our rational thoughts, and even worse, our memories.

And yet, who was I to be critical of what I saw in the shadows? After all, I was looking forward to my meeting with Caterina, and its secret nature, relatively so, heightened the thought of it. That thought drove me from the pensione. I barely said a word to James before I left.

Outside, the streets were busy in the late afternoon, as townspeople hurried to get their business accomplished before the curfew. I wandered without real direction, thinking I might see if Il Diavolo was in his home; of course, I wanted to find out if he had arranged a meeting with Caterina.

The little clusters of men from the town were gathered in the small piazza in front of the church. I gave them a nod before I went in the building where Il Diavolo lived.

No one answered the door to his room when I rapped on it. No sounds of music or other sources came through the door when I put my ear to it.

As I left his building, I was looking in the direction of Stradivari's workshop. When I didn't see anyone outside, I looked the other direction as I was taking a step. I nearly ran into Lt. Laurent.

Luckily, I caught myself before I exclaimed something not in French.

"Hello, Rémon," he said calmly. "What a coincidence finding you here."

I was sure it was anything but coincidental. He must have been following me, whether from the pensione or having seen me by happenstance along my meandering route.

"Lieutenant. A pleasure."

He gave me a sly, ironic smile and glanced up at the building. "You must be visiting your violinist friend?"

"Yes," I said, quickly calculating if my seeing Il Diavolo would be cause for concern. I added, "Mr. di Amico has been very helpful in my business of procuring the instruments for specific compositions. And he knows the local luthiers all very well."

Lt. Laurent glanced toward the Stradivari workshop. "So, you haven't settled on Stradivari?"

I smiled, trying to cover up my trepidation. "I remain certain Antonio Stradivari is the right luthier. Let's say we're still negotiating."

The officer made a "tch-ing" noise. "I hadn't realized the purchase of a few musical instruments involves so many considerations."

"As I imagine is your role as lieutenant. So many considerations."

"I suppose."

"Well, Lieutenant, I don't wish to keep you."

"As it happens, I'm off duty. Would you join me for dinner?"

I was taken aback by his offer and was immediately torn between accepting and declining. Accepting presented an opportunity to gather information directly from the lieutenant, assuming he would be open. On the other hand, he was likely trying to get me to be open, perhaps to trip me up.

In the end, I accepted, deciding that a refusal would add to whatever suspicions he might be harboring.

We went to a dining hall where there were only officers eating, it wasn't crowded as it was still early evening. We sat at a table that was away from the main cluster of officers.

The lieutenant ordered for us, looking at me, saying, "It's really the only remarkable dish I've found here." He gave me the knowing look of a connoisseur.

The wine was good, likely from a private stock for the officers. I wondered if he knew about the excellent wines in the cellar under Father Cozzoli's church.

Lt. Laurent sipped his wine delicately, savoring each drop. I took this behavior as that of a man who dwelled on the details of things, searching for a deeper meaning, perhaps in what others might consider shallow or even unimportant.

Not unlike Dr. Newton.

Similarly, his gaze never left me for long, which made me ponder everything I spoke, my every facial expression, and how I drank my own wine. Naturally, all that deliberating made my conversation style stiff as if I were translating every word.

Furthermore, that awareness brought me back to our first conversation at the Po River gate into Cremona. What was it that I said that raised suspicion? I'd thought of it a few times, but nothing came up. But it could have been something I wasn't aware of, something that I overlooked in our planning and practice.

To get the lieutenant talking more, I asked him if he liked music.

"Do I like music ..." he said with due deliberation. "I suppose the real question is, 'How could anyone not like music?' Perhaps one might not like a kind of music, or a certain piece, or a composer, but I don't suppose anyone would say they wish there would be no more music in the world."

I rephrased the question I believed was obvious. "Do you have any particularly favorite music?"

He took another dainty sip of wine while he thought. "I enjoy dancing. So, music that is played at a dance."

Not quite what I had in mind. "Dance music is enjoyable."

"I've only heard a large orchestra playing long pieces a few times. It's impressive, I will say. But I get restless, or sleepy. But I did enjoy the concert during your last visit."

"Good. I hope to arrange another and I shall invite you to it. If you can get away from your duties."

"I have little time but would consider your invitation."

"Excellent."

Our dinners were placed in front of us. The lieutenant became well focused on eating, taking small bites that he chewed thoughtfully. I ate at his speed. When we were almost finished, the hard edge he had earlier seemed to have softened—so I asked him how he thought the war was going.

He considered an answer for a few moments. "I fear it will be protracted."

"Protracted," I said in a tone that might lead him to elaborate.

After another pause, he said without elaborating, "That's what I fear."

"I shall pray that it's not."

The lieutenant gave me long look. "Bravery, valor, and strong leaders are needed more than prayers."

I would have agreed with him according to my experiences. "Then that's what I shall wish for."

W e parted shortly after finishing our dinner. Walking back to the pensione, I felt I was sinking into a deep mountain lake, drowning in its cold, dark water.

James was there when I managed to make it home. A carafe of grappa was on the small table in our room.

"Just in time," he said, pouring me a glass as well as one for him.

After a drink, I told James I'd eaten dinner with Lt. Laurent.

James gulped down the rest of his drink. As he poured another glass, he said, "A risky repast. Did you find out anything of military importance?"

"The only thing he came forth with was that he feared the war would be protracted."

"Let's endeavor to prove him wrong."

We drank to that.

With the wine and grappa of that evening, and the malaise that had seemed to settle over me, I no longer felt like talking. But James pressed on.

"Did he say why he thought it would drag on?"

"Not directly so." I told him about the lieutenant's comment on bravery, valor, and strong leaders.

"He's saying his military lacks those qualities?"

"Implied that, yes. But I suppose most lieutenants in any army would say the same."

James didn't respond, instead lay back and was quiet for several moments.

I waited him out, sipping my grappa.

Finally, he said, "So, it went well then?"

"Well enough, since I was taken off-guard by the invitation in the first place. I even invited him to the next concert we will have with the Stradivari instruments, assuming I can get back in Mr. Stradivari's good graces."

"You haven't been able to see him since returning?" James asked.

The morose heaviness I felt before the dinner returned. "I must apologize. I haven't handled this very well. I shouldn't have gone to the forest with Mr. Stradivari and let him surmise we aren't French bureaucrats. But before that, there was our first encounter with Lieutenant Laurent. I sensed he had caught on to our subterfuge. Yet, I did not say anything. And that is the worst mistake of all, James. I should have told you. I should have given you the option of abandoning our mission."

James was staring at the wall, as if he could see through it. After a moment of silence, he turned to me. His eyes were heavy-lidded, dull with drink, or lack of sleep, yet he also looked curious.

Going on, I said, "It only takes a tiny error in judgement, a mere slip of the tongue, a bare moment of distraction for the course of events to go horribly wrong."

I waited for a response.

"True," James said under his breath. "But——"

"My cousin, the son of my mother's youngest sister, my aunt Vivienne, was a fifer[2] in one of our regiments. Only sixteen, too young to be a soldier, he desperately wanted to fight. As with all

---

[2] The high-pitched tone of the flute could be heard over the loud but dull sounds of a battle. *PW*

members of our family, he, Franz, received musical training from a young age. He demonstrated a precocious talent for woodwinds, even whittling a simple flute from a piece of elder wood. More than once I thought about throwing it in a fire, as he played it constantly.

"His mother questioned me at length about what it meant to be a fifer. I explained they learned a set of commands and were expected to play them with absolute correctness and at sufficient volume. She listened intently, asking me to explain further. Finally, she said that Franz had made up his mind, and there was nothing she could do to convince otherwise. She asked only that I would take care of him. I promised her I would."

After a swallow of grappa, I told the rest of the story quickly, not so much that I wanted to get it over with, but that I didn't want to dwell on any details. But if I had it might have taken hours swollen with minutia because I remember every moment.

My regiment had been mired in a protracted and desultory battle for a scrap of land surrounding a rise of land, not much more than a molehill but nonetheless strategic in its own way. The other officers and I had been unable to find a weakness in the French forces. No weakness and no pattern to their strategies. They might attack at the darkest of night during a new moon, or at the brightest sun at its noontime peak. They might feint toward our left flank then pivot to a full attack on our right. Or vice versa. Or probe then retreat. They might appear to be in full retreat, only to turn and attack.

The French also deflected our attempts at surprise when we went on the offensive. They were so successful, I wondered if they knew our minds. A few officers, growing restless and frustrated, suspected a spy in our midst. Not believing this to be true, I knew we did need to bring the siege to an end, if not to end the loss of men and supplies, but to improve morale.

As I thought of what the French could be doing next, I realized that it wasn't as if they had no leader. Or too many leaders. It finally occurred to me that their general was allowing each of the officers to devise and lead a plan. I looked at the previous strategies and put them in categories. Each of the categories could be those of one of the officers. With that in mind, I could determine a pattern, which would allow me to predict which officer would be in command of the next plan. I presented my case to the other officers, which was met with much skepticism, but in the end, no one had anything better to propose.

The predicted attack would come in three waves in a wedge, and I drew up the counterattack. To protect my cousin, I positioned his unit in what I deemed to be the safer position. The more I went over the plan, the more confident I became.

Two days later at dawn, the attack began. At first it appeared to be exactly as predicted. The fifers signaled the beginning of our counterattack, which also seemed to go perfectly.

Then there was a collapse of the wedge, overloading one side of our defenses. I had erred. Quickly, I sent orders for the retreat of that side and for reinforcements to come to their aid. The fifers trilled out the commands.

Except for Franz.

I had to take pause here, before I could say, "My error cost him his life."

James was silent for several moments before saying, "I'm sorry about your cousin, but such is the fate of war."

"Fate or not, it was my error."[3]

Again, James went silent, but this time, he remained so.

I thought of the last time I saw Franz's hand-carved flute, resting on the hearth at his mother's home.

_____

[3] To fully understand life's arc, one should accept and embrace flaws and gifts. _LS_

chapter 23

In the morning, the old man at the pensione delivered a message from Il Diavolo. He handed it to me solemnly, as if it were a missive of death. I thanked him and he shuffled off.

The note said I could meet Caterina Stradivari that evening at the violinist's home. He was going to be out all evening, so it would just be Caterina and me. The appointment was after sunset, but depended on when Caterina could get away.

The note immediately lightened my mood.

James, getting dressed, asked what was in the note. I told him the hoped-for meeting was arranged, adding that it would lead toward a reconciliation with Mr. Stradivari.

"Are you sure you can trust him?" James asked.

"I do," I answered quickly. "If he was going to inform the French about us, he would have done so by now. And we would be in prison. Maybe already hung."

"Unless they are finding out more about us. Giving us more rope to hang ourselves."

"I hadn't wished to think that but perhaps it's true."

"Whatever your plan may be," James said, "we need to be gone from here soon with the information we have."

He was right. "Although it would be good to have one more piece."

"The exact date of an offensive?"

I nodded.

"How should we get that?"

"I don't know yet."

After a day of staying close to the pensione, venturing out only to verify the change of the guard and patrol movements through the gates, I made my way to Il Diavolo's home. Caterina opened the door when I knocked. She smiled, pleased to see me, at least I felt so.

We went into the sitting room, where there was a plate of delicious-looking refreshments, along with a bottle of wine and two glasses.

"I've missed you," she said, pouring the wine into the glasses.

"I've missed you as well," I said, although it sounded formal and stiff, contrary to the warmth I was feeling, being with her in a private place. "Very much so," I added.

She smiled again at that, and we sipped the wine.

"How have you been?" she asked me, just as I was about to ask her the same.

"Well enough, considering I seem to have fallen out of favor with your father. It's entirely my fault," I hastened to add.

"He hasn't said anything about it, but I sensed something happened."

As I had told James only a few hours earlier about my lethal error, my fatal decision, what I should tell her—that is, the full truth or not—seemed like another monumental decision.

As she looked at me with expectation, an innocent yet demanding expression, I knew I could do nothing but be utterly forthcoming.

I said, "I'm afraid I didn't handle a certain situation well."

Her brows squeezed together in confusion.

"What I mean is ..." I hesitated.

Now smiling, she shook her head. "Dear Mr. Rémon, you can be honest with me. I won't do anything to disrupt your plans, whatever they may be."

My only recourse was to tell her the truth. "To begin with, I can't tell you, or your father, the whole truth of my presence in Cremona. Not only because I'm on a secret mission, but also to keep any innocent residents of Cremona, especially those helping me, free from danger being in my association. This is even more critically important for you and your family who have been so generous to me."

Caterina was nodding slightly as I spoke, urging me on I felt, showing me she knew what I was saying was being understood. Perhaps she meant that my words were unnecessary, already known to her.

I went on, "My real name is Phillipe Wolf. I am a captain in the Austrian military. Jacques is Captain James Brookfield, with the English military. We're here to gather information on the French forces."

Caterina slowly stopped nodding, although neither did she look surprised by my admission. Then there was a foreshadowing of something other than surprise.

Disappointment?

That made me quickly add, "But it's not the only reason we are here. I'm truly here to purchase instruments, most importantly a wondrous violin, which will elevate the music I'm composing."

I paused to judge if the second half of my admission was erasing her disappointment, if that's what I perceived. Fortunately, her expression did lighten.

Curious what her father might have told her about me and our trip to the forest, I asked, "Is this what your father told you? Did he say something about why I haven't been seen at the workshop?"

"Actually, he hasn't said anything at all. Well, no words. When someone asks about you, he only shakes his head."

She rolled her eyes at the thought.

"So," she went on, "imagine my surprise, and pleasure, when I heard from Mr. Diavolo that you wanted to meet with me."

"Your father doesn't know?"

"No. I gathered from the tone of your message it wouldn't be wise to tell him."

I doubted if he would have let her meet me.

"But why did you want to meet with me?" she asked. "Other than to confess your real identity and mission?"

"As you can deduce, I'd like to continue working with your father. That part of my reason for being in Cremona remains firm. My wish is that you'd be able to help me return to his good graces."

She sipped from her wine glass. "You are supposing that I have sway with my father."

I laughed a little. "Admittedly, I'm supposing that. I believe he said that you did."

Her eyes flashed. "Perhaps you don't know my father, as he doesn't know about you."

I apologized, and told her that she was correct.

"However," she added, as her gaze softened, "my father has spoken highly of you. He described you as 'intriguing,' which I have never heard him bequeath on any other person. I believe he already knew you were more than you said, so I don't think his silence is because he's afraid of your other mission. It's that you didn't tell him about it from the first time you met."

I didn't think I could have told him then, but now see that it would have been the right thing to do.

With an honest and contrite bow, I said, "I apologize to you and your father. I should have been forthcoming from the beginning. What can I do to rectify my mistake?"

"Now that you've apologized to me, I'll talk to my father to see if he will hear your apology in person."

"I deeply appreciate that."

She smiled broadly now. "Good. Let's finish our wine and food, then enjoy the time alone."

It was only the next day when James and I arrived at the Stradivari home in the early evening. Caterina had been successful talking with her father and invited us to join the family for dinner.

The house was again full of wonderful smells. Mrs. Stradivari greeted us and showed us to the sitting room where Caterina and Omobono were waiting. Mr. Stradivari wasn't there; Mrs. Stradivari said he was still in the workshop. Caterina served us wine and food. I felt more tranquil than I had in several weeks.

After some conversation, Omobono escorted us into the workshop. Mr. Stradivari and Francesco greeted us. Spread out on worktables were several unfinished instruments—violins, violas, violoncellos. There were also many pieces of instruments in various stages, as well as a stack of wood blocks. At one end of a table, a few drawings were spread out, some were Dr. Newton's.

Without any other words from any of us, Mr. Stradivari said, "As you can see, we have taken a great deal of time to provide you with some options I believe you'll find to your satisfaction. First, we did study your composition to understand your musical ideas. For example, here," he pointed to a section of the score of my composition where the notes stretched from a high C to a low C, and a section that started fast and then slowed. "We need to have a very flexible body to cover the differences, and in particular, the bass bar must be perfectly sized and placed."

He gestured to Francesco, who picked one of the violins and played a few notes at the lower end.

"Similar to this," said Mr. Stradivari, "but with an even greater foundation. We will also have to increase the dimensions to accommodate the sound you desire. Exactly how much, I can't say at this point as it depends on the wood, as I'm wont to say."

He picked up one of the diagrams of the belly of a violin. Several lines, dimensions, and notes had been drawn. I surmised it illustrated the points he was trying to make. I tried to think what Dr.

Newton would make of it, likely he would have tried to understand the differences.

Mr. Stradivari paused then asked me, "My apologies for speaking so fast. Are you able to follow?"

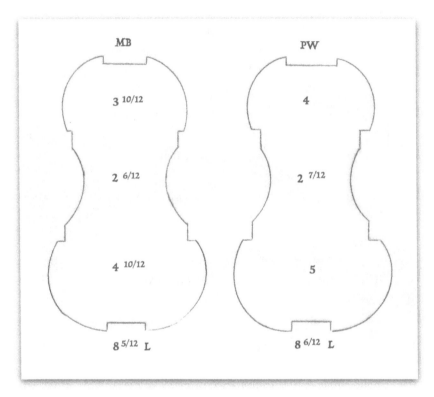

"Yes, I do understand. I appreciate the effort you've taken to accommodate this composition of mine. May I have copies of these drawings to take with me?"

"To show your friend?" he asked.

"Mostly for me, but yes, I'll show him."

Mr. Stradivari said, "You may show them to him, but he'll undoubtedly have something to say about my methodology. I want you to know, that on the whole I disagree with his approach to creating a violin. Particularly one with the most superior sound, and one that matches your desires. If there is one thing that your friend can't do is touch what is beyond science and mathematics, that which is in your heart driving you to create this beautiful expression of emotion."

I couldn't disagree with him. His words resonated deep into my being, and I barely heard the rest of his explanation of how he would create the other instruments.

At this moment, he asked everyone to leave the workshop, except for me. "We'll join you for dinner soon," he called out.

Alone, he pulled over a stool next to his at the workbench.

We discussed the financial arrangements for the violin. The fee was high, even more than Mr. Penbrook's price for the violin I purchased from him. But then I had no room in which to bargain. I also agreed to put a down payment of half the agreed cost.

"Excellent," he said.

"I do ask that you not start on the prime violin until I can show my friend your drawings and discuss with him what I have learned from you."

Mr. Stradivari thought about my request for a moment, then said, "It seems unnecessary, but if that's what you wish. We can finish the others."

"Yes, that's fine. Thank you for that accommodation. One other request, if agreeable."

"I shall hear what you ask."

"I would like to hold another concert. I've been working with Il Diavolo on my composition and would be grateful to hear it in a proper concert hall with superior musicians, of course, playing your instruments. Il Diavolo will select some of his works and perhaps other composers. I would also like you to invite some townspeople, if you feel that's a good idea."

"It's a fine idea. I shall be happy to arrange it."

I thanked him, then said, "Before I ask one more thing, I must first apologize for not telling you from the start of my other mission in Cremona. I don't know if Caterina told you what I confessed to her, but I'll tell you anything you wish to know."

Mr. Stradivari nodded. "I care little about your other mission. My only desire is to provide you the best instruments, especially a violin. However, a French officer named Laurent visited us, and asked about your dealings with me. I assumed he's suspicious of you. I told him of our professional dealings, as well as my previous dealings with your royal musician's office. He seemed satisfied, at least for now."

I was relieved. "Thank you for taking care of his visit so perfectly. I'll endeavor to keep my two missions separate. But I do wish to ask if we could invite him and other French officers to the concert."

Mr. Stradivari looked confused but said, "I don't want to know why. Let's join the others."

The concert was arranged and during the days leading up to it, I worked with Il Diavolo on the music and the practice sessions with the musicians. I was able to spend some time with Mr. Stradivari going over his plans for the instruments, especially the prime violin. He did not offer any particularly insightful comments on his reasoning for his choices in the many elements going into his creations. I could hear Dr. Newton's voice in my head: "Ask him why he wants to reduce the length of the body. Better yet, ask him for his reasoning, and how he applies it when creating an instrument. Do not accept an answer that has anything to do with his empathy with the musician, or the soul of the wood, or anything else not directly observable. When he does speak in more rational terms be precise in recording what he says."[1]

But I didn't follow Dr. Newton's imagined orders. I felt that Mr. Stradivari had had his fill of those questions.

---

[1] Exactly how Sir Isaac Newton would have phrased these statements as imagined by Captain Wolf makes an interesting epistemic inquiry. Certainly, Newton would have admonished Wolf and likely more severely than Wolf imagined. *TS*

While I was playing my role as composer and purchaser of fine musical instruments, James gathered as much intelligence on the French forces as he could. In the evenings, we shared information, and I recorded it on the musical score. We were both becoming anxious in overstaying our visit, especially making a fatal mistake.

The night of the concert came, and it was in our fortune that the fog made its presence early and strongly. I thought of that night when Caterina and I watched it crawl through the city and up the walls of her home, chasing us into her room.

As the concert began and sitting next to Caterina, I realized I'd fully lost the stabbing of jealousy of seeing Catherine kissing Mr. Montagu. As I had more than a few times, I wished Catherine were there to hear the concert, especially the newest version of the concerto. Il Diavolo had improved it, so much so, although I still felt it lacking in a way that I couldn't articulate.

The hall was nearly full. Unlike the concert at the Montagu home, the attendees, even the French officers, appeared to be listening to the music, some intently so. That livened my spirits even further.

We lingered in the hall afterwards, all but James, who left halfway through the concert. I gratefully received the praise of the attendees who were gracious enough to seek me out. Even Lt. Laurent gave me a quick nod of his head.

When I returned to the pensione much later, James wasn't there. I waited for him to return, but after a long while, I went to search for him. I got as close to the headquarters of the French forces as I could, but it was well-guarded. I managed to avoid the night patrols on my way back to the pensione.

My search had been in vain; James was in our room.

"There you are," I said. "Where have you been?"

He groaned.

He shrugged when I asked him if he were all right. He held up a hand that was wrapped in a dirty cloth, blood seeping from its edges.

Opus 5

calculus of Infinitesimals

chapter 24

U pon returning to London, and before I could call on Catherine or her uncle, I was summoned to meet with Austrian Consul Lupine. I arrived at his home punctually, barely having time to freshen up from the last leg of our journey. The consul was dressed as usual in a perfectly tailored suit. Also as usual, a neatly efficient fire had been laid in the hearth. After only a word or two of greeting, he got to the point.

"Did your mission to Italy go well?"

In the end, yes, it was successful, simply because James and I left Cremona with our lives and secret identities intact. For a second prize, we brought with us vital information about the French forces, all coded onto sheets of music. For a third prize, I was able to repair my relationship with Antonio Stradivari, with the help of Caterina. And a final prize—James' injury was not debilitating.

While James related his tale, I cleaned and dressed the wound, which luckily hadn't caused major damage. During the concert, James used the back entry into the military headquarters. The concert invitations worked to keep many of the officers away. James slipped in the main officers' room where he quickly set out to find plans, maps, documents, anything that would spell out the specific terms—forces, attack points, timing. He'd only been able to search for a few minutes, finding very little except for the log of one of the officers, much of which he committed to memory, when he heard voices coming down the corridor. He quickly hid behind the thick curtains in a far corner.

Two officers came in and sat at a table. They poured from a bottle into glasses. As much as James could hear and understand, their conversation started with usual complaints: unappealing assignments, the incompetency of superiors, the dislike of the Irish contingent.

James, feeling his legs go numb from standing awkwardly still, was worried he wouldn't be able to hide much longer. He tried to imagine of an escape route—perhaps the officers were inebriated and wouldn't notice him crawling along the floor to the window that opened onto the narrow ledge leading to the larger, and hopefully empty, meeting room. He peered carefully around the edge of the curtain. Unfortunately, he was in the line of sight of one of the officers. Fortunately, the officer's head drooped with his eyes half closed. The other officer talked on blithely, despite his fellow officer's sleepiness.

Just before James' knees buckled, the officer folded his arms in front of him on the table and let his head fall into the cradle. The other officer, with his back to James, rambled on for a moment or two, before clasping his hands behind his head and leaned back in his chair and within a few breaths started snoring.

At last James could breathe, and he slid down the wall into a squat. He got to his knees, lowered himself onto his stomach, until he could slither from desk to desk. Tantalizingly close to the door, James was about to make a bolt toward it, when the snoring officer woke up with a snort.

Instead of going back to sleep, the officer started talking, again rambling on about a trivial matter. The sleeping officer didn't respond or contribute, so James assumed he was still asleep. James remained cramped under the desk until the officer went quiet.

James resumed his escape, this time making it to the door, where he exited quietly. Out of the office he began to retrace his route inside, only to find a guard posted at the end of the next hallway. He had no choice but to backtrack. He ducked into the large meeting hall. Fortunately, it was empty. After taking a few breaths, he crawled out onto the window ledge. In the dark, he carefully made his way to the back of the building. There he climbed down the drainage conduit.

At the bottom, a startled figure came out of the shadows with long knife drawn. James lunged away, but the man slashed and caught James in the forearm and hand before running away. He wasn't a soldier, rather he was a local resident trying to pilfer from the storeroom.

I answered Mr. Lupine's question, "I consider it successful. We gathered several important pieces of information, which I passed along to the command in Vienna. The French have been stymied in northern Lombardy, but are planning an offensive push from Cremona."

"Then time is of the essence for us to have the English as allies."

I knew that having the English involved in the war at this early stage would most likely shorten the conflict, at least turn the tide in our favor. The alliance could divert French forces away from Italy, and demoralize them further.

"Agreed," I answered.

Mr. Lupine stared at me, perhaps waiting for me to elaborate. When I failed to do so, he rose, poked at the fire, and poured us a drink. He brought mine over to me, which I accepted gladly and immediately took a sip.

"Will you be to see Montagu soon?" he asked.

"I don't know," I answered in all honesty.

After a sip of his drink, he voiced what I knew he was going to say. "Montagu is still one of the key persons in our efforts to ally with England. He remains what seems to be a foe in the effort to have England enter the war, or at best, he is indifferent to joining us as an ally. What would be valuable to us," he said, looking me directly in the eye, "is to know exactly where he stands. If he's against joining, we need to know his reasons and how he might be swayed.

"Keep in mind," he continued, "what he says in public, might not be what he says behind closed doors. My personal belief is that his support depends on how much he can personally benefit."

"Benefit how?" I asked.

"Precisely what we need to know. The benefits could be financial. He could be putting in place ways for him to funnel war funds into his pockets. It could be political power, which we know is critical to Montagu's position.[1] Or, maybe it's something more personal."

Mr. Lupine stopped here and looked at me again. I didn't know what he meant by the look, not exactly. But if he was implying that Mr. Montagu's stance on the war was to spite me personally, I was taken aback. Surely, whatever personal feelings he might have against me wouldn't affect his stance on declaring war.

"Personal in what way?" I asked.

He got up again and poked at the fire. A shower of sparks disappeared up the chimney. "I wouldn't be presumptuous to say something I don't know for true. But it seems to me the English will go to the ends of the earth to satisfy even the most trivial grudge."

Several more days passed before I was able to meet with Catherine. James and I were obligated to spend countless hours in meetings with the English military—field commanders, intelligence officers, generals. Catherine had obligations as well, I heard through James through Rose, as Mr. Montagu kept his household busy entertaining guests.

James and I arrived at Rose's home, where she and Catherine were waiting for us. We had only a few minutes to get reacquainted before the four of us took a carriage to a music hall for a presentation of the work of the German composer Johann Pachelbel. The selected pieces were not only his harpsichord and organ music but also his

---

[1] Montagu's history of being in and out of favor is described well by John Macky: "But as all courtiers, who rise too quick, as he did, are envied, so his great Favour with the King, and powerful Interest in the House, raised a great Party against him, which he strengthened, by seeming to despise them." *TS*

concertos. The concert was excellent, but the joy for me was sitting next to Catherine.

At dinner afterwards at Rose's home, we discussed the music, especially the Canon in D. Catherine thought the contrapuntal elements would have sounded better at a slightly slower tempo, and when she gave a little demonstration, I agreed with her change, which added a greater depth of emotion. How the instruments entered in sequence was more dramatic, for instance.

When Catherine and I found ourselves conversing just the two of us, I asked how she had been faring since I last saw her.

"I wish I could tell you of adventure after adventure, but there have been few of those. Well, none. I've discharged my duties as they've come up. There's been some music, theater, and reading, which are always good for the soul, but those aren't adventures."

"I believe you have many adventures. You wouldn't let life be otherwise."

She gave me a smile of appreciation.

"How's your uncle?" I asked.

"Now, he has many adventures. Every day, I'd venture. I do worry about him, though. For a man of such great intelligence, he can find himself with trouble."

"Is there anything I can help him with?"

With a smile, she said, "Probably, although I was only speaking of his ways with affection."

"I've yet to talk with him since we've been back, but need to make time for him, especially concerning the counterfeiting ring."

"He hasn't mentioned it to me lately, but I don't believe it has been resolved. He would have to be the one to tell you."

Catherine listened intently as I talked about the plan. When I finished, she complimented me and expressed her gratitude for helping her uncle. "I'll tell him tomorrow you've returned. I'm sure he will be pleased to see you again, for that matter as well as the other—

the violin. I assume you were able to make progress on that while you were in Italy? So, now it's your turn; what adventures did you have?"

There was much to tell, as well as much not to tell. "I thought of you many times when I wished you were sharing the moment with me."

I told her a few—the discussions with Mr. Stradivari about his methods and beliefs, working with Il Diavolo on the concerto, the trip to the forest, the concert.

Catherine said wistfully, "To have been there … You'll have to tell me more."

"We'll need many times together for me to tell you them all."

"Yes, lovely. Did you agree with Mr. Stradivari on how the superior violin is to be constructed?"

"I'd like to believe that to be the case. Mr. Stradivari enlightened me more on his ideas on materials and crafting an instrument, for instance, his selection of individual trees, treating them as if they were his children. And there's his attention to the most minute aspect of his craft. I also believe he has learned more about what we are aiming for in the music and the violin. I'm curious what your uncle will make of what I learned."

"I'm curious as well," Catherine said. "And I can't wait to hear the progress on your concerto. What about your other mission? Was it as successful?"

"We shall see."

After a pause, she asked me in a low voice, "I know you can't tell me much of it but I hope you didn't encounter undue violence this time."

"Indeed, no," I said, not mentioning James' injury which left him with a scar. "We used our heads this time."

Catherine laughed.

When James and Rose rejoined us, we indulged in the bottle of fine brandy on which James and I splurged. Maybe it was the brandy, or the wonderful company, soon we were chatting about anything, and laughing about all of it. We soon found ourselves dancing, to what music, I didn't know—whatever was in our heads. When I happened to look around, over Catherine's shoulder and filtered through her hair, I saw James and Rose embracing more than dancing.

I closed my eyes and held Catherine closer, and she responded with a sigh of pleasure.

After a few moments, I opened my eyes and saw that James and Rose had disappeared—they had become very good at vanishing. Alone, I kissed Catherine and slid my hand down her back.

She pulled away and took my hand and led me to the sofa. We sat close together, turned toward each other and kissed.

Again, Catherine pulled away. She said, "I find my passion for you difficult to resist."

"You shouldn't have to resist, should you?" I said, hopefully more than insistently.

"But there must be some resistance on my part. If there is none from you then I must double mine."

The seriousness of her tone reduced the effect of the brandy. When I'd thought about it for a few moments, I said, "I understand. I'm destined to leave you again, likely to go to war."

She closed her eyes for a moment. When she opened them, she said, "I'm not so shallow to believe in a rigid standard of behavior, nor in some wholly defined, predestined future. Life isn't that simple. No, it's full of rich mysteries, so many that I never see falling into the shallows."

The full meaning of what she said escaped me. Whether my lack of understanding was because of the brandy, or my lack of intellect, or lack of emotional empathy, but I knew I must find out the meaning of what she said, or I would be wasting my life.

chapter 25

I arrived at Dr. Newton's home in response to the invitation Catherine had arranged. With me, I carried the notes on Mr. Stradivari's proposed violin, including the annotated drawings the luthier drew in response to Dr. Newton's science and mathematics of sound and stringed instruments.

The two of us had dinner together. I was pleasantly surprised by this social side of Dr. Newton, which I hadn't yet experienced to an intimate degree. I assumed the dinner together was because of my assistance with the counterfeiters, or less likely due to his respect for my musical quest. More probably, Catherine had spoken in my favor, convincing him an evening with me was worth his time. Whatever the reason, he seemed accepting of my presence more than any previous time.

During the soup course, I asked Dr. Newton about the status of the counterfeiting ring.

"Unfortunately, they continue unabated with their crimes."

"James and I could renew our undercover roles."

Dr. Newton stared into his soup. "Your further assistance would be of value. If you have the time to do so."

"I'll make time. I shall ask James if he's also willing, though I'm certain he will be."

"I'll accept your decisions," he said then sipped a spoonful.

During the main course, Dr. Newton said, "I hear you presented a formidable presence at the Kit-Cat Club."

I couldn't imagine why he was bringing this up now, as it occurred several months ago. I said, "I don't know if that's an accurate description but thank you."

"Most wilt under the pressure of that rabble-rousing group. Anything above utter failure should be considered a success."

I didn't know what to make of the compliment, if that's what it was. "Thank you, again," I said. "You must have heard this from Mr. Montagu?"

"Lord Halifax … yes, indirectly from my niece. The war, and our inevitable involvement at this point, can only further drag down our nation."

It was the first time I heard him express any political opinion.

I said, "As well as Austria's. It only would be worse if the French can consolidate their power."

Dr. Newton thought for several moments. "That's the prevailing theory. Unfortunately, it doesn't provide testable hypotheses. We can't create an experiment to verify their truth or falsity. We can predict, based on previous observations, a possible course of what would occur given one outcome or another. But we can't create alternative worlds where both situations can run their course."

"Would it never be possible?"

My host's mood changed from dark to light. "I'll allow that question," he said. "But the universe is set. The mechanics of the natural world are fundamentally occurring as created and is unchangeable. There's no power that could create a similar world and change one or more fundamental variables or laws of nature."

"Which only God could change?"

"God would have no need to create such an experiment. Although I suppose we might already be in one now."

"Then we're fundamentally only doing what we are predisposed to do?"

Dr. Newton thought, then nodded. "That could be largely the case."

The turn in the conversation brought me back to what Catherine had said the first night we met, about the course of one life, its unrelenting nature, and its unfathomably inevitable end.

As if hearing my thoughts, Dr. Newton said, "We must finish our dinner so we can go to the workshop."

I did as commanded.

In Dr. Newton's workshop, I showed him the documents from Mr. Stradivari. He immediately focused on the notes refuting or questioning his mathematics concerning the pressure waves inside the body of a violin.

"Of course not!" he exclaimed loudly, as if addressing Mr. Stradivari across the continent. "I wasn't neglecting the shape of the belly or back. He doesn't understand at all what I was describing. The 'plank of wood' he is throwing back at me is *not* what I proposed at all."

He fumed under his breath while he examined the documents.

I regretted showing him Mr. Stradivari's comments. I should have given him my understanding of them.

"I think what he meant—"

"He doesn't understand that my diagram refers to a small section of the wood, nor does he understand my calculations are based on the summation of infinitesimals across all of the surface."

Dr. Newton continued his complicated explanations in considerably more detail and with increasing vigor, at the heart of which were his mathematics that determine the shape or area of a curved surface. In this way, I could see how Mr. Stradivari had misunderstood Dr. Newton's theory, or rather my interpretation of it.

When there was a pause, I said, "I apologize. It's most assuredly my fault in not adequately explaining your thoughts of how the physical properties of a violin affect the quality of the sound. It was clearly my lack of preparation that caused the confusion."

My apology seemed to calm him. He proceeded to give me a lecture on his calculation of infinitesimals[1] including sketching out the main points on a piece of paper. I could understand what he was saying, at least to a point, yet I was still having trouble associating the mathematics with the design of a violin.

---

[1] What we refer to now as calculus. *TS*

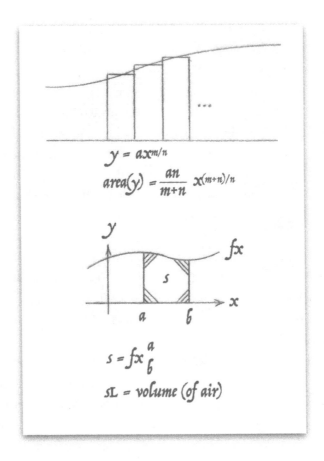

$$y = ax^{m/n}$$

$$area(y) = \frac{an}{m+n}\, x^{(m+n)/n}$$

$$s = fx\,{}^{a}_{b}$$

$$sL = volume\ (of\ air)$$

Dr. Newton didn't pause to see if I was grasping his lecture. He was already ahead of me, showing me how the infinitesimal change in curvature amplified the vibrations or created new kinds of vibrations[2] that would be unique to the way the violin was constructed. These vibrations occur as waves caused by pressure variation, which work together or against one another.

---

[2] These types of waves or vibrations are measured as *frequencies. TS*

"For example," Dr. Newton said, gathering up a length of thick twine. "Hold one end of this."

I did as he told me, and with the other end, he moved across the room. "Now hold the twine still," he said and then gave his end a quick up-and-down flick.

A clearly defined, sinuous wave traveled through the twine across the room to me, then back to him, and repeated with smaller heights two or three times. He then gave the twine another flick, but when the wave reached my end, he gave another flick. When the two sets of waves met in the middle, they stopped. He flicked again, but this time flicked a second time when the waves had returned to his end. The height increased and I could feel the increased pressure on my end.

"This time," he said, "you also create the waves."

We both began to flick our wrists and there was chaotic move-ment, sometimes strong, sometimes weak. It was a telling display. I suddenly recalled what Mr. Stradivari had told me about the thick-ness of violin plates.

As he put away the twine, I said tentatively, "The wood must be carved and polished to a very specific thickness, differing depending on the location along the surface. Thinner is better, but not too thin as the wood needs certain strength to handle the forces. I suppose it corresponds to your principle of equal and opposite forces."

"Correct," he said, relieving me of some anxiety. "Correct to a point. Actually, the more rigid the wood, the more pressure it takes. But a balance must also be maintained, as the twine showed when we were both inducing waves. Without the correct reactions, the tone created by the vibrations aren't in harmony."

I believe I understood, and that emboldened me to say, "Excuse me but I must ask, how does one take this knowledge and apply it to the precise construction of the violin? Particularly in the case of the real wood being used, which can vary considerably? Mr. Stradivari contends it's only through understanding the wood to an intimate degree can a superior violin be created."

Dr. Newton grimaced, no doubt exasperated. Trying to join the thoughts of the two great men was like the twine jumping madly when both of us were flicking it up and down.

In the end, he didn't respond; instead, he turned from me and began to write on a piece of paper. I didn't interrupt his writing, not wanting to press him, even though I had more to tell him about my discussions with Mr. Stradivari. During those minutes, my thoughts began racing, tripping over one another. At one point, I believed I was grasping Dr. Newton's arguments, then suddenly my confidence evaporated and I felt lost, as if I knew nothing, and could never know anything.

chapter 26

James and I left the Royal Mint just as the sun was setting. We each carried a small bag of counterfeit coins personally prepared by Dr. Newton. The coins were precisely assayed, which would allow them to be identified as to origin, which in turn would allow them to be traced with greater accuracy than false coins with a random mix of metals. Dr. Newton had only a brief amount of time to explain this to me, so I hope I've relayed it accurately.

With our bait, we went to the Kilwraith Tavern. We scavenged a table in the corner so we could watch the patrons and watch for Mr. Button and Mr. Ague. A few nights ago, we had left word with the barkeep that we would want to see the two men about our arrangement—assuming they were still working for Mr. Percy. I was sure that they would have received the message by now, so all we had to do was wait.

"Do you suppose they've laid a trap for us?" James asked.

"I don't believe they would. We have much that they desire, at least their employer does. No, they want all of our coin, not just the little bit we carry."

"But I do believe it was their gang of ruffians who attacked us before we left for Cremona."

I wasn't sure if that were true, but I had no better thought on who had initiated the attack. "Perhaps the ruffians are here now," I suggested. "Waiting to pounce on us again."

With his ale raised in front of his face, James let his gaze survey the patrons, all rowdy and gnarled with drink and rough work. I let my gaze do the same.

"Do you see anyone resembling the attackers?" I asked him.

James took a drink, then held the mug in front of his mouth while he spoke. "The one leaning against the corner of the bar, wearing the three-corner hat," he said quietly, then added, "Perhaps so."

I turned my head slowly as if working out a kink. The man was hoisting his ale. When he set down the mug, I did see why James thought he resembled one of them. But I couldn't be certain.

"Perhaps so," I agreed. "It would make sense that Mr. Ague and Mr. Button would have a gang at their back."

We waited, talking about only mundane matters in case someone's ears picked us out for being other than one of them.

Finally, about halfway through another ale, Mr. Ague and Mr. Button arrived. The two walked past the ruffian at the bar, but they didn't exchange words, nor even a sideways glance. Still, James was right, he seemed to be keeping an eye on us, even if only a droopy-lidded eye.

The two men found us and came over to our table. Mr. Button said as he sat down, "I was beginning to think we'd never see your faces again."

James answered, "It takes time to forge good coin, not like your bits of rubbish."

Mr. Ague snarled. His thin red hair swished around as he shook his head.

After a surprising chuckle, Mr. Button said, "You shouldn't anger my colleague. It affects his poor constitution to no end. Our coin isn't to be disparaged, no matter what you say. It did the job it was intended to, and all of us were doing fine. Until you came along."

James said, "Your 'fine' was not fine enough. You're fortunate that we are willing to work with you at all."

Mr. Button again chuckled. "Coin is coin. It's the way it's distributed."

Mr. Ague, recovered from his paroxysm, said, "And that's why you need us."

James said, "And we're bringing you an even bigger web of distribution along with the superior coin."

Mr. Button raised his hands mockingly. "We appreciate you gentlemen deigning us your presence."

Mr. Ague laughed.

I was surprised the man could appreciate sarcasm. "Let's get down to business."

I opened my jacket a little to reveal my bag of coins. The two leaned toward the bag in anticipation. I slipped two fingers into the bag, grabbed a coin, pulled it out, and slid it causally across the table.

Mr. Ague picked it up and studied it, front and back. Seemingly satisfied, he handed it to Mr. Button, who repeated his colleague's inspection.

James said, "We did the roughing ourselves this time. And we did it correctly."

The two said nothing.

I said, "I hear no objections. Shall we move outside so we can give you two bags of sample coins?"

Without a word, they got up. James and I did as well. We then followed them out to the back of the tavern and down to the barrel yard house. I resisted the urge to turn around and see if the ruffian in the three-corner hat was following us. Or anyone for that matter.

In the yard house, empty except for the broken barrels awaiting repair, Mr. Button and Mr. Ague, waited with their arms crossed. James and I took out our bags and handed one to each. They busied themselves in the dim light checking the coins. After their thorough inspection, Mr. Button exhaled a grunt of approval, and said, "We shall take this back to our governor for his approval. When can we expect the full complement you promised months ago?"

"That depends on what a full complement means."

The two men looked at each other but made no declaration. Finally, Mr. Button said, "That we shall find out."

Our business completed, there were no further words between us, and we parted company. James and I made our way out of the district, until we separated, in case we were being followed.

W hen I could escape my official duties, I was able to meet with Rose. I wanted to discuss our mission of the counterfeiters with her. I was particularly eager to learn more about how the day's takings at a brewery and the drink houses were collected and distributed.

She was happy to help, and in detail, she laid out for me the standard procedures she knew, especially who gathered the taking and made the official entries, who checked the figures at which stage, where the final balances were placed, and how profits were distributed.

She finished with this statement: "I would say that the procedures would be exactly the same, or nearly so, at other breweries."

"Thank you," I said.

"You're very welcome," she said, then added, "Are you all right? You seem very distracted. I hope you aren't preoccupied with the war or something as awful."

"There's much going on," I said. "I'm sorry to be distracted."

"I suppose it's about Catherine? I know you have a strong disposition toward her. But she may not be able to give you what you need. She's witty and smart, but there's much more under the surface. She only reveals more of herself to those whom she can trust completely. Trust, I believe, is what she values most in this world."

"I see," was all I could say. I knew that Catherine sometimes seemed to offer me her affection, and sometimes her affection seemed to be the last thing she could give me. I believed she was more than a housekeeper for Mr. Montagu. I knew that she had a deep regard and concern for her uncle, Dr. Newton as she always spoke of him with reverence and affection.

With those thoughts, I suddenly realized I was being selfish in my feelings. That realization not only made me feel horrible, but also gave me a new look toward the composition I was working on. My approach was entirely wrong.

"What is it?" Rose asked.

"I'm sorry, Rose. I don't know what to say, or rather, how to say it."

"Phillipe, you need not say anything. I'll always be available to discuss any matter."

For that, I told her I was grateful.

"As long as you continue to watch out for James," she said.

"Of course," I said honestly, hoping that I could.

I thank you again for helping my uncle with the counterfeiters," Catherine said, the next time I was able to meet with her. "I hope you aren't in any great danger."

"I'm afraid we're in constant danger," I answered with a grin. "Yes, very grave danger."

We were in the drawing room of Mr. Montagu's home. He was again at his estate in Yorkshire[1] where he attended to business every few weeks.

"Oh, my heavens," she said. "Then I'm most grateful you managed to escape with your life."

"I am as well," I said, then laughed. "No, I never felt much danger. Oddly, it was like a walk in a quiet park, certainly easy enough. Your uncle had planned it all to a precise degree. Would that he could plan all things. The world would be a better place."

"Still, I worry about him; his life hasn't always gone as he planned."

---

[1] Yorkshire County, where his estate was in Halifax. Hence his title Baron of Halifax, then the First Earl of Halifax. *PW*

"I find that difficult to believe."

She reached out languidly and drew me close for a kiss. It filled me with delight.

When she broke away, she said, "Despite your worldly ways, you really only wish the best in everyone, don't you?"

"I never would have thought that, but if you believe it true, then I must."

She gave me another sweet peck, then sat back on the settee. "My uncle did suffer a great illness of body and mind when I was younger.[2] He couldn't sleep and could barely eat without causing him distress. He became most quarrelsome with friends and foes alike. He seemed fearful they were stealing his ideas, at least taking credit for what he originated."

"My belated sympathies," I said.

She shook her head. "Now, I didn't see much of this myself, being young. But I heard my mother talking about it often. I heard and understood enough to know there was great concern for him."

"What did your mother do to help him?"

"She had little sway over him. But she tried to get him to spend less time brooding and enjoy the pleasures of life. She thought it not good for him to be caged in his study and laboratory, with all the smelly liquids and vaporous gases.[3] I've seen the room where he sequestered himself. He left drawings on the walls! He didn't eat regularly, nor eat the right foods when he did."

"How well did he respond to this treatment?"

Catherine said, "There was some improvement, but not as much as she hoped. She told me about the time he was sequestered at his home away from Cambridge during the time of the plague. He ac-

---

[2] Newton suffered what we might colloquially call a nervous breakdown during the years 1692–1693. *TS*

[3] Indeed, he may have been suffering from toxicity from his working with substances such as mercury and lead. *TS*

complished so much in his time at home, he called it his *annus mirabilis.*"[4]

Recalling what Rose told me, I said, "You care greatly about him."

"He has boundless intellect, but I worry about him reaching too far into matters that might cause him pain."

"Yet, his work at the Royal Mint does just that."

"But it also saved him, I believe. It gave him a steady life, both with income and something to occupy his mind beyond his science and mathematics."

"And Mr. Montagu—Lord Halifax—provided him with this position?"

"He secured him with the position as Warden of the Mint, prior to my uncle's current position as Master. They knew each other well at Cambridge. I understand my uncle had few friends there, not that he can't be a friend to someone, not at all. He can be very loyal and accepting. Be he also doesn't abide much in the way of falsehoods or attacks on his work or person."

"Which are difficult for any two people to avoid, friends or not."

Catherine smiled and nodded. "That Mr. Montagu would remain at my uncle's side says as much about my employer as it does about their friendship."

At this moment, I realized why she worked so loyally for Mr. Montagu.

I knew the answer to any question of her being with me would not be what I wanted to hear, and because of that the rest of the evening was blurred. I remember she was as delightful as always, as we discussed many things, especially the war and Mr. Montagu's role

---

[4] "Miracle year." Although, actually closer to two years. *TS*

outside the government's role in joining it.[5] I didn't know as much as she about the politics and economics, though I did know that the issue was extremely complicated. I also knew that my own country's safety was affected by the French incursion into Italy and that we could ill-afford to be isolated from the rest of Europe.

After a light meal, we completely changed the course of our conversation, switching to music. We exchanged views about the newer style of music, as it seemed to be leaving the current ones behind,[6] entering a new age of brilliance and fearlessness, as part of the time of reasoning that was upon us. A new age of enlightenment being led in part by her uncle who could see the world, the universe, and explain it in ways no one else had. The music was beginning to reflect that insight, ironically so considering Dr. Newton had never expressed much interest in music, at least not to me.

The talk of music led us into discussing the concerto. I told her more about working with Il Diavolo and showed her the major change he proposed of writing the main parts for two violins, rather than a violin and a viola.

"Ah!" Catherine said. "That's very intriguing. I can see why that makes such a difference."

She hummed some of it as she looked through the score. "I shall look forward to playing it with another violinist. And someday with Mr. Stradivari's violin."

"I shall look forward to that day myself," I said.

5 However, in England many argued that the acceptance of Charles II's will was preferable to a treaty that would have seen France extend its territory, including the addition of Naples and Sicily which under French control would pose a threat to England's Levantine trade. After the exertions of the Nine Years' War the Tory-dominated House of Commons was keen to prevent further conflict and restore normal commercial activity. *PW*

6 I.e., Baroque. *TS*

Then the words tumbled out of me as I described in great detail the discussions Mr. Stradivari and I had, the trip to the forest, and the designs he showed me. Catherine remained attentive all through my soliloquy, and when I paused, she encouraged me to go on. We were able to spend much of the night together as she had given the night off to the servants who remained in the house instead of accompanying Mr. Montagu. I confess to being nervous worrying that Mr. Montagu would unexpectedly cut his trip short, but soon Catherine had me forget all about him.

As I should have long ago.

chapter 27

James and I received word at the Kilwraith Tavern, via Mr. Button and Mr. Ague, who were apparently back in Mr. Percy's good graces, that Mr. Percy was ready to meet with us. We arrived at the appointed hour at Mr. Percy's office. We were escorted through his library, where I again saw Dr. Newton's *Principia*. I was tempted to ask him what he thought of it.

"Welcome, gentlemen," said Mr. Percy, standing up, fastidiously adjusting at his coat sleeves. "May I serve refreshments?"

We politely declined.

"Then to the business at hand," he said and sat down.

We did as well, and waited for him to begin.

"First," he began, "we should make clear that the coins you provide going forward will be of the same quality. You aren't going to entice me with the good coins I've inspected, and then deliver scum."

I glanced at James; we gave each other a smirk. To Mr. Percy, I said, "I can assure that what you see is exactly what we will deliver. You have my word, the word of my colleague, and the word of our producer."

Mr. Percy tapped his fingertips together.

I said, "You said, 'first,' so there must be a second condition?"

"Indeed," he said as he leaned forward. "Second point, do you guarantee the number of coins that you can deliver on a regular schedule?"

"That depends," I said. "How many do you think you can handle, and at what pace?"

Mr. Percy rocked back into his chair. "Five hundred pounds sterling per week."

James said what I was about to say, "That much? Wouldn't that cause suspicion if they were all put in circulation at the same time?"

Mr. Percy shook his head. "I have a diverse distribution network. In addition, you mentioned your brewery connection. I assume that's still on. That's my third condition, by the way. I'll agree to our arrangement if you tell me more about how the coins are handled and passed through their establishments."

Speaking in opaque terms to not give away the origin of my knowledge, I gave a brief retelling of what Rose told me, mentioning the takings handling, the accounting, payouts, and tax payments. After I finished, Mr. Percy nodded once sharply, apparently satisfied.

He then asked us, "What is your rate for the coin?"

"Forty-five,"[1] James said, loudly and firmly.

Mr. Percy grinned. "Hardly. Fifteen is the best I can do."

James and I looked at each other, then rose from our seats. "Good day, sir," I said.

Mr. Percy shook his head, not as in shutting off the deal, but as in futility. "Gentlemen, let's not be so hasty."

James and I paused our exit.

Our host spread his arms wide. "I'm feeling generous as it were."

S oon after we agreed to the terms, James secured an invitation for us to attend the next Kit-Cat club meeting. Before we went, I met with Mr. Lupine. He hadn't heard of a change in the English position on entering the war but had been unable to discover much of the lack of motivation. I told him I would do my best.

The comforting aroma of baked pies greeted us at the tavern door before we were escorted into the reception parlor, where the evening was well underway for those who had already arrived. There

---

[1] Likely 45 percent, e.g., 45 cents on the dollar in terms of US currency. Unless it was 45 shillings, where twelve pence equaled a shilling, and twenty shillings a pound. *TS*

was no formal announcement of our presence, and I didn't see Mr. Montagu, our inviting host.

James and I made casual conversation while sipping mead, which was not really to my taste but pleasant enough. I soon found myself talking with a playwright who believed he knew me from somewhere. "Backstage, perhaps, at of one of my plays?" he asked.

I told him perhaps that was the case, although I was certain I'd never seen him before.

"It must have been at my play *The Admiral's Affair*," he said, more insistently now.

I'd never heard of it, but did nod and shrug at the same time, hoping to appease him. That seemed to satisfy him, although he lingered near me, likely waiting for me to expound on how much I liked *The Admiral's Affair*. I was about to do that, making up some vague, general praise, when Mr. Montagu arrived. He strode up to the first person he encountered and engaged in a short but lively conversation before moving to the next person.

The playwright noticed my attention was diverted and stopped pressing me for praise. He turned enough to see it was Mr. Montagu. His lip curled a bit, as if in disgust it seemed to me.

I said to him, "Your play was thoughtful and entertaining."

His attention returned fully to me. "Thank you, sir."

I took a chance, based on the title, saying, "The basis for outsized self-pride is such a thin, brittle seed, is it not?"

"Indeed!" said the playwright, gazing back to Mr. Montagu, following his movements through the crowd. "You've captured the essence of the play perfectly. It does resonate throughout much of the land. And the room."

I knew we had a common enemy and, more importantly, I suddenly had a strategy for dealing with the evening.

When Mr. Montagu reached the table, we were called into the back room to take our seats. There was a frenzy of loud voices and our hosts satisfying the requests for drinks and food. When at last we were called to order, all seemed enlivened by drink and it took several shouts of "Quiet!" for the din to die.

The master of the evening, Mr. Peter Thorn, seated next to Mr. Montagu, called out, "Gentlemen, we have guests in our presence. Shall we welcome them?"

"With a poke in the eye," someone said, followed by a hoot or two.

"Excellent, but who says give a poke must take a poke," said Mr. Thorn.

"Though not in the eye," came a response.

Laughter roiled through the room.

Mr. Thorn raised his glass, "Forget the poking ... for now. Welcome to our guests."

There were three of us, and when it came to me, Mr. Montagu said, "You're back for more?"

I merely bowed.

"Cat got your tongue?" he said.

I raised a pie. "One of Kit's cats."

My attempt at humor received a few snickers.

"Then place your tongue on it and bite down," said Mr. Montagu.

A cat call rang out, along with some groans.

"I'm afraid it would ruin the flavor with my sweet tongue."

More groaning.

"Enough, enough," demanded Mr. Thorn. "I believe our Mr. Lancester has something to get off his chest?"

A heavyset man stood up.

"And a large chest it is," someone yelled.

Unperturbed, Mr. Lancester found the insult hurler and said, "Large as the rest of me ... so says your wife."

The laughter was loud and long.

"But that's a topic for another day, or night," he said, raising his hand for silence.

He launched into a soliloquy about the unification of England and Scotland, forming a new Britain.[2] There followed dissents and assents, some attributing it to the corralling of loose cattle, others questioning the timing, others saying it will be a relief to no longer fight them in battle.

That discussion flowed to another of the club members, who raised the possibility that the king[3] was ailing. Perhaps, near death.

"As much as your mind is ailing," shouted a dissenter.

For several minutes, there was a back-and-forth, and it seemed the room was split evenly on the likelihood King William would soon be gone, or that he was as robust as ever. Mr. Montagu spoke little on the matter, but he seemed on the side of an eminent passing, likely hoping it might happen soon.[4]

When he noticed I was looking at him, he stood and waited for the room to quiet. "Long live the King," he said somberly.

The others mumbled it after him.

"We cannot know the providence of God in taking our King, or not, but we must continue to persuade him not to throw our good lives away on a war we have no reason to be counted as a promulgator. But then what do I know?"

Someone shouted, "It's not what you know for we all know that it's a mere pittance." And after a pause for chuckles, he added, "We must determine where lines should be drawn."

"The lines that should be drawn?" Mr. Montagu repeated, as if in singsong to a child. "Strictly speaking, when you begin to draw lines, the war is already started."

---

2 That would be the Acts of Union in 1706 and 1707. *PW*

3 William III, who died in 1702. *PW*

4 Montagu would be more likely to rise in power with a new monarch. *TS*

That statement raised several shouted responses in affirmation, which caused Mr. Montagu to return to sitting, his arms spread out defiantly, a broad smirk on his face. He saw that I was watching him, and the smirk grew into a grin.

I returned the grin. Then with a glance at James, who gave me a sly look of humor, I stood up. "Excuse me, gentlemen." When the voices trailed off, I said, "Mr. Montagu, with all of his *wisdom* about lines, has never been at the most important line, and I don't mean the line for his dinner."

There was an explosion of laughter. I caught the eye of the playwright, who gave me an affirmative and mischievous raise of an eyebrow.

The laughter died quickly when Mr. Montagu raised his hand. "Please, gentlemen, I wish to hear more from our music man."

A titter of laughter trickled through the room.

"Thank you, Mr. Montagu," I said. There was a bit of a gasp when I did not use his official title. "If I die being known as a music man, then I shall rest in peace. You speak of lines, of borders, or power, of commerce, while I speak of battle lines. Where men kill or die crossing it. Yet we must not be fearful. For if our cause is just, then we shall conquer the line, vanquish the line, make it disappear. If you have ever taken a fresh breath of air after being shut in a closed room, or taken a draught of cold water when thirsty, then you might know only a tiny bit of the pleasure of seeing the battle line vanish."

The room was silent.

Mr. Montagu was not looking at me, instead gazing toward the opposite side of the room, as if to make me vanish.

"But," I continued, looking around the room, "if I might be so bold to ask, which lines would have to be crossed to draw you into the war, to support your allies against the French?"

Mr. Montagu spoke up before any of the others. "We shouldn't speak of these so-called lines in front of our music man, despite how he seduces you with false valor."

James spoke up at this point, coming to my aid. "There's nothing false about it. I've seen the captain in action as I've told this assemblage before. I've heard his stories of war."

Mr. Montagu now flushed a blotchy pink-and-red. He stayed in his seat while he spoke in a low grumbling voice. "Then why is the music man here and not out erasing his battle line? Is it not true that he made grievous errors that cost men their lives at one of his lines? Why does he now play at making fiddles while his so-called compatriots fight across the line? Why does he cavort with women whenever he has the chance, rather than draw his sword to fight?"

He took a deep breath, while the room remained silent. He now fully stared at me and said, "Perhaps he knows he has crossed another line, a line of the heart, which, no matter how much he battles, may never disappear."

chapter 28

I arrived at Dr. Newton's home and his housekeeper straightaway escorted me to his workshop. It was the first time I wasn't kept waiting while watching Huygens' clock. Dr. Newton had invited me to his home after we met at the Mint a few days prior. I'd been there to report on our progress with the counterfeiting ring.

Now in his workshop, with only a glance at me when I was deposited by the housekeeper, Dr. Newton said in his most direct tone, "I shall report on a few experiments I've been performing."

Spread out on his work benches were all manner of measuring devices, vials of liquids, strings and wires, bells, pieces of wood, glass scopes, and other instruments I didn't recognize. Papers filled with sketches and mathematical notations were tacked on the walls, or spread out on the limited space left on the work benches.

Immediately in front of Dr. Newton were three sections of violin eviscerated from its body. Next to the sections was a cylindrical drum lined with paper, and a metal stand on which were attached metal nibs filled with ink.

"The problem with creating sound in a violin is that the volume of air in its body is small. In order to make an adequate sound, the volume of air must get moving substantially and accurately for the ear to register the notes."

With a glance at me, seeing if I understood, which I did, but before I could acknowledge that, he said, "Wave your finger in the air."

I wasn't sure he meant by "wave" and my expression must have been dumbfounded, for he made a clucking sound to scold me.

"Like this," he said, demonstrating.

I copied the movement, like wagging my finger at a child, except more vigorously than would have been necessary to get a point across.

"What do you hear?" asked Dr. Newton.

"Hear?"

"Yes, *hear.*"

Not hearing anything, I strained to find any bit of sound. But all I perceived was the sight of my finger making its silly motion.

"You don't hear anything, do you?"

I confessed I didn't.

"Of course, you can't, there isn't enough air movement. Now put your finger next to your ear and wag it."

I'm certain I look even sillier now, but I could report that I heard a sound.

"And what is that sound?"

"Well ... I suppose it's the sound of air moving?"

"Now wag your finger faster," he commanded.

I did so. "The sound is louder."

"And?"

I listened more carefully, varying the speed of my wagging. "It changes the pitch too."

"Exactly. Your finger can't move much air by itself, but even this crude experiment demonstrates what's happening inside the violin." He waved at me to stop wagging. "Look over here."

He showed me a sheet of paper with lines drawn lengthwise. At first, they were straight, then they began to jiggle up and down. "Do you know what this is?"

I didn't at first glance, but looking at his contraption, I guessed that there was a connection. "The lines are similar to the wagging of my finger had it been attached to a pen?"

Dr. Newton gave me the briefest of smiles. "You're on the right course."

He paused. I assumed he wanted me to continue to show my ignorance. Surveying the contraption further, I deduced that the section of violin could be the "wagging finger." Looking closer, I could see a metal arm attached to the wood, at the end of which was one of the nibs.

I ventured this, "The section of violin acts like the finger when it's in play, and the nib at the end of the arm draws a line on the paper."

Dr. Newton quickly filled in the gaps of my explanation. "The drum must be rotating at a constant speed to measure the vibrations correctly. No small feat in itself, unless attached to something like a clock mechanism, which I haven't had time to do. If only Huygens were here."

He gave himself the briefest laugh then paused, likely waiting for me.

"I see," was all I could think of in response.

"Why go to all this trouble?" he asked.

Good question, I thought, mocking my own fumbling of the matter. Thinking back to the wagging finger, I said, "You're measuring the response of the violin to its movement according to time? Similar to how the faster I wagged my finger the louder and higher in pitch it became?"

Dr. Newton gave me a little nod, which I was surprised to see, then began a lecture on his experiment, the importance of which, I gathered,[1] was to precisely measure the ability of a violin, at least one section of the wood, to produce varying levels of movement caused by differences in speed of the vibrations and the amount of air in the body. He showed me what he called "preliminary calculations," lines of mathematical sentences that were as foreign as hieroglyphs.

---

[1] Much later I was able to remember and understand the lecture. I wrote this down and added explanatory notes. *PW*

The further explanation was lost, but based on the understanding Wolf mentions it has to do with what we now call a modulus of elasticity. *TS*

He concluded by explaining that his calculations showed the wood needed to be as thin as possible to move the air with enough force to produce adequate sound. His equations used his calculus of infinitesimals, which I was still struggling to understand.

I said to him when he paused, "Mr. Stradivari told me the thickness of the wood was critical to the correct sound."

"Then he must have made similar calculations."

"I can't say that he did," I answered, trying to be as careful as I could. "I can't recall seeing any experiments or mathematics. But that doesn't mean he didn't use them."

Dr. Newton looked down his nose at me. "How would he begin without them? There are too many variables to account for merely by trial and error."

Before I responded, I thought back to what Mr. Stradivari would say about going back to listening to the wood, to perceiving the wood with all senses. I knew that would not be a satisfactory response, and Dr. Newton would take me to task for not asking the luthier more probing questions. Not that Mr. Stradivari would have given me more of an answer than he did. This knowledge was his tightly-held secret.

But in an effort to keep Dr. Newton appeased, especially to keep him helping me, I said, "It's my understanding from Mr. Stradivari that he begins to know the wood's characteristics from when it's still a growing tree. When it's cut, he can tell which sections will be the best for his instruments. The wood itself is treated and then prepared for further cutting and shaping. Each step involves many decisions and his experience and skill."

Dr. Newton started to speak, then stopped, and began to think in his trance-like way. I waited for several moments, before I got up and went over to one of the other tables. On it were several jars of liquids—varnishes by the smells. They were of differing colors, some in layers, some like thick tar, others like water. Pieces of wood were coated with the varnishes as might be concocted by an alchemist.[2]

Dr. Newton launched into another lecture, speaking more rapidly than previously. He had been experimenting with different kinds of varnishes. I picked up a few bits of his results here and there—the composition and application of varnish varied immensely but did seem to provide a slight difference in how the wood became more or less stiff. He asked me if I had discovered Mr. Stradivari's ingredients.

"Unfortunately, he wasn't willing to give me a list of his ingredients, although he didn't seem that it was a great secret. I can say that the color has changed from earlier violins to his current style, from golden to red."

"Does the color make a difference in sound, or is it purely for aesthetics?"

"He never said. Nor did I ask that question."

Dr. Newton sighed in exasperation. "I'll have to consider if the color change was due to a particular ingredient that improved his varnish. I can't assume otherwise."

He suddenly picked up the samples and bolted to the door. I set after him without waiting for an order to do so. We hurried into his library, where he had previously shown me his prism experiment. This time, he had me help him set the pieces of wood into the holder, then place the contraption into the path of the sunlight streaming through the pinhole. Without a word to me, he looked at the samples from every angle as the focused light made the varnish gleam.

As suddenly as we left the workshop, we now left the library. Back in his workshop, Dr. Newton started making notes. I could only make an assumption that the light shining through the varnish caused him to observe something of interest. While many of the details of his methods escaped me, I knew that he spent considerable

---

[2] Newton was known for practicing alchemy, although his experiments were a step closer to what we call chemistry. *TS*

time investigating my obsession with the violin. But, the further he delved into the investigation, the more complicated it became. Indeed, my quest seemed more and more hopeless the longer I sat in the workshop.

Time dragged slowly, as if I were trying to pull a horse from mud. I was about to let myself out when Dr. Newton suddenly perked up from his writing. "Captain Wolf, we have an experiment to conduct."

At his work table, he showed me how to operate the revolving drum with the lined paper attached to it. There was some skill involved, as my part was to turn it at a precise speed. I struggled to satisfy Dr. Newton's required consistent revolutions per time until he said to me, "Good Lord, aren't you a composer?"

I knew instantly what he meant. When I converted his revolutions to a musical tempo of *adagietto*,[3] he was satisfied—at least he complained no further. When that was resolved, he demonstrated how to fill the pen nib with ink, and then move the tip onto the rotating paper drum when cued. That further took a few practice attempts to get right.

When satisfied, Dr. Newton placed a sample of wood onto the clamping device that held it tightly in place. That secured, he gently placed the needle-like post attached to the arm of the pen. In his other hand, he held a small mallet.

"Ready?" he said.

"Yes, ready."

"Start rotating."

I began my adagietto-paced cranking, and when he said, "Now," I moved the nib onto the drum. A thin line of ink began to flow onto the paper. Almost immediately, he tapped the wood sample, and the arm began to wiggle, forcing the nib to dance and draw a patterned flow of ink.

---

[3] Rather slow, 70 beats per minute. *PW*

When he said, "Stop," I pulled the nib away from the drum.

He removed the paper from the drum and with a studied eye pronounced, "Good."

While I replaced the paper on the drum, he adjusted the sample to a new position in the clamps—forward a measured amount. Then we repeated his experimental process with different positions and different samples. I wanted to ask him what he was measuring, what he was finding, but he was silently intent on his experiments and I didn't want to distract him. I'd seen Mr. Stradivari working in such concentration.

Through the night we repeated the procedure, until it was nearly dawn and I could no longer turn the drum even once around.

chapter 29

The coffeehouse was crowded one afternoon that was damp with drizzle and dark with clouds of speckled grey like freshly-caught prawns. My time apart from Catherine had crawled along until, finally, she was able to meet with me for a short while. I too had obligations, so in the end we could spend only two hours together.

In the private room at the back of the coffeehouse, Catherine rose to meet me, and we exchanged a quick kiss. We ordered coffee and chatted as two friends would, catching up on the days' events. Her life had been filled with her household duties—there always seemed to be a gathering to plan, or a problem in the house, or servants to manage.

"I continue to lack adventures as those in your life," she said.

I sipped my coffee that tasted so wonderful that afternoon. "Admittedly, life has had its moments since we returned."

"Well? Let me live some of it," she said, squeezing my hand. "I assume you've been working with my uncle in his capacity at the Mint? I haven't spoken with him recently, although I did hear that Rose has been assisting you."

"Indeed, she's been very helpful." I told her of our progress infiltrating the counterfeiting operation of Mr. Percy, and how we intended to ensnare him and his ring through a brewery.

"Even that little part is more exciting than my days in sum."

"I'd trade all that excitement to spend one day in total with you."

That bit of frivolity made her laugh. "Tell me more," she said. "What of the war?"

"There's much I can't say of that, but suffice to say, it's becoming more than a nuisance."

"As I hear," she said. "My employer speaks of it often."

"He does? I suppose he mentioned James' and my presence at the Kit-Cat Club meeting."

"He mentioned you attended. He said you told him to say 'hello' to me."

I couldn't recall saying that. What was his motivation for making up such a statement?

"I appreciate his passing along the message," I said, not exactly contradicting him. "There was a lively debate about the war. Your employer is leading the side against joining forces, at least publicly."

She appeared unconcerned about the last phrase I spoke, though it sounded to me like I was fishing for more of their private dialogue.

"From all he imparts to me," she said, "he doesn't wish to bring our country to war, but then he doesn't say that we'll never take up arms again."

Moving further onto the thin ice, I said, "Has he mentioned what might cause him to move the other direction?"

"He is drawn one way or another by many motivations," she said. "Be they loyalty, or financial, or patriotic sentiments."

"And in this case?"

Now she gave me a glance. To say it was suspicious would be too strong. But I could sense she had become wary. I waved away my question. "Sorry, I'm prying. Perhaps we should talk about something more enjoyable."

She smiled, likely more in relief than happiness. "How's the concerto composition coming along?"

"Sadly, it's been hindered by my lack of attention."

"What can we do to rectify that sad accounting?"

"I'd be grateful to hear some suggestions, if you've had a chance to think about it."

She sipped her coffee and said, "Shall we put another concert together? Then you shall have a date upon which you must have it finished."

"That would certainly create an urgency. But I would rather not go to the trouble again of a concert."

"I understand," she said, then quickly asked. "How far along are you now?"

"Perhaps two-thirds finished."

"Excellent. That's very far along, I would say."

But, in truth, I lacked faith in what I had composed, certainly I knew I hadn't achieved the ultimate concerto I dreamt of at the beginning. Yes, there were some flashes of inspiration, and the work with Il Diavolo helped. But lately, I'd lost the rapturous feeling I'd had when I first conceived of it. Perhaps my loss of fervor was because of Mr. Montagu's speech directed at me—crossing the line of the heart.

Catherine said, "I enjoyed hearing you talk about it before, especially the changes you made while in Italy. If I can help in any way, please, tell me. I'm anxious to play it. Perhaps you should set a date to finish it for me." There was a flash of encouragement in her eye when she made the suggestion.

With as much enthusiasm as I could muster, I said, "Yes, let's put a day on which I shall deliver. Shall we say, two weeks?"

"Good," she said happily. "I shall look forward to it."

While we finished our coffee, Catherine asked me what her uncle had been working on regarding the violin.

"Certainly, he has devoted much time to the project. For that I'm grateful beyond words. His experiments and calculations are brilliant, well beyond my ability to understand in most cases."

I described his rotating drum experiment and the ink line drawings it produced.

"Utterly fascinating!" said Catherine.

"It relates to the thickness of the wood and in turn how that relates to the movement of the air inside the violin. He created some mathematical equations from his experiments that further explained it more precisely. He is using what he calls his calculus of infinitesimals. It's been difficult, not unlike learning a new language."

"I've heard of his method of calculation," she said. "But I haven't studied it enough to help with your understanding."

"It seems very precise and powerful. Unfortunately, I don't know how I can interpret that for Mr. Stradivari."

Catherine said, "From your recounting, you're able to speak very well with Mr. Stradivari."

"We've had some good discussions, notably when we were in the forest with his special trees. Other discussions were difficult, particularly when I press them toward Dr. Newton's science and mathematics. On the whole, the luthier remains largely secretive, his explanations murky."

"That's so utterly lovely, despite his secretive nature," Catherine said in a hushed tone. "You speak so warmly of him. And of his family. They've taken you in as one of their own." She paused then said, "You can't speak the same of us when you are away."

"I can't in Italy, but I would if safe to do so," I answered. "In all sincerity, you've drawn me into your lives more than I could ever have imagined."

"In a way, perhaps. But not warmly as one of our own."

I couldn't deny that. "The circumstances are different. Perhaps one day, they may change."

She gave me a little nod while she sipped coffee. I couldn't tell if it was a nod of agreement or of sad acknowledgement that circumstances would not change. At least not favorably.

When I had time, I worked on the concerto and studied Dr. Newton's calculus of infinitesimals. On neither of which I had made much headway, so I was not unhappy when my struggles were interrupted by the news from Dr. Newton that the supply of counterfeit coins was available. The following night, James and I met him at the Royal Mint to secure the contraband.

The counterfeits came supplied in wooden crates, each of substantial weight, which James and I barely managed to lug to our carriage. All of this subterfuge took place after midnight, when the Tower's ravens were dead asleep.

Our crates loaded in the carriage, hidden with canvas and strapped down with cable rope, we took off into the night. Fetid clouds billowed from the horses' nostrils, mingling with the waterfront fog that brought me back for a moment to Cremona and its murky night air. Unhappy with the late hour, the horses refused to gallop in syncopated percussion. Instead, their hooves clip-clopped, clop-clipped on the hillocks of cobblestones.

But without other annoyances, we arrived at the barrel yard house where Mr. Ague and Mr. Button arranged to receive and pay for the counterfeits. While James kept the horses settled, and guarded the illicit treasure from scoundrels, I entered the yard house, edging along a row of barrels.

Across the yard house in one corner, lighted by a single poor torch, with tendrils of coal-black smoke swirling above the flame, the two gentlemen rested on their arses on barrels, between them a bottle of something to keep their bellies warm, and their minds as was the night air—engulfed in fog.

"Greetings," said Mr. Button, chirpy like a bird at dawn.

"A bit dark in here, no?" I said.

"More torches, more chances of sparking a fire. Barrel wood is like tinder," Mr. Ague said.

"Granted," I said. "However, will you be able to make your inspection of the coins in this light?"

Mr. Button said, "Why? Should we worry about the quality of them?"

"No smidgeon of worry should you feel. But I refuse to hear a complaint later in daylight."

Mr. Ague fumed, responding irrationally, "We'll complain when we feel like it's time to complain."

I saw there was little to discuss at his ground-level intelligence. "All right then. Shall we get on with it?"

Mr. Button said, "I say so. Bring in the coins."

"It would be expeditious if you could bend your backs to help with that task."

The two men took a swig of the liquor then followed me out.

We lugged in the crates under their smoke-pissing torch. They proceeded to open the crates. Mr. Ague took out a weighing scale that was perched on a barrel. James and I watched while they counted, inspected, and weighed our perfect, if otherwise fake, coins. They mumbled between themselves, complaining about imperfections—imagined ones in my opinion, as Dr. Newton would not let anything leave his sight with one out-of-place blemish or mark. Unless intentionally placed.

While their belly-aching grew louder, and they set aside more coins claimed to be poor, I whispered to James, "They're setting themselves up to pocket a sham cut of the coins."

James nodded and we turned back to them.

"Gentlemen!" James bellowed. "What antics are you engaged in?"

"Huh?" said Mr. Button, looking up, lusty greed clouding his eyes. "We're doing the job demanded by our employer."

"I think not," I said.

I reached over to the stack of separated coins and picked one up. I held it to the feeble light. After inspecting the front and the back, I said, "There's nothing the matter in any respect with this coin. No difference from the others. Put it with the others. Put all of the others together. Your job needs to be only to count the coins."

Standing up, with fists balled, Mr. Ague said, "You have no business telling us our business."

Well put, I thought. But emphatically untrue. "There's nothing that's more our business right now. Keep your minds on the simple task of counting."

His face as red as a boiled beet, Mr. Ague swung his fist toward my jaw, or maybe my nose, while at the same time lunging at me like a graceless drunk. It took little effort to swat him away and kick one foot out from under him. He dropped like a sack of potatoes. But surprisingly, he sprang to his feet, ready to fight on.

James stepped toward the fray, his fists ready to plunk the man. Before he had the opportunity, Mr. Button grabbed his colleague by the collar and pulled him back like a dog on a leash.

"Whoa, whoa," he said. "I'm sure we can settle this to our mutual satisfaction."

Mr. Ague gnashed his teeth, spewed spittle. "Doling out a fat lip would be just satisfaction."

So that's where he had been aiming. Not wishing that, for me or him, I raised my hands, open in surrender. "Please, sirs, the only necessary condition for satisfaction is for you to finish your counting, pay us, and then we'll be on our way."

Mr. Button uncollared Mr. Ague, who shrugged and tugged his jacket back into place. In silence, the two returned to checking and weighing the counterfeits. While they did, James went out to the horses.

Eventually, they got smart and divided the work, Mr. Button counting and Mr. Ague weighing. After every stack they did some calculating in their heads, then each announced a figure. If agreed they went to the next stack, otherwise they repeated the process.

They were interminably slow; perhaps Dr. Newton's calculus of infinitesimals could help them with their mental effort. I pressed them to hasten their work, but they ignored my exhortation.

After what must have been an hour, they were just inspecting the last stack of counterfeits when James came in to check on the work. His squished, tired expression mirrored my own annoyance.

"Finished," said Mr. Button in an undeserved proud announcement.

Mr. Ague was bundling up the coins like an egg monger before market.

"Good," said James. "Give us our payment and we shall get home before dawn."

Mr. Button looked perplexed. "But you should know we wouldn't carry the payment with us."

James and I shared our own perplexed glance.

"You must be making a poor attempt at humor," I said.

"No humor at all," said Mr. Button. "Our governor does not want to make the transfer of payments here."

James stepped over to Mr. Button. In his face, close enough so their breath mingled, "Then we'll take our coins and be gone."

Mr. Ague produced a club from his long coat, raising it above James' skull. I grabbed his wrist and twisted it.

With a grin, Mr. Button pushed me and his colleague apart. Mr. Button said, "Let's not go down this road again. You'll be paid by Mr. Percy himself. You only need to go there now."

With an exaggerated grin of my own, I said, "That's not how I understood our arrangement. If our money is not here, then I'll go get it with one of you. My colleague will stay here with the coins."

The two delinquents, stupefied by the change, said nothing. I said to James, "Let's get our coins and go."

Mr. Button said, "Not so fast. I agree to accompany you to the governor."

With that, he and I took off, the horses in a quick trot. We rode in silence to the metals yard. Once there, Mr. Button and I went up into the offices. Mr. Percy, seated at his desk looking over a ledger in the candlelight, did not appear surprised at my presence, but he said, "Is there a problem with the transaction?"

Mr. Button started to speak, but I interrupted. "Our transaction has failed to proceed with due propriety. It was only by a cat's whisker that we did not take our coins, never to see you again."

Mr. Percy gazed at me for a moment in silence, then turned to Mr. Button, who was shaking his head and waving his hands as if stricken with the dancing plague.

"We're only doing what you told us to do—check their coins," said Mr. Button.

Mr. Percy looked back to me.

"Which they did," I said, with more than a lilt of exasperation. "I guaranteed our coins would be as good as the samples we provided. It was our understanding that we were supposed to be paid and on our way to our beds by now."

"Mr. Button was indeed doing my bidding. How do I know you would be bringing us the same kind of coin? Really, I don't know you from a vagrant in a gutter. If I were to deal directly with the producer of your counterfeits, I might have more trust."

I scoffed at his suggestion.

Mr. Percy said, "I'm taking all the risk in this transaction."

"A gross exaggeration," I said. "We all have risk."

Mr. Percy stood in silence, and I joined him in his statuary pose.

I waited him out until he went over to his desk. Putting his hands in a drawer, he removed a canvas bag. After dropping it unceremoniously with a thud on the desk, he said, "Do you wish to count it?"

I smiled. "No need. I'm working directly with the governor."

"There's one other thing you owe me."

Yes, I did. I told him the name of the brewery and the account to deal with—our Mr. Ravenscroft.

With that, I reached out to pick up the bag. Mr. Percy put a cold hand on mine.

"Just a warning," he said. "Don't make me regret doing business with you."

I shook off his hand. "And the same with us."

Mr. Percy looked amused. "You don't want to pick a fight with me."

On cue, Mr. Button stepped over to me.

"I never pick a fight," I said. "I've never backed down from one either."

Mr. Percy gave me a cold glance, then gestured with his head to Mr. Button, who backed away.

"By the way," I said, "I noticed you have a copy of Dr. Newton's *Principia*. Ironic that the Master of the Mint's book is in your library."

"Curiosity. That's the reason. Trying to understand what's in his head."

"And what is it you found?"

Mr. Percy said, "Incomprehensible ideas, even bizarre in places, all of which makes him unpredictable. And thus a dangerous enemy."

If he only knew how dangerous.

chapter 30

While I was working on the composition, a military messenger delivered two sealed notes. One was from Mr. Lupine, requiring me to report to him that evening. Politely so, but still it was an order. The other note was not signed. It read:

> *One's spirit flags, in the desultory rain of a dark afternoon.*
> *A private room, a blooming hearth, warm laughter.*
> *Blood flows afire.*
> *From a porcelain mug, sipping coffee.*

My blood was not afire, rather, a river of ice in my veins chilled me from head to foot. I ran to the door, looking for the messenger, to find out who sent the poetic horror, even as I knew he would not know who brought the message to deliver. He would have been given a stack of messages by the base postmaster. Even before that, the author would not have delivered it in person; an assistant would have performed the errand.

All that supposition wasn't necessary. I knew the author was Mr. Montagu, the poet that he was. More importantly, Mr. Montagu knew about my afternoon coffee with Catherine, and perhaps our other meetings. As infrequent as they were, the knowledge of our intimacy must have set his blood afire.

Was the message a threat? I could show it to Catherine. She could study the words and the inking to tell me if it was written by her employer. She could interpret the meaning of the poem, if it carried real threats.

Even if it wasn't Mr. Montagu's work, someone knew of our meetings. The knowledge could be passed to him. Perhaps that was the point—a prelude for blackmail?

Not likely, I decided, since I had no money to speak of. I doubted Catherine had much of her own. Although, her uncle's resources certainly bore close to a fortune, if not one outright.[1]

Without knowing the author's identity with utter certainty, I couldn't think of a coherent strategy, other than to be careful with my time with Catherine. I went about my daily routine until I came up with an idea.

Taking leave of my post, I secured a carriage to the Fountain Tavern. There, I went inside and down the corridor to the hall where the Kit-Cat Club met. I stood in front of the collection of poems, found the one about Catherine. I held up the message to the writing. Immediately, I noticed similarities—the slant of lines, the fully curved rounded letters, the embellishments at the end of a line. But most of interest, the tone of the poem, and the phrasing, were similar. Although the message was shorter, more clipped, it *sounded* the same, especially when read aloud.

A pair of gentlemen passed by and gave me a look of amusement. I nodded to them before I retreated.

During the remainder of the day, my mind was filled with thoughts of what to do, from nothing to bringing my suspicions to Catherine to directly confronting her employer. I hadn't decided the best course of action when I arrived at Mr. Lupine's home. I took a roundabout way, now fearing I was constantly under someone's gaze. Even though visiting the Austrian envoy wasn't entirely an unusual event, I didn't want my movements and the people I met to be in danger or under watch because of association with me.

Mr. Lupine greeted me with more enthusiasm than I'd seen of late. We sat in front of his fire and drank his Austrian brandy. He asked me how I had been.

"Well enough," was all I said.

---

[1] At the time Newtons' salary and commission at the Royal Mint was substantial; in 1702 the combined amount was £3500. *TS*

"Well enough," he said, then repeated it softly, as if trying to understand the words, "Well enough."

Knowing what his first question of me would be, I went right into my report of the Kit-Cat Club meeting, and the strong opposition still in place with Mr. Montagu and his backers. Mr. Lupine did not seem concerned, at least he did not change his expression. He asked me for specific words used in the speeches. I relayed them as best I could recall—about the desire to remain out of the war for economic and political reasons. I didn't mention Montagu's personal attacks on me.

He nodded in understanding when I finished. "That's valuable to know those reasons. And what of the countering arguments?"

I mentioned the statements referencing that England would be drawn into the war sooner or later, and that sooner would be better. I added that I believed those in favor seemed to be in the majority, if ever so slight. Then, guilty though I felt repeating Catherine's private thoughts, I told Mr. Lupine of Mr. Montagu's motivations for changing his position.

Again, he nodded. "Your reports are excellent. I shall now tell you the Spanish are planning a preemptive strike against the English fleet."

"Wouldn't that force the English into the war?"

"It depends on the outcome," he said. "If devastating, then it would keep the strong English navy out of action. If only partially effective, it might draw the English in as retaliation. The latter being most likely."

This time I nodded. I knew what he was going to say. I said it first. "Assuming the attack is imminent, then the French will likely begin an initiative, as the past has shown. We need to set in motion a quick offensive to demonstrate to the English the war can be won. This might also spur the Spanish to begin their attack."

Mr. Lupine nodded. "You have the perfect cover in place to assist such an offensive."

"You're saying I'll be off soon to Italy?"

He said nothing as he refilled my glass.

D ifficult as it was to be preparing to return to Italy so soon (seemingly so, as it had been more than three months since we returned), I went about the preparations with due seriousness. James and I began meeting daily with the military commanders, including the Earl of Marlborough. With all the elite activity, there seemed to be a push toward war, despite Mr. Montagu's continued reluctance.

Our preparations were interrupted by an urgent message from Dr. Newton. James and I hurried to the Tower of London. We were escorted to the Royal Mint and ushered into the Master of the Mint's office.

Gathered around his desk were three gentlemen. We were introduced to them—two members of the Mint's sentinel division, and the chief criminal prosecutor with the unlikely name of Mercy.

Dr. Newton said, "Thank you for arriving promptly at my behest, Captains. We moved quickly on the counterfeiters, predominantly because I hear you may be leaving the country soon."

I wondered how he heard that. Catherine's doing through Mr. Montagu, perhaps?

Dr. Newton went on, "We need to press you into service once more." To the prosecutor, he said, "Please proceed."

Mr. Mercy's voice was deep and ponderous, which I imagined would be of great value in a courtroom. "Captains Wolf and Brookfield, thank you for your time. I need to record a detailed account of your actions with three criminals detained in the matter of distributing counterfeit Royal coinage. Are you so prepared to do so?"

"Yes, sir," we said.

James and I gave our statements separately, taking more than an hour. In mine, I gave the details of our dealings with Misters Percy, Ague, and Button. The details of dates and times, meeting locations, and what was discussed and otherwise admitted to by the three. I used my coded musical scores to be precise.

Dr. Newton reviewed the statements, and asked a few questions, largely to add precision to the details we offered. He was particularly interested in the portion of my statement describing the inclusion of *Principia* in Mr. Percy's library.

"I fail to see how reading my book would further his cause as a counterfeiter," muttered Dr. Newton.

After the statements were signed, the prosecutor said, "Thank you. Now I must ask you to identify the three men who are now incarcerated in the gaol below the Tower."

James and I shared a look of concern.

The prosecutor said, "It's absolutely a necessity. Without that, the judge won't be inclined to accept the statements."

We had no choice, apparently, and followed the guards and prosecutor down the spiraling stone staircase. The smell grew putrid the further we went, as if the sewer had long since stopped working. Then we heard the plaintive moans of those imprisoned, one of them proclaiming innocence over-and-over, so much so I was sorely tempted to find and release the man whether telling the truth or not.

The three acquaintances of ours were in the same cell. Mr. Ague had his hands over his ears and Mr. Button his sleeve to his nose. Mr. Percy on the other hand sat on the stone bench as if waiting for a round of ale to be delivered.

All three, however, gave us the naked glare of violent hatred.

The prosecutor went quickly about his business. "Mr. Ague," he announced.

He stood up, almost as if expecting to be released.

James and I told the prosecutor that he was the same Mr. Ague referred to in our statements.

We did the same with the other two unfortunates.

As we were leaving, Mr. Percy said, quietly but sharply, "You two shall regret this to the day you die. You'll experience the compounding pain of those who possess an ounce of meaning to you."

I arranged to meet Catherine, who most certainly had more than an ounce of meaning to me, at Penbook's musical instrument shop rather than the coffee house. It didn't seem prudent to go there again after the poetic threat, and I made the excuse that I wanted to see if Mr. Penbook was serious about purchasing a set of Mr. Stradivari's instruments. It gave me a legitimate reason for being there, and a legitimate reason for Catherine to be assisting me with the matter.

"Hello, Captain Wolf," she said after stepping from her carriage.

"Hello, Miss Barton."

"Lovely day, isn't it?" she asked as we stood outside the shop. In the window was a single violoncello, gleaming on red velvet.

"Indeed," I said. "And thank you for meeting me here."

"It's my pleasure. Shall we go in?"

I opened the door for her.

"Such a fine gentleman you are, despite what they say."

I laughed, although I'm sure there was truth to her humor.

Mr. Penbook was standing in front of a row of violins when we entered. He hurried over to his chair. When he saw it was us, he came forward a step.

"Welcome back," he said. "It's been a long time. How's the violin playing? Satisfactorily, I pray."

Catherine assured him it was playing fine, admitting she lacked time to play it very often. She glanced at me and added, "I'm waiting for a new composition to be finished."

I gave her a little nod.

"I hope to hear it soon as well," said Mr. Penbook. "And what can I do for you today? Would you be interested in the violoncello in the window? It's a brilliant instrument from an estate just settled. No? Perhaps a new bow?"

I told him of my travel plans.

Hearing that I was going back to Cremona to settle on a violin from Mr. Stradivari's shop, he seemed most keen. "That's exhilarating news," he said. "Come, let's sit over at the table and tell me more."

As we walked over to the table, I saw Catherine out of the corner of my eye and noticed her forced smile.

I said, "I wouldn't characterize the news so grandly. I hope it will be a quick and productive trip. I have to thank Miss Barton for introducing me to her uncle who has helped me understand what I need to be asking Mr. Stradivari in the way of crafting a most excellent violin."

"What does he say?"

"He says much," I said, "and sometimes nothing."

Catherine did smile graciously at that.

"Dr. Newton uses his science and mathematics to predict how changes in the many variables will affect the instrument's sound. He also makes many observations and performs many experiments. I hope I've retained a good fraction of his ideas in order to discuss them with Mr. Stradivari."

Catherine said, "Captain Wolf has been very diligent in his efforts and has been very generous with my uncle. I'm sure he'll return soon with an excellent violin and an equally wonderful composition. Won't you, Captain?"

"As is within my power to do so, yes, I shall."

Mr. Penbook looked from me to her, and then said, "So then, what can I do for you?"

"Since I am going to Italy, I wished to verify your desire to purchase an instrument or perhaps even a set from Mr. Stradivari?"

Mr. Penbook blinked. "I would indeed be interested in such a purchase."

"Excellent. What shall I tell Mr. Stradivari?"

He pondered my question with considerable thought before he said, "I could sell a set consisting of a violin, a viola, and a violoncello. And I might have a buyer for a superior guitar."

"I believe all four are possible," I said. "Mr. Stradivari prefers to know the player's preferences before he creates an instrument."

"I see," said Mr. Penbook. "I shall have to contact the person interested in the guitar. Of the set, I don't have particular players in mind." With his eyes on Catherine, he said, "Perhaps Miss Barton would be so kind as to give her opinion as to the kind of instruments she would like to play or hear played?"

Catherine smiled. "I'm flattered you think me capable of such opinion. I shall have to think about it."

Mr. Penbook assured her that her insights would be most valuable. "As for the payment?" he asked me. "Do you know what he would want to be compensated?"

"I can't say. But if you give me an idea of what you would pay, then I will see how well I can negotiate."

"Yes, I can do that. When will you leave for Italy?"

"I don't know yet, but in not too many days, I believe."

"All right. I'll determine a figure and let you know."

"I won't leave without it."

That settled, Catherine and I left. We walked along the streets for a while, nearing the Tower of London. At the sight, I said, "I should warn you that the men in the ring of counterfeiters were apprehended, and James and I had to witness them and give evidence against them. When we were finished, the leader threatened me."

I told her word-for-word what he said.

Catherine said, "I can only thank you again for helping my uncle. Don't worry about me, however." She took my arm as she had the first night after the concert, and said, "Assuming you are saying that I have an ounce of meaning to you."

Before we parted, Catherine invited me to dinner with her and Dr. Newton. I accepted, of course.

"And sincerely," she said as she squeezed my arm, "don't worry."

"I'll try not to."

She laughed. "I don't believe you. So then, please, focus on your mission."

Mr. Lupine and I met in the shadows of St. Paul's Cathedral, still shiny new from its reconstruction.[2] He paced in a little circle while he told me that his home had been ransacked.

"I was out at the time. They didn't appear to find anything of value, either monetarily or politically. Those kinds of things are hidden safely. It was likely just a message."

"A message to stop trying to influence the politics of the state?"

Mr. Lupine gazed up at the steeple, the architecture clearly influenced by the great cathedrals of the continent, of arches etched in heavy stone and faced with gold leaf. Was he looking for divine intervention?

"I believe so," he finally answered.

I didn't tell him of my own threats, real or imagined, or at least unsubstantiated. "This isn't a positive turn of events," I said. "How will it affect our plans?"

Now he looked around as if to see who might be listening. There was no one within hearing range whom I could see.

"We have to diligently continue our pursuit. Are you leaving for Italy soon?"

Before I could answer, he said, "I think the sooner, the better."

"Yes, I think that as well," I said.

---

[2] The reconstruction of Christopher Wren's design was consecrated for use about four years earlier. *PW*

Although construction continued in the 1720s. *TS*

"Good," he said. "If I don't see you before you go, I wish you the best of good fortune in your mission."

He said that in a quiet, uncertain voice, his head turned to the side as if he didn't believe it possible.

chapter 31

T he housekeeper at Dr. Newton's home greeted me as warmly as an old friend, though perhaps because her employer's niece was there, her presence softening the severe mood when it was only the great man and me. Shown inside, I found Catherine in the sitting room, along with James and Rose, their attendance previously unannounced. They laughed when they saw my surprise.

Several fine wines were opened for the occasion. After some banter, Catherine told me that her uncle wanted to see me in his workshop for a few minutes before joining us. I wondered where he was, although neither was I surprised by his absence.

Catherine escorted me into the workshop, where Dr. Newton was bound up in writing.

"Uncle Isaac," she said softly, "Captain Wolf is here."

Dr. Newton glanced up while continuing to write. Without a word, he looked back down and finished his thoughts. Catherine gave me an affectionate smile.

Finally, he put away his quill pen. "Over here," he commanded.

Catherine and I obeyed.

From one of the drawers in a cabinet, Dr. Newton took out a bound set of papers about a thumb-width high. "I've added this to my previous notes on the matter of the violin. It's still incomplete as more could be done, but it's the current sum of my knowledge."

He handed it to me. The title on the cover, written in his bold hand, was *On The Design Of a Stringed Instrument*. I peeled back the cover and skimmed the first few pages of the manuscript that recapped his experiments and the conclusions he had drawn. I could see I'd have to spend many hours going through it.

"Thank you, thank you," I said, stumbling over my gratitude.

At the time, I believe he gave me a little nod, although I'm certain now that it was a mere blink of his eye.

Catherine filled in the silence. "My uncle is most appreciative, especially your assistance in the matter at the Mint. Am I correct in saying this, uncle?"

Dr. Newton made a little gurgling sound in his throat and sputtered out, "Yes, of course. Most appreciative."

Catherine insisted we move to the dining room where we were served a hearty dinner with the excellent wine. The lively conversation went on for hours, with much laughter, and nothing of politics or the war or our impending departure, although, the latter draped a heavy cloak over my heart.

Dr. Newton left the dining room first, without so much as a word.

Before the night became too late, James and I had to return to our quarters in anticipation of early morning obligations. We went into separate rooms for our personal goodbyes. In the shadows of her uncle's library, Catherine kissed me tenderly.

"A truly wonderful evening," she said.

"Yes, I hope one of many more."

"Yes, certainly," she said brightly.

Catherine and Rose walked us out to our carriage. I watched Catherine as we traveled down the street. When she vanished from view, my heart was seized with dread, then despair.

W e were about halfway into our journey to our quarters when the carriage stopped unexpectedly. All was silent for a moment. I started to investigate when the doors were thrown open and James and I were dragged from the carriage. There were two men on each of us.

I was dragged toward a wooded patch. When I struggled, one of them kicked me in the back of the knee and I collapsed. They hauled me to the nearest tree.

They slammed me up against its rough bark. One of the thugs had a coil of rope draped over his shoulder. When he partially released me to find the end of the rope, I took advantage and burst away from them.

They cried out that I had escaped. I heard the others cry out in answer and I ran toward them.

James had already been halfway secured with rope to a tree. When one of his captors charged toward me, James was able to free himself from the other. We turned to fight them off. They regrouped and advanced toward us. In the light of the moon, I could see another of them had his own coil of rope. Rather than be hung, drawn and quartered, we decided it would be better to take our leave.

And so we ran.

Opus 6

The Battle of Cremona

chapter 32

After a quick decision, James and I got horses from the military headquarters and rode to the Tower of London. A guard was quietly bribed, and we entered the cell in the bowels of the Tower. Mr. Button and Mr. Ague sat on their benches, their jaws clenched. Mr. Percy was lying on his bench, his hands folded peacefully on his chest as he gazed up to the soot-stained ceiling

James ordered the other two to stand. When they didn't comply, I walked over to them. "Believe me, it's in your best interest."

They glanced at each other, then stood up.

James gave them a crisp order, "Follow me."

Now they looked at Mr. Percy, who gave them a nod.

When they were out of the cell and into another, I closed the cell door. I approached Mr. Percy, who remained still.

"Would you like to retract your threat?" I asked him.

Mr. Percy let out a long breath. He inhaled another, and when his lungs were full, he slowly folded his legs and swung them off the bench until his feet were on the floor. He sat up, his hands gripping the edge of the bench, his head hanging down. Slowly, he looked up at me.

Then he lunged, more quickly than I imagined him capable. Just as quickly, his thick hands were around my neck, his grip strong. I gave him a moment to change his course of action, but he didn't relent.

I tensed my neck muscles, fighting against his grip. Then my hands were around his neck, my grip more powerful. In only a few moments, his eyes bulged, his mouth opened, but he could suck in no air. Before I could release my hands, his eyes rolled back in his head. He went limp and dropped to the floor. I knelt over him, slapped him across the face, but he was already dead. He hadn't been without air that long.

His heart must have given out.

W e were back at our quarters before dawn. There we collected our travel baggage and began our journey.

I was certain Mr. Percy was behind the assassination attempt, although it could have been, I hypothesized,[1] Mr. Montagu's doing. I didn't tell James that, as I'd never spoken to him about the threat from Mr. Montagu, poetic and as subtle as it may have been. Also, I didn't want James to consider that he might have had anything to do with the threat, indirectly so, of course. He'd introduced Catherine and me, and encouraged us by arranging times we could be together. In the end, though, if it was Mr. Montagu, an escalation to assassination was due to his envy and jealousy, about which I could do nothing.

Despite that possibility, even if true, Mr. Percy's threat was still too vicious to ignore.

That settled at least for the time being, the rest of our journey went with seemingly great speed. No doubt we were driven by the assassination attempt, but also because we knew we were not heading back to Cremona to merely gather more information. There was the urgency of forthcoming action.

Riding side by side, James and I traded stories, egging each other on, exaggerating details or events whole cloth, as if trying to wipe away our near deaths.

"How many did you have to fight off? Even as you were half-blind with blood streaming from your head wound?"

"A half dozen? I don't know. I didn't take the time to count."

---

[1] Thank you, Dr. Newton. *PW*

The stories sped up time, bringing to mind Huygens' clock, whirring and ticking in Dr. Newton's home. Was time really constant? If Huygens' clock was with me, would it have sped up as I so perceived?

I wondered what Dr. Newton would think about my experiment. I could hear his voice in my head, in his rising pitch as he listed the fallacies and illogical ideas of my thinking. Or maybe he would just go silent and brood. Yet, my thoughts of him were now more ones of affection, rather than fear or frustration. I had a sudden desire to turn back, ride straight to London for one more dinner with Dr. Newton. And Catherine.

V ienna came into view before we knew it. We arrived at the military headquarters and found open bunks. Too tired to say another word, we fell asleep without food or drink.

I woke early, having slept soundly for a few hours. I found a bath and soaked in steaming water, as hot as I could stand. The soak and scrub made me feel as if I were starting my life anew, or at least rid of the odor of horse and saddle leather.

When the water grew tepid, I dried off and dressed and shaved, then rousted James. After a robust Austrian breakfast of three kinds of sausages, bread and cheese, and roasted apples, we reported to the officers to whom we were assigned.

They were a dry group, full of questions on the state of the English predilection toward war, the readiness of the English military, likely battlefronts, and the odd question that sticks in my memory like a spike in a tree, its wooden flesh growing around it. One of the younger officers asked, "What do English women prefer in lovemaking?"

James and I laughed off his inept question. "You'll have to find out for yourself," James answered.

The rest of the day we reported to other officers as required, always higher up the rankings, until we found ourselves arriving in the large hall to meet with the leader of the Austrian forces, Prince Eugene of Savoy,[2] and Field General Vaudemont along with his retinue of officers. They were engaged in a lively discussion that we were obliged to wait for a pause before we were introduced.

Prince Eugene, a slight man in his late thirties, had a countenance as gray as the fog of Cremona and eyelids that drooped with heaviness but did not fully obscure his intense gaze upon us. He stood up and the others did as well.

"Welcome, gentlemen," he said in English.

A map was spread out on the table around which we were seated. Prince Eugene ran the meeting with all due seriousness, asking pointed questions of us and the officers, the tone was both questioning and interested in every opinion. The gist of the matters included a push from the north, likely driving the French into Cremona, where James and I would perform our surveillance and report the best way to attack the city.

Those broad strategies established, the meeting was over except that Prince Eugene asked me to stay behind. The others continued their exit as we sat in silence, while I was worried about the thrust of our private interview.

The prince sat pensively tapping his fingertips together until we were alone. He came straight to the point: "When did you last see our envoy in London?"

"Mr. Lupine? A few weeks before we left."

"How was he?"

"Concerned. His home had been searched. He told me that the conflict was building against the war."

"I see," said the prince. "We've lost touch with him."

---

[2] Prince Eugene was thirty-seven at this time, gray with worry as our forces were outnumbered and lacking resources. *PW*

"That's terrible news. You suspect he was …?"

"We'll continue to investigate. But it doesn't look like a favorable outcome. I wish you were there to assist. But you have a more important mission. I've heard of your excellent work, in London as well as in Cremona."

"Thank you, sir."

"Before we part, I want to say I was sorry to hear about the events that caused the death of your young cousin. I understand how that affected your career. Please accept my words as true and genuine. Losing any soldier in our command is painful enough."

I tried to voice my appreciation, but only a little murmur came out of my throat.

He nodded. "I'd like to pay my personal respects to your aunt before I go to Italy. Do you believe I would be well received?"

"Undoubtedly," I said.

The prince nodded, then was silent. I took that as my cue to leave.

T he late afternoon fog had already crept over the banks of the Po River and enveloped Cremona's walls, greeting us like an old friend as we approached the gate.

"Our second home," I said in French.

James said, "I have to confess, I've become fond of the city."

I had as well.

We were pleased to be processed without much ado after waiting in a line that wound up from the fields to the gate. Lt. Laurent was, so far, nowhere to be seen. James and I again hired a carriage to take us to the pensione. As we traveled, we took stock of the city.

The French platoons marched less in their languid pace than before, and more as if they had important business. Likewise, the locals strode quickly, purposefully, as if rain was starting to fall.

At our pensione, the old porter dragged our bags for us into our room without a word. We thought about staying in another place this time, but that might look suspicious, and we would likely be found anyway.

We settled into the room, took a short rest, then went out in search of a meal. We went to the taverna where Omobono Stradivari had taken us. It was nearly empty and we relaxed with a glass of wine while waiting for the meal.

I said to James, "You must be missing Rose."

James groaned and sat back in his chair. "I try not to think about her. I'm sure she's happily working in the brewery offices with all the men there."

"I don't think you have to worry about that. She doesn't seem one to be swayed by shallow words of seduction."

James nodded in agreement. "I hadn't expected to be with anyone as wonderful as Rose. The thought of never seeing her again drives me mad."

"I have no doubt you'll see her again."

James smiled. "I'll hold you to that. And you? I'm certain you miss Catherine."

"Yes," I answered without hesitation, "but it's not the same with us. Catherine's life is complicated with her employment, with her famous uncle."

"She obviously favors you above all."

"Would that be true. I don't believe she's in a place to make such a choice."

James shook his head. "Perhaps not in her mind, but when it comes to matters of deep feelings, the heart wins, especially with the hold you have over her."

"I'm sure you're right in most cases. But not in this one, I'm afraid. Yet I keep hope."

We finished our meal and began a scouting trip. We ventured to stroll toward the Po River gate, which was well guarded all hours of the day. The citadel's stone walls loomed into the fog, as if monstrously emerging from a cave, then disappearing into the gloom. I made note of the doors and gates and slits for weapons as far as I could see and imagined shot raining down on the militia attacking from outside.

W e woke early despite our late night out. James seemed anxious, pacing and looking out the window as if hearing a battlecry. I left him to his vigilance. I was excited to see Mr. Stradivari and his family.

Walking along the narrow streets, still quiet in the early morning, I felt a tranquility I hadn't experienced for a long time. The peacefulness led to a longing for Catherine, who would surely feel it as well, for if nothing else, she possessed more than one person's share of empathy.

When the streets began to fill with residents and soldiers marching, I hurried to Mr. Stradivari's workshop. I carried the book presented to me by Dr. Newton, my latest version of the concerto, and the rest of the funds I owed the luthier.

I hadn't been able to fully read Dr. Newton's book on the journey from London to Cremona. Glancing through it, trying to grasp his intricate drawings and perplexing mathematics, my first impression of it was that it was a masterful work and hinting at something grander, something that spoke to the heart of humanity. I could only grasp a few of the details, and those because of my discussions directly with Dr. Newton. The precise calculations of pressure waves continued to confound me, even as I now understood the general ideas. I was particularly slow in understanding his calculus of infinitesimals applied to the design of the curved surfaces of a violin.

Dr. Newton's theory of varnish and how it affected the wood surface and consequent transmissions of the vibrations was equally complex, but the specific effects he proposed I felt that I might understand in principle. However, his alchemy of ingredients and ratios, thicknesses and drying times, seemed derived from experiments to account for all the confounding variables, like the squiggly lines drawn on the paper during the experiments I helped him complete.

I nearly laughed aloud as I could hear Dr. Newton's voice in my head congratulating me on learning one thing, then chastising me for my ignorance on the rest. So when I reached the door of the Stradivari home and workshop, I lacked much confidence in what I might be able to convey to Mr. Stradivari. I hoped he would add his insight into Dr. Newton's experiments and formulas.

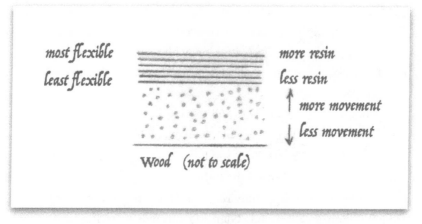

Omobono met me at the door, clapping me on both shoulders, as if I were a favorite brother returning from battle. The news of my arrival spread through the family and they came to greet me—Mr. Stradivari, Mrs. Stradivari, and Caterina, who gave me a warm smile. We were all talking at once until Mr. Stradivari waved his hands and demanded they release me.

He took me into the workshop where Francesco was working diligently but stood up to welcome me as well.

Mr. Stradivari and I sat at one of his workbenches. "Mr. Rémon, how have you been?" he asked me.

"Well enough. Many things have happened, many good and some less so, but I survived."

Mr. Stradivari nodded in agreement. "I can say the same. Life has been more strained. There are more soldiers, and thus more shortages of essentials as the military commandeers the first of every-thing—food, cloth, wood, and wine."

I shook my head. "The hazards of war."

"Sadly so," he said then asked, "Will it change soon for us here in Cremona?"

"I can't say for sure, but I imagine things will get worse before they are better."

He shook his head as he waved his hands in the air. "I know that to be true, but I didn't want to hear it. Enough, let's move on to your instruments. We've made great progress, exceeding your expecta-tions. I'll be happy to show you."

"I'm excited to see them."

He grandly motioned for me to follow him. We went to a corner of the workshop. There I could see the makings of the set of instru-ments—a violin, a viola, and a violoncello. He explained the state of each, all in differing phases, yet I could see all were well along toward their exquisite completion.

"I haven't started on your principal violin yet," Mr. Stradivari said. "As we agreed."

"I'm prepared to discuss that with you." But the first order of business was to give him the balance of his funds owed. I put the coins on the table.

Mr. Stradivari said, "It goes without saying I appreciate your payment."

He called for Omobono to take the coins and write a note of payment received.

After he picked up the coins, Omobono said, "We'll have to go out again to celebrate with Jacques."

"I'd like that," I said.

When Omobono left, I said to Mr. Stradivari, "The next item to discuss is my concerto. It's not fully finished yet, but far enough along for me to let you have this copy. I hope it helps with the design of the violin."

He accepted the score and glanced through it. "I'm sure it's brilliant. I'll have my musician friends appraise it."

"Excellent. I've arranged for another set of your instruments to be purchased by a seller in London who pointed me to the Italian violins in the first place."

I told him of Mr. Penbook's desires.

"Excellent," said the luthier. "We are eternally grateful."

"Lastly," I said, taking Dr. Newton's bound manuscript out of its bag, "my learned friend, whom I can tell you his name since he put it on the title page, Dr. Isaac Newton, has found the idea of violin construction so fascinating that he created this book."

I put the manuscript on the table. Mr. Stradivari immediately leafed through a few pages. He looked up at me. "This is clearly a monumental work. I can't comprehend it without further study."

"It's very complex, yes, I don't understand all of it myself, even though he explained most of it to me. But I do grasp some of the basic premises. For example ..." I turned to the page with the pressure waves and started to explain how sound travelled and how this fact affected all of the parts of a violin.

I didn't get very far before Mr. Stradivari waved his hands as if in surrender. "I appreciate your attempt to explain your learned friend's brilliance. But if you don't mind, I'll have to spend some time with the manuscript before I can say more about it."

"Of course," I said. "Please take all the time you need."

After Mr. Stradivari and I had finished our dealings, we were served a full meal as wonderful as usual. I felt guilty partaking given the circumstances of the occupation. Mr. Stradivari urged me to enjoy the meal, as if he sensed I was reluctant to take advantage of the hospitality.

I did enjoy the meal while Mr. Stradivari talked more about his work, including an extended description of the violin commissioned by Il Diavolo.

"I was under the impression he was happy with his Amati," I said.

"He told me his style is changing, as well as people's tastes in music. They want music with more passion, a bigger voice, played in larger halls."

"Interesting," I said, vowing to myself to discuss this with Il Diavolo.

Caterina returned to the dinner table and asked if we needed anything else. I said I needed nothing, and Mr. Stradivari excused himself to return to his workshop. Caterina and I went into the courtyard.

I said, "It's good to see you again."

"I must say the same."

"How have you been since we were last together?"

She thought about the question for a long moment. "I can't say I didn't miss you. I know that you have your mission, so I don't want to say I thought about you every day. That would be too much for either of us. So, I'll merely say that life goes on."

I supposed that was good, at least good enough. But I didn't know what to say in response.

"And how have you been, Chief Financier to the Royal Musicians Office?"

I smiled at her barb at my false identity. What could I tell her? My time away had been fraught with intrigue, counterfeiters, war strategy, personal threats, and an assassination attempt, along with experiments in science and learning the mathematics of Dr. Newton. Not to mention my time with Catherine.

In the end I answered with, "I've been well also. As you portrayed your life, mine also goes with much that is required of me."

"Duty over love?" she said quietly. And astutely.

"Duty is always at the forefront, is it not?"

Caterina got up and walked over to me. "Let's forget duty."

We went up to her room, climbing a stairway that was hidden around a dark corner; one would have to look carefully to see it. The stairway was narrow and dark, and we walked up with our sides touching. Soon our hands were joined.

We said nothing more as we climbed to her quiet room under the attic.

After we were unentangled, Caterina, lying on her side, her head propped in her hand, said, "Father won't let me try anything in the workshop. Yes, I can take care of the household, and the young one, especially since Mother was down for several weeks with the baby.[3] I help him with the business, such as ordering materials and keeping accounts, but none of that takes talent. Not like actually shaping wood, or playing a violin, or composing, as you do."

"I think you have great talent to be able to do all that you mentioned. But talent, I think, is merely a passion, an obsession, something one spends considerable time nurturing."

She gave me a peck on the cheek. "You believe that some true talent resides in all of us, something we must discover as it's deeply hidden?"

I gave that question some thought. "Perhaps, so. Consider your father, for example. When I ask him how he creates his instruments, he doesn't tell me directly. Rather, he alludes to his skills and knowledge metaphorically."

She lay back on the pillow, and pulled the sheet up. "Yes, I know what you're saying. It's maddening for my brothers. He can't tell

[3] Giovani Baptista Giuseppe, born 6 Nov. 1701 *PW*

The "young one" likely referred to Francesca Maria, born September 19, 1700. Unfortunately, Giovani Baptista died at eight months. *TS*

them how to do something correctly, only that they aren't doing it right."

"I've seen that with my friend in ... London," I said with a guilty pause. "Dr. Isaac Newton, himself a genius, has the same problem. In fact, he becomes very angry when I can't understand what he's telling me."

"Please, tell me more."

Where to start? I told her the highlights of what I knew of him, of trying to read his works, of how he conducted experiments on the eviscerated violin. I told her of his position at the Mint and how he near single-handedly rescued the English monetary system from collapse. I told her about the help James and I provided in capturing the counterfeiters.

Caterina listened, attentively, and when I stopped, she kissed me on the lips and we further indulged ourselves.

L ater, Caterina asked me, "Something's on your mind, keeping you away from here at this moment. It's the real reason why you are here, yes?"

"The real reason?"

She didn't say anything.

"Possibly," I said without further explication.

"Or something else? Maybe someone else?"

This time I didn't respond.

After another long while, she asked me, "Have you completed your composition?"

"Nearly. I thought it would be finished by now, but I find it difficult to end it."

"It must not be ready to be ended."

Indeed.

chapter 33

Back at the pensione, James said, "So, you're alive. I was beginning to worry you'd run afoul of the French."

I ignored him.

"How is Mr. Stradivari? And family?"

"All are well." I said no more than that. Instead, we discussed intelligence gathering, drawing up maps and troop numbers, movements and artillery placements. It was clear that the French had been in retreat since our forces began advancing. As predicted, they were making Cremona their stronghold in the Lombardy region as the numbers were unquestionably greater than our last visit.

James said, "It's good they're concentrated in the city. But not good because of their numbers."

"An element of surprise will be needed to even the odds."

"How shall we do that?"

I had been thinking of a plan. "As we've been able to make our way through the underworld of the counterfeiters, we could make our way in the underground of Cremona. I'll show you."

Our first stop was at the stores of the military that was along the wall near one of the gates to the city. Two guards were on duty.

"Good morning," I said to them.

"Is it?" one spat.

"I wish I could take your place," I said. "To give you a day off."

The guard gave us a loud guffaw. "That's a big fat lie. What do you want, besides bothering us?"

I said, "My colleague and I have a soirée later this evening with a pair of sisters who have fine palates."

One guard said, "Ah yes, those sisters. We know them well."

We laughed at his sarcasm.

The other guard said, "What of it?"

I said, "If we had a bit of cheese and bread, perhaps some cured meat and pickled vegetables …"

"You want us to assist with your soirée?"

"If you could be so kind."

"Kindness has nothing to do with it."

"No, of course not. We shall give you some coin."

James pulled a bag out of his pocket and jangled it.

"How much?" a guard asked.

I nodded at James who took out some of the coins and displayed them on his palm.

"That will get you dry infantry rations," the guard sniffed as if he could smell the amount. "If you want something from the officer's supplies …"

James dipped into the bag and removed more coins.

The guard shook his head. "Put it back in the bag."

James complied and the guard held out his hand. James looked at me and I nodded again. James handed the bag to the guard. They told us to wait and they went into the warehouse.

After only a short while, one came back. He peered around, looking for anyone who might see. Satisfied it was clear, he handed us two burlap sacks.

"Leave quickly," the guard said. "Go down the alley, not the main street."

We did as directed. We dropped off one of the bags at the pensione, and then walked to the southern edge of the city wall to the Parish of Santa Maria Nuova. Inside, a few locals were quietly worshipping. James stayed with our bag in the back shadows while I went to find the priest.

Father Cozzoli was in his office and when I went in he immediately recognized me.

"Welcome back," he said. "What news do you bring?"

I replied, "We have something to show you and also a request."

"I pray it's not another gift of a dead soldier."

"It's much the opposite."

The priest and I went out to the rectory where I motioned for James to bring the burlap bag, then at my request the three of us went down the stairway beneath the parish. In the wine cellar, I opened the bag and showed him our spoils.

"Officer rations!" he said. "Incredible. How did you get these?"

"I won't say, but we'd like to trade them for a few bottles of wine."

He laughed. "Done."

"There's something else," I said. "We might need a larger favor from you than we have the right to ask."

The priest tilted his head. "What would that be?"

"Would you consider allowing us a surreptitious entrance to the city?"

The priest turned away, thoughtful for a few long moments. Or maybe he was praying.

James spoke up, "We'd also like to make a substantial contribution to your parish, if that helps you decide."

The priest turned back toward us. "We're a poor parish, always in need. But we don't want to run afoul of the French military."

I said, "We can make it appear that you had nothing to do with anything that might happen."

James took out another of his bags of coins from his pocket. He handed it to the priest.

Feeling its weight and then looking inside, the priest was satisfied. "Please inform me in advance of when something might happen."

"We will," I said.

"Let's open a bottle of wine to salute our agreement," said the priest.

James and I didn't protest.

On the way to the Stradivari home carrying the remaining contraband, I witnessed a procession of officers parading through the city. In front was the leader of the French forces in Cremona— Marshal François de Neufville, the duc de Villeroi. One of the officers marching just behind the Marshal was Lt. Laurent. Perhaps he had been promoted to a higher rank, one that awarded him the privilege of being close to the Marshal. The officers appeared to be making a show of force and confidence, rather than doing anything of importance.

I avoided the procession and arrived at the Stradivari house unchallenged where Caterina greeted me. I presented her the food and wine. She was as surprised to see the bounty as had the priest. Caterina asked, "How did you get this?"

I shrugged.

"I see," she said, returning my shrug.

Mr. Stradivari came to welcome us, and he immediately took me to his workshop. We sat at one of his worktables, where a space had been cleared for Dr. Newton's manuscript.

Mr. Stradivari opened it to a page. "I've been reading this carefully, and if I understand it correctly, or even a small amount, it's an approach to understanding how a violin creates sound, particularly the quality of the sound. Your friend, Newton, tries to show how small changes in any of the design or materials or craftsmanship can produce large differences in tone."

He pointed to the open page on which was replicated three of Dr. Newton's graphical sheets. "This looks interesting, these traced vibrations, although I can't say I understand the purpose of it. How were they obtained?"

I wished I could have been more articulate explaining the experiments. I showed him the differences in the graphs where the smooth lines indicated less unwanted vibrations. I pointed out the differences in length of tone and peaks indicating more or less power.

Mr. Stradivari studied the page for several long moments, before he closed the manuscript, stood up, and motioned for me to follow him. "Do you have a few hours to spend with me? I'd like to take you somewhere and show you a few things outside of the city."

"Yes, I have the time."

"Good," he said and asked me to wait in the sitting room.

He came back in a few minutes carrying a basket. "Caterina put together some food for us. Omobono is arranging a carriage for us."

We went outside. The fog was lifting and the sun was an ivory white disk behind its remnant. We went to a livery stable where Omobono was waiting with the carriage. He looked wild-eyed, as if excited to be out of the workshop for a few hours. I hoped he didn't drive with the same wildness.

Despite my worries, he drove steadily and we were soon over the bridge and out into the country. The fields were fallow and not many people were out. The flat, empty terrain was good for an advancing force, but they would be exposed if not under cover of night or fog.

Mr. Stradivari and I talked about the scenery, asking if it compared to my home. I said few places in Austria were far from views of the mountains.

"It must be beautiful," he said.

"Yes, it is."

After that conversation died out, I asked him how he arrived at his methods of crafting his instruments, hoping the general question might lead him to telling me something more specific about his craft.

"I have to say I didn't conceive any of those features common to all of the stringed instruments, and especially not the violin, the pinnacle of achievement. In particular, Amati contrived the basic length, the f sound holes, the sound posts, or the scrolling neck. I can't say who concocted the original recipe for the varnish.

"But what I have done, since Amati's design over a hundred years ago, is incessant improvement with each element, hearing what the differences make for the sound. Certain changes in materials or size or other aspect will make a change in sounds. A larger violin will have a lower and more powerful tone, for instance. Other changes can be subtle, or surprising."

I wanted to press him for more details, which Dr. Newton would want to hear. But before I could, Mr. Stradivari announced our first stop.

Looking around, I didn't see anything I would associate with the making of stringed instruments. There were only a few scraggly trees, some marshy wetlands. While Omobono secured the carriage, we walked down to the marsh. "There," he pointed ahead of us.

I wasn't sure what he was pointing at—the water, the rocks, the mud, or various plants growing in the marsh. "I'm sorry," I said, "where should I be looking?"

He motioned for me to follow as he began to walk further. He stopped and knelt down in front of thin, reedy plants.

"Horsetails,"[1] he said.

With their fern-like explosion of green at the top, the plants did resemble horsetails. Mr. Stradivari sorted through them until he found one he apparently liked and plucked it out. He gave it to me and said, "Feel the stalk."

It was slightly rough, yet silky and pleasant to the touch at the same time.

The luthier said, "I use this in the final polishing stages or varnish as it provides a light touch. However, when it needs to be used and how much, can only be judged with a sensitivity developed through experience."

And not by mathematics or science was my assumption as to the underlying meaning of his statement.

----

[1] Latin name – *equisetum. PW*

Also called scouring rush or puzzle grass. The plant fibers contain silica. *TS*

We walked further along the edge of the marsh until we came to the Po River. We stopped at the bank and Mr. Stradivari said, "And what do you think I get from here?"

I answered the obvious. "Water?"

He laughed. "Not here. The water's foul. Well, it was an unfair question of me, since you can't actually see what I get from the river."

Then I recalled seeing something that looked like the dried skin of a fish on one of his workbenches. I mentioned that to him.

"You're correct. In this river are dogfish, whose skin provides a perfect roughness for a secondary stage of polishing the wood. I don't imagine you would find mention of horsetails and dogfish in your learned friend's book, would you?"

"No, there was no mention of horsetails or dogfish. I suppose, though, he might never mention any of the details of how a violin would be crafted, certainly not down to the type of marshy plant or type of fish used for its skin."

I thought of Hyugens' clock and Dr. Newton's comments. In fact, he would have said focusing on construction details would take up valuable time in finding the true nature of things.

Mr. Stradivari made no further comment on my response.

Back in the carriage we headed away from the river, higher up a hillside where the weather cleared and the sun hung low above the horizon. Soon we stopped again and this time, we walked to a grove of trees, which I assumed was our destination. Omobono tied up the horse and followed us with the basket of food. We sat under a maple tree and had our lunch.

While we ate, Mr. Stradivari said, "The maples in this area aren't the best, but this maple tree is special. It birthed several trees whose wood has been used for the back plates of violins."

I could see the stumps around the grove along with maples of varying girths.

"Some of these maples now growing will be perfect. Most will not." He went over to a tree and rested his hand on it.

The same as with the spruce trees, I thought.

"The maples grow fastest in the spring, making its wood more flexible. Growth in the winter is slower, but it's usually stronger. Does that make sense?"

"Yes. Which is better for violins?"

"Ah, that's the point! Might there not be a need for both?"

I thought that the answer might be in the affirmative, but I didn't speak.

He answered for me. "Both are desirable qualities, you see. As I showed you in the mountain valley, I've been watching and listening to the trees since I first started making instruments. I had to learn for myself where they grew, how they grew, and how to select the best ones. No, not the best, the *only* ones that could become instruments. I could show you how to listen to them."

He paused and looked off into the distance, as if he could hear them now.

A fter the trip into the country, I met James at the pensione. He told me about his observations of troops entering the walled city, and I told him about the trip outside those walls with Mr. Stradivari.

"He showed me where he gathers wood, plants, even a fish to make his instruments. But I also found some terrain that was clear and protected for advancing forces with minimal danger of being observed from the city walls."

"Perhaps he knows something will happen soon," James said. "And that's why he took you there."

I hadn't considered that. "Possibly so."

"You still believe he presents no danger?"

"He doesn't. I'm sure of that. We shouldn't present a danger to him either."

We rested until it was dark, after curfew, then went out into the city, sliding through the dark until the advance of marching soldiers echoed around the corner. Plunging back into a narrow alley, we waited for the platoon to pass. But it wasn't just one, three marched past our hideaway. They weren't the infantry we knew were already in Cremona; they were from a different troop, likely from the northern outposts, maybe from as close as Soncino, less than a day's ride.

When they were gone, James said he was going to follow them. I said I would go the other way to see if there were more platoons from the new troop.

I saw no other platoons and walked toward the Stradivari home. Before going in, I first stopped to see Il Diavolo. He opened the door, but only after I knocked several times and was about to give up, even though I heard rustling inside when I put my ear to the door.

"Rémon! Come in." The violinist looked more disheveled than usual.

I followed him in and immediately noticed a travel trunk, open and half-full.

"An impromptu tour," he said. "I'm decaying here, like a pile of autumn leaves. And then there's the oncoming military offensive."

I couldn't hide my surprise that he would know about it. He gave me a clucking sound of reproach.

"We all know," he said and resumed his selection of music, "considering more troops are arriving daily. There are more restrictions placed on us. The soldiers are on edge."

I couldn't argue with him about his observations. "Where will you go on your impromptu tour?"

"The great music capitals in Europe," he answered in longing tones. "It's time for me to reacquaint myself with the passions of the world."

"Musical passions?"

"Of course, although there are all the other passions that one must experience, or one's own passion will extinguish."

"I hope to hear one of your concerts."

"I hope to see you at more than one."

He selected more scores to include in his trunk, then turned to me and asked. "Shall I include your concerto in my repertoire?"

"Unfortunately, it's not finished."

With a shake of his head, he said, "That's unfortunate. Was my advice not helpful?"

"The fault is all mine. It's become a jumble of notes and melodies and counterpoints, with no coherent theme and structure."

"Have you lost your passion for it?"

I hadn't considered that possibility, but I didn't believe so. I thought of the concerto constantly, as I often thought of its inspiration.

"I don't believe that's the case," I finally answered. "If anything, it's grown stronger. It might be that my passion overwhelms my ability to complete it."

Il Diavolo gave me a wry smile. "Better that than the other way."

chapter 34

The Stradivari family invited James and me to an officer rations dinner. While the meal was being prepared, Omobono was sent to invite Il Diavolo after I mentioned that he was leaving for his grand tour. Caterina suggested the violinist might bring some of his friends so they could play music in exchange for a share of the meal.

"If that's all right with you," Caterina said to me. "The meal is your doing, after all."

"That's more than fine with us," I said.

Mr. Stradivari led James and me into his workshop to show us the progress on the set of instruments. With just one look at them I could see even the most minute details had been attended to with precision and passion.

I said, "So beautiful! You haven't sold your soul to make these such beautiful instruments, have you?"

"I do that with every instrument," he said with a laugh. He then rapidly described the features of each instrument. I later noted as much as I could remember of those details.[1]

Just as he was finishing, we were soon summoned for dinner, which was a most enjoyable meal. Afterwards, we were entertained by the musicians, who played a few of their favorites before they played my latest version of the concerto.

Later, Caterina and I shared a few moments in private where she said, "Your concerto is marvelous. Even if you don't believe so, your strong emotions come through the music. I feel there's love and compassion, punctuated by loss and grief. An event has deeply affected

---

[1] For example, the main dimensions, the angle of the cross grain, the arching. *PW*

you. But I also agree you have yet to fully capture what you need to say with your concerto."

Her insight was penetrating. "Thank you."

After a moment of silence, she asked me, "I assume you're composing your concerto for someone?"

A hard lump grew in my chest. Quietly, I responded "Admittedly, yes."

"Say no more," she said with bravado. Then, matching my quiet tone, said, "Perhaps someday—"

Our conversation was interrupted by a loud banging on the door to the Stradivari home. From the shadows of the courtyard, I saw Omobono open the door to find Lt. Laurent.

"Good evening," the officer said to Omobono. "Is the master of the house at home?"

I started to rise, but Caterina tugged me down by the sleeve of my jacket.

Mr. Stradivari came to the door. "Good evening, sir. To what do we owe this honor?"

Perhaps, I thought, he had finally gotten word that there was no Phillipe Rémon of the Royal Musicians Office, or that there was no Royal Musicians Office at all. If not that, maybe he discovered our bribery of the storehouse guards.

"Good evening, Mr. Stradivari," said Lt. Laurent. "I happened to pass by earlier and believe I heard music."

Mr. Stradivari said, "Yes, sir. A little music was played."

"Excellent. I hope to be invited to your next concert."

"Of course! You'll be the first to receive an invitation."

"Thank you," said Lt. Laurent. Before leaving, he sniffed the air. "What delicious smells coming from your kitchen. Much better than the lowly meals we get in the officer's mess."

Mr. Stradivari said, "My wife and daughter do wonders with what we can manage to find."

On hearing that, Caterina and I suppressed our laughter.

J ames and I redoubled our efforts to become as familiar as we could with the renewed military presence without endangering ourselves. We took to the streets at dawn, and stayed out late into the day. We made special accommodations where we could: loosening a bolt to the guard tower door, finding places of ingress that were less guarded, noting the times when fewer guards were on duty.

Early one morning, when the pre-dawn cold was murderous and the last thing I wanted was to get out from under the blankets, we got up and went to the storehouse. We solicited the warehouse guards for more officer rations. They demanded twice the amount, and when they wouldn't negotiate their demand, we paid it. We divided our spoils, leaving half with Father Cozzoli, and half with the Stradivari family.

When we returned to the pensione, the innkeeper said to us: "I've been asked to tell you to go out the Po River gate just before sunset."

A message from Austrian forces had gotten through the French defenses.

We stayed in the room until the sun was setting, then hurried through the streets to the gate. We saw no one except passing soldiers after going through the gate, but we had to wait only a few moments before a man approached us ghostlike out of the deepening shadows.

Dressed as a farmer, he carried a sack over his back as if out to harvest some of his crop. With a nod, he led us back in the direction from which he had appeared. His pace was swift and James and I were nearly running to keep up with him.

We came to a narrow path off the main road which he turned onto, glancing back to make sure we were still following. Our breaths bloomed as clouds as we kept up with him, goat-like, on the path.

At a bend and up a slight rise in the path, we came to a small grove of trees. I could hear the breaths of horses, a good and welcoming sound, as I hoped we would ride to our destination.

Ride we did. Our guide took us cross-country at full gallop. The terrain was hilly and we stayed close to the tree line. I didn't see anyone until we came to the entrance of a valley. Lining the ridge were sentries. We rode through the gap and crossed a shallow stream. In the back corner of the valley, in a secluded break in the forest, the main Austrian forces were encamped. We rode past the soldiers who looked up at us with faces gaunt from battle. I felt soft as a lambkin compared to them.

We dismounted at a cluster of tents. The guide took away our horses and an officer showed us into the largest of the tents. Seated around a portable table were Prince Eugene of Savoy, General Vaudemont, and two other officers.

"Welcome," said the prince, then getting straight to the point asked, "What can you tell us?"

We gave them the general conditions in Cremona, describing the considerable rise in the numbers and the movements in and out of the city. We told them that the French troops were exhausted from battle, especially their defeat and hasty retreat from the northern Italian front. As we had witnessed, most of them spent evenings in the taverns, and if not on patrol during the day they were sleeping off their carousing in their barracks.

We updated the officers on the concentrations of French forces and their defenses of the city gates, especially of the Citadel across the Po River. Using our coded maps, we pointed out their warehouses and armories, designated watch towers, and stables.

The prince murmured his understanding at several points, and when we had finished our report, he said, "Excellent. That's one of the most detailed accounts of enemy placements I've ever heard. Correct, gentlemen?" he asked the other officers.

They all agreed; although whether they really did or not, I couldn't tell.

General Vaudemont said, "Unfortunately, the report reveals a well-fortified city. Good heavens, according to your count, there are more than seven thousand French troops and maybe a thousand Irish inside the walls. An attack would likely be very costly, despite our successes against them at Brescia, Chiari, and Soncino. We are undermanned and not supported this far from Austria."

The prince asked the other officers for their opinions and the discussion that ensued was lively and full of disagreement.

I felt it was my turn to speak up. "What if we have the element of surprise?"

General Vaudemont shook his head. "Trickery fails to impress me. It's a fool's game."

The prince raised his hand. "Tell me more, Captain."

I told them about the wine cellar under the parish and the willingness of the priest to help us.

General Vaudemont asked, "How can we trust this priest? Perhaps he's in collusion with the French."

I said, "He's no friend of the French. He admitted that to us. He has helped us in the past, when we had to dispose of a soldier whom we believed discovered our true identities. We've had other dealings with the priest as well."

The prince asked James his opinion.

"I wholeheartedly concur with Captain Wolf," said James.

General Vaudemont protested, "But to secret all of our forces through a wine cellar into a small parish?"

The prince said, "No, that wouldn't be wise. There should be a portion of the forces going through the tunnel, while the others will attack from the other side when the forces inside have opened the gate and reduced the forces inside as much as possible."

The other officers voiced their agreement.

The prince said to Vaudemont, "General?"

After a long pause, the General said, "Yes, that does make strategic sense. But how can we bring our forces close enough to strike quickly without being discovered?"

I said, "There is a less traveled back way." I told them about the forest with Stradivari's maples and the Po River marshes.

"I don't like marshes," said the general. "Too easy to become impeded."

"True," I said. "That's why the French avoid it. There will be no patrols to discover our march. But I believe it passable."

General Vaudemont, finally, had nothing to say.

The next day, I went to the Stradivari household. Caterina, holding her young half-sister, let me in, a worried look on her face. I asked if she were well.

"I am," she answered. "My little brother is feeling poorly."

I heard the infant's cry from inside. "I'm sorry to hear of his illness. I hope he recovers soon."

"Thank you for your kindness," she said quietly. "Father is in the workshop."

Mr. Stradivari was working with Omobono and Francesco, his white smock covered in wood shavings, his knit cap pulled down tightly. He greeted me, then asked if he could continue to work while we talked. "I have in mind what needs to be done with this piece, and if I sleep, it might be gone in the morning."

I watched him for a while as he polished and checked measurements with a fine wire gauge. He worked with such practiced precision, it seemed impossible anyone could learn how to achieve the same results.

"If I could interrupt your work for just a moment, I'd like to tell you something important."

Without looking up, he nodded.

"For the next few days, you and your family would be wise to stay away from the marsh where you get the horsetails, away from the maple grove. Please, stay close to home." Hoping it was unnecessary, I added, "I'll do everything in my power to keep you and your family safe."

Again without looking at me, without pausing his work, he nodded.

I hoped he took my warning in all seriousness. Not only did I wish him no harm, but selfishly, I needed him to create my violin.

chapter 35

T he evening before the attack, James and I moved into the parish. We guarded the entrance to make sure the French stayed away. While we watched, I rambled about our last dinner with Dr. Newton and Catherine and Rose. James agreed it was a most excellent evening. He reminisced about our times in London, our roles in bringing down the counterfeiters, our attendance at the Kit-Cat Club, and then, less rambling and in almost a whisper, told me that Mr. Montagu wanted him to make sure I never returned to England.

Although I wasn't surprised, the revelation sent a tremor through me. "At what lengths did he want you to go to ensure that?"

"He didn't specify the methods, but it was clear I was to do whatever was needed."

"I hope you'll receive adequate reward for accomplishing your mission."

"There was no mention of reward, but I assume there would be if I asked. Of course, if I fail, there will likely be retribution."

"Undoubtedly. Did he say why he wanted me to be banished from England?"

"Not directly, but vaguely about mistrusting your motives."

"I'm sorry you've been put into this position," I said. "I'll be watching my back from now on."

"As well you should," said James, with a grin I could see even in the dim light.

"It's my affair with Catherine," I said.

"I suppose it is," he said.

We left it at that.

At midnight, the priest left the wine cellar door unlocked before he retired for the night. James and I barred all doors to the sanctuary and side entrances, and extinguished all candles. While James stayed in the sanctuary to make sure it was safely locked and deserted, I hurried through the catacombs to the wine cellar where I opened the door to the dry moat. The night air was cold and damp, perfect conditions for fog to form. When all looked clear, I went out, crossed the moat, and climbed the other side. The effort warmed me and I hurried as quickly as I could in the dark.

I followed the path until I came to the waiting forces. Prince Eugene met me there. "All is as planned, Captain Wolf?"

"Yes, sir. We're ready."

"Good," he said then turned and paced along the line of grenadiers. "As a soldier, you are never fully prepared for battle, just as a man is never fully prepared for life. Yet both must be fought and lived. We will never be fully prepared for battle; we must only be more prepared than our enemy. Tonight, we have more than a single advantage. We have an elite fighting force, the best on the continent, and we have the element of surprise."

Whether the soldiers appreciated his speech, I didn't know. But it was true only if the surprise attack was executed with precision. What could go wrong? Of course, there were many things—Father Cozolli might have second thoughts, or had been working with the French from the beginning, or he was tortured into revealing the plan. Or the French might be more alert than assumed. The attack might unravel and collapse because of unforeseen delays or random bad luck.

Finally, when the night seemed the darkest, and the fog was as thick as it would ever be, Prince Eugene said to me, "Lead us from here. Two lieutenants are at your command. And here ..." He motioned for one of his officers to come forward with a sword in a scabbard and a flintlock pistol with powder bag and shot.

I acknowledged his trust, and thanked him for the weapons. When I had secured the weapons, I issued the one-word order: "Forward."

Leather boots creaked and packs shifted as the soldiers began their march. One soldier muttered a brief prayer, "God help us." Others laughed nervously.

I led the way on the path. In a few minutes the men were breathing heavily keeping up with my pace. As the air grew colder, the soldiers' exhaled breaths condensed into clouds obscuring their faces.

Within sight of the wall of the city, I motioned them to stop. I surveyed the wall for any light or movement that might betray a trap. I saw nothing and tapped the shoulder of one of the soldiers who darted ahead through a thicket to the cellar door. After a moment he reappeared and waved his arm that all was clear.

I gestured for the next soldier to move forward. When they were moving into the catacombs, I followed the line of soldiers into the cellar, lighted with the yellow, flickering glow of a candle. I walked along the narrow tunnel passing the wine cellar. Along the sides of the tunnel were caves carved into the rock, lined with brick and filled with stacks of bottles. The stale air smelled of damp soil and layers of dust that had settled on the bottles.

At the head of the line, I clapped the lieutenant on the shoulder. He went to the end of the tunnel where the stairs led up to the door into the parish. Pulling on the handle, the door creaked open enough for him to look inside. Then he opened it fully and disappeared inside.

After a few moments, the lieutenant returned with James who motioned that all was clear. I waved the men through and up the stone steps. We gathered in the darkness of the parish, filling it wall-to-wall with more than three hundred men.

The soldiers' rustling, coughs, even their breathing was loud. Prince Eugene hushed them with a quick hiss. When it was dead quiet, the prince, the two lieutenants, and James and I gathered near the front door.

We reviewed the status of the forces defending Cremona. Only a handful of sentries were at the lesser gates, while a contingent of Irish was quartered at the Po River gate. The French officers, including Marshal duc Villeroi, supreme commander, were lodged at Offredi Palace[1] near Cremona's main plaza.

Prince Eugene split his advance forces into two—one heading to the main barracks of the French soldiers, the other to open the gates and allow the rest of Eugene's forces to advance to the Offredi Palace. James would guide the first half and I the other. Our halves would then rejoin to take over the Po River bridge and gate and allow General Vaudemont's forces to enter the city. James would take the first shot—the signal for us to attack as well.

When we verified our understandings of the plan, Prince Eugene and the lieutenants divided the forces, then gave the order to attack. Before we moved out, I wished James good luck. "I will see you soon!" he answered.

I clapped him on the shoulder.

Sneaking hundreds of soldiers through the night seemed an impossible task once we started filing out of the parish. The city was filled with our footsteps, creaking leather, and breathing. With Prince Eugene at my shoulder I led our group through the deserted streets. Eventually we encountered a local tradesman up early to begin work. Startled, he froze. I waved him back into his shop. He did that, shutting the door behind him.

When we neared the gate, I motioned for the men to stop and stay still as possible. I went ahead with a lieutenant toward the gate, found the loose bolt to the guard tower lock and removed it. With our

---

[1] Now known as the Cavalcabò. *TS*

pistols drawn, the lieutenant and I stole up the steps. We surprised the young sentry who was half-asleep perched over one of the tower openings. Startled, he raised his musket.

I aimed my pistol at him. "No, sir, do not," I said in French.

Sheepishly, he lowered his weapon to the floor and raised his hands. We tied and gagged him, then opened the gate for the remainder of the advance force.

Back with the others, we made our way toward the Offredi Palace. Anticipating the upcoming confrontation, my heart was pounding, lungs heaving. As we neared the palace in the dead of night, in the thickening fog, I saw a dull flash and then not long after, the muffled crack of a musket shot. The delay at the precise distance from the barracks, I estimated, thinking back to my first meeting with Dr. Newton. Of course, the wet fog would affect the speed of sound, slowing it as the air is denser, I assumed.[2] Then I wondered if the wet air also affected the speed of the light from the muzzle.

I suppressed my errant thoughts.

James' signal shot ignited the battle. We ran through the streets, and quickly reached the palace. No soldiers were yet outside, still soundly sleeping. We gathered the forces in attack-and-defend positions around the Palace entrances, then without a pause, we broke down the doors and rushed inside.

I followed the second wave into the lower levels of the palace. We quickly spread out. I heard a shout, then the loud crack of a shot, a moan, then silence. The first casualty; I hoped it was not ours.

The volley woke the entire force inside the palace. Musket fire was now exploding everywhere. Screams and grunts and moans filled what little voids of sounds were left. I moved into the battle and soon

---

[2] Thinking about it later, I came to the correct conclusion that while the air is denser, which lengthens the time for the sound wave to start moving, the increased density helps the wave go faster. Of course, as Dr. Newton pointed out, the air temperature also affects the speed as it affects density. Such complexity ... *PW*

saw the defenders pouring out of their sleeping quarters, most un-dressed, unprepared for what they likely couldn't believe was happen-ing. I reached the frontline with Prince Eugene just behind me. As the corridors become more well defended, I shot my pistol. The prince then fired his while I reloaded.

Clearing a path to the stairway up to the officer's quarters did not take long, but the soldiers and officers at the top of the stairs had the advantage of being able to shoot down. To counter their firing, we formed several wedges and sent volley after volley of shot toward their positions. When they retreated, we were able to reach the top of the stairway.

The French officers backed further into their quarters. We again formed our wedges, and advanced from both directions. With their backs to the walls, the French officers fired wildly. We advanced quickly, the prince and I heading to the quarters of their general, a handful of the best following behind us. Reaching the doorway, we lined up on both sides. I slowly entered the room to find three of his guards pointing pistols at us. I ducked quickly back, but as I did, I noticed movement behind the men, and saw that the window was open.

With our soldiers leading the way, we charged into the room, rapidly dispatching the guards. I ran to the window and looked out. Two figures had dropped in the courtyard. I eased myself over the windowsill.

The prince said, "Be careful."

I let go and dropped to the ground. Landing awkwardly, I rolled to absorb the rest of the force. I scrambled to my feet and ran after the two. They were well ahead of me, but I pushed forward until I got to the end of the courtyard and the back gate. It took them sev-eral moments to get it open and I was able to catch up with them.

They both turned, and I saw one was Marshal duc de Villeroi. The other was Lt. Laurent.

They both bore pistols. I raised mine, as they did theirs. A volley of gunfire distracted them, some of the musket balls hitting the wall to the left of me. I managed to step to the right, avoiding the fire. They turned to flee out of the gate. I raised my pistol again and fired as they made their escape. My shot hit Villeroi in the thigh and he spun down. He shouted at Lt. Laurent when he stopped to help, commanding him to escape. Lt. Laurent growled like a mad dog, then ran off into the fog.

I wanted to chase him, but instead stayed with our trophy, the duc de Villeroi, grand marshal of the French forces.

B y sunrise, the French forces at the palace were subdued, and the Marshal and most of the officers under arrest. Prince Eugene and his officers set up headquarters in the Hotel de Ville, taking over the room where James and I once hid. When all was established there, I went to search for James.

I found him outside the barracks. There were dozens of dead and injured, more French than ours. Most of the shivering French were dressed in their nightclothes and barefoot.

James looked relieved to see me, and I him. He had great splatters of blood but when I expressed concern, he insisted it wasn't his.

"How was the attack?" I asked him.

"The surprise was successful."

I heard a volley of musket shots inside the barracks.

James said, "We still have pockets of resistance. But most have laid down their arms. All must have gone well with you, since you are here."

I briefly told him what happened at the Offredi Palace and that the prince was directing the battle from the Hotel de Ville.

"Good," James said. "What about General Vaudémont? Has there been word yet if he is attacking from the Po River gate?"

"That question I can't answer," I said. "We must bring a few men with us to find out what's happening."

We gathered a platoon of soldiers and ran to the gate. We did not hear any great confrontation as we neared. Instead there was an unnerving quiet, and I felt as if we were being watched. I held back in the narrow streets.

"What is it?" James asked.

"I have a feeling the Irish battalions protecting the gate have spies."

James looked around. "That could be."

"Let's proceed alone," I said.

James nodded. He and I went ahead, staying close to the wall and in the dark doorways. As we neared, we could hear the voices of Irish outside the guard towers. James said they were talking about the need to stay to guard the gate, rather than join the battle.

James and I retreated. Obviously, General Vaudémont's forces had not yet made it to the city. We headed back to the Hotel de Ville to report directly to Prince Eugene.

"Vaudémont should have launched his attack by now," he said.

I said, "Shall we ride out to see what is delaying him?"

"Yes, go," said the prince.

James and I found horses and rode out through the gate we opened earlier. The fog was already lifting except for the low areas where it was a thick winter blanket over the marsh. We picked our way slowly through the winter terrain of fallow fields and bare trees.

We arrived at the spot where we met the forces before. A platoon had camped there, and when they saw we were not the French, they greeted us, asking for news of the secret attack. They told us that General Vaudémont's forces were stalled by the terrain, especially the cannon, which were bogged down.

We waited until a messenger arrived. He told us they were moving, but very slowly. It might not even be today that they could arrive at Cremona. The messenger also reported that a relieving French battalion was on its way to Cremona. That was not good to hear either.

James asked the messenger, "Which force will make it first to Cremona—the Austrians or the French?"

"I can't say with confidence either way," the messenger said. "I can only watch and report what I see."

I said, "Please gather more about the situation, and send it to Prince Eugene."

The messenger rode out to complete his mission. James and I returned to the city. When we arrived, there was still sporadic fighting in the area of the barracks. James and I reported to the prince.

"That's most vexing," he said after our report. "We can't hold out forever, despite our immediate advantage."

I said, "We can at least make it seem our forces are near—if we take the Po River gate and open it."

Prince Eugene said, "We barely have enough forces to keep the remaining French under control. How could we attack the gate? The Irish are tenaciously guarding it."

I said, "What if we don't have to fire a shot?"

James knew what I was going to suggest. "A bribe? That's a good idea. The Irish get paid less than their French equivalents. We can surely entice them with coin."

Prince Eugene said, "Yes, we should try that while we have the upper hand."

James said, "I should be the one to make the offer. I know the Irish better than most here."

I said, "But they best not know of an Englishman already fighting in the war."

"I doubt that would make a difference. We'll likely be in the fight soon. No, it must be me."

With the prince's agreement to provide the funds, James and I went to the Po Gate. James presented himself with a white flag to the guards. Without a look back he disappeared into the guardhouse.

I waited for James to return with an acceptance of an offer. But he did not. I thought of going to the guardhouse myself, but knew it foolhardy. I returned to the headquarters and reported to the prince.

Perturbed, he said, "If they're not to be moved with money, we shall have to move them with force."

I wanted to say that such action would put James at risk. But I couldn't, and I volunteered to lead the men. The prince granted that request and I gathered the soldiers I could take away from their duties guarding the French in the barracks. There were only a hundred of us, against maybe four hundred of the remaining Irish.

We split out into two groups, attacking the gate from the flanks rather than full on at the front where most of the defenses were positioned. But the Irish had set the bridge on fire. It was clear that we would not be able to take the guardhouse and I ordered a retreat. I made it back to the headquarters, disconsolate at not having rescued James.

The prince said, "It was the correct course of action. Every one of our soldiers is needed."

We tried to agree to another strategy, but it was clear that if the French reinforcements arrived before ours, we were doomed.

Nearing the end of daylight in the late afternoon, with still no word from General Vaudémont, and the French gradually retaking control of many of their posts, the prince announced we would have to retreat. We would take with us the Marshall and the captured officers. As we made the preparations, the platoon leaders reported that the French had lost many soldiers, but we had also lost many.[3]

---

[3] The dead numbered about 400 (around 1500 total casualties) for the Austrians, and 1100 for the French. The Irish brigades suffered 350 casualties. *PW*

As the short-lived conquering army of Prince Eugene made its retreat, I stayed behind in Cremona. When they were gone, I made my way through the wreck of the battle to the Stradivari house.

chapter 36

As usual, Mr. Stradivari recollected to me, he rose before dawn to organize the day's work. He hated to lose one moment of daylight. His life was passing too quickly and he had much to accomplish before he could no longer hold a saw or chisel or horsetail. His technique, he believed, was improving with each violin, viola, violoncello, but the path to perfection was long and required infinite patience.

The musket shots and shouts caught his attention but even without my warning, he wasn't surprised. No Cremona resident capable of thought should have been surprised. Who didn't suspect that the Austrian troops were massing on the Po River plain, readying their battle plans to attack the French occupiers of Cremona? No one cared too much, on the contrary, life was mostly good. Farmers and merchants were supplying both armies with bread and wine, cheese and meat, fruits and vegetables to fill their commissaries. Before the French occupied Cremona, the city-state had been under the rule of the Spanish Hapsburgs. One was as bad as the other. Taxes were taxes, laws were laws.

As the battle grew more intense—the French obviously getting the worst of it—he portioned that day's work for himself and Francesco and Omobono. There was the rough shaping of two back pieces left for Francesco, and gluing the ribs onto blocks for Omobono. Mr. Stradivari was working on the final smoothing of a violin belly, delicate work, done with feel. This he left for himself. Neither son had yet developed the sensitivity required. Whether they ever would was a question he couldn't answer.

The battle sounds grew louder, closer. He could make out grunts and shouted commands. Curiosity got the better of him and he went up to the secadùur. Peering over the short wall, he could see the flash of muskets fired through the fog.

He thought of telling Antonia to bar all the doors and windows—but there was no need, she would have already secured them. Observant and calm, she ran their household with efficiency and frugality.

He went back to the workshop, keeping his ears open to the battle. What he would do if it came to his house, he had no idea. He had no weapon other than his tools, and none would serve him well in that regard. As he used his thumb plane to shave pieces so thin, they were nearly invisible, he grew more concerned that the battle, the war in general, would affect his business. A prolonged conflict might depress the market for his instruments. That would be tragic as he was excited to start each new commission.

The shooting became more frantic, seemingly from all directions. What a bad stroke of luck if his life was ended by a stray musket ball. He tried to put the thought out of his mind to concentrate on the delicate shaving.

Almost as suddenly as it started, except for some sporadic shooting, the battle seemed over. The Stradivari household settled into their daily routine as well as they could. The rumors began to filter in —all of the French were dead and the Austrians were pillaging the city, or the Austrians were all dead and the French were pillaging the city.

"What's the true story?" Mr. Stradivari asked me when I was in their home.

"Something between those two," I answered. I told him of the early successes then how it fell apart and that James had been captured. "He tried to resolve the standoff peacefully. I'm sure he's being tortured for his efforts. That's why I'm still here."

"I'm sorry to hear about your friend," Mr. Stradivari said. "Can you rescue him?"

For that question I had no answer. I didn't know what happened to him when he went into the Irish guardhouse. I didn't know if he was alive, but I had to assume he was and likely now in French hands. Whether they had found out his true identity, I couldn't speculate one way or the other.

"I wish I knew," I said.

Mr. Stradivari said, "Perhaps I can help."

I was struck by his offer, but also concerned. "You've done so much already for me. I can't put you in danger."

"I don't want that either, but if I could do it without arousing suspicion."

"If that's possible, I would be most grateful. But please, if it can't be done safely, then abandon the quest. To add to that, if my mere presence here is putting you or your family in danger, tell me and I'll leave."

Mr. Stradivari waved his hands. "No, no. I respect you even more now that I know the full truth of the matter. My own truth is that I'm grateful you're still alive. Perhaps if we disguised you as a worker here, you'll remain safe, and we won't be in danger."

"It might work," I said, although I was skeptical.

In my wool cap pulled low, leather apron enveloping me, my face dabbed with wood dust, I might pass for an apprentice, an old one, so said Caterina who laughed as she put together my disguise. As an apprentice, I started at the lowest rung of the luthier ladder—sweeping the floors, and while I did that, Francesco and Omobono went about their duties. Francesco was the focused worker, diligently and skillfully drawing and cutting the ribs. Omobono, working less diligently on sharpening chisels, caught my eye when I neared him, and for the first time since I met him, he didn't smile when he saw me. Instead with a frown set in stone, he pressed me for details on the battle. But I couldn't accommodate him in that regard as they weren't pleasant recollections, and I could only think of James.

While Mr. Stradivari went out to be my eyes and ears, I finished my apprentice duties and then helped Caterina with dinner preparations. She was quiet, and occasionally shivered, as if cold, but I knew it wasn't that.

"I'm sorry for the war that has affected you and your family."

"It's horrible. How can you exist by fighting battles?"

"It often becomes just that, existing through them. Simply mustering strength, thinking ahead."

She gave that some thought while stirring the soup. "Still, it must be horrible."

More often it's worse than that, I thought.

Just as dinner was ready, Mr. Stradivari returned, reporting on the continuing chaotic scene after the battle. The dead were being loaded on wagons. The wounded were spilling out into the plaza, struggling to stay alive in the cold while waiting for their treatment in the hospital. A few captured prisoners were pushed along in the streets, but he didn't see James.

A French battalion had arrived to reinforce the defenses of the city, but there was still chaos. The soldiers were taking it out on the citizens, leaving them with nearly no food or other goods.

"We'd best stay out of their way," he said.

I knew he was correct, but I couldn't imagine James in the hands of the French for a moment more than necessary.

I asked Mr. Stradivari, "Did you find out where the prisoners were being held?"

"There was no word of that."

"It wouldn't have been good to raise suspicions by asking either. Was there any talk about the surprise attack?"

"There was much talk about how the Austrians appeared from everywhere like magic."

It must have seemed that way.

We finished our simple dinner, then worked into the evening. My mind was on how I would find out where the prisoners were held captive. Even so, I was also intrigued to watch Mr. Stradivari working on a violin, finishing the final shaping and polishing of the belly. He constantly checked the thicknesses with his gauges, turning the wood this way and that, as if his eyes were more accurate than his gauges —likely they were. His patience and care were so much more than I could ever imagine that I would have.

Seemingly satisfied, he suddenly stopped. He turned to me and said, as if he had been thinking of this all while he worked, "Your Englishman, Dr. Newton, is seeking a revelation of sound as the voice of universal truth. Not as in a divine being, no, but as in something that exists naturally and made perceptible only through our clumsy attempts. Every once in a great while, in many centuries, the very essence of that universal truth is made transparent. We believe we are on the cusp of such a time.

"He's searching for the ingredients and materials of universal truths, obtained from his observations and experiments, his principles of motion and mathematics that describe them. These are like the ingredients and materials I need to create a musical instrument except they aren't on paper. I scour markets and fields and forests, meeting with merchants and wood cutters and if I can't find what I need, I will create it myself."

He showed me one of his gauges. "I had to commission a tool maker to create a special set of calipers. The standard ones didn't meet my needs. I've come to this realization that your Englishman and I are more alike than either of us would like to agree."

His words gripped my heart, as much as Catherine's words had when we first met. They commanded as much attention as did all of the great words Dr. Newton had said to me. They were all part of some great symphony. And I realized what I had been composing had been so shallow compared to what Catherine, her uncle, and now Mr. Stradivari were saying that I felt crushed beyond insignificance.

New music was playing in my head all night. I wrote down the score by candlelight, furiously scratching my pen over makeshift score paper. It was magnificently different from anything I'd ever composed before, unlike anything I'd ever heard. It was a cry for the universal truth, for the essence of humanity, the unfathomable meaning of love.

It was my lament.

In the morning, I left my room in the Stradivari house and went down to the workshop. Mr. Stradivari was there alone, already preparing for the day's work.

"You don't have to get up this early," he said.

"I haven't been asleep."

I handed Mr. Stradivari a note I had written in French. It read: "To Lieutenant Laurent of the French army. I know the whereabouts of the man you seek, and also the knowledge of the surprise attack you desire. If you come alone tonight to the Parish of Santa Maria Nuova, you'll find both."

I told him, "Of course, don't deliver it yourself, please. You can't be connected with this in any way."

"I understand," he said. "I'll make sure it's in his hands."

When he left, I turned to my apprentice tasks, first cleaning up from the work last night, then helping Francesco with the placement of the ribs in a viola. I asked him what he thought of his father as a luthier.

He said, "I don't understand much of what he says or does. He shows me how to do it. But when I try it, I can't do it exactly the same, no matter how many times I try. He will not show me again, believing that if I can't grasp the technique or the idea with one explanation, then I'll never be able to ever grasp it. I don't think that's true, but he won't change. So I'm relegated to the simple parts. But I'm working on my own violins now, when I have time."

"Is this how he learned, do you believe?"

"He can't say how he learned. Whether from another master, such as Amati. Or if he learned on his own. I don't know."

"His skill must seem unattainable by anyone else."

Francesco thought about this for some time. "Perhaps it is," he said, and went back to work, resigned to his place in the Stradivari workshop.

W hen Mr. Stradivari returned, he gave me a quick nod. We finished up the rest of the day, had a meager dinner of stale break soaked in broth. When it was well dark, I said my goodbyes and left on my mission. I said I would be back, when concern darkened the faces of the family.

Dressed in a worker's smock and coat, I carried a basket as if scavenging for food. The city was still in chaos, with many out looking for food and other essentials. Bodies were stacked along the wall where they had fallen. Blood had congealed into black stains. The gate and guard station patrols had been tripled.

I made it to the parish without being challenged. Inside the rectory, a few of the Cremona residents were seated staring ahead to the altar, or at the floor. A few were praying on their knees, an older woman fervent in her prayers.

I didn't see the priest. He could be away or in his office or he had fled with our retreating forces. Nor did I see Lt. Laurent. I waited in the back shadows, watching the parishioners come and go. When there were only a handful left, the lieutenant stepped into the church.

He looked around, then took a few steps inside. I walked past him and whispered, "This way."

He followed me to the side door; I held it open for him. He hesitated, then went in, turning around so he could see me.

In the dark, I doubted he could recognize me. Closing the door, I said, "Let's go down to the wine cellar."

"Rémon!" exclaimed the lieutenant. "You didn't turn tail and run with your fellow Austrians?"

I said, "I'll answer your questions later."

There was a candle and a flint lighter in the catacombs. I lit it and we went further into the cellar.

"Shall we open a bottle?" I said.

"We may as well," he said.

I found one and opened it. I poured the wine into mugs.

We took a drink. The lieutenant smacked his lips, then shrugged. "It will do. So, what do you have to tell me?"

"I'm sure you would like to know more of what happened in the attack."

"I'm curious, yes, but it has already happened and I cannot change that. I would like to know what has happened with Marshal duc de Villeroi."

"I'd like to exchange that information for information about my colleague, Jacques Marchand. He was taken by the Irish."

The lieutenant hesitated before he said, "I can't speak for the Irish, whom they might have, or whom they don't."

"I don't believe that. I'm sure they've reported to you and turned over any captives."

Lt. Laurent took a long drink. "I speak the truth. I only want the marshal returned to us. What do you want in exchange?"

"The return of my friend. That's all."

"You have the power to make this exchange?" he asked.

"I have the ear of Prince Eugene of Savoy."

He gave me a long gaze. "The Irish are using their success in the defense of Cremona to increase their pay, provisions, and other doles. They may not want to turn over any prisoner until their demands are satisfied."

"Give them what they want," I said.

"If it were up to me——"

I lost my patience. "It *has* to be up to you. There's no choice for what must happen now."

"I don't think you are in the position to make demands. You aren't much more than a rat in hiding. In fact, I believe it's time that you join your friend in our prison."

The lieutenant pulled a pistol from inside his coat. "I'm confident with you in our custody as well, we will have more power to negotiate the return of the Marshal duc de Villeroi."

"So, you do have him in your custody?"

Lt. Laurent waved his pistol at me. "Of course. We wouldn't let the Irish hold him. You can see him for yourself. Let's go."

I turned to walk out of the wine cellar. As we went past one of the niches in the catacombs, a blur of a figure came out of the shadows. The man grabbed the lieutenant's arm, twisted it, and the pistol flew away before he could get off a shot. I whirled around and together we tackled the lieutenant and had him on his stomach, and trussed his hands with catgut.

My co-conspirator was Antonio Stradivari.

In the lieutenant's uniform and in the residual chaos of the battle, I was not challenged and gained access to the prison where I transferred James into my custody. When we were safely back in the wine cellar, he told me about his capture and imprisonment. The cellar underneath the Offredi Palace, the French headquarters of the occupation, served as a prisoner of war dungeon. The dank and cold walls were depressing, but not as much as the continuous darkness. The guards were sullen and indifferent to him, neither cruel nor sympathetic. They disliked the time they spent in the cellar too. The guards on duty, both French privates, likely undistinguished in battle or serving a punishment for insubordination, came for him shortly after the morning meal, the only way he could keep track of the passing hours and days. They escorted James into an office where the bright sunshine streaming through the windows blinded him. The guards pushed him into a chair. James steeled himself for another round of torture. His ribs ached, and his bruises refreshed their dull throbbing pain.

"May I offer you a glass of wine?" said a voice.

James shaded his eyes until he could make out a tall French officer standing in front of him. "Is it poisoned?"

Lt. Laurent spoke as if reprimanding a child for a prank. "A Frenchman poisoning wine? Never mind then. Let's get straight to the point. Where have they taken the Marshal?"

"I'm a humble assistant with the musician's union," James said.

Again, the lieutenant laughed. "Don't insult my intelligence. You are one of the leaders of the surprise attack. That much I know. You are immune to torture as well according to reports. I wish you were under my command."

James said, "No one is immune to torture. I simply have nothing of value for you."

"I'm sure you were part of the surprise attack. Why else would you be the one trying to bribe the Irish into abandoning their posts?"

James said, "I was only trying to stop further bloodshed."

The lieutenant struck James across his cheek with the back of his hand. "I want to know where they're holding the marshal. I want to hear if another attack is imminent."

"You want to know many things. Perhaps if you had done your job the first time, none of these questions would be necessary."

The lieutenant turned red, struck James again, then left him with the other inquisitors.

I pointed to the lieutenant, now tied up in the corner of the wine cellar, his head drooping until his chin rested on his chest, and said to James, "You can take your revenge now."

James shook his head. "He was doing his duty."

"You're fortunate," I said to Lt. Laurent.

The officer shrugged casually, as if his life were spared every day. "Would that I first acted on my suspicion."

"What did raise your suspicion?" I asked him.

He shook his head a little. "You spoke more like a confidant military officer than a lowly bureaucrat."

"Lowly!" James laughed.

I found it humorous as well.

We finished a bottle of wine, then I motioned for James to follow me. Out of earshot of the lieutenant, I said, "I must visit Mr. Stradivari before we leave. I'll return quickly and we can be away with our prisoner before sunrise."

"Be careful," James said

I was able to sneak through the city still in the lieutenant's uniform, and I arrived quickly at the Stradivari home. Mr. Stradivari was still awake in the workshop.

I said to Mr. Stradivari, "I must leave now. But my heart is heavy that we were unable to liberate your wonderful city. I have to leave the instruments you made for me and the other documents. I don't want to be caught with them in case that should happen."

"I'm sure you'll be safe," said Mr. Stradivari. "You are most resourceful."

"I promise to return when this war is over. I hope it will be a short conflict."

"As do I," he said. "War is not good for business."

Nor is it good for love.

coda

There was a time I'd been impatient watching Huygens' clock while waiting a few minutes for Sir Isaac Newton to allow me an audience. By the time a treaty was signed,[1] eleven years had passed since the Battle of Cremona. Another four interminable years dragged on before the last battle was fought. Even then, there was so much to do to ensure peace would be lasting, and thus it was another year, a total of sixteen, before I could return to Cremona.

As I rode up to the Po River gate, sadness overcame me, a wave of realization of so much lost time. Since James and I departed the city through the parish wine cellar tunnel along with our prisoner, I'd been in Prince Eugene's military. Based on the trust the prince put in me, I quickly moved up the chain of command until I was a field general commanding two battalions. The pressures of the war were punishing, with many successes and failures, before the war ground down into a stalemate, both sides declaring victory.

There were no guards at the gate, yet with a shudder of dread I recalled the last time I went through it, wondering if a French lieutenant named Laurent was lying in wait for me.

Past the open gate, the streets of Cremona were bustling. I stabled my horse and walked through the city that seemed changed. For one, all the buildings, streets, and piazzas appeared much older than I remembered, although a few facades were being renovated.

But the Stradivari house was seemingly untouched from the war and time. I didn't immediately approach the house. I must admit I felt a certain uneasiness in entering the Stradivari home and workshop. I didn't know what I would say, nor did I know what I wanted to see. There hadn't been a day that I hadn't thought of Antonio Stradivari and his family, especially Caterina, contemplating what I learned from them. I hoped them to be well and happy, of course,

---

[1] While the Treaty of Utrecht, signed in April 1713, established a broadly applied notion of peace among the nations involved in the War of Spanish Succession, there were several conflicts and individual treaties to be concluded. *PW*

and to have had continued success making their great and wonderful stringed instruments.

Equally, rarely had a day passed that I did not also wonder where Sir Isaac Newton's genius was taking him—somewhere beyond my understanding I was certain. As with Antonio, Sir Isaac's voice stayed in my mind, ready to critique my reasoning before I ordered one action or another on the battlefield, or in life. For one thing, thanks to what I learned from both Antonio and Isaac, I was able to suggest improvements to the construction of our artillery and other equipment.

Pressure! It all came down to pressure.

And the thoughtful, empathetic skill of finding truth, even if it was in the humble horsetail plant.

Memories of Catherine also sustained me. Especially when all ebbed to a low point, her bright enthusiasm and wit, her grasp of the human condition, lifted me up. And I often thought of the concerto I finished before the Battle of Cremona and left with Antonio. I did no more work on it, at least not on paper. In my head, I fought my personal battle with the score, but hadn't found a change that would stick, none that would make it better. Also, the boom of cannon and the crack of musket fire interfered with the beautiful melancholy of the concerto.

Someone opened the door of the Stradivari home—a boy about ten years old, carrying a pail filled with sawdust. He was already getting tall, still thin, but with a bright, curious expression as he gazed at me. I could see both Antonio and Antonia in his appearance.

"Hello," I said in Italian.

"Good morning, sir. May I help you?"

"I would like to speak with Mr. Antonio Stradivari."

"Father is in his workshop. I can take you there."

"That would be wonderful."

"Follow me, please."

The smell of bread baking and fresh wood shavings filled my memory with warmth. There were other smells and sounds—a rich mix of varnishes cooking, saws sawing, many voices speaking at once.

We turned into the workshop. There, Omobono, Francesco, and two other boys were at work.

"Father," said the boy, "this man would like to speak with you."

Antonio Stradivari, only slightly aged from our last time together, looked up from the violin belly on which he was tracing a line of purfling. There was only the briefest moment of perplexity in his eyes, of wondering who I might be.

"You!" he exclaimed as he jumped up.

He greeted me as a long-lost lover with an embrace. Omobono and Francesco jumped up as well and we all exchanged long greetings. Antonio introduced me to his sons Paolo,[2] the boy who showed me in the workshop, and Giovanni and Giuseppe, the young apprentices.[3]

All work stopped. We went into the main part of the house where Antonia and Caterina were coming into the workshop to see what was causing the commotion. They also greeted me with surprise and great warmth. We started talking at the same time, exchanging bits of our lives since the last time we saw each other.

In only a few minutes, we[4] all gathered around the family table, heaped with more food and drink than I had ever seen. At least the end of the war was good for the stomach. They wanted to know what had happened after Antonio had helped me escape with James. I briefly told them that we quickly caught up with Prince Eugene and

---

[2] Paolo was born in 1708. *PW*

[3] Giovanni was born in 1703, and Giuseppe in 1704. *PW*

[4] Besides Caterina and the sons, Francesca, born in 1700, was still living in the Stradivari home. *PW*

retreated away from the advancing French forces, then we went our separate ways as I stayed close to Prince Eugene throughout the war.

Antonia said, "I'm sorry to say that many times we assumed you were ... gone forever."

Omobono said, "As in dead."

I laughed at that and said, "That wouldn't have been an unrealistic supposition."

I compressed the ensuing years into a manageable tale. When I finished, I asked them to tell me what had been happening in the workshop and in Cremona.

Antonio said with a smile, "For one thing, we managed to finish your set of instruments. Thank you for giving us a little extra time."

We all laughed.

I said, "I'm surprised you still have them."

Omobono said, "Admittedly, we tried to get father to sell them several times."

"I wouldn't have blamed you if you had. I should pay you for storing them for so long."

Antonio waved his hand in refusal. He related their tale, one of survival in the aftermath of the Battle of Cremona and the few years under French rule until they had to abandon northern Italy. Life was hard, but they maintained their workshop output at a healthy level.

"We were fortunate," he said.

But I didn't believe luck or providence had anything to do with their success.

When we finished chatting and eating. Antonio took me to their storage room. "We've been taking very good care of your instruments. Our local musicians have played them to help with the curing process."

"Thank you. I wish I could have contacted you, but, the war ..."

"There's no need to apologize. We would have kept your instruments forever. Besides, you paid in full!"

In the storage room, several instruments were on stands or racks. A tag with a name dangled from each. Four of them read: "Phillipe Rémon, Royal Musicians Office." As I looked at each, I was speechless, without a breath of air in my lungs. The depth of beauty in the varnish drew me in like a magical sea, refracting light into colors as seen through Sir Isaac's prisms. The body lines were perfect, the purfling as exact as the edge of a crystal, and the scroll like a living rose.

Especially the wondrous, my perfect, violin.

I finally caught my breath. "They are so incredible, as if made in heaven."

Antonio chuckled. "It was more like hell, trying to understand and use your Englishman's science and mathematics. And then trying to create the instruments to best match your music composition, also caused me many sleepless nights."

"I'm sorry to put you through that," I said.

"I was speaking largely in jest. It was inspiring and stimulating. I don't know how well I met your expectations, but to me it was just having the chance to expand my thoughts. In the end, however, I could only rely on what I've learned over many years, which materials provide the purest sound, which techniques will bring out the best in the materials."

"I understand," I said. "I'm certain what you have created here is beyond any of my meager requirements."

"I don't know if that's true," he said. "The only thing that matters is the pleasure the violin induces. Shall we set up a test concert for you?"

"I'm more excited than I can say to hear them."

"Then let me arrange it."

During the time Antonio needed to set up the concert, I stayed with the Stradivari family. I reacquainted myself with Sir Isaac's manuscript. The first time I looked at it after so many years, I realized I'd only understood so little of it. But after studying it with benefit of time, the science and mathematics began to make more sense. So much so, I started to make notes, adding them to the account I'd started writing not long ago.

The concert was held in a new hall, rising from the disruption of the war. When the evening arrived, Omobono and Caterina ushered me in. The hall was full of patrons. On stage were four musicians. In the midst, of them, Antonio announced my presence as not only a hero of the liberation of Cremona and the composer of a wonderful concerto, but also a man of science, mathematics, and philosophies.

All boundless, but appreciated, exaggerations.

When the applause died down and I was in my seat, I had a sudden fear that the concerto would be received as the first attempt had in Mr. Montagu's home. Introduced one at a time, the musicians held one of my Stradivarius instruments. The last was the stunning violin I had been waiting so much time to hear. When fully introduced, the musicians held the instruments in the air to acknowledge the loud applause.

Antonio Stradivari gestured for the musicians to arrange themselves in playing position. He said to the audience, "Please enjoy," then walked off the stage and sat next to me.

The first violinist raised his bow and the others nodded, and they began to play.

Before I was able to return to Cremona, I traveled to Gibraltar to arrange final offensives in Spain and Portugal with the British military stationed in that region. After arriving, I was introduced at a gathering of officers and other officials. The day was one of full sun and a warm breeze. All those in attendance were in good humor, despite lingering tensions between the British military and Austrians.

We talked about the remnants of the war that needed to be dealt with from the military standpoint. We discussed what the leaders of the countries, or those in power behind the scenes, wanted to see the finish of the war to look like, essentially who controlled which territory and, likely more importantly, which trade routes.

"In the end, it's who profits most."

That astute observation was proffered by a young English officer, John Conduitt,[5] whom I sought out after one of the meetings in which he was in attendance. His demeanor and insightful comments caught my attention, much more than those of anyone else at the meetings. Particularly, his knowledge of British politics was astute, not only because it would be helpful, but it showed his mind was sharp, his speaking voice articulate beyond his years, and that he could hold his own in any argument.

Captain Conduitt and I dropped in the officers club which overlooked the strait and shared a bottle of Port.

"Whom do you feel is profiting most from this realignment of power?" I asked as the ruby liquid warmed me smoothly.

He placed his glass on the table. His fingers were long and sinewy. Fingers a violinist would love. He looked to be about thirty years old, about the age I was when I was in London. Now, I was certain most would say that I looked twice his age. My face was creased with lines from worry and lack of sleep, but worse, battle scarred from the war.

"We, the British, will profit most," he said without hesitation, "much more than Austrians, I'm sorry to say, General Wolf. As a re-

---

[5] Conduitt was serving as Deputy Paymaster General to the British forces in Gibraltar. He had been a captain in a regiment of the dragoons serving in Portugal, and had served as judge advocate—a lawyer who advises a court-martial on points of law and sums up the case. *PW*

sult of the war's outcome, we opened our shipping and trading routes, and are expanding into others. It's the end of the Spanish and Portuguese domination, and of course, Austria is landlocked."

"No apologies needed," I said. "I know that's true. But what about individual members of your country? Who's profiting most?"

He thought for a moment or two, eying me, for what reason or reasons, I didn't know. Wondering how much he could trust me? Wondering whom I knew and didn't know? Or just speculating on my motive for asking?

His answer was thoughtful and measured. "Profit is usually in the hands of those in seats of power, wouldn't you say?"

"Yes, I agree. I haven't been in England for many years, so I don't know who holds the power, or what that power includes." I mentioned a few names from my time in London, members of the Kit-Cat Club especially, ending with Mr. Montagu.

"Charles Montagu? The Earl of Halifax?"

"One and the same. Although, when I knew him, he was not the Earl of Halifax." I told him the years when I was in London.

"He wasn't substantially in power then," said Captain Conduitt. "But he rose swiftly when King George[6] ascended to the throne. Indeed, he rose all the way to the First Lord of the Treasury."

"The First Lord of the Treasury," I repeated slowly. "By 'all the way,' you mean that the position is as high as he could go?"

"Exactly. The highest position in the government."[7]

---

[6] George I. *PW*

[7] The position of First of the Treasury has little to do with the financial aspects of the treasury but is the head of the elected government. Montagu, the Earl of Halifax, was the first to be recognized as such. The First Lord of the Treasury is the position that became also held by the Prime Minister. *TS*

"Interesting. I knew he had ambitions, but he was against the war at first." Then I smiled ruefully in recognition of his switch of support. "When he could see a way to his benefit …"

"Yes." He explained further some of the minutia of the ways of England and especially the Whigs led by Montagu. "But in the end, it's unfortunate he could enjoy his seat for only a few months."

I was perplexed. "He lost his position as First Lord of the Treasury so quickly?"

It was Captain Conduitt's turn to appear perplexed. "You don't know that he recently died?"

"No," I said, as my heart jumped staccato in my chest. "How did he die?"

"That I don't know, other than he passed from a sudden illness."[8]

"That's tragic," I said.

"True," he said, then went into lengthy detail on the chaotic rush to fill the power void.

My mind was occupied with its own chaos—a furious gallop of thoughts, explosions of memories, veiled and revealed threats. And when the chaos dissipated to a dullness, an ache overtook me.

We continued our conversation into the night, over dinner and then further drinking port and whatever else came across the bar in the officers club. John Conduitt could well-hold his drink, and I further learned more about him, from his travels, to his happpenstance in

---

[8] The Earl of Halifax died from lung disease. Alexander Pope wrote a poem pointedly commenting on Mr. Montagu's death ("Farewell to London in the Year 1715"):

The love of arts lies cold and dead
In Halifax's urn,
And not one Muse of all he fed
Has yet the grace to mourn.

securing increasingly responsible and lucrative positions, to his deep interest in history.

When we exhausted our topics and energy—and surprisingly, outlasted the dark of the night—we parted ways. After a brief sleep, I awoke surprisingly refreshed in body and mind. There were further meetings that morning and into the afternoon, rehashing much of what was already discussed or agreed upon. I was getting tired by then, and with my mind like gruel, I begged off the next round of meetings and went to my quarters.

I didn't sleep so much as trudge through a quagmire of half-dreams and half-memories. They were disturbing enough for me to realize I needed to write down what happened, not for anyone but for me, so that I would have a true and complete account of what I learned and experienced.

Before I went out in search of paper and pen, I sought out Conduitt. I found him in his office in the British headquarters. His office was expansive, enough space to bivouac a platoon. Shelves of neatly stacked books, polished cabinets labeled with contents, lined the walls. His desk was equally large, but on it was only a neat, short stack of papers, and an inkwell.

He looked up, then carefully dabbed the nib and placed the pen in a holder. He smiled and rose from his chair. He appeared to have had a full night's sleep, unlike how I felt and no doubt appeared.

We sat on a pair of chairs in a corner of the office. We exchanged a few pleasantries, both agreeing that we had a fine evening together.

"And I hope for many more," I said. "If I could prevail upon you, would you have a blank journal, or two, that I could purchase?"

He went over to one of his cabinets and pulled out a stack of journals. He put them on the table. "Please, take what you need. Without charge, of course."

I thanked him and took two.

"What did you need them for?" he asked casually.

I didn't know what to say exactly, as it was indeed a long story. I started with my immediate thought. "After speaking with you last night, I awoke realizing I must make an account of my experiences."

He sat back into his chair. "I'm intrigued. Please tell me more."

I really didn't know where to start, or even that I should say anything at all. My mind was again in a quagmire.

"I'll tell you someday, maybe I'll let you read what I put down.[9] But for now, I have a question for you. What do you know of science?"

"Science? A fair amount. I'm immersed in antiquarianism."[10]

He stopped there without further explanation, as if waiting for me to express interest in his continuing. I asked him, "What particular area of antiquarianism?

"The analysis of ancient manuscripts—Greek and Roman. I'm most interested in a critical analysis, rather than an interpretive one."

That struck a chord with me, along with his position as paymaster. "What are your plans after you finish here?"

He gazed at me, perhaps considering the intent of the question. "I have no definite plan. But I'll likely return to London."

"I have someone you should meet when you return," I said, thinking of Sir Isaac.

Another three months passed in Cremona before I could arrange shipment of the instruments and make my way to London. While in Cremona, I learned all I could about the violin, as much as Antonio would tell me. The belly had indeed come from the spruce

---

[9] But will it ever be finished? *PW*
Or ever fully and faithfully translated? *TS*

[10] Antiquarianism focuses on empirical evidence, as summed by the eighteenth-century antiquary Sir Richard Colt Hoare, "We speak from facts, not theory." *TS*

named Lonesome, and the back from one of the maples outside the walls of Cremona. The wood had been treated after partial curing in water made viscous with a fine, sandy powder. I documented all of the dimensions I could find to measure. As for the varnish layers, I learned the first was actually a layer of glue, likely sealing the porous wood and binding all the pieces together. I tried to relate all of these aspects to Sir Isaac's precise drawings and formulas, but I doubt I could answer more than a few of the questions he would ask me.

When I arrived in London, I moved into an inn for an extended stay. My room seemed luxurious, as I was used to austere quarters even as a commander. I usually had the often meager rations our troops were fed.

I settled into my room, tired from the journey and the uncertainty of what I was doing in London after all the years that had passed. James and I lost touch—he was caught up in the war as England entered it not long after the Battle of Cremona.[11]

When I recovered from the travels, I went out into the city, walking through the neighborhoods, parks, and other places I remembered, and when I came upon this place or that I especially recalled a fond memory, like Catherine's favorite coffeehouse, I was shot through with wistfulness.

I came to James' home, the location of which I obtained at the military office. When I asked about James, I was told he retired from active duty two years ago. His little home was tucked into the end of a street opposite a small park. I walked up to the door and knocked.

James answered the door. We recognized each other, yet not, as the blood of hundreds directly and thousands indirectly had soaked into our flesh.[12] A physical scar traced a line on James' face. I was

---

[11] Officially in May of 1702. *PW*

[12] The total deaths in combat are estimated to be four hundred thousand, with likely twice that number of deaths due to disease and other causes. *TS*

reminded of Mr. Lupine. James' right leg was stiff with a limp when he rushed to embrace me. He dragged me inside his home. Rose, he said, was visiting her mother with their children, Angelica and Barrow. I heartily congratulated him on his family, and asked if he was going through the alphabet with children's names.

He laughed. "Yes, but sorry, it's a long way to 'P,' Phillipe."

"Thank you for the thought," I said.

As we drank ale, we traded tales of the war, James outdoing me by far, having received his scar in a hand-to-hand tussle, and a musket ball that knocked off a small chunk of his kneecap.

"What brings you to London?" he finally asked.

"I suppose it's to finish something I started, and to make my apologies. One being that I let you go into the Citadel in Cremona and be captured by the Irish. It was poor judgement on my part."

James waved away my concern. "What I learned in Cremona about French military, the tenacious Irish, and your secretive techniques were invaluable to me. I was able to make strategies and command men with confidence."

I appreciated hearing those words, more than I could express. "I learned as much from you, if not more. I also apologize for not keeping up correspondence."

Again, James waved away my apology. "We were in the midst of war. I don't hold any malice toward you for that."

"Thank you. I admit I felt regret and remorse over that, and the main reason was that I didn't want to hear the news of what was happening in London."

James thought for a moment, then nodded. "But now you want to know what has happened?"

"I believe so."

I arrived at the Newton home in a carriage, hauling the set of Stradivarius instruments. Catherine moved to her uncle's home, reasonably so but not without controversy, as James told me. In his will and testament, Charles Montagu, the Earl of Halifax, left a large amount to Catherine specifically for her loyal service and "excellent conversation." More than one acquainted with Montagu and Catherine implied the "conversation" was a sexual metaphor. In fact, a rumor circulated that they had secretly married.[13]

But if my hopes had been raised with the news of Mr. Montagu's death, they were squashed by the news that Catherine had married only a year ago, and after only being in acquaintance with her husband a few months. She married a young officer and deputy paymaster who returned from his last post in Gibraltar—John Conduitt.

Conduitt was now working with Sir Isaac at the Royal Mint, and living in Sir Isaac's home with Catherine. I girded myself to see them after so many years with no communication. I wouldn't have been surprised if I was met with dead silence. When I knocked on the door, I was met with anything but silence.

"Phillipe!" exclaimed Catherine. She embraced me with such fervor I nearly broke down and wept. Her uncle standing behind her to her right without great expression. To her left was her husband, Conduitt, who stood in rigid pose, surprised to see me, likely in shock at seeing his newly-wed wife embracing me.

---

[13] Voltaire wrote in an essay about Sir Isaac, many years after his death: "I had a notion in my younger days that Newton had made his fortune by his extraordinary merit. I made no doubt that both court and city at London had created him, with one common consent, chief manager and supreme director of the coin of the kingdom. I was herein greatly mistaken; Sir Isaac Newton had a pretty niece, called Mrs. Conduite [sic], who had the good fortune to please the lord high treasurer, Halifax. Had it not been for this handsome niece, his doctrine of gravitation and infinitesimals had been wholly useless to him, and he might have starved with all his talents." However, as mentioned, Newton secured his position before Catherine arrived in London. *TS*

Catherine released me and I shook the hands of her uncle and husband. We went into their parlor and conversed rapidly, at least Catherine and I did. As I had with James, I condensed my service in the war to a few highlights.

Sir Isaac was most interested in my last meetings with Antonio Stradivari. He mentioned that over the years he thought about our discussions, which I remembered more as frustrated lectures, delivered from the brilliant master to the wretchedly dim-minded student. He described with equally great enthusiasm that "our" experiments and philosophical reasoning had helped him explicate his ideas of the nature of light, which led to his publication of his book *Opticks*.[14]

While we chatted, the Stradivarius instruments in the carriage were unloaded and carried into the parlor. As they were revealed, my heart was filled with the joy of seeing them arriving safely, and even more joy at seeing the wonder and astonishment in Catherine's eyes.

D uring the following weeks, two events had been arranged. The first was a presentation to the Royal Society,[15] *On The Nature of Sound as Exemplified by the Construction of a Stringed Instrument*. Given Sir Isaac's role as president, I was appointed to give the presentation. Of course, he helped me write the correct concepts, but I was able to include my experiences in Antonio Stradivari's workshop, as well as the luthier's discourse on his craft.

------

[14] The most popular of his publications, written in English, rather than Latin, and in a more understandable style than *Principia*. *PW*

[15] While the Royal Society, whose charter was to provide a forum for the fledging sciences flourished under Sir Isaac Newton's presidency from 1703-1727 (his death), he was not above wielding his power, especially in his dispute with Gottfried Leibniz over who discovered the calculus of infinitesimals. Newton formed a committee to look into the matter, but he wrote the final report giving credit to himself. *TS*

The second event was a concert after the presentation to the Royal Society. Catherine put together the musicians, reserving the first violin for herself at my request. Initially she refused, explaining she had not played much in the last few years. But when I showed her the Stradivarius and she played but a few notes, she needed no further convincing.

The scientific presentation went well enough, despite my nerves. The roomy was stuffy, and I was afraid the Royal Society members would be soon asleep. But they appeared to be paying attention, and asked pointed and complex questions. Sir Isaac assisted me by rephrasing the difficult questions that led me to the answer.

I was also afraid the concert would be a disappointment. But Catherine was delightful in her introduction to the long history of the Concerto for Violin in C Major. She gave a brief account of the life of the instruments from Cremona, especially the violin she held. When the music started, I realized I was holding my breath for several bars. Catherine's violin playing then took over my entire being, and, as I had in Cremona, could feel the soul of Antonio Stradivari singing in the violin.

No one in the audience was not enraptured with the heavenly sound coming from the instruments. Whether they liked my music or not, I believed they knew something beyond reason was happening. And when it was over, as in Cremona, they were silent for a long moment before erupting in applause and cheers.

At the reception afterwards, when I had received congratulations and had to retell the story of Cremona many times, Catherine finally rescued me, and with her arm entwined with mine, led me away from the throng and said, "General Wolf, your delightful composition needs a more evocative title than Concerto for Violin in C Major."

The Royal Society Of London
For Improving Natural Knowledge

A Lecture By

General Phillipe Wolf

"On The Nature of Sound As Exemplified
By The Construction Of a Stringed Instrument"

Author's Note

Many people, references, and resources helped during the several stages of writing this novel. My considerable appreciation goes to Marie-Lise Assier, Christian Urbita, Mariangela di Maggio, Stephen Thompson, Christy O Harris, Lawrence O'Toole, Ann Morstad, Garrett Hongo, Wendy Tokunaga, Richard Mawhorter, and Linda Shimoda.

Antonio & Isaac (The Annotated Account of Phillip Wolf, Composer & Spy) is a work of fiction. There are, of course, historical characters and facts in the story. Fully explicating all of the facts versus fictions would likely take as many words as the novel itself. Sweepingly, the novel includes real people and events, as well as real science, mathematics, and facets of violin making, in particular what is known about Stradivarius violins and other instruments. While I have tried to maintain the coherence of these facts with reality, their edges have been bent to nestle them into the novel.

To wit:

Phillipe Wolf is fictional. Of the other main characters, Isaac Newton and Antonio Stradivari are real historical figures as is Catherine Barton, Sir Isaac's half-niece. In London, Charles Montagu (the 1st Earl of Halifax) and John Conduitt are historical figures. James Brookfield and Rose Harrington are fictional, as is the Austrian envoy, George Lupine, and the music instrument vendor, Penbook. In Cremona, Antonio Stradivari's family members are real, as is the priest, Cozzoli. The violinist, Il Diavolo d'Amico, is fictional, as is Lieutenant Laurent. Other historical figures who make cameo appearances include Jonathan Swift, Prince Eugene of Savoy, French General duc de Villeroi, the 1st Duke of Marlborough, and by reference the luthier families of Cremona.

The real historical events include Newton's tenure at the Royal Mint and the Kit-Kat Club's role in a shadow government. However, the counterfeiting ring and Kit-Kat Club meetings portrayed in the novel are fictional. The recounting of the Battle of Cremona is fictional but based on much fact. A spy for the Austrian forces did infiltrate the city, although posing as a farmer. The priest, Cozzoli, did allow Austrian forces to invade the city through his parish's wine cellar.

In all of Newton's works and personal records, there's barely a mention of music. The specific true reference in the novel is Newton's comparison of the visible light spectrum to a musical scale. There's no recorded mention by Stradivari regarding science or higher-order mathematics such as calculus, but that's not to say he couldn't have used or understood the subjects.

Finally, there's no record that Stradivari and Newton had any knowledge of each other.

The numerous references used include these main sources, listed below by person and topic. Any errors in the novel contra to the facts or due to fictionalizing of these references are mine.

Antonio Stradivari

Anthony Stradivari: The Celebrated Violin Maker, François-Joseph Fétis. Dover Publications, 2013, original English edition published in 1864.

Antonio Stradivari: His Life and Work, Henry W. Hill, Author F. Hill, Alfred E. Hill. First edition 1902. Dover Publications, 1963.

Antonio Stradivari, Reports and documents, Carlo Bonetti, Agostino Caval-cabò, Ugo Gualazzini. First edition, Comitato Stradivariano, 1937. English edition, Editions Cremonabooks, 1999.

Antonius Stradivarius, Dirk J. Balfoort, translated by A. G. Doyle-Davidson. The Continental Book Company,

Museo del Violino in Cremona. https://www.museodelviolino.org/en/

Stradivari, Stewart Pollens. Cambridge University Press, 2010.

Stradivari's Genius, Tony Faber. Random House, 2004.

Tariso's *Cozio Carteggio,* various authors, articles on Stradivari, violin making, performers, and other topics. https://tarisio.com/cozio-archive/ Representative articles include:

> Antonio Stradivari: https://tarisio.com/cozio-archive/browse-the-archive/makers/maker/?Maker_ID=722
>
> Francesco Stradivari: https://tarisio.com/cozio-archive/browse-the-archive/makers/maker/?Maker_ID=723
>
> Omobono Stradivari: https://tarisio.com/cozio-archive/browse-the-archive/makers/maker/?Maker_ID=724
>
> The "Sancy" Stradivarius and Ivry Glitis: https://tarisio.com/news/ivry-gitlis-sancy-stradivari-film/
>
> Rugeri family: https://tarisio.com/cozio-archive/cozio-carteggio/the-rugeri-family/

The "Secrets" of Stradivari, Simone F. Sacconi. First edition, *I "Segreti" di Stradivari*, Libreria del Convegno, 1972. English edition, Eric Blot Edizioni, 2000.

Wikipedia. Numerous articles.

Isaac Newton

All Was Light: An Introduction to Newton's Opticks, A. Rupert Hall. Clarendon Press, 1993.

Isaac Newton: The Last Sorcerer, Michael White. Addison-Wesley, 1997.

Never at Rest: A Biography of Isaac Newton, Richard S. Westfall. Cambridge University Press, 1980.

Sir Isaac Newton: His Life and Work, E. N. Da C. Andrade. Anchor Books, imprint of McMillan Company, 1954.

The Life of Isaac Newton, Richard S. Westfall. Cambridge University Press, 1993.

Wikipedia. Numerous articles.

Music, Science, Other

Burn & Learn, Eric Paul Shaffer. Leaping Dog Press, 2009.

Cremona Violins, A Physicist's Quest for the Secrets of Stradivari, Kameshwar C. Wali. World Scientific, 2010.

"Epistemic forms and epistemic games: Structures and strategies to guide inquiry," A. Collins and W. Ferguson. In *Educational Psychologist*, Volume 28, pages 25-42, 1993.

Musimathics: The Mathematical Foundations of Music, D. Gareth Loy. MIT Press, 2007. Science & Music, Sir James Jeans. First edition, Cambridge University Press, 1937. Dover Publications, 1968.

Opticks, Or a Treatise of the Reflections, Refractions, Inflections & Colors of Light, 1730. Isaac Newton, Dover Publications, 1952.

Science & Music, Sir James Jeans. Dover Publications, 1968, original edition, Cambridge University Press, 1937.

The Ten Most Beautiful Experiments, George Johnson. Alfred A. Knopf, 2008.

The Vibrating String Length of Today's Violin. And *Le violin de l'Abbaye*, Christian Urbita.

Wikipedia. Numerous articles.

Notes and credits on drawings and photographs
Credit by author unless otherwise noted.

1. Title page - Window in luthier workshop (photograph by Marie-Lise Assier, Christian Urbita workshop)

2. Title page - Tower of London door (screenshot of video by Christy O Harris)

3. Title page - "Half-and-half" Stradivarius front image of violin ("Francesca" by Wiki Commons) and a Newton schematic facsimile

4. Chapter 2 - "Pure tone and string chord" - Comparison of a single pure, uniform note (for example, from a tuning fork) and the chord of multiple notes of a vibrating violin string (based on Sir James Jeans, *Science & Music*, 1937, Dover Edition, p. 76)

5. Chapter 4 - String force energy and a cross-section of body through bridge, showing bass bar and sound post (based on Jeans, ibid., p. 101, 104-105, Sacconi, *The "Secrets" of Stradivari*, Eric Blot Edizioni, 2000, p. 70)

6. Chapter 7 - Map of Cremona, showing the location of Antonio Stradivari's home and workshop, and other luthiers (based on Carlo Bonetti, Agostino Cavacabò, Ugo Gualazzini, *Antonio Stradivari: Reports and documents*, 1937, Editions Cremonabooks, 1999, p. 33)

7. Chapter 7 - Stradivari's violin mold "MB" (based on Sacconi, ibid., p. 48)

8. Chapter 8 - A musical code developed in Cremona for recording troops and positions (map of Cremona 1702 excerpt based on photograph by Andrew Fare)

9. Chapter 12 - Newton's prism color bands and musical scale correlation (based on Sir Isaac Newton, *Opicks*, Dover Publications edition, 1952, p. 155)

10. Chapter 16 - Thickness variations across violin cross sections (based on Sacconi, ibid, p. 63, 66)

11. Chapter 16 - Pressure-force diagram of a violin

12. Chapter 18 - Asymmetrical transmission of sounds and differentiation of tone

About the Author

Todd Shimoda has previously published five novels described as "philosophical mysteries." Born and raised in Colorado, he now lives in Southern California. He is currently working on a handful of new novels, and he also designs educational technology applications. For more information, please visit these websites: shimodaworks.com and toddshimoda.com.